DEVOTED

BY LUNA MASON

THE BENEATH THE MASK SERIES
Distance
Detonate
Devoted
Detained

THE BENEATH THE SECRETS SERIES
Chaos
Caged
Crave
Claim

THE BENEATH THE BLAZE SERIES
Inferno
Ignite
Intense
Indulge
Instinct

DEVOTED

BENEATH THE MASK

Luna Mason

kensingtonbooks.com

KENSINGTON BOOKS are published by:
Kensington Publishing Corp.
900 Third Avenue
New York, NY 10022

kensingtonbooks.com

Copyright © 2024 by Luna Mason

This book is a work of fiction. Names, characters, businesses, organizations, places, events, and incidents either are the product of the author's imagination or are used fictitiously. Any resemblance to actual persons, living or dead, events, or locales is entirely coincidental.

To the extent that the image or images on the cover of this book depict a person or persons, such person or persons are merely models, and are not intended to portray any character or characters featured in the book.

All rights reserved. No part of this book may be reproduced in any form or by any means without the prior written consent of the Publisher, excepting brief quotes used in reviews.

All Kensington titles, imprints, and distributed lines are available at special quantity discounts for bulk purchases for sales promotions, premiums, fundraising, educational, or institutional use.

Special book excerpts or customized printings can also be created to fit specific needs. For details, write or phone the office of the Kensington sales manager: Kensington Publishing Corp., 900 Third Avenue, New York, NY 10022, attn: Sales Department; phone 1-800-221-2647.

The K with book logo Reg US Pat. & TM Off.

First Kensington Trade Paperback Printing: September 2025

ISBN 978-1-4967-5748-7 (trade paperback)

10 9 8 7 6 5 4 3 2 1

Printed in the United States of America

Electronic edition: ISBN 978-1-4967-5752-4 (ebook)

Interior design by Leah Marsh

Content warnings: explicit language; alcoholism, drug addiction, and withdrawal; domestic emotional abuse of FMC (not by the MMC); death of family members; murder; graphic violence (including murder, torture, kidnapping, arson, stabbing); sexual assault of FMC (not by MMC); use of safe words; and cheating. This book is explicit and has explicit sexual content, including praise, breath play, edging, exhibitionism, anal, spitting, food play, and rope.

Without limiting the author's and publisher's exclusive rights, any unauthorized use of this publication to train generative artificial intelligence (AI) technologies is expressly prohibited.

The authorized representative in the EU for product safety and compliance
is eucomply OU, Parnu mnt 139b-14, Apt 123
Tallinn, Berlin 11317, hello@eucompliancepartner.com

To all my dirty girls who think hand tattoos are just
pretty necklaces. This one is for you.

Mr. Russo will see you now . . .

AUTHOR'S NOTE

Devoted is a dark, standalone mafia romance. It does contain content and situations that could be triggering to some readers.

This book is explicit and has explicit sexual content, intended for readers 18+.

The MC and FMC for a period of the book are in arranged/forced marriages; therefore, there is cheating. However, *there is no cheating between the main characters*, nor do they sleep with their "fiancé(e)s."

This book does contain graphic descriptions of a previous sexual assault on the FMC. This is primarily described in chapter fifteen.

A full list of triggers can be found on the author's website, http://lunamasonauthor.com.

Chapter One
LUCA

I sit back in my chair as my men walk into my dining room. Grayson and Frankie, two of my best, take the seats on either side of me.

"Boss." Grayson's blue eyes meet mine.

He tugs on his collar then reaches over for the bottle of scotch in front of us, pouring his own before hovering over my now empty glass.

"Refill?"

"Please."

When the last guy, Enzo, who runs our security services, closes the door, I clear my throat, all eyes now on me.

Their leader.

The top tier of my organization take their seats; the further twenty surrounding the table stand to attention. There has been word among the group that there is unease since the departure of my foster brother, Keller.

Our masked hitman, our main asset. The man who put the fear of God into our enemies.

This was never the life he wanted, but it was the one we were forced into. I gave him his freedom; it's not something I will ever have. I had to let him go, to finally have the family he deserved with Sienna.

I stand and clap Grayson and Frankie on the shoulders.

"Marco's kidnapping of Nico is an act of war. As such, we will respond in that way. None of us will sleep until he is home. We will bring him back to his wife. We hold no prisoners. Any Falcone fucker who crosses our path will die. This city is ours, and no Falcone can take that from us."

The men cheer. "How are we taking Marco out, boss?"

"We keep breaking him down. Every shipment, every warehouse, every man who steps into our territory, we kill. He might have numbers, but there is no power behind them. Not like us. Right now, nothing comes into or goes out of New York without my say-so. We have the commissioner in our corner, so we fight."

I knock back the rest of my scotch, the empty glass banging back down on my oak dining table. I nod to Enzo. "Any more intel on Marco?"

He runs a hand through his jet-black hair. "I'm digging into his past family dealings. I think if there's anything to find, I'll have it soon for you, boss."

If anyone can find it, it's Enzo. There isn't anything he can't tap into.

I raise my voice so my words are crystal clear. "We take Marco when the time is right; we fold them, we break them."

The room goes silent. After Keller's rampage over the Falcones, torturing and killing fifteen of Marco's men, they hit back, stealing our cocaine shipments, burning our warehouses, and now, taking Nico.

I ball my fists.

"Vince, Ramos, I want you keeping tabs on Carlo at all times. Oversee every single fucking shipment. I'm not losing anymore. If I'm missing a single gram, you're paying the consequences."

Ramos gulps. "Got it, boss."

"In the meantime, Grayson and Frankie will be leading the takedown operations. You listen to their orders. Every building those fuckers own will be burned to the ground. Enzo will be working the security to keep finding their warehouses, their hideouts, and feeding it through."

Grayson rubs his hands together. He loves an explosion.

"Now are you ready to hunt?" I throw my arms up victoriously.

The room erupts into cheers and grunts of my men.

"Fuck yes." Grayson looks up at me with a devilish grin.

"I SAID, 'WHERE the fuck is he holding Nico?'"

He claws at my calf, gasping for air, his eyes ready to burst out of their sockets. I release the pressure of my foot from this Falcone fucker's neck.

He spits a mouthful of blood on the leg of my Armani pants. I sigh and press back down on his throat with my body weight.

"Let's try this again. Last chance. Where is—"

I pause as gunshots ring out to my left. My ex-Marine right-hand man, Grayson, is firing some asshole's brains out.

He gives me a menacing smirk as he wipes the blood spatter from his forehead.

"These dumb shits don't know a thing, boss," Grayson grunts.

The jackass under my foot coughs. "Oh, sorry." I lift my knee momentarily, leaving him wheezing on the warehouse floor, and I crouch down, pulling my knife from the sheath on my ankle.

"Where was I? Ahhh, yes."

Tears stream down his cheeks. I chuckle as a dark patch appears on his gray sweatpants.

"Don't worry, it will all be over soon," I whisper while pressing the tip of the blade under his chin.

"Where the fuck are they holding Nico?" I grab his greasy hair and tilt his head back.

"I-I don't know," he croaks out.

I half believe him. Marco has an army of utterly useless men, and this one is no different.

"Well, that is a shame." I stab my blade up through his throat and slide it back out as he goes limp in my grip.

After wiping my blade on his sweater, I stand, dusting off my suit.

"Frankie?" I call out.

"It's all clear, boss." His voice echoes through the large building.

He comes around the corner with a grin, holding a handful of phones. His kill count multiplied tonight, by the looks of it.

"Get those delivered to Enzo. Let him work his magic." With all the people here, I find it hard to believe they were *all* clueless.

Frankie nods, running a crimson-stained hand through his chestnut hair.

"Are we ready to light this shit up?" Grayson asks from behind me.

"I wouldn't dare stop you," I chuckle.

Commissioner O'Reilly will no doubt have something to say about yet another warehouse fire. But it's either that or twenty dead bodies for him to deal with.

Grayson douses the building in gasoline while Frankie and I wait in my Bentley. I spark up a cigarette and take a deep inhale, resting my head back.

Another night, another dead end. But, one step closer to ridding New York of the Falcones.

Frustration forms a hard knot in my head as the flames start to consume the building. Grayson jumps into the back seat, slamming the door shut with about as much grace as a six-foot-four killing machine can do.

"All good?" I look at him in the rearview mirror.

"Nothing like a burn-out to end the night. I can't go for a drink to celebrate, though; I've got somewhere I need to be." He shifts to pull out his cell and glance at it before meeting my eyes.

"You mean, you've got someone you need to be in?" I retort, biting back a grin.

Frankie sniggers next to me while Grayson's shooting me a death glare.

Grayson and Maddie, the worst pair on the planet at hiding their relationship. The man who swore off kissing a woman for almost eight years sure as hell kissed her. The truth is, everyone can see what they have is the real deal, no matter how they try to hide it from us.

A whole year we've had to put up with them avoiding each other, and now it looks like they've finally caved. I've got a ten-grand bet with my foster brother, Keller, that they will screw by the end of the year. I probably should up the bet to married by the end of the year.

I've known Grayson since the moment he stepped foot into New York seven years ago. I gave him a life here when he ran from his own in Chicago. The best decision I've made. I gained another brother and right-hand man.

"Fuck you," he grits out.

"I'd rather you stick to fucking Maddie, thanks."

Frankie slaps his palm against his thigh. "Who's Grayson fucking?" He turns to me.

"Maddie, Sienna's best friend. You know, the blonde one. She's sassy as hell."

I can feel Grayson's gaze burning into the back of my head.

"Ohhh, getting down and dirty with the best friend, nice." Frankie gives him a wink.

Grayson stiffens in his seat, and I can't help but laugh.

"We're just giving you shit, G. You know I'm happy for you."

And I am. Much like Keller, Grayson has found his person. Happiness suits the grumpy Marine.

I turn on the ignition and put the raging inferno of a warehouse behind us.

When I pull up to the curb at his place, Grayson nearly jumps out before I even stop. He must be itching to get out of the car for his *date* with Maddie.

"Have fun *not* fucking Maddie," I call out as he makes his way toward his building.

I drive to my estate with Frankie. Once inside, I head straight toward the liquor cabinet in the kitchen.

Taking his scotch, Frankie lets out a sigh as he leans against the marble counter.

"Boss, Marco isn't going to let up. We need to hit harder,

do something that will break him. These men don't mean shit to him. They are nobodies he's plucked off the damn streets."

I take a moment to savor the smooth burn of my own drink. He's right. In all these months, Marco has been unpredictable. But no matter what we do, he just recruits more.

It's always been hostile with the Falcones, since the day I was given the keys to the kingdom after my birth father's death.

He must have seen me, the little street rat, as an easy target. Well, I've proven that fucker wrong. I've managed to keep the power in my hands all this time.

Things were at a standstill until he made the world's greatest mistake. He orchestrated the kidnapping of Keller's wife. He started a war that I fully intend to finish. The commissioner's even backing me.

"We need to do something big. But we can't risk Nico's safety. I mean, we know Marco is unhinged." He steps into the next room and lowers his tall frame to the black leather couch. Crossing his ankle over his knee, he looks more comfortable in my living room than I feel most of the time.

"Enzo sent over the files on Marco's daughters." I briefly looked at them this morning, but I haven't had a chance to dig deeper yet.

The cushion creaks as he leans forward and his dark brows rise.

"He doesn't hide them well." I pull out my phone and open the email, clicking on the first picture. Two Italian girls stare back at me.

"Eva, the youngest, on the left. Rosa, on the right," I mutter, reading the contents of the email.

The redhead on the left is younger, not by much. She looks nothing like the woman on the right, whom I can't take my eyes off of. Smaller than her sister, she has a waist that looks like it's begging for my hands and a set of hips that I bet would fit mine perfectly. Her big brown eyes are staring right at me over a set of deep red fuck-me lips. I can't deny it—despite being the daughter of the enemy, she is beautiful.

Rubbing my hand along my day-old stubble, my eyes still fix on her. Rosa. My cock starts to twitch against my zipper. I shuffle in my seat to try to rectify it. What the fuck is going on with me?

This isn't how we do things. We respect women, always. It's non-negotiable. My foster mom would rip my heart out of my chest for bringing harm to a woman.

"This could break him." Frankie takes another long sip, watching me closely over the rim.

This could be the way to end this.

"It shouldn't be hard to find them. I'll get on it with Grayson. It's a bold move. They could kill Nico," Frankie says, breaking me from my haze.

Doubt stabs into my chest. "Or they take another one of ours. Hell, they could take Maddie next. They've proven how low they will stoop. I can't do that to Grayson."

His gray eyes meet mine, and he nods.

"Come on, let's go. I need to get a real drink." I pocket my phone, letting out a ragged breath.

I need to down some scotch and then sink into a woman. Preferably of Italian descent. With big brown eyes, long, curly jet-black hair, and a killer body.

Chapter Two

ROSA

"Rosa, get your ass here now!" The deep resonance of his voice carries up the balcony.

"No!" I scream down the stairs at my dad.

I slam my old bedroom door shut, leaning against the heavy wood. This is why I never come home. As if it wasn't enough having me followed around by his spies, now he wants me married off. None of that holds my interest. I only come home for one reason: his supply.

Pain sears through my spine as I am thrown onto the floor when he barges through the door. It's dulled by the fact that I'd already raided his vodka stash before he caught me.

"Get out!" Kicking my legs, I push myself across the smooth floor, away from him.

He yanks me up by the arm. His dark eyes, much like mine, bore into me. His brown hair is graying at the sides, but there isn't any weakness as his fingers bruisingly tighten into me.

I try to tug his hand away, but he holds me in place, towering over me. "You need to sort yourself out, girl."

"I'm not doing anything wrong. I'm just having fun." It's the lie that everyone around me knows. The mafia princess without a care in the world, who goes out to party every night.

"You can't keep running, Rosa."

I straighten my spine. "From what, *Dad*?" I spit out the word with venom.

"You know what."

I let out a laugh. "You can't even say it, can you? You can't accept what happened to me! If you can't speak about it, how the hell am I supposed to deal with it? Do you have any idea how fucking hard it is?"

I snatch my arm from him. He sighs, taking a step away from me. Emboldened, I press closer. The one advantage of being constantly drunk and high: the courage that comes with it.

"I am dealing with it the only way I know how. You decided to let him live; you didn't protect me. The same way you didn't protect Mom or Nonna."

His eyes flash with anger, his face reddening. He lifts his hand and I flinch. It doesn't take away the fact that he is completely responsible for their deaths. What happened to me was due to his failure.

"Clean yourself up. Next week, I am discussing a marriage arrangement for you. No one is going to want to marry a junkie."

I bow my head. Tears sting in my eyes. I don't want to be this way, chasing my demons away with any poison I can find. Anything to make me feel numb, to stop the nightmares, the fear. The embarrassment.

No one understands. Not even my own dad.

"Well, I won't be getting married, then. Like you said, no man wants a woman like me."

"Go to therapy, to rehab. You have to find a way. You can't live like this."

It's the only way I know how.

"It's either you or Eva." He crosses his arms across his chest, and his jaw tightens as he stares at me down his nose.

My younger sister, my light in the darkness. I've protected her since Mom died. She's the one person I try to be better for, the reason I keep myself alive. I can't leave her with Dad on her own. I don't trust his men. I don't trust this life. I will never let anything happen to her.

I narrow my eyes. "You wouldn't."

"I need to try to forge a deal with Romano. I need his backing to take down that son of a bitch, Russo." He grits his teeth as he speaks, his fists clenching by his sides.

Wow, that Russo guy has really gotten under his skin. Good.

"That isn't my problem. I thought Romano was the enemy?"

"He was. The accident was a long time ago. This is my way in." The accident. He means my mother's death.

"You can't make me marry anyone," I whisper.

I know deep down he can. Like every man—they can take away your choice with the snap of their fingers.

He tips my chin up aggressively. "You'll do as I say. And no more stealing my coke. I've locked up my supply. If you're that desperate, you'll have to find your own way. Forget the past and grow the fuck up."

He lets go. I stumble back and watch as he storms out and slams the door behind him. I pull at my hair. Shit. He can't be serious.

My hands start to shake as anger and panic rush through me. I don't want to feel. I need my fix before the world creeps back in.

I pull out my phone and call Liv, my best friend. She's the life of the party; she'll know where to get the good stuff.

"Girl, where are you?" I can barely hear her over the music.

"I can't get anything from Dad's," I whisper, biting at the skin around my nails.

"Well, Miss Mafia Cocktease, looks like you'll have to bat those lashes at the men at the bar tonight, because I'm out until Carlo can sneak me more."

My heart sinks. I hate having to do this. Talking to random men, no matter how drunk I am, puts me on edge. My friends call me "the cocktease" because they think I'm using these men for the drugs but won't go any further. Everyone thinks I'm a virgin, saving herself for marriage. It's an easy lie in this life.

They have no idea it's because I'm petrified of being intimate with a man. That I'm tarnished. That I haven't been touched by anyone since *him*.

And I'm not sure I ever will.

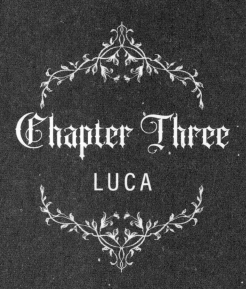

Chapter Three

LUCA

Smoke meanders from the lit end of my cigarette over the steering wheel before slowly drifting out the open window where I rest my elbow. I take another drag and loosen my tie.

Today started off in the worst way possible. A box was delivered two days ago with a gruesome surprise: Nico's mutilated body. My blood boils with the need for revenge.

"How are things looking?" I ask Grayson as he hands me some of the surveillance pictures he's taken.

"All good, boss. Should be an easy grab. She's shitfaced most of the time. I've never spent so much fucking time in crappy clubs in my life. There are a couple of bodyguards; nothing we can't take care of, though."

I nod, a grin forming on my lips as I turn to face him.

"I'd love to see Marco's face when we take his precious 'princess.' We're going to make that asshole pay." He might have thought he one-upped us by delivering Nico's remains to my doorstep. No wonder none of his men had a clue where Nico was; he was probably dead by then. What I have planned is going to rock his world.

"Taking his daughter is a good start. What are your plans with her?" Grayson has a mischievous glint in his blue eyes.

"Depends on how Marco behaves. If he doesn't back down, I'm not opposed to ridding the world of another Falcone." I shrug.

Frankie clears his throat in the back seat. When I look through the rearview mirror, I notice my green eyes are bloodshot. I don't know the last time I slept properly; definitely not since Nico's death.

He runs a hand through his chestnut hair, and I raise a brow.

"Everything alright back there?"

Frankie is my newest recruit, who has quickly become one of my top guys. He's ruthless, like Grayson. But has the mafia experience. He worked with Romano Capri in Italy for a few years. The top organization in Europe.

"Is taking his daughter really the best next move? He has backed off since we've obliterated nearly all of his facilities. We've killed over half of his men. He's weak." He slides to the center and pushes a knee against each of the front seats.

"Exactly. I don't just want him on his knees. He'd come back like cancer. I want him broken, watching everything he loves die. Only then will I kill him." I can hear my own voice almost crack, trying to contain the rage bubbling inside of me.

"But—"

"How about you remember who the fuck you're talking to." I cut Frankie off, swinging my head around to face him. "Do you have a problem with how I lead?"

Grayson sniggers next to me.

I'm doing this so the next time it's not one of my family. I will always protect them, no matter what.

Frankie chuckles and lifts his palms up in a sign of retreat.

"Glad we cleared that up," I huff, turning back to Grayson, who is biting back a laugh.

"Shut it." I don't have the patience for his humor today. "Okay, so when is it taking place? I need it done yesterday."

I toss the cigarette butt out of the car onto the driveway of one of our warehouses. I've had a complaint about how we're packing our coke, so I'm about to go in there and slap them into shape.

"Friday. She has plans to go to Trance with a couple of friends. We're scoping it out tonight and will work out the best course. She seems like she'd take well to you, boss. Just flash her a little bag of the good stuff and she'll chase after you." He gestures at the squat brick building we're parked in front of.

I laugh. "I won't have a problem. You don't think you're up to the job? Lost your touch on getting women already?"

Grayson runs a hand along his perfectly manicured stubble. "I— Uh." A hint of red works its way over his cheek.

"You're pussy-whipped. I think that's what you want to say?" I bite back a grin.

"Fuck off, Luca." Grayson clenches his jaw and stares out the window.

Frankie bursts out into full-bellied laughter in the back.

"You two are like a fucking married couple."

We both turn to look at him. "Don't be jealous, Frankie. There's room for you. Don't they call it a throuple now?" I wink at him before turning back to Grayson.

"I'll be ready Friday. Send over any information you have

collected on her. I want to know who and what I'm dealing with. Mafia princesses can be pains in the fucking ass. I don't have time for that."

"Will do, boss." Grayson nods.

"Good, now back to work. I'm going to go beat the shit out of Ramos. Useless fuck can't even pack coke right."

I swing open the door, straighten up my dark suit, and tighten my tie.

Grayson hangs out of the window and calls my name.

"Did you forget something?" He's waving my black gun in the air with a grin.

Shit.

I need to get my head back in the game. "Don't kill him. Poor kid is only twenty-one. He'll get there," Grayson says, holding on to the Glock.

I roll my eyes and snatch my weapon out of his hands, holstering it in the waistband of my pants.

"No promises. Now, you two fuck off and get back to work."

Chapter Four
ROSA

I tug down my tight black dress as I walk through the doors to Trance, our favorite spot for a Friday night. Bobby, one of my bodyguards, opens the door for me. As I walk through, he grabs my wrist. I turn to face him with a scowl. "Don't touch me," I spit out.

"I promised your father I won't let you make a fool of yourself. He has a big meeting tomorrow, and the last thing he needs is to clean up after you again." His breath, tinged with whiskey, chokes over me.

I huff and snatch my arm back. Like my bastard of a father cares. He stopped being my dad the day my mom died.

He didn't want to accept what his man did to me. He couldn't bear to be around me after I told him. All he is is a power-hungry thug.

"Well, he doesn't need to worry. I'm totally fine. Just having a good time, living my life."

20 ~ LUNA MASON

I cross my arms and straighten my spine. I've gotten good at pretending to be okay. I do it every time I leave the house.

"Look. He cares about you; he just has a lot going on at the moment."

"Are you serious? He's had a lot going on for years!" I can't disguise the hurt in my voice. "I'm not having this conversation with you."

He frowns, and I turn my back on him and keep walking, the urge to shoot some vodka taking over. If I'm sober, I feel. I feel so fucking much it cripples me.

He shakes his head and assumes his position for the night to watch me. I storm off and search for my friends in the sea of faces. Spying Liv's bouffant blonde hair, I head to their table at the back of the room.

The top is lined with drinks. Liv and Jas eye me suspiciously as I toss back a shot before even saying a word, letting the vodka set my body on fire. Making me numb.

Just how I like it.

But it's not enough. Nothing is ever enough. This is my life. Day after day, drink after drink. It's the only way I can stop the recurring nightmare of *him*. Even just temporarily.

"Hey bitches!" I say, plastering on a smile for them.

"Stressful day?" Jas asks, looking over her nearly empty glass with a grin.

"Something like that," I mumble.

"What's the plan for tonight?" Liv says, flicking her blonde hair over her shoulder.

A smile creeps up on my lips. I spy Bobby to my left, watching me like a hawk by the entrance to the bathroom.

"The same as all the other nights. Get fucked up, pass out, maybe find some guys to keep us up," Jas interrupts before I can reply. She finishes her glass of wine, then licks her bright red lips.

"Come on, little mafia princess, you had best head to the bar. You look like you need to catch up." Liv slides toward me.

I can't remember the last time I even had a hangover; that's mainly thanks to the cocaine. Since flunking out of college, the three of us moved in together, and we've partied hard since. The second I start to sober up, I can feel his teeth biting into my flesh, the weight of his body pressing me into the mattress. His cold hands gripping my hips.

I shiver in my seat, almost feeling his warm, whiskey-laced breath gagging me. Bile rises up my throat, and I swallow it back down.

Alcohol is not going to cut it tonight. The memories have been creeping back in more and more frequently.

"You're right. I need some shots and maybe something more."

My friends both look at me with a knowing smile.

"You best get to the bar and find us a guy; they always give it up for you. Little Miss Perfect Tits and Ass. Hell, how you get away with not sleeping with them for it, I'll never know," Liv giggles and downs her shot.

I scan the bar area, filled with suited men. One of them is bound to have what I need. I hate doing this, but when Dad cuts me off the desperation takes over.

"Fine," I huff out.

My drug lord father apparently draws the line at me taking what he supplies. What he doesn't know is that little line of white powder is the only thing keeping his daughter sane.

He wants to act like nothing happened to me. Fine. But I can't forget the moment my life was shattered by one of his men.

So I've found my own way to forget. Being that wild child, living up to my reputation.

"Well?" Jas questions, shaking me from my thoughts.

"I'm on it," I say and stand, shuffling my dress down over my ass and readjusting my bra so my tits perfectly fill the plunging neckline. I prop my arms up on my favorite place and signal to the fairly attractive dark-haired bartender.

"What can I get you, love?" The bartender grins.

"A vodka and Coke, please." I bat my eyelashes at him.

He nods and starts pouring. "This one's on me," the bartender drawls, snapping my attention to him.

I bite my lower lip, wondering if he has what I'm looking for.

"Thank you."

He gives me a wink and starts taking the next woman's order. I stir my straw around my glass and take a sip. Maybe if I drink it fast enough, I can call him back and ask him if he knows who I should talk to.

I just need a few more of these and a bump and *he* won't even be on my mind at all.

A deep voice booms from behind me.

"Asher, double scotch on the rocks, please."

Asher immediately stops what he's doing and starts pouring the scotch. I turn around, trailing my gaze up the tailored black suit until I am struck by emerald eyes.

Wow.

His dark hair is that perfect length I could run my fingers through. Day-old stubble frames his sharp jawline. He kind of has that sexy, rough-around-the-edges vibe.

"Why's a gorgeous woman like you ordering her own drinks?"

I stare at his full lips as he speaks. I blink a few times and shake my head to refocus.

Straightening my spine, I pull back my shoulders and meet his eyes. "Because it's the twenty-first century?"

He closes the distance between us, and I feel like I'm drowning in the heady scent of his aftershave.

What the hell is happening right now? This isn't me. Men don't get to me.

I close my eyes as he leans in, his lips brushing my cheek.

"Is that right?" he murmurs.

Heat spreads along my chest in a wave and crawls up my cheeks.

I turn my face into his and whisper, "There is something I need, though."

He chuckles and my heart rate picks up. The cut of his suit and the easy way he pulls his black Amex from his wallet screams money. They are always the ones with the good stuff. Just what I need to numb my brain.

His arms frame me against the bar. I can feel the heat of his body surrounding me as he leans his full lips near my ear. "And what is that, then?"

He raises a brow and gives me a boyish grin, his hand going into the inner pocket of his designer suit jacket. I notice a tease of a tattoo sticking out beneath his cuff as he pulls out the little baggie of white powder.

As he leans back in, his breath hits my cheek. "So, do you have a big night planned?"

Bingo.

"Yes." I bite my bottom lip and play my role, batting my lashes at him.

He takes a step back, his eyes roaming my body. He runs a hand over his stubble and lets out a ragged breath, his glance flicking to the bathroom. The now bodyguard-less bathroom.

"Not here." His voice is low.

He holds out his hand, but I hesitate for a second. His green eyes pierce into me, making me feel weird things in my chest.

Fuck it. If it means I can be numb again for the night, I'm taking it.

The second our palms connect, a spark flies, enough for me to try to jerk my hand back. But he doesn't let me; he just squeezes it tighter.

I follow his lead toward the bathroom. Not my place of choice, but it'll do for now. Excitement courses through me.

"Hey, what's your name?" I ask out of curiosity.

"Luca."

He doesn't look at me, he just walks us through the little hallway toward the fire escape. As he goes to push open the door, I ask, "Don't you want to know mine?"

He turns back to me and raises his brow.

"I don't need to ask. I know. *Miss Rosa Francesca Falcone.*"

I stop in my tracks, looking him up and down again.

The power, the suit, the Italian look.

"Shit," I whisper.

"Yes, shit indeed." He exhales and turns to face me.

His eyes bore into mine. Gone is the grin, the playfulness.

Panic chokes my words. "Please don't do this. I can speak to my dad. Whatever it is you want, he can give you—"

"Too late for that." He cuts me off, opening the door and dragging me out. The shock of moonlight burns my eyes. As the glare fades, I spot blood splattered on the ground. "No!" I see Bobby's lifeless body behind the Dumpster next to me.

Before I can take a lungful of air to scream, a hand clamps over my face from behind, smothering me. I flail around as much as I can, fighting for breath. But I give in; my life isn't worth fighting for.

Chapter Five
LUCA

I run a hand through my hair as I watch Grayson put an unconscious Rosa in the back of Frankie's car. The fear in those big dark eyes of hers didn't give me the thrill I thought it would.

"Boss, let's go!" Grayson shouts and taps the top of his car, startling me from watching Frankie speed off with Rosa.

I read through the notes that Grayson gave me, and I stared at her pictures for days. Grayson wasn't lying when he said there were men lining up for her. When I walked up behind her tonight, seeing her in the flesh, I realized the pictures didn't do her justice. She was dressed up with her long jet-black hair cascading down her back almost to her perfect, round ass. But when she turned to face me and her full red lips brushed against my cheek, my heart actually fucking fluttered.

So much so, I actually debated whether there was time to take her in the bathroom on the way out. I forgot who I was and what I was doing.

26 ~ LUNA MASON

I wipe my sweaty palms on my pants and head over to Grayson to slip into the passenger seat of his Audi.

"That was too easy." Grayson rips off his tie and puts on his sunglasses. "Frankie's taking her to your place and he'll put her in the basement. I have big plans with Maddie tonight."

"Who's going to watch Rosa? Frankie?"

He side-eyes me as we peel out of the parking lot. "Can't you do it?"

Shit.

"I have to go meet the commissioner. I'll call in Ramos to help with Rosa for a couple of hours until I get home. Get Frankie on sending the message to Marco." Digging into the pocket of my jacket, I pull out my pack of cigarettes. Why does a simple grab have my hands shaking like this?

"On it. Shall we send a body part? She doesn't need all ten fingers anyway." Grayson grins at me and looks at me over his aviators.

My eyes go wide. "No," I reply too quickly. "What the fuck is wrong with you? You know we have rules, even for the bratty daughters of our enemies."

"I was joking. She doesn't seem like your typical mafia princess. If anything, she's running from it." The dark outline of the club fades in the rearview mirror.

Why is she trying to get away?

"Hmmm."

I can't shake this feeling, this weird ache in my chest. This woman is going to wreak havoc on my life.

I CHECK MY tie in the mirror and swipe back my hair. Commissioner O'Reilly has summoned me in. Which can only mean one of two things: he wants more money, or he knows something.

I stand and wait by the docks, sparking up a cigarette. The pungent smell of the water slowly hits less as I try to burn it out of my nostrils. Dull shouting and the grinding sounds of machinery are drowned out by his heavy footsteps appearing behind me. I smirk at how recognizable his steps sound. "George."

"Mr. Russo."

He stops next to me, and we watch over the cargo ship as the boys load up the latest shipment.

"You have been causing quite the mess out there, Luca." His knuckles whiten as he grips the rail.

I roll my eyes, taking a drag.

"It's a busy time. You wanted the Falcones wiped out. Now isn't the time to start telling me to stop. Is that what you summoned me here for?"

I turn to face him, in his full NYPD outfit, badges lined up. Fucking joke that is our police force.

"The Capris, they're coming for New York. The Falcones have a shipment tomorrow night. We need you to intercept it. We can't let Marco or Romano run this city. I won't let it happen. So, once you take Marco out, you need to make the message loud and clear to Romano that he isn't welcome here." George clenches his jaw as he looks out over the ships.

"Why the Capris?" I keep my face deadpan, waiting for his answer. There is always more with him. But he's caught my interest.

He turns to me, leaning his hip against the rail, and crosses his arms. "They're the scum of the earth. Arms dealers, human traffickers. You name it, they do it. They need to stay on the other side of the pond with their poison." As if to emphasize his point, he spits onto the ground near his polished shoe.

"But you work with me?" This guy is confusing sometimes.

"Your father, believe it or not, was a good man. He saved my ass a few times. You are the lesser of two evils, Luca. You're humane, you respect women and children. You have a heart. That's why you need to run this city. Not Marco. And certainly not Romano."

I take in his words and swallow. He doesn't know I have Rosa tied up in my basement.

"I can do it."

I've heard enough about Romano Capri to know that stealing from him isn't going to be taken lightly. Like hell am I letting Marco think he can start running guns in my city. If anyone is, it will be me. And it sounds like the commissioner wants to keep it that way.

"You do that. Keep me posted. You know where I am if you need me." He stands and extends his hand, palm up.

I nod and stub out my cigarette on the gravel and slip out the envelope of money from my suit jacket. "This month's cut."

He slides it under the lapel of his uniform and straightens his tie. "Pleasure doing business with you, Mr. Russo."

I watch as he walks heavily along the docks and into the shadows.

Chapter Six
ROSA

My eyes flutter open, my mouth drier than waking up after a three-day bender.

The pounding in my head makes my vision blurry. I blink a few times and take in my surroundings. Plain gray walls with only a metal cart in the corner. I suck in a breath, spotting the bloodstains etched into the white-tiled floor.

"Shit." I pull against the ropes on my wrists binding me to the wooden chair.

As I look up at the door, I spot a red dot flashing.

A camera.

I take a moment to look at my arms—not a single scratch. I pull against the restraints again and try the ones around my ankles. I let out a defeated sigh when they don't budge.

The door squeaks open. It's not the guy from the club, Luca.

No, this guy is far younger, kind of eastern European looking. His gaze is fixed on me.

Batting my lashes at him, I put on the sweetest voice I can muster. "Please, could you untie me? I need to use the bathroom."

He doesn't respond, just grins and crouches next to me.

A chill runs through me, and I swallow down bile as he traces his index finger along my bare calf.

I'd rather he shot me between the eyes than touch me.

"You are a beauty," he whispers, sliding his palm up my slender legs.

My heart is lodged in my throat as he trails his finger past my kneecap. I squeeze my eyes shut.

Please no.

If I've survived this long, I can do it again. I repeat this mantra to myself over and over.

I know I'm lying to myself.

His face will just merge with Dante's in my nightmares.

A bang makes him jump, and he scoots back.

I turn my face away from him. He doesn't get to see me. To know my fear. Men like him thrive off it.

"I'll be back for you," he says as he stands. His tongue darts out to move over his lower lip.

Chills run down my spine, his heavy footsteps followed by the door slamming closed.

I was taken from one hell into another.

Chapter Seven
LUCA

Turning my attention to the monitor, I kick back in my chair and sip my scotch.

Rosa, Rosa, Rosa.

She fascinates me. She hasn't even flinched. She hasn't cried or screamed.

I underestimated her strength.

That tight little black dress is showing off all of her curves. She won't be able to wear that for as long as I keep her.

Musing what it would be like to have my hostage naked, I send Keller a quick text asking to borrow some clothes from his wife for my guest.

I'm glad he doesn't ask; I don't know if I'm ready to fill him in on this little adventure quite yet.

Taking a drag of my cigarette, I watch as she tilts her head back, letting her dark tresses flow over the back of the chair. I had to go and kidnap the most beautiful woman I have ever laid eyes on. When her breath tickled against my cheek in the club, my dick was throbbing.

The door opens, which catches my attention. Flicking my ash in the ashtray, I sit upright in my chair and watch.

Ramos stalks toward her, and she doesn't move. Her eyes are still on the ground.

I haven't asked him to check in on her. I only came upstairs to get changed before releasing her from the basement. Two hours is more than enough time for her down there. She isn't a threat to me.

I lean forward, propping my elbows on the oak desk, and turn the sound up.

"I told you I'd be back for you, pretty girl."

She tugs at the bonds on her wrists. It's the first response I've seen from her.

He leans over her, trailing a finger along her cheek. Pulling on her long hair to make her face him. But she doesn't; she looks straight past him to the camera and straight into my soul.

Pure fear radiates from her features.

Her chest heaves and all the color drains from her tanned skin.

Snatching my gun up from the desk, I rush down the stairs.

"Please don't. I'm begging you. Do anything to me but this. I won't survive this again." I can hear her as she screams hysterically through the door.

Again.

Tightening my grip around the gun, I push in the code to open the door to the basement.

I have to get to her.

How did he get her untied so quickly?

She's already on the floor, and all I can see are her legs as he straddles her while fumbling for his zipper.

"Shut the fuck up," I can hear him grumble as he puts his weight against her shoulder, driving her harder against the floor.

Her scream rips through the small room and fills my ears until they're ringing.

Rage completely consumes me.

"Get the fuck off her. Now!"

Ramos spins his head around to me with a shit-eating grin. Rosa's legs thrash as the scream turns to sobbing. This overwhelming need to protect her kicks in.

"Boss, I'm just having some fun. You can't bring a little thing so beautiful and not let us have a taste. The slut has been begging for it. I mean, look at that little dress she has on."

I stride toward him, my gun behind my back.

"Stand up," I command. Rosa falls completely still beneath him.

He does as I say, his loose pants hanging low on his hips, revealing his bare ass.

"Boss, what the hell? It's just a whore."

That does it.

I pull the gun out and aim it between his eyes.

"No man in my organization treats women with such disrespect. Men like you don't deserve to walk the streets."

He opens his mouth to respond, and I pull the trigger. Blood splatters up the wall. I give him a hard shove and he thuds to the ground.

Piece of shit.

I throw my gun down and it clatters against the concrete floor. I put my hands up to show her that I'm unarmed and walk toward Rosa. She's now huddled against the wall, tugging up the front of her dress.

"I'm sorry about him."

Her piercing brown eyes meet mine, and all the oxygen is sucked from my lungs.

As I approach her, she doesn't flinch. Her eyes scan me up and down.

"Can I help you up?" I hold out my hand, palm up, and wait for her acceptance.

She stares at my extended fingers for a moment before slowly reaching out and placing her cool hand in mine. Electricity jolts through me as she stands. Damn, he must have really tugged on her. I unconsciously rub the red marks on her wrists. She snatches them away.

"Don't touch me," she sniffles.

I take a step back and hold up my arms again in a sign of peace.

"You can trust me, Rosa. I won't hurt you. I swear on my life." I place my hand across my heart and smile at her.

Those chocolate-colored eyes narrow as she stares at me. "Right . . . coming from the guy that kidnapped me in the first place."

I shrug.

"But I did just kill one of my men for you." I let my arms drop, gesturing to the embarrassment to my organization that now lies stiffening beside us.

She looks down at Ramos's lifeless body on the ground and back at me and rolls her full lower lip between her teeth. Her brows furrow as her wary gaze meets mine.

"Why?"

"Because he tried to hurt you. He touched you without your permission," I answer honestly, leaning against the doorframe.

She hugs her arms over her torn dress until her fingers dig into the soft skin above her elbows. "And what's to say you won't hurt me? I can't trust you."

I don't know why I am bothering to argue with her over this. I could just pick her up and take her upstairs. Yet something stops me. The way she screamed *I won't survive this again* has my mind reeling. My gut is telling me I have to tread carefully with her.

When I lift my arm to run a hand through my hair, she flinches. What the fuck happened to her?

"Well, how about this? I only need you long enough for Marco to agree to stop dealing with the Capris. While you're here, you can live in my house. What's mine is yours. I'll make it up to you for what that asshole did. You'll be the most pampered captee ever." I try to flash her my most charming smile.

"Or you could let me go home?" She bats her lashes and gives me a coy smile.

"You know I can't. You know how this life works, Rosa." Her name rolling off my tongue sounds so natural.

She throws one hand up in a wave.

"Pfft. My dad's obsessed with power. He won't stop until you're dead. He's not interested in me."

I can sense the pain in her voice. I know what it's like to be unwanted. It must be a theme for the children of mafia bosses.

"Noted."

She bends and picks up her shoes, letting them dangle at her side. Without the heels on, she is tiny in comparison to me.

"Come on, I'll give you the grand tour." I offer her my hand again and she accepts, placing her manicured hand in mine, and damn, my cock twitches.

She throws one more glance at Ramos before I lead her out of the basement.

"I can't believe you just did that to him." I can feel her shudder through her palm.

"I meant every word. Any man who treats women like that deserves to die. Earlier on, you said you couldn't survive this again?"

I stop short as she plants her feet into the ground, slipping her hand from mine. I turn to face her, and her eyes are shining with tears.

Shit.

"Hey, it's okay. If you don't want to talk about it, we won't. No more tears today." I close the distance between us.

She sniffles and smiles at me. I can't help but smile back at her as I hold my hand out to her once more.

She grabs it and my heart skips a beat. *What the fuck is this?*

I lead her to the grand hallway and through to the lounge. My place has the highest security known to man. She isn't getting out of here. So it's not going to make a difference if she's in the basement or roaming around the house.

"Go take a seat. I'll make some coffee." My hand feels naked without the heat of her fingers. A part of me wants to keep dragging her with me. But the shakiness in her steps tells me she needs to relax.

"Got anything stronger?" she calls out after me.

I ignore her. Grayson warned me about her habits. I don't know what she's running from. I have every intention of finding out. I need to make up for what Ramos did, and part of me wants to protect her. I owe her.

Chapter Eight

ROSA

As I sip the coffee, my hands shake uncontrollably. *What the hell?* I just need something stronger, anything, to settle my nerves.

"I need a drink, Luca."

Luca switches his attention to me from his phone and frowns. The black cabinets and white walls start to swirl. I need some air.

Nausea washes over me as I put the coffee down. I don't know how long it's been since I've had anything. Last night? I struck out at my dad's house.

Shit, I don't feel well at all.

I stand and stumble forward, catching myself on the coffee table. Swallowing past the excessive saliva now in my mouth, realization hits. God, I'm going to be sick.

I'm too scared to move. Everything is wavy. *Am I dying?*

"L-Luca? I don't feel well."

Before he can reply, my body shudders as my stomach feels

38 ~ LUNA MASON

like it's twisting on itself. I bend over and try to hold back the gagging that takes over my throat. I lose to my body and projectile vomit all over his marble floor. That doesn't lessen the cold sweats washing over me.

"Drink, Luca. I need a drink, or a bump? Please?"

I swallow the bitter taste in my mouth, the tremble in my hands only worsening. Rubbing my hands over my face, I dart toward the sink in the kitchen as another wave comes over me, my head feeling like someone is hammering at my skull from within.

I throw up, over and over again, until I am gasping for air.

I grip the counter to keep the room from spinning. "Drink . . . Luca." I can barely speak.

"Here." He puts a glass into my hands and helps me take a sip. As the flavorless liquid enters my mouth, I shake my head.

"No, I need something stronger. You don't understand."

"Rosa, you need to ride this out." His tone is soft but firm. He takes my hand and leads me into a bathroom covered in white marble.

"I can't." I'm not strong enough to do this. My whole body aches. I start to cry as the bile rises again, my insides burning.

"P-please, help me." My legs give out and I collapse onto the cool floor. The porcelain toilet is almost inviting.

"I promise I won't leave your side."

That isn't what I mean, but the second his hand strokes my back, the comfort is there, despite feeling like I am dying.

I throw up until I am dry heaving. My stomach still cramps in its efforts to expel the tiny sips of water that Luca keeps feeding me. All I can think about is finding a way to get out of this. Just one more drink and I'll be okay.

Weak and shaking, my body finally gives up from

exhaustion. My limbs are heavy and sweat beads on my fore-head. Luca is just a fuzzy shape in the periphery of my vision.

"Rosa? Rosa?" His voice is laced with panic, matching my own frenzy of emotions.

I try to open my eyes, but it's no use. I'm just so tired.

Chapter Nine
LUCA

Fuck. Her body goes limp against the toilet. How can she be so completely gray yet still so sweaty?

Shit, shit, shit.

Lifting her into my arms, I lay her down on my bed. One of my pillows gets pushed against her back to keep her on her side, just in case she throws up again. She's completely out of it.

Grayson told me he thought she might have a bit of a problem. I assumed it was just her partying hard.

What she's going through now is complete addiction withdrawal. The panic sets in when I realize this could kill her.

I stand at the edge of the bed, running a hand through my hair. What the hell do I do? I can't let her die, but I don't have a clue what can help.

Her dark hair sticks to her sweaty face, even as her fragile body shivers violently. I gently place the back of my hand on her forehead. "Shit."

DEVOTED ~ 41

She's boiling hot.

My heart twinges as she starts to heave, and I quickly lift her to a seated position. As I hold her upright and pull her hair out of her face, she spills acrid bile all over my floor.

"Rosa, it's going to be okay," I whisper.

She shakes her head, moaning as she clasps her trembling hands on her knees.

"I need a drink." Her voice is croaky. I can't give her a drink. I don't know why this urge to help her through this takes over. I don't know this girl, but something is telling me she needs to overcome this. Whatever it is she's running from is going to kill her if she doesn't get clean.

"You're so fucking strong, Rosa. You've got this, okay?"

I really hope she does.

MY BACK IS aching and stiff as I sit on the chair in the corner of my bedroom watching Rosa sleep. It's been an exhausting night of rushing her to the bathroom and holding her hair as she throws up, then carrying her back to bed.

The hardest part has been her screaming at me for a drink, clawing at my chest as I carry her and begging me to put her out of her pain.

I grew up on the streets; hell, I sell the stuff. I know how powerful that little white powder can be. Rosa, however, doesn't strike me as a typical junkie. She might be a mafia princess, a party girl, but this level is way beyond that. I'm not even sure she realized she was an addict.

As the sun starts to rise, I get my phone out and use my app to put the blackout blinds down. She needs to sleep. So do I, but I won't. Not until I know she isn't going to die on me.

42 ~ LUNA MASON

She needs someone to protect her, to care for her, and that person is me. Even if my heart is in my throat the entire time.

When she starts to groan in her sleep, I jump out of my chair and crouch beside the bed. I clasp my hand over hers. She's still warm, but not the furnace she was.

She coughs, and it spikes my panic.

"How are you feeling, Rosa?" I keep my voice calm, even though I feel like screaming right now.

Her voice comes out hoarse. "Like I've jumped in front of a bus, had my insides set on fire, and I have someone living inside my brain hammering on my skull."

She rolls onto her back and stretches out. I need to get her into some fresh clothes. Hell, even a shower.

Despite her deathly looking complexion, her beauty shines through. The silky fabric of her black dress rides up her thigh, and I can't pull my gaze away from her slender legs. I shake my head, trying to rid the dark thoughts stirring around seeing her on my bed.

"Do you still feel sick?" I can't stop myself from touching her forehead to check her temperature again.

Her eyes widen as she watches my hand. "A little. Nowhere near as bad."

Relief washes through me, exhaustion taking over. "I'll get you a glass of fresh water." When I return, she sits up, digging her heels into the mattress to scoot back against my headboard. Her cheeks pale, and that shake in her hand is still visible. I don't know if she can even hold the cup.

The bed dips as I sit on the edge. She won't even look at me; her fingers knot in her dress as I lean closer.

"Rosa, it's okay. I'm here to help you, not judge you."

She nods, avoiding my gaze. The quiver as she tries to drink has water sloshing over the rim, so I hold the glass up to her lips, and she takes a small sip. I'm mesmerized watching her throat bob as she swallows, making me shift uncomfortably next to her.

Something is clearly wrong with me.

She barely drinks half when I'm carrying her back to the bathroom and the water makes a swift reappearance. I sit on the tiled floor next to her, rubbing her back as she sobs, holding the toilet. I pull her into my arms and place her between my legs, holding onto her tight while her tears soak through my T-shirt. Her body shivers, and with shaking hands, she's grabbing hold of my top when I feel her go limp again.

"Shh, it's going to be okay, I promise you. You will get through this."

I'm pretty sure she won't recall any of the last twelve hours. Which can only be a good thing. The place she is at right now is the pits of hell. I just hope I can help her claw her way out.

Her breathing becomes regular, and I know she's back asleep. Lifting her easily, I carry her back to the bed and pull the thick comforter back over her. Taking my seat across the room, I pull out my phone. I'm in over my head and a hospital isn't an option. So I dial the only person I know that can help me.

"Luca, it's basically the middle of the night. What happened?" Her voice is muffled and groggy.

I check my watch—it's six a.m.

"I need your help, Mom. Can you come to my place?"

She sounds much more awake as a tinge of panic laces her words. "Of course, son. Give me half an hour."

I look over to the sleeping Rosa and let out a sigh.

"Thank you. Can you swing by Keller's on the way? He should have a bag of clothes ready for you."

"Should I even ask?"

"I'll explain when you get here."

I CAN HEAR the sound of soft steps and something being rubbed against the walls before Mom stops at the doorway to my room. Her mouth drops the same as the bag when she sees me. Her gaze switches between Rosa and me, making her eyebrows knot closer together with every glance. I'm cradling Rosa against my chest again. She started crying out in her sleep and thrashing around to the point I was scared she was going to hurt herself.

She rolls again, her arms wrapping around her stomach as a small moan escapes her lips, piercing into my heart.

Mom rushes to the side of the bed, tucking her long gray hair behind her ears before gently cupping Rosa's sweaty face.

"What's happened to this poor girl? Who is she?"

"She's going through withdrawal. I had no idea she was an addict. She's Marco's daughter."

"Luca!" She raises her voice and stands up to put her hands on her hips.

Rosa flinches in my arms, and I shake my head at mom, giving her the *not now* stare. She can shout and scream at me all she wants after Rosa has gotten through this.

"I just need your help, Mom. So does Rosa. I haven't slept or eaten since yesterday. She's been throwing up, sweating, and has been in and out of consciousness all night. I can't do this on my own anymore." I hate having to ask for help. It makes me feel like a failure.

Mom's face softens, and she nods, then pulls my head against her to ruffle my hair.

"Well, I'm glad you stepped up to help her. Go and get

some rest. I'll take over." I let Rosa down gently against the pillow, but it rouses her from her restless sleep.

"Nonna? Is that you?" Rosa's voice quivers as she speaks.

I shrug at Mom. At this point, I don't even know if Rosa knows her own name. Every now and then, there are moments she seems to have it together. This doesn't seem to be one of them.

Mom smooths out the wild hair around Rosa's face. "It's okay, dear. Do you think we can get you freshened up?"

Rosa shakes her head and nuzzles herself further into my chest, grabbing my shirt so tightly I can feel her nails digging into my skin.

"Don't leave me, Luca."

Her voice is soft, but it's like a kick in the gut. I hold her petite frame against mine and stroke her back.

"My mom is here to help you, Rosa. It's just for a little while."

When I manage to peel myself away, she sits up and watches me. Then, her face pales before she sways and droops back against the pillows.

Mom sits down on the bed next to her and places her hand over Rosa's. "You are going to be just fine. Come on, let's get you showered."

Thank you, I mouth and sneak out of the room, letting out a lungful of air as I do.

I don't want to leave Rosa, but I have to sleep. I have no idea how long her symptoms will last, so I have to be ready for the long haul. I won't let her down.

A light tap on the guest room door wakes me. I sit up and see my mom's furrowed brow and down-turned mouth greeting me.

"How is she?"

46 ~ LUNA MASON

"She's sleeping. I gave her some more water with some vitamins and electrolytes to keep up her strength. My God, does she need some. This stage should pass in a day or two. I don't know how far you're willing to go to help her, son. But she is going to be struggling with this every day for the rest of her life. I can see she has that fight in there deep down, but it's going to be tough. On both of you."

I swallow the lump in my throat and nod.

I can't explain it. I want to help her, and I am willing to do whatever it takes. I'm already itching to go back in there and check on her.

"I had no idea."

"She is going to be fragile, Luca. I don't know what happened to her. Just be gentle with her."

"You think I should let her go back home?" It would mess up all of my plans for Marco, but right now, I don't even care. Seeing her this sick makes my chest hurt for her.

Mom shakes her head. "No, not if that life is what put her in this mess. Right now, you are her best option. I know you'd never hurt the girl. Just be careful with this." She places her hand over my heart, the warmth from her palm burning into my chest.

I tilt my head while looking down at the creases framing her eyes. "I don't think that will be an issue."

I've never given my heart to anyone. I am certain this is the same. Just because I want to help her doesn't mean I'm going to be madly in love with her. Even if she is the first woman in a long time to cause a spark in me just by being near her.

"Call me if you need anything. I'm heading to my Zumba class. Here is a list of everything you need to order for Rosa."

She hands me a slip of paper that is covered on the front and back with her delicate handwriting.

"Love you, Mom." The light smell of her chamomile soap envelops me as she gives me a quick kiss on my forehead.

"I love you, too. Now get back in there; she needs you." The bracelets on her wrist jingle as she pulls the door closed behind her.

After a quick shower, I almost feel human again. Tiptoeing down the hall, I peer through the crack in Rosa's door to see she's sound asleep. Good, I have a little while. My own body is starting to itch from the lack of nicotine.

I head out onto my balcony, closing the sliding glass door behind me, and spark up. Kicking my feet up on the little glass table, I watch as the clouds float by above my head. The last twenty-four hours have been a fucking eye-opener. My heart hurts for the suffering of that woman on my bed.

She might not have anyone to protect her, but while she's here, I will step up.

I get my phone and start on a mission. I need a therapist and some research. I need to know exactly what I'm dealing with and the best way to help her.

Chapter Ten

ROSA

My head is pounding, making me groan, as I crack my eyelids to see the sunlight streaming into the room. My face slides against the silky pillows, the unfamiliar sandalwood scent a fast reminder I'm not at home.

Shit, where am I?

I bolt upright, and my eyes land on Luca. His elbows are resting on his knees, holding his head up. How long has he been here?

"How are you feeling?" His voice is gravelly, like he's tired.

I rub my forehead. The headache is so intense I can barely even think through it. "I'm okay, I think. How long have I been out of it?"

His sharp jaw clenches as his green eyes darken. "Don't worry about it. You're okay now."

I don't totally remember the last few days . . . weeks . . . ? A lot of throwing up and so much pain. I feel absolutely disgusting. When I pull back the covers, I'm surprised to see myself in an oversized black T-shirt and dark sweatpants that I don't even recall getting into.

Swinging my legs over the side of the bed, I suck in a breath to stop the room spinning. I've never been so weak in my life. I never, ever want to experience this again.

When I slowly push myself up, Luca jumps across the room with his arms out like he's ready to catch me if I fall. Leaning against the mattress, I steady myself.

He stands right next to me. "I'm here to help you, if you need it."

I grab onto his arm, my legs are so wobbly. "This is fucking embarrassing," I mutter to myself. Even if he is my captor, no one should have ever seen me like this.

"You're good, Rosa. You've got this." He's like a rock, firm and steady next to me.

I hiccup. My emotions are too much right now.

"I'm sorry you've had to deal with this. I bet this wasn't what you signed up for when you kidnapped me."

His warm palm covers my hand resting on his. "This isn't about me. If this is what it takes to heal you, then I'm glad I did it."

He doesn't know what I'm running from. I bet if he did, if he knew how tainted I am, he wouldn't be saying that. No one would.

As I take a step forward, my footing falters and I crash into his chest. His strong arms wrap around me, and for the first time in my life, I feel safe. I probably shouldn't, knowing who he is. My dad's enemy, a mafia boss. But right now, he is all I have. Of all the evils in my life, Luca is my best option. I close my eyes for a second, letting the sound of his heart calm me, his chest rising and falling steadily.

"How about I run you a bath and go and make you some

breakfast?" The rumble of his words vibrates soothingly against my cheek.

Both options sound heavenly right now. The fact that he's so willing to go out of his way for me, to care for me, has me wanting to cry. It's so unfamiliar, but it's the best feeling in the world.

"I'd like that."

After a long, relaxing soak in the bath, I look at myself in the mirror without a scrap of makeup on. My skin is a little less gray and my eyes look less dead. Maybe I am getting somewhere. This is the longest I've gone without a drink in years. The tremble in my hands reminds me I am nowhere near out of the woods yet.

When I open up the walk-in closet, it makes me gasp. Luca told me he had clothes delivered for me, but I wasn't expecting a full wardrobe's worth. I run my fingers along the fabric— sweaters, jeans, pretty lace shirts, in every imaginable color. His suits are neatly hung at the end. I'm assuming I'll need to move all this into another room at some point. There's no way he'll be okay with me taking over his life. I open up the drawer inside and find a variety of underwear all neatly folded. All black.

I shimmy on some panties and throw on some leggings and a hoodie. There are even scrunchies and a bag of makeup and skin-care products left on the bedside table. He's seen me at my absolute worst, so I can at least try to make myself a little bit presentable. Even if it's just to get that worried look off of his face.

I snatch up the bag and head into the bathroom again, working my magic, making my skin glow, and shove my curly hair into a messy bun.

As I head down the stairs, the smell of breakfast cooking

makes my stomach rumble. Luca is whistling to himself and flipping pancakes. How did I not notice before that he was just wearing a tight-fitting black T-shirt and gray sweatpants that show off every damn muscle?

His head turns to see me and his face lights up.

"Wow," he whispers, before smiling and returning to the stove.

My cheeks burn as I sit up on the barstool over the kitchen island. He scatters fresh fruit over the pancakes with a practiced flair, and I lick my lips as he places a plate down in front of me.

I can't even think of words worthy of how delicious it smells. "This looks incredible."

He winks at me and slips onto the seat next to me. I can't help but keep peering over as he eats, watching his muscles flex as he cuts into his meal.

After a moment, he pauses and his eyes meet mine. "What's the matter? You aren't hungry?"

His voice shakes me from my daydreams. How long was I staring at him?

"Y-yes. I——" Shit. I avert my gaze and quickly shove food in my mouth to avoid any conversation. His soft laugh when he turns back to his plate sends a warm shiver into my belly.

I manage to make my way through the whole thing. The sugar is already battling my exhaustion. Feeling like I need to repay him for his kindness, I start to take the plates, but he places his hand on my arm, stopping me. Tingles erupt on the contact, and I find myself staring at the touch.

He pushes his chair out and pulls the dish from my grasp. "You stay where you are. I've got this."

"I want to help. I don't want to be useless anymore. You've done so much."

He huffs and steps away. The second his hand is gone, I miss his touch. What the hell? This is new. I've never wanted a man's touch, yet his makes me giddy and safe.

As he loads the dishwasher, I put all the fruit scraps into the garbage, humming away to myself.

"I have to go to work today. I'm not sure what time I'll actually make it home tonight."

I can sense the unease in his voice. God, I must have really been a mess for him to sound this worried about leaving me.

"I'll be fine, Luca." The water almost scalds my fingers as I wet a cloth to wipe the counter.

He leans against the closed dishwasher door and crosses his large, tattooed arms across his chest. "Are you sure? Because if not, I can cut out my training session with Grayson, so I'll be with you most of the day."

"I swear, I feel better today. I'll just watch some movies, maybe sit outside and get some fresh air. Going through all of my new clothes will take most of the day."

I bite back a grin, pulling on the sleeves of my sweatshirt so he can't see my hands shake.

He pulls out a phone from his gray sweatpants and holds it out to me. His eyes narrow as he stares at me. I'm frozen in place, struggling to focus on anything other than those green eyes and their little flecks of brown.

"This is locked to my number only. If you need me, for anything, you call me."

I take it from him and hold it tightly, letting its warmth from his body seep into me. "I will. Now go get ready. I can finish up here."

He takes a few steps away and stops, spreading his broad palms on the island countertop. "I mean it. Please call me."

My heart flutters over his protectiveness of me.

"Promise." My finger makes a cross over my heart.

We gaze into each other's eyes. I have no clue for how long we stare in silence. The air around us almost feels electrified. The spell is broken when he clears his throat and backs away.

"I'll see you later, then, little one." He winks and snatches up his keys.

It leaves me sagging against the counter, wondering what the hell is happening.

Chapter Eleven
LUCA

I swing open the doors to King's Gym, Keller and Grayson's boxing club. Tossing my bag down next to the ring, I watch as the two owners beat the shit out of each other.

The ladies' kickboxing class in the far corner has stopped their training to ogle the two sweaty beasts sparring in the ropes.

"Time's up! My session starts in"—I check my Rolex—"forty-five seconds."

They stop and Keller clocks Grayson on the side of the jaw and laughs.

I'm desperate to unleash some of this anxiety brewing inside of me. I'm still not totally okay with leaving Rosa on her own, despite her assuring me she will be fine. She is so fragile, it's hard to feel comfortable being gone.

I don't know how to cope with this overwhelming need to protect her. When I'm with her, I forget about myself. She is my focus.

"Asshole," Grayson grunts, rubbing his jaw.

I may not have any blood family, but these two are my brothers. Keller, my foster brother turned heavyweight boxing champion of the world. The "Killer" himself. His title fight brought in enough money to pay this place off so I could let him retire from my organization. He left some big shoes to fill as one of my enforcers, so I'm fucking lucky I had Grayson there to take his place.

They're both lethal. And both are angry. I'm glad they're on my side.

Keller unlaces his gloves with his teeth. "Brother," he pants out, resting his huge, heavily tattooed frame on the ropes.

I stand there for a moment watching him catch his breath. "Being a dad got you out of shape already?"

He scowls at me. I might joke, but he has never been happier. He and Sienna have a perfect family with their kids Max and Darcy.

Grayson jabs Keller in the arm. "He's back in fighting shape. Your next opponent will be lucky to get out alive."

Keller's come a long way from fighting on the streets. That's how we grew up, with no parents or home. We fought for everything. Food. Money. Hell, even for our lives, in some cases. We always had each other's backs, and always will.

I jog up the steps and duck under the ropes.

"Everything okay?" Keller asks after he takes a drink. I can hear the concern in his voice.

Just because I probably look tired, it shouldn't be a sign of something wrong. "Yeah, why wouldn't it be?"

Grayson chucks over some gloves for me.

Keller crushes the empty plastic bottle in his large hand. "I heard you've got a certain Falcone daughter residing at your place."

I flick a glare to Grayson, who shrugs.

"Don't worry about me. I have it under control. I'll see you tomorrow night for dinner. Can you make that chicken dish? I've been thinking about it all week."

"I'll ask Sienna." He grabs my shoulder and brings his face level with mine. "All you have to do is ask if you want my help, Luca. Family first. Always. We've had each other's backs, nothing has changed there."

But it has. He has something I can't let him lose.

"Keller, Mom would rip me limb from limb if I let you back. We're good." I scowl at Grayson past his shoulder. He shouldn't have told Keller about Rosa.

I'm not dragging Keller into this. He would tear the world down to protect his family. He would die for them. I won't put him in a position to do that.

I jog away from him and put up my gloves, motioning Grayson to join me.

Grayson holds up the pads, and I start to throw some jab combinations. Left, right, left, duck. Over and over again.

"Ready to fight?" I wipe the sweat from my forehead.

His eyes light up. "I'm always happy to knock you on your ass, Luca. I've only got twenty minutes. Maddie is meeting me here."

"You two straightened out your little argument?"

He scrunches his face up, "Maybe, let's see if she shows."

"She will."

It's so obvious they are in love. It's sickening.

"I would have paid millions to see her pull a gun out on you," I chuckle.

He shakes his head. "Shit, it was scary and hot all at the

same time. I always said she'd try to kill me one day. Honestly, just wait until you meet your Maddie. I would have let her shoot me. That's the scary part."

"I don't think that's in the cards for me yet. Although, if I do, I'll be snatching that gun out of her hands and shoving it up her pussy until she's screaming my name."

I burst out into laughter as Grayson bites the inside of his mouth, sporting a grin, and shrugs.

"You filthy fucker. I'm jealous." I have tears running down my face.

"Whatever. Let's box. When you're in the ring, I'm the boss." His hands come up under his chin as he bounces closer.

"Well, now I can't concentrate. I won't be able to look at you holding a gun the same way again." Dropping my arms to my sides, I'm laughing so hard I don't have the strength to pick them up.

I snap my mouth shut when his glove hurtles toward my face. I duck out of the way, but he nails me on the side of the head. It's the kind of pain I need to distract myself from life right now.

I KILL THE engine and am shrouded by darkness. The flame of my lighter illuminates the inside of the car briefly as I light up a cigarette while I wait for Frankie and Vince. Grayson's too busy taking Maddie on a date in London.

They pull up in a dark box van next to me. Silently, we climb out of our vehicles and grab our gear.

It's time to steal guns from the biggest crime family in Europe.

The three of us weave our way through the stacked

58 ~ LUNA MASON

cargo containers before I give the signal to stop. Dropping to one knee, I peer slowly around the corner. There are three men guarding our goal, the guns slung across their backs reflecting the spotlights. They're facing away from us, watching as the boat pulls up. Vince clambers up to a better vantage, his silenced sniper rifle strapped snugly across his shoulders.

I look at Frankie, who doesn't take his eyes off the men.

"He sent his fucking rookies to a gun deal," he mutters.

"Handy for us." They aren't ready. We are.

As the boat docks, Vince fires a quiet shot and the guy in the middle thuds to the ground. The other two jump away, aiming their guns in the air randomly. The wrong way.

"Let's do this," I grunt to Frankie.

We crouch and move toward our targets. I gesture to him at the Falcone straight ahead of me. Pulling the knife from my pocket, I creep up behind him, grab him around the throat, and slash from left to right. Warm blood spills across my forearm, and I toss him to the ground as he clutches at his throat. I watch the life drain from his eyes and then turn my attention to Frankie. He has the last guy in a headlock. When I hear the snap, I cringe and Frankie drops him.

"Ouch," I whisper to him with a grin.

"Says you." He looks down at the dead guy on the ground next to me.

Footsteps signal Vince joining us, and we walk toward the boat.

There's only one guy that I can see, and he's tying up the boat.

I press my gun against the back of his head, and he stills.

"Guns," I bark at him. "Load them in that van. Now."

"Eh?" He turns to face me, the tip of my gun now at the

center of his forehead. He looks past me, to Frankie and Vince on either side of me, and then down.

I laugh as the shock appears on his face when he spots the bodies. "I see you've spotted your friends back there."

"I-I am not part of this. I'm just the delivery guy." His voice quivers.

I jab the barrel hard enough to leave a half-circle cut on his head. "Load the guns into the van. Tell Romano there is only one way to ship his guns into New York and that's through Luca Russo."

He steps back, nodding frantically and calling in Italian to someone in the boat.

Frankie pulls his own pistol up as a young guy appears at the steps, shaking like a leaf.

"Go on, then." I shove the old man with my gun.

Once they load up the back of the van, Frankie slams the doors shut.

"You sort out the mess here, V," I say while I'm texting the quantities to Enzo.

"You got it." The short Russian herds the two boatmen back toward the docks.

Frankie hops in the truck. Not a single hair is out of place on his head. This life comes naturally to him.

I hit send on the text and look up at him. "Good job. Get those back to our warehouse. Keep them hidden; the less people that know about this, the better."

He doesn't say a word, just drops his chin before firing up the diesel and backing out of the alley.

My boots kick along the gravel. I should have gone with him to make sure everything gets well covered.

Something is screaming at me to get home.

To get to her.

BY THE TIME I get there, it's two in the morning. I'm careful as I creep past the guest bedroom, not wanting to disturb Rosa.

I head into the en suite and wash the blood off my hands. The water swirls a deep red. Gripping the side of the sink, I stare at my reflection in the mirror. My hair is tousled, with splatters of blood smothering my white shirt and speckled all the way up my neck. My jacket and shirt get tossed in the ever-growing pile of laundry. It takes forever to scrub the dried crust from under my nails.

Turning on the shower and cranking the heat up, I stop as I go to take off my pants. I swear to God, that sounds like yelling. I rush out of the room into the hallway.

Screams rip from Rosa's room.

"Get off me!" I can hear the panic in her voice.

What the fuck? I dart back into my room and snatch the gun off of my bedside table. I slowly push open her door with my weapon at the ready, then flick on the light.

Her cries get louder. I scan the room and she's in bed, wrapped up in the blanket, but rolling around and shrieking in agony.

Oh shit.

My gun clatters to the floor. I rush over to her side and crouch down. Sweat beads on her forehead, and her eyes are squeezed shut as if she's in pain.

"Please, no," she whimpers.

I reach out to touch her but stop myself.

"Rosa," I whisper.

Her body flails around the bed. It's like she's possessed.

I can't watch this; her wails are eating me alive. It's pure, guttural misery.

Without thinking, I get on the bed and pull her body into mine. Carefully, I hold down her arms and wrap her in an embrace.

"Shh, Rosa. It's me, Luca. No one can hurt you here," I whisper into the top of her sweaty head.

I can stop anyone physically hurting her, but I can't fix what's tormenting her on the inside. If I could take some of her pain, I would in a heartbeat.

I hold my breath, holding her snugly.

Her screams turn into tears falling against my bare chest. I keep talking to her, telling her I'm here and that she's okay.

I don't know what is haunting her, but now I realize why she's so desperate for a drink. And why she looked at me in horror when she found out her room was next to mine.

She didn't want me to see her like this.

I sit with her, letting her settle in my arms. I'm too scared to move or startle her. So I stay exactly where I am for hours. To the point that my back aches and my arms are dead.

As the sun starts to rise, I carefully lift her head to rest it on the pillow and slip out from under her.

I take one last look as I close the door. She looks peaceful now.

My grip on the door handle tightens and my jaw clenches. Whatever demons are doing this, I want to fucking kill them.

Chapter Twelve

ROSA

I wake with a start, feeling around the bed. *Where the fuck am I?* I sit up quickly with my hand on my chest as my heart beats against it.

Come on, Rosa, get it together.

My head throbs, and embarrassment takes over. My nightmares are back. He's back. And what's worse, Luca has seen my weakness.

When I finally gather the courage to get up, I rummage through my drawers and look for a sweater. My door is cracked open. As I step into the dark hallway, I notice Luca's room is the same.

Stopping for a second, I bite my nails as I debate my next move. I don't want to talk about my nightmare; I can't. I haven't uttered the words since it happened and I told my dad. The more Luca witnesses, the more questions he is going to have. I won't be able to hide it from him.

I tiptoe to his door and peer in. The natural light streams

in, highlighting his sleeping form. I have no idea how long he stayed up with me last night, or what I screamed in my sleep. I just remember his bare skin holding me. This is the first I've seen him without his shirt on: His chest has splashes of black tattoos that follow both of his arms to his wrists. The sheet is tangled around his waist, and a part of me wants to see what he's hiding.

The floor creaks as I take a step closer, and I let out a gasp, looking at his face. His green eyes are now open and focused on me.

I back away and run down the stairs to the kitchen.

I wonder what it would feel like to have him touch me. To have his full lips pressed against my own.

But darker thoughts overwhelm me. Older memories. All I can see are Dante's black eyes glaring at me. I can feel his slimy hands on my skin and his wet lips on my neck.

My own brain hates me, and I need to stop it. I need to drown it out.

I start opening the cupboards frantically. Luca's a mafia boss. He's got to have something here.

On the second cupboard, I grab the first bottle that comes to hand and put it on the counter in front of me.

Bile rises up my throat as the nightmarish memories overwhelm me until I pop open the top and raise it to my lips.

"Rosa." Luca's stern voice interrupts me.

I let go of the vodka, like I've been caught stealing.

He storms toward me and snatches it from me. I watch in horror as he pours the contents down the sink. He then proceeds to do the same with every damn bottle in that cupboard.

Before he can finish the last one, I claw at his arm.

"I don't need your help. I don't want it. Just give me the

rest of that and I'll be fine. Just fuck off and let me live my life how I know."

I tug his arm, and he doesn't flinch. He doesn't look at me.

"Luca, give me the bottle!" I scream at him.

"Enough, Rosa!" He smashes the glass against the counter and I flinch back.

He runs a hand across his stubble, almost in annoyance.

Desperation starts to take over; my throat feels like it's closing up. I'm trapped in my own circle of terror inside my brain, and the one relief I have has just been dumped down the sink. I can't live with these nightmares. I just can't do it.

"You can kick and scream at me all you like. I'm not stopping. I will help you, whether you like it or not." His eyes bore into mine, and I slink away from him.

"This"—he points at the shattered glass—"is not your answer, Rosa. You have the strength up here." He points to his temple with his index finger and walks toward me.

My bottom lip quivers as he approaches and towers over me. "I want to help you, Rosa. I really do. But that has to stop. I won't let you do this to yourself under my watch. You've handled the absolute worst of it and you got through it like a boss. Now you have to fight it every damn day, but I will be with you every step of the way. I promise you."

His features soften, those bright green eyes meeting mine. I hold on to the barstool for support, squeezing the leather.

He wants to help me?

"Why?" I blurt out, without even thinking.

He frowns and lowers his head so our faces are level. It feels like he's staring right into my soul.

"Because I like you. Because I can feel your pain every time we're in the same room. Although you may not, I see your potential. I want to help you stop hurting. I want you to be able to walk out of here when this is over and live your life. I had my life taken away from me, and I know how it feels to not be certain of who you truly are and where you belong."

I hiccup and hold back the tears burning in my eyes. I can't talk, so I simply nod my head.

"Come here, little one," he whispers.

I look up at him and my heart flutters. He's smiling, his perfect white teeth poking through, his arms open, inviting me in for a hug. I wrap my arms around his waist, and he pulls me so tightly into him I can barely breathe. His heart pounds against my ear, nearly making the erratic rhythm as my own.

I let my body relax for the first time in a long time. Taking comfort from him, I close my eyes and just breathe. I've been running my whole life; I've never truly stopped for long enough to just live in the moment. To feel. To let anyone in to help me.

"I want to help you fight this, Rosa. If you'll let me?" he whispers, and my chest constricts.

"You have no idea what you're letting yourself in for, Luca."

Chapter Thirteen
LUCA

"Brother, you need to get hold of Grayson. He was a fucking mess about last night." Keller's deep voice booms through the speaker as I wait for my coffee to pour.

I grit my teeth. I won't let anyone hurt my family again. Last night was supposed to be a simple hit at the casino. It was all arranged with the manager and commissioner.

Turns out, Marco had more men there undercover and one decided to try to rape Maddie in the bathroom. Grayson took him out, but it was another close call.

"I'm meeting him soon. I'll straighten this out. We're close to ending this." I can taste victory. I know we're getting under Marco's skin.

There's a pause on the line. "Maddie's pregnant."

Shit. I run a hand over my face; I need something stronger than a coffee.

"That's good news, right?" I ask, confused by my brother's harsh tone.

"It would be if I didn't have Grayson in my office after nearly killing one of our new recruits this morning. He thinks he can't protect them, that he's not cut out for this. He's spiraling."

"I'll speak to him. You know I'll do anything to protect our families, right?"

He sighs. "I know. Luca, you need to let us in. Don't kill yourself over this on your own."

I stifle a yawn and we say our goodbyes. I need to get to Grayson and make sure he's okay. I'm running off of three nights of no sleep.

Rosa wasn't lying when she said she needed a drink to help her sleep. Every scream is like a punch to the gut. I am hurting for her. Last night, I held her until she calmed down and then I fell asleep cradling her in my arms.

All I want to do now is find a way to get inside her brain and take whatever memory is haunting her away. She's been on edge since I dumped the alcohol. It fucking pained me to watch my Macallan swirl down the sink. But this could be her one chance in life to fight for herself.

I just can't quite work out why I care so much about this woman and her future. Or why I spend my afternoons digging into her past from the notes Enzo shared. So far, there isn't any clue as to who did this to her.

Because I swear to God, I will hunt him down and cut his dick off. As I take a drink, I notice the time on my gold Rolex. Ten a.m.

She should be getting up any time now.

Setting aside my own mug of black coffee, I fire up the machine to make hers. She likes everything sickeningly sweet, so I grab the milk and caramel syrup from the fridge.

A smile creeps onto my face as I hear her light footsteps coming down the stairs.

I have no idea if she knows I've been cradling her in her sleep. I don't want her to know and be embarrassed.

She groans as she slides herself up on the barstool.

"Morning, grumpy," I say, handing her a steaming cup of coffee.

Dark circles surround her eyes, and her usual olive complexion is gray.

"Are you feeling okay, Rosa?" I straddle the stool across from her.

She stares past me and doesn't respond.

"Rosa?"

She shakes her head. "Huh?"

"I said, are you okay?"

"Fine." She sips her coffee and I grab my own.

"I have to head out. The fridge has been stocked back up. I'll make us some dinner when I get home."

She nods.

I sigh and take in her shrinking figure. She has been eating, but nowhere near enough. The withdrawal effects of her lifestyle are hitting her hard. Add in the nightmares on top, and I fear she's a ticking time bomb.

And I can't watch her explode. I won't.

As I walk past, her hand flies out and grabs my sleeve.

I stop and turn to face her.

"Thank you," she whispers, not looking me in the eye. I can't help but notice the pink blush spreading along her chest.

"What for?" I hold my breath. I know what she's about to say.

"I know you've been helping with my night terrors, Luca. I've never had anyone to help me through those." She takes in a breath and snaps her lips together.

My chest aches. I can't imagine how hard this is for her. "How long have you been dealing with them?"

She bites her lower lip. "Six years."

I cover her fingers with mine and squeeze her hand.

"I'm so fucking sorry," I say quietly.

She drops her hand from mine, so I take a step forward and tip her chin up. Those big dark eyes gaze into mine, stealing my breath away.

"Give me the name, Rosa. I need his name. I can make him go away."

Fear flashes across her face and she chews on her lower lip. A tear rolls down her cheek that I swipe away with my thumb.

She squeezes her eyes shut as she shakes her head slowly. "I-I can't. Don't make me say it."

"Shh, it's okay. One day, when you're ready, you'll tell me the name, and I promise I will end him."

My jaw tics as I think of all the ways I'll punish that man, but I keep my touch light on her face.

She looks down and plays with the hem of her shirt. "Luca, I'm not your problem to fix. I'm just the woman you kidnapped. Once I leave here, I'll go back to being the broken girl trying to claim back a sense of control. That's just my life."

This protective feeling I have over her surges within me. She sounds so fatalistic. Something isn't sitting right with leaving her, not like this.

I'll make sure I wrap this meeting up in record time so I can get back to her. Maybe I shouldn't even go. "Are you sure you're feeling alright? I can stay home if you need me?"

Her bottom lip trembles, and she shakes her head as little beads of sweat form on her forehead. I thought we had gotten past this stage of the withdrawal. Since the nightmares started, she's become a shell of herself.

Chapter Fourteen
ROSA

I pace around the kitchen, my mind reeling from this morning. I can't stand these nightmares. It has been so long since I found my drinking *cure*. I forgot how real they feel; it's like Dante is there in the room with me, and I'm that innocent seventeen-year-old again whose world is about to be ripped apart.

I itch at my neck. I can't let Luca see me like this again.

When he touched my face, it was like everything melted away for a second. It's more than that. It's his comforting strength and the way he holds me through my nightmares.

It's like he sees me.

He just knows what I need and doesn't falter.

But he doesn't know me. No one does. The pain that I endured is impossible to understand.

I throw open the next cupboard on my hunt for some

alcohol. The one thing I know can "fix" me for now. I can't be feeling these things for Luca.

My body is a furnace, and the sweat is dripping off my forehead. I can't focus on anything else right now except something that will make this stop.

Packets of pasta? Jars of sauce? There's a bottle in the back, but when I reach for it, it's soy sauce. There's nothing here that can help.

"Fuck!" I shout.

Taking a step back, I look at the chaos in front of me. Every cupboard door is open, food is thrown all over the countertops and floor. Anyone seeing this would think he's been robbed. Running my shaking hand through my hair, I wonder, *What am I doing?* What has happened to me?

I don't want to drink. I don't want the torture of weaning myself off again. I just need Dante to go.

Acid burns its way up into my throat, and my trembling hands lace around my neck as I try to swallow it down.

Taking a step back, I pick up the glass container and hurl it against the wall while letting out a scream.

I'm so broken and I don't know how to fix myself.

How do I get *him* out of my brain?

Rushing over to the sink, I grab the marble counter and throw up. My stomach heaves as I try to catch my breath. I start to panic when I can't stop. My whole body quakes as I pull at my hair and thud down onto the floor. The shards of glass scratch into the flesh of my thighs. Bringing my knees up against my chest, I close my eyes.

Dante's jet-black eyes stare back at me as his hand muffles my mouth to stop my screams. His heavy frame pins me underneath him. I squeeze my eyes shut, and bile rises up my throat again as I remember the way he ripped off my towel and bit me, drawing blood. Then, the moment he flipped me over and held me down.

"This virgin cunt is mine. Only mine." The words replay on a loop in my head. And it's always followed by the pain.

Tormenting me.

Chapter Fifteen
LUCA

As I open the front door, her cries echo through the house. I slam it shut and run.

"Rosa!" I choke out her name as I round the corner into the kitchen. She's curled up on the floor, knees pulled up into her chest, rocking back and forth. Her long dark hair is in tangles, like she's been knotting it for hours. As I scan the room, it looks like a war zone with stuff strewn everywhere.

Shit, this is bad.

I go to her and drop down onto my knees, pulling her tiny body against mine. Her hands latch onto my white shirt. "I-I can't get it out of my head," she sobs, pulling at my collar. "Over and over. He's all I can see. All I can feel. I can't take it anymore. I just want this nightmare to end."

I stroke her wild, dark hair as her tears soak my chest. "Shh, little one, everything will be okay. He can't hurt you anymore. I won't let him."

I wish I fucking knew who *he* was.

"He can and he is. He's inside my head. If I can't drink, I can't get rid of him."

I wrap my hands around her waist and stand, lifting her with me. Like it's the most natural thing in the world, her being in my arms.

I take us up to my bedroom, kick open the door and lay her down on my bed. I press the button to lower the blackout blinds while tugging off my tie and jacket. I get on the bed next to her, pull her into my side, and stare up at the ceiling.

"This is your safe space. Your sanctuary. And I want to listen. Give me your demons, Rosa. Let them out of your brain and into mine. Let me take some of this pain from you."

I can't bear her suffering like this.

And one thing I've learned through the years of battling with my own mind is you have to talk about it. I can be her person—someone that will just listen.

"None of this is your fault, Rosa. You can tell me as much or as little as you'd like. Okay?"

Her hand rests lightly on my chest, just above my heart, and it sends my pulse racing. So I flatten my palm over hers and hold it.

We lay there in silence for what feels like a lifetime. Her frantic breathing is the only thing I can focus on.

She takes a long, shuddering inhale before releasing the words I knew she had caged inside. "I was raped."

I squeeze my eyes shut and try to fight the flare of rage that threatens to overtake me. I fucking knew, but hearing it come out of her mouth makes me feel murderous.

"Oh, Rosa, I'm so sorry," I whisper, giving her hand a reassuring squeeze.

"He worked for my dad. He was five years older. I thought it was cool he was giving me, a little seventeen-year-old virgin, attention. He would always flirt with me behind my dad's back, telling me I was beautiful."

The asshole.

"And then one night, my dad was out. He came into our house and tried to kiss me. I said no. I wanted to save myself for 'the one.' But really, he was kind of creeping me out."

Clenching my jaw, I wait for her to continue.

"He stormed out, and I thought that was the end of it. But two days later, my dad went to get Eva from Sicily. She had stayed with my aunt over the summer. I had exams coming up, so I stayed home. Our mom died a few years before that, so our dad was barely home. He shipped us off most summers."

She stops and her body starts to tremble next to me, so I pull her in closer with my other arm and stroke her bicep.

"I just got out of the shower and he was sitting there, waiting for me on my bed." Her voice quivers, then falters.

I try to wait patiently, but the silence grows. Maybe she needs a little reassurance.

"You're doing amazing, Rosa."

She takes a deep breath, and I brace myself.

"I told him to leave, that I'd call my dad. He had my phone in his hand and shoved it in his pocket. I darted for the door, and he grabbed me before I could get out. He squeezed my wrist so tight, I can still feel it now." Her hand twitches against my chest as if she's fighting his grasp.

"I-I don't know if you'd want to hear the rest, do I need to do the graphic details?"

"You tell me as much or as little as you'd like. I can handle it, I promise you. If you feel letting out everything will help, then do it."

Her hair tickles my neck as she nods.

"He yanked me back by my head and threw me down on my bed. When I tried to climb off, he ripped the towel off of me. Pinning my arms over my head. And then he, uh—bit me."

I clench my jaw so hard my teeth grind, anger rolling through me.

"It left scars of his teeth marks. That's why I have this tattoo on my collarbone." She raises herself onto her elbow and pulls down the neck of her shirt.

"Jesus," I hiss.

I look down at the array of dark flowers that runs across the top of her shoulder and my eyes start to water. This poor girl.

"He told me that my 'virgin cunt' would always be his. When he flipped me over, he held me down. He was so heavy I could barely breathe. I tried to scream and cry and kept telling him no, but he wouldn't stop. It burned and hurt so bad it felt like he kicked me in the stomach. When he was finished, he kissed me. Then he said he would be back for me." Her words come out in a rush. Each tumbling faster than the next, like a dam has broken inside of her and she needs to get it all out.

"Fuck, Rosa." I run a hand over my face and let out a ragged breath.

Turning on my side to face her, I pull her in for a hug.

"I'm so sorry, Rosa. I can't even imagine that pain you're going through." She nuzzles her face into my neck, her nails digging into my skin.

"I'm so proud of you. You are the bravest woman to walk this earth. I promise I will make sure he never comes back. I swear on my life."

Her tears fall against my throat, her body jerking from the sobs racking her. All I can do at this moment is hold her.

"Where is he now?" I can call Enzo in the morning to find this monster.

"I don't know. My dad just said he took care of it. He refused to speak about it again with me. When I asked if he was dead, he shook his head. He let him live, Luca. If my uncle was there, he would never have let that happen."

She loses herself to her tears, and I rest my head on top of hers while she lets it all out.

I've wanted to take Marco out of power for years. But now, I won't stop until I kill that asshole. His one job in life is to protect his daughters, and he failed.

"All this time, you've been worrying about him coming back for you. Is that why you drink? Is that what the nightmares are about?" It's a struggle to keep my voice even with the fury burning so hot inside of me.

"He will come back, Luca. The look in his eyes—he's a psychopath. I drink to blur it all out. After it happened, I raided my dad's liquor cabinet, and the rest is history. Then when the alcohol didn't quite cut it, I took it further."

"The coke."

"Yes. It let me drink even more. So I'd completely black out and not be able to remember a thing." She buries her face against my chest. "It's embarrassing."

"You're a survivor, Rosa. You did what you needed to fight. You have nothing to be embarrassed about. Not with me, not with anyone. No one can tell you how to deal with your own trauma."

I deal with my demons by fighting and killing. She uses other means. Everyone uses something.

"I was so alone. I messed up my college, my future. He took everything from me. No matter how hard I try to regain some type of control over my life, he always wins."

She lifts her head, her hands pressing on my chest to sit herself upright.

"I want to be better. Maybe go back to college and do a photography course. Make some new friends. I don't know, maybe even get a boyfriend. I just want to be normal, without him holding me back, without living in fear."

I stiffen at her words. Or one word: *boyfriend.*

"You can do whatever you want to do, little one. I'll help you in any way I can, I swear."

I place my hand on my heart, and she covers it with her own.

"Thank you for listening. I never knew how much relief I would feel just saying it all out loud to someone willing to listen." The light from the hall creates a halo around her as she looks down at me.

"You are so strong, Rosa. I don't think you realize your own strength yet. I will always listen. I might not know exactly what you're dealing with. But I do know what it's like to be left alone. To fight with yourself every damn day. To feel like you're suffocating in your own thoughts, that you will never quite be good enough. Watching everyone else around you move on and have these perfect fucking lives and you're just stuck."

I let out a breath, and her hand strokes my cheek, making me smile.

"Well, who needs a therapist when we have each other, right?" She hiccups.

It's the cutest noise I've ever heard.

"I can get you the best in the country, if you would like?" I've already made arrangements for when she is ready.

"You would?" The surprise in her voice is clear, and it

breaks my heart. All this time, she really has had no one on her team.

Well, today, that changes. What she doesn't know is Dr. Jenkins, a top psychologist in her field, is lined up to visit when I call.

I rest my forehead against hers.

And, for some reason, it feels like home.

Something I've never truly had.

Chapter Sixteen

LUCA

My cock twitching wakes me up. I groan and rub my . . . pants?

What the hell?

Relief washes over me as her sweet coconut scent fills my nose. Last night comes flooding back to me. She fell asleep in my arms. I didn't want to wake her. I must have passed out at some point, too. I was anticipating another nightmare after everything she unpacked last night.

Her arm wraps around my chest. As I slowly slip out from under her, I watch as her full lips slightly part and a deep breath flutters out. She is perfect.

Gently resting her head on the pillow, I tiptoe out of the room.

As I am about to leave, I somehow find myself standing outside my bedroom door. Maybe I could get Maddie and Sienna over to keep her company during the day? Surely being on her own for so long could be making it worse.

DEVOTED ~ 81

I pinch the bridge of my nose, willing away the ache at my temples.

My phone starts vibrating against my chest in my jacket.

"Hello?"

"Mr. Luca Russo, I assume?" A thick, gravelly Italian accent greets me.

"Who's asking?" My stomach sinks with the options.

"Romano. You wanted my attention. Well, now you have it."

Fuck. My mind isn't with it for this. "Did you get my message?"

He laughs on the other end. "Do you have any idea who you're dealing with?"

"Do you?" I spit back.

"If the Capris want to run guns into New York, we don't need anyone's permission." His voice raises.

Now it's my turn to laugh. "That's not how it works here."

He pauses with a small chuckle. "You've got balls, I'll give you that."

I roll my eyes.

"Look, what do you want? I'm busy," I say, as I hear Rosa closing the door to the bathroom.

"I'll start with getting my guns back. Once I have those, I might have some information that you'd be interested in having."

I don't give a shit what he knows. "No deal."

I end the call. I don't have time for this right now.

RIPPING OFF MY tie the second I walk through the front door, I follow strange noises coming from the living room.

82 ~ LUNA MASON

She's shoveling in popcorn, giggling to herself. At this moment, this is a carefree version of Rosa. My cheeks start to hurt from smiling at her. That weird warm fuzzy feeling stirs up in my chest, making me rub it.

"Are you going to stand and stare all night, or do you want to watch with me?"

She doesn't look away from the movie as I drop down on the other end of the couch. She side-eyes me and hands over the bowl, but not before taking another huge handful.

"What are we watching?" I mumble around a mouthful.

"*Bridesmaids.*" She doesn't elaborate, and we sit in silence for a moment.

"So, it's about some wedding?" That gets her attention as her head swings around to face me, her jaw hanging open.

"You haven't seen *Bridesmaids*?" she says in disbelief.

I toss one of the buttery morsels at her, aiming for her gaping mouth.

"Hey!" It misses and lands where her shirt flares over her chest.

"I usually just watch boxing videos. Is there a fight in it?" I can't help but tease as I stuff a handful in my mouth. Her eyes sparkle with menace as she clambers over and snatches the bowl back. Her hand brushing mine sends jolts of electricity through me.

"I guess you'll just have to watch and find out." She settles beside me, with the bowl resting in the gap between her legs.

We sit in comfortable silence. I spend most of the film watching her. The way her face lights up, the way her neck bobs when she drinks. The way she snorts when she laughs too hard.

I reluctantly stand after the film ends. I have to be at the warehouse to meet Carlo, our drug shipment coordinator, tonight.

"Luca?" Her voice halts my footsteps.

"Yes, little one?" I lean against the doorway, watching her cheeks flush. They always do when I call her that.

"I was thinking . . ." She trails off, her forehead creasing.

"Hmmm?"

She chews on her lower lip. "You know how you end up cuddling me to sleep most nights, anyway?"

I bite the inside of my mouth, liking where this is heading already.

"I do." It's a struggle to keep my tone neutral.

"What about if we just slept in the same bed?" She looks down at the empty popcorn bowl and coyly rolls it on her lap.

I suck in a breath, rolling my bottom lip between my teeth as I feel blood rush to my cock.

"Not anything like that. I just like you cuddling me to sleep. You keep my nightmares away." She shrugs, making a pout with those lips I am so desperate to kiss.

I take a pause; I want to give her the impression I have to contemplate it. "Yes."

Her head tips up and her bright smile forms. It's the one that makes my heart race. "You really don't mind?"

I shake my head. "Trust me, I don't mind."

My cock might have to learn how to behave, and possibly my heart. I'm starting to realize there's not a damn thing I'd say no to this woman for.

* * *

MY PHONE VIBRATING on the nightstand wakes me. I pull Rosa tighter into me and nuzzle my face into the crook of her neck, taking a deep inhale.

A perfect way to wake up. Well, minus the irritating buzzing next to my head.

I groan and roll over, careful not to disturb the little beauty still snuggled against me. As I move, the cover lifts and I catch a glimpse of her perfect body framing mine. My cock starts to throb, so I snatch my phone up and roll onto my back. Grayson's name lights up on the screen at—I squint— six a.m.

"Grayson. Everything okay?" I whisper.

"Yeah, sorry, I— Fuck."

I squeeze my eyes shut. "Try again? It's early."

Rosa stirs next to me, and I pull her tighter against me, letting her settle again.

"I think I'm going to propose to Maddie." His words tumble quickly. I don't think I've ever heard him sound so nervous.

"About time." A smile forms on my face. He deserves this; they both do. "When? Need any help? I'm a good singer?"

He chuckles. "No, thanks. I don't know. I had the ring made in London. I've been waiting for the right time. I might take her to dinner this weekend."

"I'll get some guys on security. Just let me know where and when." Frankie will keep them safe.

"No, I can handle it. She is already on edge about my life-style; I don't want that ruining our engagement. It's just one night."

I roll my eyes. He's so stubborn sometimes. He can protect himself, without a doubt. It doesn't mean it sits well with me, especially now that Maddie is pregnant.

I hear Maddie calling his name in the background and chuckle. Both of us have been whisper-talking this entire time. He doesn't have a clue it's because I have Rosa tucked neatly into my side with her ass pressed up against my hip.

"I gotta go. I'll speak to you later," Grayson says.

"Have fun."

As I toss the phone to the foot of the bed, Rosa rolls over to face me, her features still serene in sleep. I glance down at her and smile that she had a night without a nightmare. Even if it's another night my cock painfully aches. But it's worth it to see the glow shining through on her skin.

That perfect smile that makes my heart race.

I wrap my arm back around her and close my eyes. These moments of tranquility don't happen often for me.

Chapter Seventeen

ROSA

When I get up, I find him already in the kitchen. "Good morning. What's on your agenda today, Rosa?" He opens up the cupboard, pulling out a black mug.

"I don't know? A walk out in the garden? Can you get me some books? Maybe take me out on a job with you? Just sit and talk?"

I snap my mouth closed after the last option. He checks his Rolex with a frown and opens the fridge. "What about breakfast?" he asks.

I slide onto the barstool and watch him bring the coffee machine to life.

"Breakfast sounds lovely," I reply.

His black Armani suit fits him like a second skin. It's snug enough I can almost see his biceps straining against the material. But it's those damn tattooed forearms I can't stop looking at as he rolls up his sleeves.

DEVOTED ~ 87

"Omelet okay?" he asks, turning to face me.

His deep, gravelly voice is doing things to me I've never experienced.

"F-fine," I stutter.

He nods and cracks the eggs into a mixing bowl.

"How long have you been the boss now?" I rest my chin on my palm and watch as he cooks.

"I've been around for a while, seven years or so, since my biological father was murdered."

His back is to me, so I can't read his face. Biological father? "Oh, wow." What a strange way to talk about his dad.

"I never knew Marco had two daughters," he says over his shoulder as he pours the egg mix into a pan. My eyes widen in surprise. It's interesting my dad kept us hidden.

I swallow the lump in my throat. "He didn't want us around much," I all but whisper.

A few moments pass in silence as he fries the omelets.

He slips one from the pan onto a dish with practiced ease. "You know, I never knew my real dad. I grew up on the streets. I was a foster kid."

"Oh, I'm sorry. That must have been hard."

He shrugs, placing my plate down in front of me. The smell alone makes my stomach rumble.

He stops and frowns. "You aren't eating enough, little one."

I gulp, unsure of what to say.

"I go through phases. Sometimes I'm starving, other times I feel sick. It's getting better though."

In this case, it's neither. I'm just too distracted by him.

I pick up my fork, and his eyes dart to my shaking hand.

"You need to eat properly. Popcorn isn't a meal." His voice is stern.

He grabs his own plate and sits next to me. I'm overwhelmed by the smell of his masculine cologne.

I poke my fork around the plate.

"So how did you go from foster kid to mafia boss then?" I ask, hoping to change the subject.

He looks down at my cooling omelet. "Eat and I'll tell you."

My mouth waters as I swallow down a mouthful of eggs. I pull on the sleeves of my sweater, trying to fight the nausea bubbling in my stomach.

"I was left in an apartment on my own as a baby and got taken in by Social Services. My mom was a junkie that OD'ed. They found her next to me. They couldn't find my dad."

He takes a bite of his food. "Another mouthful." He stares at me until I take another timid bite.

"I was tossed from place to place until one family sent me to Tony's boxing club when I was eight because I had a temper." He shrugs. "What they didn't realize, Tony ran an underground fight club. So when everyone else gave up on me, I always had a place to go. But that's where I met my brother, Keller. Tony took him in, too, and we spent our teens fighting for food and for survival."

A smile lights up his face. "And then Mrs. Russo took us in when we were sixteen. An older Italian lady who'd just lost her husband. She tried to whip us boys into shape, and we fucking love her for it, and her cooking. Our bellies were full, we had a warm bed, and we had a real family. So as soon as we turned eighteen, we changed our last names to Russo. We were her sons and always will be."

"Aww, that's so sweet." I stuff another mouthful of eggs. I can't help the pang of sadness at the mention of mothers. I miss mine so much.

"So how does that lead to the mafia boss?" I say with my mouth full.

He chews his bite slowly, and I watch his Adam's apple move as he swallows. "Well, turns out my dad wasn't a runaway junkie like my mom. He was the head of the fucking mafia. Giuseppe Luciano."

My mouth falls open. That's a name I recognize. The fights my mom and dad would have always involved that man's name growing up. Mom wanted us to go back to Italy, but my dad was obsessed with taking over power from Mr. Luciano.

Luca watches me. "You knew him?"

I shake my head. "No. Just heard of his name. I was kept away from my dad's business."

"Hmm." His chest rumbles and makes my heart jump.

Ignoring the flutters in my stomach, I try to stay on topic. "So your dad made you take over the mafia? Why?" I push another forkful of food into my mouth. I want to know more, and that's how I can keep him talking.

"That, I still don't know. I'll never know. His advisors found me and dragged me in the back of an SUV to my dad's gated mansion. Told me the will he had drawn up stipulated power goes to his only surviving son."

I cough as I try to hold back a laugh. "Wait. Your name used to be Luca Luciano? That's a mouthful of a name."

He chuckles. "Russo is much better."

I tap my fork against my lips as I try to picture a young Luca being dragged into his dad's empire. "That must have been hard."

His lips thin as he looks at his coffee cup pensively. "My life has never truly been my own. I've been fighting my whole damn life to survive. This is no different. I'm at a place now where they respect me. I have more money than I know what to do with. Once I take down your father, the city is mine."

"Something is still missing?" I can tell he doesn't look happy about his current mission.

His eyes search mine as he leans back in his chair. "Maybe. Maybe not. I never know what's in the cards for me."

I push my half-eaten plate of food away from me. "My dad was never the same since Mom was murdered."

I blink back the tears. It isn't easy to speak about my mom. I never speak about any of my agony.

His warm palm rests for a moment on my knee. "I'm so sorry."

I look at his broad hand with the tattoo peeking beneath his white cuff. "There was an explosion at our house. I was only fourteen. It happened so fast, I don't remember much. Eva and I were making up dance routines in the garden. The next thing I knew, I woke up in the hospital. My mom, Nonna, and a few others were killed."

I choke on a sob. After her death, my dad wouldn't even mention her name in the house. All the photos are gone. He even pushed me away because I had her dark eyes.

"All he cares about is power. We lost our home in Sicily because of his war with the Capris. And then he brings us here and breaks us all over again."

I bury my face in my hands.

"Oh, Rosa." His voice is soft and comforting.

I jump off the barstool, my chest feeling tight. A feeling I know too well.

I can hear him calling after me as I dart to my room and slam the door shut.

I WAKE UP with a yawn and snuggle into a shirtless Luca's side. He puts his strong arm around me and pulls me closer.

In the last two weeks, I've only had a couple of nightmares. Both times, he's wrapped me up in a hug and whispered. "It's me, Luca. I'm here. You're okay, little one. No one will hurt you." Then rocked me back to sleep.

I feel like a new person. One who actually sleeps and wakes up not hungover.

"Morning, little one." His voice is husky as his breath tickles over my head.

I roll my eyes. "I'm really not that small."

He moves onto his side and gives me a smirk. His dark hair is messy on top, and I have a strange urge to run my fingers through it.

A fire heats up in my core, a completely alien feeling that has me clenching my thighs together. I want this man, I just don't know what to do about it. He would never want a broken woman like me.

"You slept well last night." He grins, his green eyes sparkling mischievously.

"Why do you say it like that?" I tilt my head to get a better view of his face.

He bites his bottom lip. "You may or may not have grabbed my dick in your sleep."

"No! I did not!" I gasp.

Embarrassment washes over me. My cheeks are now on fire.

"You did. It woke me up."

"Oh my God, I am so sorry." I cover my face with my hands. He pulls them away and his lips turn up in a smile.

I start to panic. What if he makes me go back to my own room? I'm enjoying these peaceful nights of sleep.

"Hey, it's fine. Don't worry. I can think of worse things than to be groped in my sleep by the little Italian beauty I have in my bed." He puts one of his tattooed arms behind his head, propping himself up as he watches me.

He thinks I'm beautiful?

I bat my lashes at him. "I am sorry."

He laughs and slides toward the other side of the bed. "Come on, we have to get up. I have something for you downstairs and then I have to get to work. The quicker I get it taken care of, the sooner you can have your freedom."

My real life. It's like a kick to the stomach. I guess he's just humoring the poor little recovering junkie. I knew there was no way he'd be feeling the things I am for him.

I sigh and scoot away from him, getting myself out of bed and grabbing my black silk robe that hangs behind the door. As I turn around, I catch him staring at me intently, his eyes scanning my body, which makes my stomach flutter.

"Well, what's downstairs for me?"

He throws off the comforter, revealing his muscular frame. Dark ink scales down his right arm and across his chest. He throws on a pair of gray sweatpants and a black hoodie. He might always be dressed to kill when he leaves the house, but the second he's back home, he's in his comfy gear and ready on the couch to watch a marathon of films.

I open up the door and lead us downstairs. As I reach the last step, he catches my hand, which makes me stop. "Hang on, I want to check it's here first."

"Okay." I laugh. "I'll wait then."

He nods and heads toward the lounge. I step over to the side table opposite the stairs that's filled with pictures. Him, Keller, and Grayson when Keller won his championship fight. In another, Luca is sitting smiling and cuddling his niece, Darcy, with her brother, Max, cuddled into him on the other side.

And a picture of Luca, Keller, and an older lady I assume is Mrs. Russo. I squint—I swear she looks vaguely familiar.

"Ready," he calls.

As my foot hits the final stair, I stop in my tracks as I find him beaming like an idiot, pointing a massive camera at me.

"Umm, Luca, what are you doing?" I tighten my robe reflexively.

Laughing, he walks toward me and hands me the camera, a high-end Canon. "This is for you. You told me the other day you'd love to be a photographer. So, I've enrolled you in an online course," he says, shoving a new laptop in my other hand.

Tears threaten to spill as I look at the two most thoughtful gifts anyone could ever buy me. "I-I don't know what else to say, other than thank you." This could mean a future outside of the mafia.

He beams at me and takes the camera and laptop out of my hands, placing them on the glass coffee table behind him.

I shake my head. *Thank you.* I can do better than that.

I walk up to him and wrap my arms around his waist and squeeze him tight. He returns the hug right away. His heart hammers against my cheek.

"I thought it would be good to have something to keep you busy during the day. Something you can continue when you're free."

I look up at him through my lashes and notice a pained expression etched across his features.

"It's the best gift I've ever had."

He gives me a small smile, and his arms tighten around me.

"You deserve everything, Rosa," he whispers, sending goosebumps across my skin.

"So do you, Luca." Unshed tears sting my eyes.

His lips skim along my cheek as he brushes away my hair over my shoulder. Every cell in my body reacts to his touch. "You need to get ready for your appointment. Dr. Jenkins will be here soon."

Nerves pit in my stomach. My first shrink appointment. I start to release my arms, and Luca holds me firmly.

"You are going to be just fine, little one. I promise you." His soft words fill me with confidence.

***

AFTER DR. JENKINS leaves, it's a strange feeling. I'm a ball of nerves, yet there is an element of relief washing over me. I did my first session, I didn't break down, and she didn't think I was crazy or a junkie.

I head to the en suite in my room and turn on the shower. I might sleep in Luca's bed, but I've moved my stuff into my original room. I don't want him to feel like I'm completely intruding on every aspect of his life.

I open the door to grab some more towels and crash straight into Luca's hard chest.

His large hand catches my elbow, keeping me from falling.

"How was your first session?" He smiles down at me.

"Good." I take a step back, giving us some distance. But it's really to stop my skin from overheating from his touch. He scratches the back of his head, a silence clouding us.

"I was going to make some hot chocolates. Want to watch a movie?" He shifts his feet and watches me.

I bite back my smile. "I'd like that."

By the time I shower and get in my pajamas, Luca has two hot chocolates smothered in whipped cream on the table and a massive bowl of popcorn ready for us. I join him on the sofa and sit on the adjoining cushion. I'm itching to move closer; our bodies are only inches away.

It's his turn to pick, so I settle in, resting my head on one of his gray cushions.

As my eyes start to flutter closed, I shake my head, trying to combat the exhaustion.

Luca chuckles and I look over to find him watching me with amusement, stuffing popcorn into his mouth. "Not a fan of Superman?" His eyebrows raise as he turns to me.

"Umm, who isn't a fan of Henry Cavill?" I laugh. "I'm just tired. I think all that talking today drained me."

"Talking is good, right?"

"Hmm, we didn't go deep today, just some basics around my habits, how to combat the cravings initially, how to cope with my—" I pause. "—trauma."

His smile softens, and his warm palm pats my knee. "I'm here if you want to talk. No matter when."

Tears sting in my eyes. I've never had anyone say this to me. But I can't; I don't have the words yet. "Thank you, Luca."

He gives me a sad smile, reminding me just how broken I am. I don't want people's sympathy—I just want to feel normal again.

I bring my knees up and cuddle them, turning my attention back to the TV.

"Little one, what's the matter?" The concern in his voice has the tears I'm holding back almost hurting my cheeks.

I stare at the screen, a blur of pixels at this point, my mind wandering back to *that* day. I hug my knees tighter, holding my breath. I can hear Dante's voice rolling around my brain. Pain starts to radiate from my collarbone with the sensation of his teeth sinking into my flesh.

"Shit." I squeeze my eyes shut. Dr. Jenkins taught me a technique today—four sides. I take in a deep breath, hold for four, and release for four, picturing the sides of the square being drawn. And not *him*.

I can faintly hear Luca's deep voice calling my name, but I zone him out. I block everything out. Focusing only on the whooshing of my breath, picturing it flowing around the square, capturing the rising fear that threatened to erupt. That craving for a hit to hide him.

After a few minutes, I look over at Luca, who's watching me with interest, his expression warm.

"What was that?" he asks quietly.

I chew on my lip nervously. "It was about to be a little breakdown, but I used the breathing technique Dr. Jenkins taught me. Four sides."

His face scrunches as one eyebrow raises. "Four sides?"

"Yep. Turns out it kinda works." Amazingly.

"Tell me how it works? You know, in case I ever have to guide you?"

My heart hammers, my skin flushing as he waits for my response. Dr. Jenkins had me close my eyes and draw the square around my kneecap to visualize the shape. "Can I show you?"

"Of course you can." He sets the bowl on the coffee table and pauses the movie.

I scoot closer to him, planting my feet on the floor so I'm next to him. I shiver in anticipation as our knees brush. "So I'm going to draw a square around your knee."

He laughs. "Okay—"

"As I'm doing that, you breathe in for a count of four, hold it for four, exhale for four, and hold again. You have to picture your breath drawing the sides of the square, as I am doing it with the tip of my finger."

"Got it." He grins as I look up at him.

My cheeks heat and I turn away, focusing on his knee. The second my finger touches, I hear his breath hitch behind me. As he rests his hands on his muscular thighs, I start to instruct him, following the same pattern with my finger.

He leans back, his arm resting behind me on the back of the couch, his eyes closed. I take a moment to admire him, even when his hair is tousled and the first few buttons of his shirt are undone. Any woman would drool over him, me included, apparently. Who needs Superman when I have my very own right next to me?

He peers out of one eye. "You stopped."

"Oh, sorry." My face flushes for a whole new reason: the fact that he caught me ogling him when he's supposed to be relaxing.

"It's fine. Can you do that thing on my knee a bit longer? It feels so good," he growls contentedly.

I swallow, my eyes wide. Knowing I can make him feel good makes me smile. I kick my legs up to the side to try to get comfy, leaning into his frame to adjust.

My head is just inches from his chest, but my eyes are still heavy. I tense my muscles in my arm and hold my weight. He asked for me to show him, not to start cuddling and use him as a human pillow.

I keep tracing the square on his knee, his gravelly humming in appreciation lulling me to sleep.

I startle myself back awake as my head hits the pillow.

Luca stands above me. "You fell asleep, and it didn't look comfortable at all. I carried you up here."

I snuggle up into the blanket. "Thank you," I manage to whisper. I can feel myself drifting off, but I hold on to wakefulness as the bed dips and he cuddles into me.

That's the moment I can finally let myself sleep.

Chapter Eighteen

LUCA

I get the coffees ready for our normal routine. Coffee on the balcony watching the sunrise. Everything is peaceful at that time.

The main reason I slip out of bed at the first opportunity is to hide my morning wood. A whole night of Rosa snuggling up against my side is almost torturous.

Picking up my phone vibrating on the counter, I hesitate to answer it with an unknown number flashing up on the screen.

I slide to accept and turn it on speaker. "Hello?" I call out, pouring in Rosa's caramel syrup.

"Ah, Mr. Luca Russo." Marco's husky Italian voice greets me. I quickly pick up the phone, sending the sound back through the earpiece.

"How the fuck did you get my number?"

"I'm a resourceful man. Your hacker's phone was quite

handy." I don't even want to imagine what he had to do to Nico to break the encryption he had on his phone.

"Are you calling to make a deal in exchange for your daughter, or are you wasting my time, Marco?"

Resting the phone on my shoulder, I start on my own coffee. I only have a few minutes until sunrise. I'm not missing our routine for this asshole.

His dark laugh makes the little hairs on the back of my neck stand up.

"I don't know why you're laughing, Marco. Your poor daughter is tied up, begging for her dad to save her. She only has a few days to live, and you haven't even made an attempt to save her."

I'm disappointed for Rosa. Her own father hasn't even tried to come to her rescue. I shouldn't be surprised. After what she told me, it doesn't sound like he makes a habit of trying to be there for her.

"You've grown weak, Russo. You don't even know I have snakes in your den. I'll get her back, but I don't have to make a deal with you. When I bring you to your knees, I'll take my junkie daughter back. But you having her is no threat to me."

I bite my tongue.

"You took the wrong daughter. Eva is much more of an asset to me. I can marry her off because she's pure. A true princess."

I tighten my grip on the phone, gritting my teeth so hard I'm surprised they don't crack.

"Wrong answer, Marco. You've just agreed to your own death. That was your last chance to stand down, and you've fucked it up. You piece of shit."

I cut the call, slamming it down on the dining table. Who talks about their daughter like that?

She means more to me than she does to her own father. Now I'm just spurred on more to kill him. Not just for myself, but to get him out of Rosa's life. She deserves better.

The orange sunrise blasts through the double doors into the kitchen. I swipe up the coffees and race up the stairs. My blood might be boiling, but I won't let her down.

I stop before I get to the glass door and watch her. She sits on the balcony in just her black satin robe, her slim tanned legs kicked up on the small table in the center. She's looking up at the sky, a completely new woman in comparison to the one who entered here.

Her eyes light up as she turns to me, her wide smile making my heart flutter in my chest. I bite back a grin and head to my girl.

Back to our happy spot, our escape from reality every morning. My home is suddenly starting to feel like less of a shell. "Here you go." I carefully hand her the steaming cup.

She tucks her hair behind her ear. "Hmm, thank you."

Taking a seat next to her, I light up my cigarette, looking out over the garden as the sky turns a beautiful shade of red.

"What took you so long?" she asks, looking over the rim of the dark mug.

I have a choice. The call with Marco confirmed my suspicions. Holding her here is doing nothing for my cause. Now, I'm keeping her for my own selfish reasons. I won't be that man, not to her.

She deserves to choose her own path now.

I clear my throat around the knot that suddenly forms. "I spoke to your father."

I watch as she swallows, bowing her head.

"And what did he say?" The fear in her voice makes me sick, murderous even.

I set down my cup and lean on my knees to look closely at her. "Rosa, he's not coming for you."

She sighs, taking a sip of her drink. "Let me guess, the 'junkie daughter' isn't worthy of his resources." She laughs, but it doesn't disguise her hurt.

"Something like that." I run my fingers through my hair. I wish I could tell her differently. That he loves her and would burn the world down to save her.

But he isn't that man.

We sit in silence, my head and my heart battling. I can keep her safe here, even from her own family. It's selfish, but I want her to stay. She is my reason for looking forward to coming home. Without her, this house is empty.

I take another drag, letting the chemicals burn their way down. "Rosa—"

"Hmm?" She doesn't look up. Her sorrowful eyes stare into her coffee.

"—it means you're free to go. I don't need to force you to be here anymore. Marco isn't backing down." Tamping out the ember in the ashtray feels like a judge's gavel striking a decision on our future.

Her eyes water and she nods. "I understand. You want me to leave."

My chest tightens. "What? No. I don't want you to leave. I'm giving you a choice. I won't force you to be here with me. It is up to you now. You can stay. I will keep you safe in our little haven while you recover, and it's still dangerous out there. Your father is making many enemies. If I got to you, anyone could."

Her big brown eyes finally turn up to meet mine. "So you're just keeping me here to keep me safe?"

"Rosa, I promised I wouldn't abandon you. I meant it. I want you here." I want her here more than anything.

I know what it's like to be tossed aside. I was that kid.

Her eyebrows shoot up in surprise. That red blush I love so much spreads up her neck.

"You're doing so well, Rosa. Your nightmares are becoming less and less. Here, you can rebuild your life, you can start to heal. But the choice is in your hands now."

She takes another sip, looking up at the clouds for what feels like a lifetime. All I can do is fucking hope she wants to stay with me.

She rolls her pink lower lip between her teeth before turning to me. "I'd like to stay."

"That's the answer I was hoping for."

She bats her lashes and I hold in a groan, my dick twitching against my boxers. I need to get a hold of myself.

I'm so proud of her; every day she's fighting a battle in her own mind and winning. As each sunrise breaks, she becomes more of the real Rosa.

When she's finally victorious, it will be a sight to behold. I just hope I'm there for it.

***

GRAYSON'S NAME FLASHES on the screen, and I smile. Tonight is the night he's proposing to Maddie. I snatch the popcorn up from the counter and head toward the couch. It's my movie choice tonight. I'm thinking Captain America sounds good. Last time, she fell asleep with her hand on my leg. I can't wait to see what tonight could bring.

I accept the call. "Did you do it?"

"Luca, he's been shot," Maddie says between sobs.

The bowl drops out of my hand, spilling all over the floor. I struggle to keep my voice even. "Where are you, Maddie?"

Taking the steps two at a time, I rush up to my office and unlock the safe.

"St. Luke's-Roosevelt Hospital," she replies.

I take out a couple of guns. He's a sitting target at the hospital. Hell, so is she. I can't let my best friend die, nor his fiancée. If anything happens to them, I'll never forgive myself.

"I'll be there in fifteen. Don't let him out of your sight."

"He's in surgery, Luca. I've locked myself in the bathroom," she chokes out. The pain in her words feels like a kick to the balls.

"Fuck!" I slam my fists down on the table. I'm going to kill every single one of these fuckers for this. I am done playing around. This ends.

I let out a breath—at least she is safe for now.

"Okay, Maddie. I'm on my way now. Just stay where you are. We have to keep you safe. Keep the door locked, and I will knock for you when I'm there."

"Luca, what if he dies?"

I suck in a breath. If he dies, we're all screwed. I knew I shouldn't have let him go tonight without any protection. One night and this happens. Panic rises in my chest and I swallow it down. I can't lose it, not right now.

"Maddie, it's going to be okay. Grayson won't go down without a fight. He will do anything to make his way back to you both. I'll see you soon."

Both.

I tighten my grip around the gun. He was so ecstatic when he told me Maddie was pregnant. He was literally months away from having it all.

And now my chaos has ruined that for him.

But I will make this right, no matter what.

I smash my fist against my oak desk, over and over again, in a fit of rage. I don't even notice Rosa appear in the doorway.

"Is everything okay?" she asks, barely poking her head through the crack. The fear is evident on her face.

My nostrils flare as I look at her, her hair still dripping, and only a white towel wrapped around her.

"Fuck. No. Not even close. Grayson's been shot."

She rushes toward me, squeezing her arms around me. I stiffen. I don't know if I have ever had someone comfort me.

I rest my head on top of hers, her sweet scent calming my inner rage only slightly.

After a deep breath, I return her hug. "I have to go."

She releases me and takes a step back, looking up at me with worried eyes. "Be careful, Luca. Please."

I blink a few times, shaking my head. Now isn't the time to worry about me.

"I'll try." I place a kiss on the top of her head and her breath hitches.

Chapter Nineteen
ROSA

"Shit," I hiss, knocking over the bowl of beaten eggs across the counter.

The bacon sizzles on the stove as I wipe up the mess.

Okay, fry the bacon and boil the pasta. Check.

Now what?

I check my laptop on the counter and reread the recipe. Spaghetti carbonara. My mom's favorite. Well, the only thing she could cook to Nonna's standards. Wiping the sweat from my forehead, I realize it's already almost noon. Luca hasn't come home since going to the hospital last night. He's texted a few times to let me know he's okay, but I know he's going to be hungry when he gets home.

Next, grate the cheese. I throw open the cupboards beneath me; the grater has got to be hiding around here somewhere. When Luca cooks, he makes it look so easy. I, however, am a disaster.

As I rummage through the cupboards, the front door slams shut.

"Luca, I'm in here!" I shout, peering up over the counter.

Weird, he always comes straight in to see me.

As I step around the corner to the living room, I find him slumped on the sofa with his head in his hands. His chest is shaking.

Is he crying?

I rush over to him and drop to my knees.

"Luca, are you okay?"

He shakes his head, yet won't let me see his face. For everything this man has done for me these last few weeks, I have to help him.

"Luca, you can talk to me," I whisper.

He looks at me through teary, bloodshot eyes.

Fuck. This isn't good.

I sit on the sofa next to him and pat my lap. He shoots me a questioning look.

"Lie down."

He does as I say, laying his head on my lap. I stroke his soft brown locks while wrapping my other arm around his body.

He nuzzles his face into my bare stomach, his tears falling onto my skin.

"Talk to me. Luca, please."

He takes in a deep breath. "He had a major surgery. They don't know if he will make it. I've been with Maddie; she's so fucking broken. And I can't stop thinking about him never meeting his kid. He was so excited, Rosa. He has everything he ever wanted, and my stupidity could have ruined everything for him."

"Hey, this is not your fault, Luca. The mafia is a dangerous place, we all know that."

108 ~ LUNA MASON

"If they had a better leader, it wouldn't be."

"Stop it with that. Soon you'll be top of the top. I have no doubt you can take down my dad's men. Then it's Luca for world domination. You've got this."

I suck in a breath and ask. "Was it my dad?"

He nods. "I should never have taken you."

A tightness forms in my chest. "Well, if it's any consolation, in taking me, you saved me."

He moves his head to look at me, and I give him a reassuring smile.

"It's true. This is the first time in my adult life I've truly felt free, happy even. And that's down to you. I know this wasn't about me. Why would he attack Grayson?"

His elbow sticks up as he wipes his face. "He wants something I've got."

"Which is?" I know it isn't me.

Luca's voice drops. "Can I trust you?"

"Weirdly enough, I trust you with my life."

He sits up and faces me, our noses almost touching. My breath hitches as I realize his cologne has long faded and his raw, manly scent covers me, making me want to press my thighs together.

"I have the commissioner's backing to run the gun shipments into New York. I just need to take the merchandise from the Capris somehow to keep them from gaining a foothold here."

"See, you're doing great." I reach out and stroke his stubbly jaw. He leans into my touch. "When will you know more about Grayson? Is Maddie okay?"

With an exhausted groan, he sits up. "Soon. I just came home to shower, change, and update the rest of the guys. I need to get our retaliation organized while we wait. I have a guy with Maddie keeping an eye on her for me."

I tuck my knees to my chest, but they feel cold without his warm heat laying across them. "I have faith he will pull through. From what you've told me, he's a fighter; he won't go down that easily."

He gives me a sad smile, and it breaks my heart seeing him like this. I roll onto my knees to wrap my arms around his neck and place a soft kiss on his cheek.

He pulls his head back, his eyes opening wide as he stares into mine. The pain he carries seems to melt a little as his thumb rubs idly across my elbow.

Breaking the spell, he clears his throat and sits up straight. "What were you cooking?" he asks.

"Carbonara." I pull away, letting my hand drift down to rest on his veiny forearm. "Don't expect much. I can't even find the grater."

He chuckles, and it makes me smile. "Thank you, little one."

"I told you to stop calling me that!" I lean back in feigned protest and poke him in the chest.

He huffs. "Fine." His warm fingers cover my hand. "What about 'tesoro'?" he asks in a hoarse whisper.

I blink a few times at the sweet nickname that fell from his lips. "And why am I your treasure, Luca?"

His full lips twitch into a smile. "It's because you are. You are my stolen treasure."

Heat blooms in my chest. "It's cute, I accept."

He laughs. "Good. Agreed then."

I unfold myself from my cushion and go to stand, but he catches my wrist, his eyes searching mine.

"Can we stay like this for a bit longer?" He pauses. "Please?"

When I give him a small nod, he shifts to one end of the couch and he taps his lap. He must be expecting me to lie my head on his leg like he had been.

I don't know what comes over me. I straddle his thighs and settle down on his lap. His eyes go wide.

"What are you doing, Rosa?" His deep gravelly voice sends pulses to my pussy.

He groans, tipping his head back against the headrest.

Holy shit. I lick my lips as his Adam's apple bobs.

"I-I don't know," I answer honestly.

My feelings for him confuse the hell out of me. He brings his face back to me; his bloodshot eyes remind me of the pain he's feeling right now.

"Oh, Luca," I sigh, wrapping him up tight, his head nestled between my breasts.

He's never faltered when it comes to me, so I will be there for him. We fight together.

"Thank you, Rosa. I'm going to be lost when you leave me."

I don't even want to think about that day, so I just hum in agreement.

His phone starts to vibrate. He takes two long breaths that end in a sigh before he leans back to dig it out of his jacket pocket. I slide away onto his knees to give him some space to answer.

The tanned skin of his face pales as he listens to whoever is on the other end, then a flush of red works its way up his neck. "What in the fuck do you mean you can't find her?"

I flinch back at the sheer anger in Luca's voice, torn between getting off his lap or hugging him closer. So I do what my heart tells me to do—I bury my face into his chest and I hold on to him as tight as I can. I just know they're talking about Maddie.

"Keep looking, we can't lose her. We have to find her before he wakes up. It will fucking kill him." His hand tightens where he grips my hip.

I keep my face pressed against his chest, my heart sinking for him. It's going from bad to worse for him, and there isn't a damn thing I can do to help. It might be wrong, but I wish my dad was dead, so this would stop for him. The cell phone bounces off the cushion after he ends the call. "I have to go."

"Luca, you've got this. It will be okay. Go out there and fight, just keep your head and don't get yourself hurt," I whisper. I release my hold and lean back, grabbing his face in my hands. "Don't worry about me. I'm safe here." I press a soft kiss to his cheek and hop off his lap.

There's a fire in his eyes as he stands. "I'll see you soon, tesoro."

Chapter Twenty
LUCA

Watching my best friend's heart rip out of his chest when we told him Maddie was missing made me realize our weakness. We don't have enough men for this fight. I promised him I will do what it takes to bring her home, and that starts now. With Sienna being so broken about Maddie's disappearance, me and Keller don't have a choice.

We need more recruits, and we know exactly where to find them.

In the place it all started for us.

I follow my brother as we push open the doors to our childhood.

Tony's gym.

The familiar smell of leather and sweat hits me, and I feel like I'm home.

Keller looks at me with a smirk.

"Memory lane." His shoulders pull back as he steps into the cool interior, like he's strutting before a fight.

"No killing anyone in here tonight." It's not often I'm the voice of reason.

We head toward the ring, both in our gym gear. Tony wouldn't let us step foot in here if we didn't intend to fight. I'm not sure what man would be stupid enough to get in a match with Keller, the best heavyweight boxer in the world. But tonight, we are here for a different reason.

"Where is the little bulldog?" Tony might be built short and wide, but he knows how to train someone to be the best version of themselves.

And that's what we need. An army full of fighters, men just like us. If we can pull this off, we will be unstoppable.

"My boys!"

Tony rushes toward us, his arms in the air. "You like what I did with the place?" He winks.

"Yeah, you spent our money well," Keller replies as he glares down a life-size cutout of himself from his prize fight.

"You're in for a treat tonight. Biggest draw in the underground in a long time."

I narrow my eyes at him. "What makes you think we're fighting?"

"You wouldn't dare come home and not show them all how it's done. The motherfucking Russo brothers."

"Rules still the same?" Keller asks with a menacing smile.

I know he's craving the blood. He might not be my hitman anymore, but you will never take the fight from him. The man was made to kill, he just chooses not to. For now.

"What rules?" Tony replies, his broad smile revealing a gold top tooth.

"Perfect. I'll go first," I say, shrugging off my sweatshirt.

"Jax is ready to fight. Calls himself the 'King of Chaos.' Reminds me a bit of this one." Tony nods at Keller.

"So he wants to cave in my skull? Ideal."

I need something to get this built-up anger out. I need to switch my overthinking mind off for a night.

But the menace in the ring, that's me.

I rub my hands together and bounce from left to right. "Let's see what he's got."

Tony ducks under the ring and slicks back his white hair as he stands.

I follow suit and stand in my corner with Keller hanging over the ropes. He wraps my hands up in heavy white tape. We don't use gloves here.

My opponent and I are fairly matched in size. If anything, his muscles are leaner, so he might be quicker. He rips off his vest like the Hulk, and I roll my eyes at Keller.

He's covered in gang-style tattoos from his neck all the way down to his ankles.

"No rules, just please don't kill each other. I can't deal with the police," Tony shouts.

Keller nods to me, his eyes darkening as I focus on my opponent. With the adrenaline flowing through my veins, I feel the most alive I have in years.

"Fight!" Tony calls and the crowd cheers.

Jax wastes no time launching himself at me. I duck away from him and jab him straight in the ribs. He stumbles back a step, and I take advantage, cracking him straight in the nose.

He stands and wipes the blood from his face.

"You cunt," he seethes.

"What, can't handle a fucking punch? Pussy," I spit back.

I dance around the ring, taunting him.

He comes at me again, this time landing a clean uppercut on my jaw. I shake my head. *Fuck, that feels good.*

"Arms up, Luca!" Keller bellows behind me.

I smirk at Jax. "That's your one and only."

As he moves forward again, I put my weight on my left leg and all the power in my right and launch my foot straight into his stomach. He groans and backs into the ropes.

I storm toward him, taking my opportunity.

As I unleash a barrage of punches to his face, blood splatters from his split eyebrow. He weakly defends with his forearms. He grabs my hand before my punch lands and pushes me back. His nostrils flare. That evil darkness Keller has, I see it lurking in Jax's eyes.

Well, shit. This is going to get interesting.

I crack my neck as we circle into the center of the ring. He pulls back his fist and slams it into my mouth. Pretty decent shot.

I spit blood onto the floor, running my tongue along my teeth. I like this guy.

"Want a job?" I say before he pulls his elbow back for another strike.

He stops and tilts his head, glancing at Keller behind me.

"Fucking lightbulb just switched on?" I circle my finger in the air to Tony, letting him know we're wrapping up the fight. I've got bigger plans for the King of Chaos here. He is exactly the kind of guy we need—dangerous.

"Meet Keller at King's Gym tomorrow." I nod to him and slap him on the shoulder.

I duck under the ropes and head to the office.

Tony shuts the door behind him, the cheers from the crowd signaling the next fight making it almost too hard to hear. Someone must be getting their head caved in.

I sit heavily in the metal chair, rubbing my jaw. "Tony, I need a favor."

He sits down on his desk chair. "Anything." He pours us two glasses of scotch. It's Tony's fault I have a taste for it.

"Any decent fighters. I mean, killers. Guys you think could join me. Send them to King's Gym." Flexing my hand, I think I may have cracked a knuckle. That Jax has a hard-ass head.

He knocks back his drink with a grimace. "What are you building, boy? A goddamn army?"

"Pretty much."

FRANKIE POURS ME a scotch and hands it over. It might be ten in the morning, but I need this. I've barely been home since Grayson was shot. I miss her.

Only being home for two or three hours at a time isn't enough. What I wouldn't give for a full night of having her wrapped in my arms.

With all of my men out searching for Maddie, I've had to step back into dealing with our shipments and keeping an eye on Grayson. He's about one more flip-out away from blowing up Marco's home. But it isn't going to bring back Maddie.

Frankie leans back and rests his glass on his crossed knee. "What's the plan, boss?"

"Good question." I stare at the pile of photos in front of me. They all run together and are useless.

His icy gray eyes bore into mine.

We have Maddie, who disappeared from the face of the earth. Grayson lying in a hospital bed. Keller is on a warpath.

I scratch my scruffy jaw and down my drink. Enzo is the best man for the job, but even he has been searching and coming up with nothing. We've been door to door. The commissioner is scouring for reports matching Maddie's details.

I've called in every favor possible with families across the country.

Nothing, not one fucking thing.

Romano's name lights up on my phone, and Frankie and I look at each other. What does he want?

"This better be good, Romano."

He laughs. "Fucking hello to you, too, Luca."

"I'm not in the mood for another debate about gun running." I sip my scotch, checking the time. I have to meet Enzo in an hour.

His voice is calm, almost teasing in tone. "Not even if I told you I had some information about your little blonde friend that is missing?"

I cough on my drink. "You know where Maddie is?" I can't hide the anger in my voice.

"I may have some information you might find useful, yes. It comes at a cost and you'll have to come here to discuss the deal first."

Frankie's eyebrows shoot up. I don't have any other options. I promised Grayson I'd bring her home. That I'd keep my family safe.

"I'll be there. Send me the details." I cut the call and sit back in my seat. Downing the contents of my glass, I hurl it against the wall, shattering it on the oak paneling. "Well, looks like I'm going to Italy. You coming?"

Frankie glances to the corner, where shards pepper the floor.

"No. I'll stay here, keep an eye on Grayson. Keller is busy training up all the new recruits. Grayson needs someone watching out for him."

I couldn't stop my brother even if I wanted to, especially not when Sienna begged him to help us find her best friend.

I don't want him in this life, so I tasked him with training up the guys Tony sent over.

Especially if this shit with Romano Capri turns south, we need every asset we can get.

I pinch the bridge of my nose, a headache already forming at my temples. "I'm out. I gotta go check in on Rosa before I leave. I'll take Enzo with me. Keep me updated on Grayson."

He salutes me. "Yes, boss."

Something clicks in me as I reach the front door. I turn to Frankie, who is sitting back, tapping away on his phone. "Do you remember what the doctor looked like that took her away?"

He leans forward, resting his elbows on his knees, and scratches his beard. "I might be able to pick them out if I saw them again."

"Good. You head to the hospital. Find that doctor and bring them in. See what they know. I'll have the commissioner do some digging on the staff there."

He nods and leans back.

I pull out my pack of cigarettes. "I'll be back in a couple of days. I'm trusting you to keep this together for me."

"You got it, boss."

Chapter Twenty-One
ROSA

It's that time of the month again when not only do I want to stab someone, I am in agony. Like a hot knife is being twisted into my stomach.

It wouldn't be so bad, except Luca also threw out all the painkillers in the house. As per Dr. Jenkins's instructions.

So here I am, curled up in the fetal position on Luca's silky black bedsheets, squeezing my eyes shut, waiting for the pain to subside.

God definitely is a man if this is the kind of shit he puts women through.

I groan as I roll onto all fours and cat stretch, wiggling my ass in the air, and try to breathe out the pain by letting little puffs of air out of my nose.

There's a thud on the floor. I lean forward and poke my head under my arms to look. Luca leans against the doorframe, a gym bag by his feet.

His eyes are glued firmly to my ass, wiggling up in the air.

A smirk creeps up on one side of his lips. "Everything okay in here, Rosa?"

Damn, I've missed that husky voice of his.

"All fine. Just some stupid stomach cramps. I've heard yoga stretches can relieve muscle tension. This is the only one I know." I lean forward slightly.

"Don't stop on my account," he growls.

I let out a sigh of relief; this is actually working.

He walks toward me and my heart rate picks up. I look up, resting on my elbows, getting a deep stretch in my lower abs. It feels so damn good a moan escapes my lips.

My eyes go wide when I realize it isn't his gym bag. It's luggage. "Are you going away?"

He stays quiet for a moment, slipping his hands into his pockets. "Italy."

"Oh, nice." Jealousy pangs in my throat. He didn't ask me to go.

"I'll only be gone a couple of days. I have to do everything I can to find Maddie." The pain behind his eyes is evident in the dark circles surrounding them.

I can't fault him for his dedication to his family.

"I understand." It hurts, but I swallow it down.

His jaw clenches as he looks down at me. "I wanted to say goodbye before I left."

I suck in a lungful of air, my body tingling as he steps closer to the edge of the bed.

I sit back, resting on my heels, and I roll my shoulders. "Is there anyone you trust who can visit me? I'm desperately craving some form of human interaction. I don't think I've ever gone this long alone without surrounding myself with people."

To avoid the turmoil in my own head. I'm not ready to see anyone in my old life yet. It's not safe out there, anyway.

The bed dips as he sits next to me. "I can arrange something."

"Thank you!" I launch myself at him and wrap my arms around his neck. His body vibrates against mine when he laughs.

My tits press into his chest. Fuck, even they hurt like hell today.

"I kind of missed you," I whisper.

He rubs his hand along my back and rests his head against the top of mine.

"Me too," he whispers, and I can hear the smile in his voice. "Kind of."

He sighs and wraps an arm around me, his hand splaying over my stomach, making little circles on my skin with his thumb. I squeeze my thighs together as heat builds in my core.

I close my eyes; I shouldn't feel this. *He's just being nice. He feels sorry for you, Rosa!*

Pain radiates from my uterus. I jab my hands into my stomach and press my face flush against his chest, letting out a groan.

"God, I hate this," I whine.

Normally, when I'm wasted, I don't feel it. I don't feel anything. That's the whole idea. So this is a hard launch back down to reality.

"Just take a deep breath in, tesoro. Just like you showed me, remember, it should work."

The way he says my nickname has me melting on the spot.

I do as he says, keeping my eyes shut and picturing my breath drawing the square.

We do this a few times, breathing through the pain. Together.

My body loosens, sinking further into Luca's side. I'm so relaxed, I could fall asleep like this.

"I need to get going, Rosa. Are you sure you're going to be okay? I can try to rearrange my flight?"

Disappointment clouds over me. In his arms, I'm safe. "No, honestly, I will be fine. I guess I will see you in a few days."

I lean forward and he slips his arm from me, leaving me empty again. I hike my knees up to my chest and cuddle them. The overwhelming sadness starts to consume me.

These damn hormones.

Closing my eyes to hold back the tears, I still as he bends forward and kisses my temple.

A lump forms in my throat that I fight to swallow past. It takes me a second to realize I haven't heard the click of the handle.

I look up to find him standing next to the door, his dark eyes boring into mine.

"Fuck it," he mutters.

My heart rate picks up as he strides toward me, the desire in my core rising with every step.

"Luca?"

"Please tell me I can kiss you."

The easiest answer I will ever have to give leaves my lips. "Yes."

"Oh, thank fuck."

All the air is sucked out of my lungs as he grabs my face in his hands, lifting my chin up, and his full lips hover just an inch away.

As I close my eyes, he presses his lips over mine. It's slow and gentle to start, his hands running through my hair. I let him deepen the kiss, our tongues now dancing, and I grip a fistful of his hair.

"You. Are. Perfect," he groans, before capturing my lips again.

Every cell in my body is set alight.

He pulls back, his darkened eyes searching mine, and I look up at him through my lashes.

"I couldn't leave without saying goodbye properly." A smile creeps up his lips, my own now tingling, and a dampness forms between my legs. I want—no, crave—more from this man.

"I'll miss you."

He takes me by surprise, kissing me again. This time I can't hold the moan that escapes my throat.

"I promise, I won't be long. When I'm home, we have some things to discuss."

A blush forms along my cheeks, and I nod.

He gives me a wink before closing the door behind him. I lay back on the bed, breathless, boiling, and with a newfound sexual frustration I've never experienced before in my life.

Chapter Twenty-Two
LUCA

I stare at the gray-haired mafia boss in front of me. The most ruthless and unhinged man in Europe. Mr. Romano Capri. They say he once cut out someone's tongue and made him swallow it for talking to him in the wrong tone.

He bites the cigar between his front teeth as he gestures to one of his men to procure a bottle. I cross my ankle over my knee and watch.

A younger version of Romano sits to his left, with slick black hair and dark aviators. Antonio is a carbon copy of his father.

"I'm glad you finally came to your senses," Romano says in a deep Italian accent. "Whiskey?"

I put my hand up and shake my head. "No, thanks. I'm here for business only."

"Suit yourself." He continues to pour until the two glasses in front of him are brimming with the dark liquor.

Sitting back, he takes a slow sip before narrowing his eyes and pointing at me with the ember of his cigar. "You stole from me."

"I was proving a point." I shrug. "The Falcones are useless; they don't control what comes in and out of New York. I do."

Stroking his white beard, he casually crosses one leg over the other while taking a puff of his cigar. "You've got balls, I'll give you that. I have information that is of the utmost importance for you, but what do you bring to the table in return?"

I flatten my palms on my knees. It takes everything in me not to curl them into fists.

"I can get your shipments into the port. I have the commissioner on board," I lie, but I'll do what it takes to get my family back together. To bring Maddie home to Grayson.

Antonio grunts next to him, and Romano shoots him a warning look.

"Tell me. How is your mom, Mrs. Gianna Russo? And your brother, Keller? He has a lovely family now with that beautiful little British girl—Sienna, isn't it?" He smirks, flicking his ash on the oak desk.

Running my tongue across my teeth, I spark up a cigarette. It's a struggle to keep my face as straight as I can, despite the rage burning through me right now.

"They stay out of this," I spit out with venom, dropping my façade of calm.

"Only if you behave. One wrong move, and you'll have a lot of funerals to plan for."

Antonio snickers, and I clench my jaw, gritting my teeth.

Assholes have a death wish.

"You expect me to let you use my organization after threatening my family? For what? Prove you know where Maddie is." I stand and toss my cigarette on the floor, the embers floating up from the checkered tiles.

His chair creaks as he pours himself another drink. Every movement is slow, unhurried, predatory. The smoke that clings to the corners stagnates as he purses his lips. "You'd have to trust I know enough to locate her."

A roar of frustration lodges in my throat. "Do you have her?"

He shakes his head. He's a liar.

"Fuck you for wasting my time." As I turn on my heel, my stomach sinks thinking of how few options I have left.

"Deals like this don't come around twice," Romano calls out after me, and I slam the door.

I'll find another way. I have to.

Chapter Twenty-Three
ROSA

Luca has only been gone a few hours and I swear I can still feel him on me. My body is still on fire, and I can't put it out. Even after a cold shower.

So I've decided to distract myself. He might have a mansion, but I've seen every square inch of the damn place.

It's all black, white, and gray.

I've managed to get through some of the photography course, going out into the backyard and snapping pictures of the vast amounts of greenery he has planted.

I've nailed the carbonara recipe.

It's peaceful here. Luca was right; it's like a retreat, where I get to snuggle with my own Greek god of a man. I don't have Bobby, or the other guards, two steps behind me at every turn. I don't have the overwhelming need to drink, thinking Dante will appear around every corner. And I even manage to sleep without the nightmares anymore.

I plop down on the couch and kick my legs up on the

coffee table, turning on the newest episode of *Brooklyn Nine-Nine*. If Luca's not here to make me laugh, then Captain Holt can instead.

I can't help but think about poor Maddie and Grayson. I don't know them, but Luca loves them like his own family. He's so torn up about this, it's hard to bear. Just because we've lived our lives in the mafia doesn't make it hurt less.

"Hello?" A female voice startles me.

I turn down the volume on the TV. "Can I help you?" I call back and stand up.

Luca never warned me of any visitors.

An older lady, with her hair in a neat bun and glasses resting on the top of her head, steps around the corner into the living room. She has two big shopping bags, one in each hand.

I rush over. "Here, let me help you with those." I take the bags from her hand and place them up on the counter.

She looks me up and down. "You look better than the last time I saw you."

"Pardon?" I take a step back.

"I'm Gianna. Luca's mom."

"Rosa," I reply, still completely confused. I keep looking at her. I can't place her, but she seems so . . . familiar. I thought I recognized her in the photos, but just assumed that was because of Luca speaking about her.

Unless—I can feel the blood drain from my face.

She saw me.

"Did you see—"

She cuts me off and gives me a sad smile. "I came to help Luca one night. He was a bit panicked and exhausted."

I cast my eyes to the ground, wishing the earth would tear open and swallow me whole. I know Dr. Jenkins tells me I have nothing to be embarrassed about—hell, Luca is very adamant about that, too. It doesn't mean there is a switch I can flip to turn off the awful truth.

It's embarrassing. His mom saw me at my rock bottom.

"I'm so sorry you had to see me like that. I wish we could have met under better circumstances."

"Don't apologize, please." She pushes a gray tendril of hair behind her ear before pulling the first bag to her and opening it.

"It shouldn't have been your or your son's responsibility to get me clean." I rub my hands along my neck as my heart rate picks up, the nerves getting the better of me.

"Well, Luca shouldn't have kidnapped you, either. Has he been good to you?" A bag of flour and a bag of sugar appear from one of the bags.

"Yes," I reply without hesitation. "Your son is a good man."

She places her palms flat on the counter as she looks at me. When she raises one brow, I can see where Luca gets it. "Hmm. He could be. He just needs himself a nice woman to keep him under control."

I open my mouth to speak, but no words come out. For some reason, I kind of want her to like me.

"Would you like a coffee?" I ask, trying to fill the silence.

"Really making yourself at home," she huffs, and I take a step back.

Okay, then.

As I make my way over to the machine, she calls out after me. "Black with one sugar, please."

Exactly like my Nonna. A painful twinge tugs in my chest at the memory.

She starts rummaging through the cupboards and tosses an apron at my head.

130 ~ LUNA MASON

"Here, put that on. I volunteered to bake cupcakes for the orphanage, and Luca's kitchen is bigger than mine. I could use the help."

A sadness washes over me, remembering cooking at home with my mom and Nonna. How mom would let me lick the spoon behind Nonna's back. It was the best part.

"What's Luca's favorite cake?"

Opening one of the lower cupboards, she starts pulling out the mixing bowls. "Lemon drizzle. The recipe with the limon-cello in, of course." She stops and looks up at me. Her tanned cheeks pale.

Shit. I cringe as the realization settles on her face.

Chewing the inside of my lip, I wait for the look of disapproval from her. Her son can't even have his beloved cake because of me.

But it doesn't come. Instead, she winks. "I have an amazing recipe without it I've been wanting to try. Maybe next time?"

A smile forms on my lips. She isn't judging me.

I stand and watch as she shuts the door and straightens, pointing to the second bag on the counter. "There are some things in here from Luca. And Sienna gave me some books for you. Luca's worried you're getting bored."

I look in the flowery duffel and I can't help but smile. A big, pink hot-water bottle, some rose oil bath salts, and enough chocolate to last a month.

"Did he—"

"Yes, all requested by Luca himself. With instructions to hand deliver and make sure you were okay."

I bite back a grin and dig out one of the Hershey bars and take a bite.

Mrs. Russo puts her hand on her hip and holds out her

empty hand with a teasing smile. I chuckle and hand her a bar for herself.

"He's learned. It's the fastest way to make a woman smile," she says, pointing the chocolate at me and winking.

I let out a sigh of relief. We're getting somewhere.

BY THE TIME we bake and drink Luca out of coffee, it's dark outside. Mrs. Russo grabs her things to leave, and I walk her to the door.

"You take care of yourself, Rosa. You're a good one." Her warm hand rests on my arm before she steps off the concrete porch.

"It was nice to meet you, properly."

"Tell that boy of mine I'll be having words with him when he decides to come home. If he comes home this time." She shakes her head and pushes her round framed glasses up her nose.

"I will." The thought of Luca not coming back sends a cold shiver up my spine.

I close the door behind her as she slips into her car and drives off.

The giddy feeling of having someone to talk to fades, so I decide to dig out one of these dark gray books Sienna sent me.

Five hours later and I'm still engrossed in this book. Not just any book—the damn dirtiest, filthiest smut. It has me blushing and giggling, and at times my mouth even hangs open. He fucked her with the handle of a knife. Am I completely wired wrong for finding that even remotely hot? I've escaped reality and entered into a realm of sexual freedom.

There's no embarrassment here, no trauma. Now, I'm itching to get to the end; I can't get to sleep until I know he groveled his ass off.

It has also reminded me of how much I have missed out on. I've never been kissed, not like the way Luca kissed me earlier. I've never so much as had an orgasm by a man. I've been so wrapped up in running from my demons, I have never lived.

I've never wanted it. I have certainly never craved it.

Until Luca.

A sadness creeps over me, and I close the book. I don't know what I want. I don't know how much I can even handle without the fear consuming me again.

What if I have sex with Luca and Dante's face flashes in my mind? What if he thinks I'm completely broken?

I curl up into a ball on the couch.

What if I really am?

Chapter Twenty-Four

ROSA

I pull the blanket up under my neck and snuggle into Luca's bed. It's so much comfier than the one he gave me. Well, that's what I tell myself. In reality, it smells like him. It makes me feel safe.

He's still not home, and it's been days now.

I miss him.

Some of his men pop in and make sure I'm okay and restock the fridge for me. They don't speak to me; they don't even really look at me.

I toss and turn with my eyes closed, trying to get some sleep. Hoping my brain doesn't take me there. Back into my inner hell.

But my thoughts instead are filled with worry for Luca. What if something happened to him?

Fuck it.

I slide out of bed and throw on my black robe and head downstairs. I'll sleep when he's home, when I know he's safe.

When I enter the kitchen, I head straight for the fancy coffee machine, grabbing Luca's black BOSS mug, which makes me grin.

The machine buzzes to life, and I jump up on the counter beside it and watch the coffee pour.

"I hope that coffee is for me, tesoro." His deep voice makes my heart flutter.

"Luca!"

I slide off the counter and run to him. He grins and spreads his arms out wide as I crash into him. As I wrap my arms around his muscular frame, he crushes me against his body.

"Did you miss me?" he whispers.

"No."

I keep my head nuzzled into his chest so he can't see my smile.

"Liar," he chuckles. "Well, I fucking missed you, Rosa."

I turn my head up to face him. His hands lower down my back until he cups my ass, his eyes searching mine.

I bite my lower lip. "I missed you, boss man."

Right now he looks every inch the mafia boss. The tailored black suit and black tie. Except, now I know him better, I can see the dark tinge under his eyes, the way his hair is tousled from when he runs his fingers through it when he's stressed.

"Did you find Maddie?"

He frowns and shakes his head. "No, but we're close. We will bring her back. How have you been? Everything okay here?" He smiles, but it's strained.

"I'm fine, just bored out of my mind. I'm missing our movie nights. I met your mom, though, she is so cute. I love her." My words tumble in a rush. I'm so happy he's back; I feel like I need to make up for lost time.

"I hear. She is very fond of you, too." He strokes a lock of hair off of my cheek and tucks it behind my ear. The feather touch on my skin sends little sparks through me. "How are you sleeping?"

His concern sets the fire off inside of me.

"Good. Surprisingly." It's either the sexy books distracting me or his scent smothering me in his bedsheets that are keeping the nightmares at bay and unleashing something new within me.

He brings his hand to my cheek. "I'm proud of you."

I nod. It's all I can manage without bursting into tears. No one's ever said that to me before.

His forehead rests against mine, our noses touching. Our heavy breathing fills the room. Something catches his attention behind me; he snakes an arm around, and I follow his hand with my eyes as he snatches up *the book* from the counter.

My cheeks are burning as he licks his lips, bringing the book between us.

"What's this about?" His eyebrows raise as he reads the back cover.

A wave of heat flashes up my cheeks. "Just a romance book. Sienna gave them to your mom for me."

His chest rumbles. "Hmm. Is that what you call this—a *romance* book?" His tone is playful.

"Something to keep my mind busy," I stammer. Embarrassment floods me, and I'm tempted to run away and hide in the bedroom.

He opens it to the center. His face goes through a range of expressions until his mouth forms a perfect O. I cover my face with my palm.

136 ~ LUNA MASON

"Oh, well, Viktor is certainly keeping her busy here." His voice is husky.

"Men in books tend to know how to do that." I bite my lip.

He growls in response and I giggle.

"Trust me, there's nothing they can do that I can't."

"And what would a book boyfriend do next, then, Mr. Russo?"

With that, he spins us around, and my back hits the cool wall. I part my lips to speak, but I'm at a loss for words.

He has a look of pure hunger as he rolls his bottom lip between his teeth.

Goosebumps erupt in the wake of his fingertips trailing down my exposed arm. I shift my hips in his hold, his hard erection pushing against my stomach.

He leans in, his lips grazing my earlobe.

"He would probably slide his fingers inside her to get her nice and wet, dripping all over his hand. At the same time sucking on her big, beautiful breasts."

He pulls his face away, his words leaving me breathless and needy.

"Then what?" It's barely a whisper, I don't recognize my own voice.

He looks deep in thought for a second before he gives me one of his playful smirks. The line of heat from his palm works its way up my arm until his thumb traces my chin and his fingers wrap behind my neck, tilting me to look directly in his deep green eyes as his voice lowers. "He would probably then hold her up by her throat, squeezing just enough to stop the air but not enough to pass out. Enough she could only focus on his thick, pierced cock pounding into her, hitting

DEVOTED ~ 137

that sweet spot that has her trembling and panting, all while she's fighting for air."

"Shit, Luca," I pant out.

"And then, right before she's about to explode, her legs trembling, her heart rate spiking, he would slide one of his soaking fingers into her asshole to set off her fireworks."

I splutter on a cough and he chuckles.

"Wow." I'm lost for words.

I'm almost orgasming from his filthy mouth. Unbelievable—a man who can get a woman off with words.

Never, ever in my life have I been so desperate for every single detail he described.

"I'm not quite done," he growls.

I bite the inside of my lip. "You're really going the whole distance with this. Carry on . . ."

He places his index finger over my mouth and my eyes go wide.

"He would take her to bed and lay her down, ripping every shred of clothing off of her, and demand she grab the headboard. Once she does, he'd loosen his tie and roll up his sleeves, leaving her waiting in anticipation. She will be begging for more. Only then will he join her on the bed, grab her perfect ass in both hands to hold himself, and lick her clean. Fucking her with his tongue, maybe even both holes. Until her hips are bucking against his face and he is smothered in her sweet juices."

A whimper leaves my throat. What is happening to me?

"Jesus Christ, Luca," I moan.

"Yes, she would probably moan just like that. But louder, she would be screaming my, I mean his, name until her lungs were burning. And then do you know what he'd do?"

138 – LUNA MASON

I shake my head. All I can picture is my hands on the headboard.

"He'd pull her spent body into his arms and kiss her. One of those earth-shattering, make-you-come-on-the-spot kisses."

His gaze locks on my lips, his dilated pupils making his eyes black.

"Show me," I whisper.

I can see the conflict cross his features, so I smooth my fingers through his messy brown locks and pull him toward me, so his lips are barely brushing mine.

"Please. I want this. I need you." I tug him closer to me. "Everything. I want it all. With you. I'm ready."

I've never been more sure of anything in my life. To show me what it's like to be owned, possessed, consumed in the best possible ways.

To unleash the woman beneath I know is there.

"Can I kiss you? I can't stop replaying it in my head," he asks, and I nod. Me neither.

"Words, Rosa. If we do this, we do this properly. I want to worship every inch of you. But it has to be completely on your terms. You are always in control."

His face is serious, but my body is on fire.

"Luca, I want this. Shit, I want this so much. Please."

I rise up on my tiptoes, my lips hovering over his, and whisper, "Be the first man to ever make me come."

"Oh fuck," he groans, his warm breath hitting my lips. "I need to get you upstairs." With that he bends and scoops me into his arms, cuddling me into his chest as he takes us to his bedroom.

He lays me down onto the bed, softly stroking my face as he bends down and kisses me, running his hands through my hair. The mattress dips as he lays down next to me, and I turn onto my side to face him.

Nerves bubble under the surface. What if I'm not good enough? What if I'm too broken? And the last one worries me the most. What if he still can't do it for me?

"Hey, are you sure about this?" His deep voice distracts me from my spinning mind.

I look at him, the hunger in his eyes, the concern in his voice, and I smile.

"I am. I'm just worried I'm not enough for you. I want all these things, I just don't know if I'm really capable, I guess."

I bow my head in shame. It's my awful reality. I've never had the touch of a man, consensually.

"It's you, Rosa. Just simply by existing, you are perfect. Even if you want to just lay here and let me worship your body for the night, we can do that. This is new for me too. What I do know is, anything with you will be everything."

He traces his finger down the side of my face, and I suck in a breath. Just that light touch alone has me squeezing my legs together. He gives me the courage to lean forward and plant my lips against his.

"Let's do this, Luca." I grin up at him, and he grabs both sides of my face and crashes his lips over mine for an all-consuming kiss.

"Baby, this is *only* about you. I want to give you everything. I don't need anything in return. I can wait. I will wait until you're truly ready for me. Even if you have to cuff me to the bed. We can't rush this." He rolls on top of me, resting his weight onto his forearm as I wrap my legs around his waist. Visions of a naked Luca, cuffed to the bed and letting me have my way with him, have me soaking my panties.

"You need to have a safe word, Rosa. If anything is too much, you use it."

His cock strains against his pants rubbing against my needy pussy, and I moan in response.

"Tesoro mio, give me a word, please."

I grin and say the first thing that pops into my head. A word that makes me feel safe.

"Treasure."

Chapter Twenty-Five
LUCA

My heart almost stops when she says the word. I don't think she realizes just how much I do treasure her.

"Good girl." I roll her bottom lip with my thumb and brush my lips gently over hers.

"What do you want me to do to you, Rosa? Tell me."

"Well . . ." She pauses.

"Come on, I won't bite. Well, unless that's what you want." I playfully snap my teeth.

She tries to look away, and I gently cup her cheek to face me.

"I want to feel alive. I've never been with anyone else—since. You would be my first," she whispers so quietly I have to stop for a second to register her words.

I go completely still. "It would be a fucking honor, Rosa." My chest swells. I can't even hide the smile.

I start kissing along the column of her neck and she tips her head to the side. I travel down to her collarbone, my lips following my fingers as I slide her black robe over her shoulders.

"You are delectable," I say against her soft skin.

She moans in response, tightening her thighs around my waist, my painfully hard cock pressing against her.

I plant kisses down the inside of her arm; I plan to kiss every single inch of her. I lick down the inside of her bicep, and she jolts just before I reach her inner elbow. When I stop and look up, she giggles.

"That tickled."

"What, here?" I nibble in the same spot that had her jumping. This one taste, though, earns me a little breathy moan.

"Hmm, yes." Her eyes flutter closed. My other hand reaches for the edge of her tank top, pulling it down as I start massaging her breast, all while kissing that new little sensitive spot of hers.

"You're beautiful, Rosa."

She truly is. In this moment, she's like a different woman from the one whose hair I held back as she purged her old life. She was even beautiful then.

Making my way back to her mouth, I press my lips over hers. Her hips start to roll, making her pussy rub against my cock. I want to watch her come to life under my touch.

She runs her fingers through my hair, tentatively pushing my head down. I kiss around her nipple, her back arching, pushing her perky breasts into my face. I alternate my attention between them both before placing one of her rosy buds in my mouth and sucking gently.

My cock begs to explode as she pants, whispering my name sweetly.

"More, Luca."

DEVOTED ~ 143

Her pulse flutters in her neck, fueling a pink flush that spreads across her chest. It takes every bit of restraint I have not to rip off her panties and sink into her. But I can't. I want this to be special for her.

She deserves to know what it's like to feel cherished. To feel special, because this woman truly is.

"I want to savor you, tesoro."

"I feel savored already, I promise."

I sit back on my heels and take a moment to soak in this beauty before me. She rests her arms above her head with her legs still wrapped around me, her hips hovering above the mattress.

I peel open her robe, revealing her little black satin thong. Fuck, she's perfect. I have to feel her body pressed against mine.

She hungrily watches as I undress myself, tossing my shirt on the floor. She sits up and runs her hands along my abs, sending bolts of electricity through me, enough to make me bite back a groan.

She traces along the V to my waist and unbuckles my belt. She stops and looks up before unbuttoning.

"Baby, I'm yours. You want my cock, you take it."

She sucks in a breath. There's a slight shake in her hands, so I help her out, undoing them for her. My raging hard-on is barely restrained by my boxers.

Discarding my pants, I bring myself back up to her, lying next to her and stroking her hair out of her face. I claim her lips, my fingers finding the hem of her panties.

She opens her legs wider for me. The best invitation I've had in a long time.

"Good girl. Shall we see how wet you are for me?"

She nods, and I go back in for another kiss—it's soft and sweet. Intimate, even, which is uncharted territory for me.

I dip under the panties, pushing them to the side, and slide down her smooth pussy.

She moans out as my index finger circles her soaking clit. I take it slow and gentle, getting the moisture from her entrance and sliding it back up. She pants beneath me, so I kiss her.

"God, Luca." Her head arches against the pillow.

"I am, yes. Now, lift those hips for me, baby. Let me in."

My lips follow along her jaw and down her neck. I work my way to her stomach, tasting her all the way down, not forgetting that little spot on her arm that has her shivering as I plant a kiss there.

My head is now between her legs, with a perfect view of her pussy. She sits herself up, her eyes wide.

"Luca—"

"Yes, baby." I plant wet kisses along the inside of her thigh.

"W-wait."

I stop and look up at her.

"No one's ever done *that* to me before." She rolls her bottom lip between her teeth as she looks down at me.

I swear to God my cock is throbbing so hard it hurts. "Oh, fuck."

I look at her glistening pussy. "Let me show you how good it can feel. Let me taste you?"

I curl a finger inside of her and she moans, her knees collapsing on the bed.

"Fuck, yes," she pants out.

Using the tip of my tongue, I lick slow circles around her throbbing clit, and her hips immediately jerk against my face.

I lick all the way to her entrance, removing my buried finger and replacing it with my tongue.

Her hands grip the sheets so hard her knuckles go white.

"Is that good, baby?" My voice is laced with a deep hunger.

"Oh, God, yeah."

"Do you want more?"

I flick her clit and she screams out. "Yes!"

"Ride my face then, baby,"

She lifts her hips a little more and I grab onto her ass cheeks.

Licking and sucking as she writhes on the bed, I keep the same rhythm, fucking her with my fingers.

She screams out my name and her legs squash against my head, quivering against me, her hips bucking uncontrollably. I carry on until she has nothing left to give, letting her ride my face and take what she needs. Even being absolutely smothered by her, I can't get enough.

"Luca!" she pants out. I pry open her legs and come up for breath, wiping my mouth with the back of my hand, and grin at her. She props herself up on her elbows, her chest rapidly rising and falling, her cheeks beautifully flushed.

"You like that?" I wink at her, and she lets out the most adorable little giggle.

"I loved that. How have I gone twenty-three years without that in my life?" She pushes a wild lock of her black hair away from her face.

"You wanna go again?" I give her my best mischievous grin.

As much as I can't wait to sink my cock into her tight and dripping pussy, I would have absolutely no problem letting her get off on my tongue for the whole night. Watching her is more than enough for me.

She shakes her head. "I want you."

"Oh, baby. I want you, too." I sit up on my knees, still between her legs, and pull off my boxers, palming my throbbing dick. Her eyes trail down my body, going wide when she gets to my cock.

I start to stroke it up and down, wiping the pre-cum spilling out of the top, knocking the metal bar I have through the head.

"Y-you're pierced?"

She licks her lips, not taking her eyes off it. I look down at the silver stud and swipe my thumb over the barbell. "Trust me, you'll love it."

Her mouth falls open, and she snaps it shut.

"Do you want to touch it?" I continue to stroke my cock, looking into her eyes.

She swings her legs around and mimics my position, pushing herself up onto her knees. She shuffles closer to me, her nipples brushing against my bicep.

The second her hand touches mine, bolts of electricity shoot through me. I stop what I'm doing and let her investigate. She's deep in thought as she brushes her finger over the head of my cock, every nerve ending reacting as she lightly touches the piercing.

"Oh fuck," I groan.

She wraps her dainty fingers around my shaft. "Luca?"

My eyes droop closed as I fight the urge to lose control. "Yes, baby."

She starts to stroke me up and down. It's fucking heaven. "You're huge. What if it won't, you know . . ."

The words every man wants to hear from their partner. But this time, there is concern in her voice.

I cup her face. "We've prepped. I'll go nice and slow. You'll stretch around me perfectly. If it hurts, we stop. I promise."

My eyes search hers. She tightens her grip and ups the pace.

"Or you can get me off like this, because fuck, it's hot," I grunt.

I lean down and whisper into her lips. "Do you want to ride me, baby? You set the pace, take what you want from me. The power is all in your hands. Always."

Her eyes light up. "I'd love that."

I nod, and she removes her hand. I lay down flat on the bed, resting my hands behind my head, my erect cock ready and waiting. I mean every word. This is about her; she deserves to have the power. Claim back a part of her that was ripped from her.

She crawls up my body and settles above my dick.

Before she can sink down, I sit up and rummage through the drawer, pulling out a foil condom wrapper. I rip the packet open with my teeth, but I stop as she puts her hand over mine.

"I have an IUD. I'm clean, obviously. If you are, too, I'd like to feel all of you. I want this to be different for you, too. To be more."

Holy shit.

I couldn't say no to that, even if I wanted to. She's thrown me.

"I've never not used one," I answer truthfully.

There is no denying the fact I enjoy sex. But I also can't deny that this whole experience with Rosa is different. It's more.

"If you want to, it's absolutely fine," she says, taking the condom from my fingers, grabbing the top between her thumb and index finger.

Which I suddenly hate.

I grab the condom out of her hands and toss it across the room.

"You can be my first," I say, which earns me one of my favorite things in the world: a smile from her.

She rubs the tip of my dick along her slit, smothering it in her wetness. That alone has me panting. She leans forward, and her hand grabs my throat to hold herself upright.

"Well, fuck, that's new," I choke out.

"Oops, sorry." She lifts herself back up, her cheeks now red.

"Leave the hand there, Rosa." I tug at her arm to put her hand back.

The sensation of her clutching the side of my throat only makes me hold my breath more. With her free hand, she grabs my dick, lining it up with her entrance. Her weight now on the hand that's pressing down on my windpipe, she slowly sinks down.

"Oh my god," she cries out, her head falling back as she lowers herself.

"Squeeze that hand tighter, baby."

Her nails dig into my neck, and I wince as she pierces the skin. Between that and her pussy suffocating my dick, I'm on fire.

"Take all of me, right up until you feel that piercing hit that sweet spot."

With a small whimper, she leans forward. I groan out as she hesitates halfway. She faces me and sucks in a breath of air and holds it.

"Breathe, baby, you're doing so well, just a little bit more for me."

She increases the pressure around my throat, which makes my balls tighten, and she takes all of me down to the base.

She lifts herself up and sinks back down a few times, each time almost sending my eyes rolling into the back of my head. The warmth on my dick as she rides me is incredible.

"So perfect, Rosa. You feel so good."

I watch in awe as she starts to up the pace, rolling her hips to hit the spot she wants. Taking everything from me. Her eyes flutter shut. Her mouth makes that perfect O as she moans.

She picks up the pace, slamming back down, making her ass slap against my thighs.

"Fuck, Rosa."

"Luca, take control. Please," she says breathlessly, pushing her dark hair out of her face.

"Yes, baby. Anything." I move my arms from underneath my head and grab hold, digging my fingers into her hips.

"Spin around for me."

She lifts up slightly and rotates so her back faces me. I bring my knees up slightly so she can support herself.

"You ready?" I ask.

"Shit. Yes," she hisses as she pushes herself up and down the length of me.

Tightening my grip, I lift her up and let her fall, moving my hips up to fuck her, watching as my cock rams into her from behind, her ass bouncing up and down.

"This is so hot." I wish I could take a picture so I can remember this image forever.

"More," she hoarsely screams.

I keep pounding into her until I can feel her walls clamp down on me, my balls going tight and my whole body tensing. Squeezing my eyes shut, I roar out her name at the top of my lungs and she joins me as I fill her up completely, spilling into her until my cock is twitching inside of her.

Sitting up, not even caring about regaining my breath as my chest burns, I lift her up and pull her to face me. Our sweaty foreheads meet, and her warm breath hits my mouth.

"That was—" I don't even have words, like an out-of-body experience.

"Perfect." She finishes my sentence for me.

As I look into her hooded eyes, a warm feeling settles over me. One that should put me on edge; it's not something I ever thought I wanted or needed in life.

But right now, it truly is everything. She wraps her hands around my neck, but pulls back quickly. Her eyes widen in shock as she stares below my jaw. "Oh my god, Luca, you're bleeding!"

"You've left your mark on me."

In more ways than one.

Chapter Twenty-Six
ROSA

Brushing my fingers along his pecs, I trail my nail all the way down, tracing his hard abs.

He leans over, his chest nearly smothering me. "What are you doing?"

I hear a drawer slam shut, and he lays back down, grabbing hold of my bare ass cheek. With a mischievous glint in his eye, he hands me a little black notepad and pen.

"What's this for?" Is this where he keeps track of the girls he beds?

"Write down everything you want to explore. All those things you read about in books that get you all hot and flustered. All of your desires you've never had an opportunity to try."

"W-why?" He would really do this for me? "You don't think it's weird?"

He grunts, thrusting the pen between my fingers. "The

opposite. It will be my new bucket list, baby. I want to tick off every single thing you write in there."

I open up the pad to the next blank page and tap the tip of the pen against my chin. It's been a few weeks since he returned from Italy, and it's safe to say our relationship is growing stronger every day—and so am I, with him beside me.

And teaching me.

"Hmm, so many to choose from." I start scribbling them down, adjusting my position so he can't spy on me.

"Hey, I wanna read!" He fake pouts at me.

"Patience." I hold the pen up and wink at him.

Anal, hand necklaces, can I squirt?, spitting, edging, sixty-nine, back door play on him?

I pause and lift my gaze to him. He's watching me like a hawk.

"Want to see?" I hold the notepad against my chest, suddenly nervous to show him.

He so far has treated me like a delicate princess, one who's broken and scarred. Is he going to think I'm crazy for wanting all of this?

"Fuck, yes." He props himself against the headboard and eagerly holds out his palm.

I offer the notebook to him, and he whips it out of my hands.

His eyes go wide, quickly filling with pure desire as he turns to me.

"This is quite the list. Shit, I need to start reading these books." Amusement laces his tone.

The paper tears as he rips the page out, tossing the pad on the floor. He pulls me into his chest, holding the scrap with the sexy list in front of us.

"Can we start on it later? If you're ready? The rules are still

DEVOTED ~ 153

the same; you're in control. We do this at your pace. But fuck, just reading this list has me ready to go again."

I slide my hand under the covers—he's not lying. I wrap my hand around his thick shaft. "What about trying a simple one before you have to go to work?"

"Which one do you have in mind, tesoro?" His hips move as he thrusts slowly into my hand.

I can feel a little drip from him, and it makes me lick my lips. What would he taste like? "Sixty-nine?"

"Oh, baby, it's like you're speaking my language here. Climb on up. Your man needs his fill before work."

He throws back the covers, leaving his muscular frame on display as he slides down to lie flat. I admire all the ink for a second before staring back at his dick with that silver bar through the head.

I climb over him, my legs on either side of his head, propping myself up on my forearms.

I take him in my mouth until I can feel the metal hit the back of my throat. I jolt forward as his tongue connects with my clit.

"Baby, I need your thighs around my head. I want your pussy to fucking smother me. So bring that gorgeous ass back and sit."

A moan escapes my mouth, still full of his cock. I start to bob my head, resting my weight on one arm so my hands can slowly start to caress his balls.

My eyes flutter closed as he licks all the way up and down, his tongue then teasing my entrance. My toes curl as his tongue slips in.

"Deeper, baby. All the way, fill your pretty little mouth with my cock." His gravelly voice sends shockwaves through my core, spurring me on.

As I find my rhythm, my confidence now building, I start to make little circles with my hips. He licks and sucks like a man starved. His grip tightens around my thighs. I suck all the way up and let it pop out of my mouth before licking the salty drop of pre-cum from the tip.

"Hmm, that's it, baby," he groans, his breath fluttering against my throbbing pussy.

Pushing myself up on my arms, I spread my legs wider and lean back. "Is that okay?"

He pulls away after another long lick. "Okay? More than okay. This is fucking heaven, Rosa."

Heat spreads across my cheeks, my eyes rolling to the back of my head as he continues to feast on me.

"Oh, fuck, Luca, I'm so close."

"Mouth. On my cock. Please." His voice is muffled.

I bend back down and part my lips, taking him in my mouth, swirling my tongue as I bob up and down, upping the pace and taking him as far as I can go, just before I gag. I squeeze my eyes shut as my climax bubbles to the surface, my body on fire. My hips buck against his face, and I suck him with everything I have.

His fingers press hard into my hips. Mine dig into his thick thighs. I'm moaning with his cock stuffing my mouth as my body explodes, my legs shaking and his grip the only thing holding me in place as he licks my orgasm from me.

I wrap my fingers around his cock and pump him while sucking. It doesn't take long for him to follow behind me, hot liquid pouring down my throat.

With a gulp, I swallow the salty taste down. He releases my thighs, his tongue still making small gentle circles on my clit as I come down from my high.

He peppers kisses along my thighs and taps my ass, enough to send waves of pleasure straight to my core.

After showering together, we get dressed and eat breakfast. Like a regular couple before their normal nine-to-five office jobs. He grabs his gun from the counter and frowns at his phone.

"Kiss, please."

He taps his lips, and I lean up off the barstool and kiss him.

"I'll see you later, gorgeous."

———————— • ————————

LUCA WHISPERING MY name wakes me from my peaceful slumber.

"Rosa, baby. I need you to wake up."

I blink a few times, and his beautiful face comes into view.

"Huh? Why?" I rub my eyes to clear them. His face is red, his nostrils flaring.

"I have guests—ones that can't know you're here."

He throws the drawer open, and I scoot up, pushing my bare back against the cool headboard.

"Guests? Who?" I try to shake the sleepy fog from my head as I watch him.

"The Capris," he grunts.

My eyes stay glued to his chiseled abs as he throws on a black T-shirt, and I let out a sigh as he pulls his gray sweats over his dick.

Squeezing my thighs together, I try to stop the ache in my pussy.

"What do they want?" I pull the blanket up over my belly.

"To talk." He plants a kiss to my lips, rubbing his thumb along my cheekbone. I melt into his touch.

"I'll get rid of them. Just, please, don't make a sound."

I nod my head. "I promise, Luca."

I swallow the lump in my throat. These men are dangerous.

"Good girl. You're safe here. I will always protect what's mine, tesoro." A darkness flashes across his eyes as he grabs his gun from his bedside table and leaves.

He called me his?

Chapter Twenty-Seven

LUCA

"You had best have a pretty good reason for turning up at my fucking house, Romano," I seethe, the grip on my gun tightening as I look through my metal gates at him.

"Are you not letting me in?" He looks around and up at the camera stationed on the brick wall pointed at him. "We need to speak. In private."

Maddie.

Fuck.

I aim my gun at him.

He holds his palm up in surrender and chuckles. "It's not that kind of party, unless you want it to be."

"Like you said, trust is earned. Prove you have the information I need," I spit back.

I don't have time for this, and I certainly don't want the Capris knowing about Rosa.

"Someone working for you isn't who he says he is. He has

Maddie, I am certain. If you let me explain, you'll see why." He calmly pulls out a thick white envelope from his jacket and waves it.

"You better not be wasting my time again, Romano."

I key in the passcode to open the gates.

I lead him to the back entrance of the house, the furthest away from my bedroom that sits above the front door.

"Take a seat." I point my gun at the dining table.

"The information I have, it never came from me."

I narrow my eyes as he walks around the offered chair, hovering by the side table filled with picture frames.

He picks up the photo of me holding Darcy, taken on the first day I met her. "Cute family you've got, Luca."

I don't like where this is going, and I grit my teeth together to bite my tongue. "Just spit it out."

"Depends if we have a deal." He looks up at me.

"I thought deals like that never came around twice," I counter.

"Things change. I want my guns in New York, and you have the shipping facilities. An alliance would be good for business for both of us."

"An alliance?" This suddenly became interesting.

He waves the frame idly. "Do you want to find Maddison?"

"Of course I do." Grayson's a mess; I've never seen him so broken. I'd do anything to make this right.

"I'm giving you one chance, and one chance only, Luca." He takes a step toward me, and I straighten my spine.

He shoves the picture into my chest, pushing me backward.

"My daughter, Maria, wants to build my empire in New York for me. She's an overachiever, you could call her. She

DEVOTED ~ 159

needs a visa, so you two will marry. She will also be there to keep an eye on you, make sure you are conducting my business in the right way here. If you fuck this up, well—" He pauses, looking at the frame. "There is nothing more devastating to a father than losing his only daughter, is there, Luca?"

My blood boils at his words, the muscles in my neck threatening to pop out. "That's my niece you're talking about, you fucking cunt."

He tuts, taking a step back.

"This—this is what I'm talking about, your irrational behavior. You think I haven't had eyes on you for a long time? My daughter will whip you into shape, carve you as one of us. Keep you in line. If you do that, then I'll send you right to Maddie. No one has to get hurt here. It's all up to you now."

He places the picture right side up on the dining table.

I squeeze the back of my neck—marrying his daughter?

"Luca, this isn't really a choice. If you don't do this, I'll burn everything and everyone you love to the ground for stealing from me. If you do this, they live, you run my guns, marry my daughter, you do as we say. You get Maddie back in return."

I lose Rosa.

I'd lose any chance I potentially had at happiness with the one woman who makes me feel anything.

But they're my family. There is nothing I won't do to protect them.

So the old asshole is right.

I don't have a choice. Family over everything, right?

"Deal. Now tell me who has Maddie."

"You might want to sit down for this one," he says.

I grip the back of the chair in front of me.

"I'm fine."

"Your new friend, Frankie, isn't who you think he is."

He rummages in his beige linen suit jacket and throws the load of paperwork over the table. I pick it up and scrunch it in my hands as I look at the photocopy of a driver's license with Frankie's familiar face on it.

My guts turn to ice when I read the name. "Mr. Francis Falcone."

Fal-fucking-cone.

That motherfucker.

My legs feel weak and I slump into one of the chairs. "Tell me everything."

He shakes his head. "It's all there. He has her, mark my words. I don't know why he decided to keep you alive, but you're lucky. He's clever. Don't underestimate him."

As he turns to leave, he pauses. "I expect a ring sent over to Maria by next week. We will sort out the details once you retrieve Maddie. Welcome to the family, son." He puts particular emphasis on the last word before he steps outside.

When the door slams shut, I let out a ragged breath, staring down at the picture left on the table. Then my gaze drifts to the frame he was holding. Darcy.

Squeezing my eyes shut, a headache forms at my temples. I frantically throw open the cupboards.

Fuck. No scotch.

So, instead, I fling the pile of papers from my reach and watch them scatter across the tile, resembling my life.

Frankie. What the hell have you done?

Chapter Twenty-Eight

ROSA

Luca paces into the room like a wild animal. He tears through the room, putting on his suit.

"Luca, what happened?"

He turns to face me. His jaw clenches so tight it looks like he may crack a tooth. He fumbles with his tie.

"Jesus fucking Christ," he hisses and gives up.

I walk over to him, without a scrap of clothing on. He told me not to move earlier.

"Let me." I take the smooth black tie in my hands. He lifts his chin as I do it for him, his Adam's apple bobbing.

"There, done." I smile up at him.

His features soften, his gaze traveling my body, giving me goosebumps as the anger shifts to pure hunger in his eyes.

"What happened down there, Luca?" I pin him with a stare.

"I've made a deal with the devil to bring Maddie home."

"What deal?"

He shakes his head. "Not right now, please." The sadness laced in his voice stops me from pressing him further.

I wrap my arms over to cover my breasts, suddenly uncomfortable that he's keeping secrets.

"You're beautiful, you know that, right?" He tilts his head to the side.

"I guess." I shrug.

I didn't ever know my beauty until he showed me, until I got clean. Now, when I look at myself, I like the woman who stares back at me. The one with glowing skin, brighter eyes, and shiny hair.

"Things are about to get messy, Rosa. Really messy." His head drops.

He looks absolutely exhausted.

"Hey, you've got this. You are Luca fucking Russo. You can take on the world." I cup his stubbly jaw and tip his head back up. Something is eating him alive.

I know it's going to come down to Luca or my dad. And I know who my heart wants to win this. The only man who has ever protected me.

"Don't hesitate when it comes down to my dad, Luca. Not for me. You keep yourself safe. I want you to come back from this. Not him. Okay?"

I blink back the tears; I can't believe the words coming out of my mouth. But I mean every single one.

I can't lose him.

He simply nods. I wrap my arms around his muscular frame and hold him tight. I never want to let go. At this moment, we're just Luca and Rosa. Our little escape from reality. It's perfect.

But I know deep down it's too good to be true.

"Go and take over the world, Luca." I swallow, my heart heavy.

He strokes the back of my hair, and his erratic pulse hammers against my ear.

"Rosa, do you have any family members called Frankie?"

I pull back and gasp. "Yes, an uncle. He left us a few years ago. I haven't seen him since the explosion that killed my mother."

He frowns.

"Your dad's brother?"

I nod. "Why?"

Dread fills me. Frankie was the ruthless one. I loved him more than my dad. He was always my protector. Until one day, he was gone.

His finger traces my shoulder. "If I'm right, I'll tell you everything. From the look on your face, I'm suspecting you liked your uncle."

"I did," I say honestly. "I don't know what my dad did to him. If he is back, be careful, Luca. Growing up, he was always my protector. He once blew up one of my bully's parents' cars for picking on me about being a virgin. I want to see him; he owes me an explanation."

He assesses me, his lips tight. "I can't promise you anything. I don't know what I'm walking into yet. I have to protect my family, and you, tesoro."

"Me?" My brain is working a hundred miles an hour with all of this information.

"Of course, you. Now, stay here. I'm sorry. I hate doing this to you. This is your home, too. But it will not be safe out there."

I go up on my tiptoes, pressing a gentle kiss to his lips.

His hand wraps around my naked body and cups my ass. His other hand lightly laces around my neck, which has me melting against him. He groans into my mouth, his tongue demanding more, and I give it to him.

"Fuck, now isn't the time to deal with this and a hard-on. But it's worth it. I needed that." He drops another kiss.

"Please be safe, Luca." My bottom lip starts to tremble, and he runs his thumb along it.

"When I have this to come home to, of course I will be," he rasps and pats my ass.

Even when the world is a mess, he makes me smile.

"I'll go get your spicy book collection from downstairs; that will keep your mind busy." He winks.

"That isn't your worst idea," I tease.

If there's ever been a time I need to escape reality, it's now.

Chapter Twenty-Nine

LUCA

"Wait there," I call out. My fingers are itching to pull out my gun and shoot Frankie fucking Falcone between the eyes.

I hear Grayson's Audi pull up, and he opens the front door, ignoring Frankie.

"What's going on?" a concerned Grayson asks.

"Just come inside."

I ball my fists together so hard they shake, using every bit of self-restraint I have not to knock Frankie the fuck out. But I need the truth. And I also need Frankie not to suspect I know.

I look between them both.

Grayson clearly appears irritated. "Well?"

I suck in some air, putting on my best serious voice. "Rosa is fucking dead."

I keep my eyes glued on Frankie. He stiffens next to Grayson and his jaw tics. He keeps his eyes on the ground, refusing to look at me or Grayson.

Bingo.

"And?" Grayson says.

"Well, she was our bargaining chip over the Falcones for Maddie."

That isn't even remotely true. Marco made clear his thoughts on his daughter.

Frankie starts to shift uncomfortably, and Grayson notices far too easily. "Do you have a fucking problem?" he asks Frankie, who rubs his hands along his stubble.

"No problem. Want me to take the body out . . . boss?"

"Yeah, fine. Go and get the supplies from the warehouse and come back. Grayson, with me."

I storm past them both, my restraint now wearing thin. I have to get away from Frankie. I head to my office and drop down behind the desk that's scattered with CCTV footage photos looking for Maddie.

"Should I send a condolence card out to Marco?" Grayson smirks.

I shoot him a look in warning as he sits opposite me.

"What do we do now, boss?"

The door flies open, and my heart is in my throat. I squeeze my eyes shut, hoping it's not her.

"Luca, I can't get the coffee machine working!"

She waltzes toward me, completely oblivious to Grayson. Her hair a curly mess, her cheeks flushed. My God, she looks beautiful. I can't take my eyes off her, in that black robe that leaves very little to the imagination.

She wraps her arms around my neck, and I suck in a breath, completely forgetting who the fuck I am with right now.

Grayson clears his throat, and I give him a death glare. I know I'll have some explaining to do. But, right now, I have a semi-hard cock and the woman who invades my mind is wrapped around me.

She leans in and murmurs, "Sorry, I assumed they'd gone. I thought you might like to join me in the bath. I really want to taste you again, Luca. I can't stop thinking about it."

She looks up at me through her lashes. It takes everything I can muster not to groan in front of my best friend. Or throw him out and spread her across my desk.

I bring my lips to her ear. I can see the goosebumps appear along her throat.

"Baby, you can suck my cock any time you like. Seeing you on your knees for me, your mouth stuffed with my dick, is what dreams are made of. So go and run that bath. I'll meet you in a minute."

I watch as she blushes and she steps out. I run my hand through my hair as the door clicks shut. I know I'm on borrowed time with her, with everything going on right now. So I want to make the most of it. My sliver of happiness will be ripped away if Romano was right and Frankie has Maddie.

"So, railing your captive. That's a new one for you."

I turn to look at Grayson, who's biting back a laugh. It's the first time I've seen him smile in weeks.

"Fuck off. It's not like that."

"Whatever, boss. I don't care. What I do care about is why you lied to Frankie."

Shit.

I pull out my phone and show him the photos of the documents Romano gave me. I can't tell him who gave me the intel. I can't risk Romano's threats. I've sent the driver's license to Enzo to investigate. I have to err on the side of caution, for now, until Enzo can confirm whether tracking Frankie leads us to Maddie or not.

"I was able to make a deal with Romano Capri after all. I think Frankie is working with the Falcones. You were right; something wasn't adding up. He appears out of nowhere, wanting to work with me. Frankie wasn't just Romano's damn bodyguard. He was his right-hand man. He left because he had family business to attend to in New York. Every damn time, he knows exactly where the Falcones' new hideouts are. He was the last one to see Maddie."

I watch as the realization settles over Grayson, his face turning red.

I continue. "He's smart. He all but ran the Capris in Europe. His reaction to Rosa's death was exactly as I suspected. He's refused to go anywhere near her. Always found an excuse for not checking in on her."

"Because she'd recognize him?"

"Exactly."

"Can I do the honors when he's back?" Grayson's teeth show in a menacing smile.

"Why do you think you're here?"

His fists knot, and he pounds them on my desk. "I swear to God, I will rip him limb from limb if he's touched her."

"I'm banking on that. How I didn't shoot him on the spot back there, I don't know. We need to get Maddie first before we kill him. I'm waiting for Enzo's call. He's digging into him for us now. If I've learned anything from you, it's that we need intel before we act."

This is Grayson's kill. If Frankie does know anything about Maddie's disappearance, I don't want to know the pain Grayson will inflict on him.

Frankie's reaction earlier was enough to confirm everything

Romano told me. Some part of me hoped Romano was somehow wrong, that he'd doctored the documents.

I place my phone down on my desk. "We are going to find Maddie. We are so close."

He has no idea what is going on behind the scenes. I've seen how much pain he's been in, not even from being shot. From losing the love of his life.

He drops down onto the sofa and throws his arm over his face.

"I need to go and check in on Rosa. Give me five minutes." I head to the door.

"Only five? I would have put you down for lasting longer than that." His voice is muffled through his jacket sleeve.

I chuckle and shake my head. "Around her, five is probably about right."

———————————

I TAP ON her bathroom door. "Rosa, baby, can I come in?"

"Yes," she calls back.

I open the door and stop. "Jesus, Rosa. Fuck me."

My eyes rake up her naked body, her tiny waist and perfect pair of tits with her nipples standing to attention, just begging to be sucked. She grins and bends over to turn the tap off on the freestanding bath in the center of the room. I groan and readjust my dick in my pants.

That ass.

I stalk toward her, and she gasps as I spin her naked frame to face me.

"I told you to stay in your room." I pin her with a glare.

"I'm not very good with orders. Plus, you left me with

some really steamy books, Luca. That was a bad idea on both of our parts."

She gives me a sly grin, and I bring my mouth down to hover over hers.

"Oh, is that right?"

She nods.

"So, if I ordered you down onto your knees to suck my cock, you'd say no?" I grip the bulge in my pants for emphasis.

Her eyes go wide as she glances down.

"Well?" I growl.

She sinks down onto her knees before me.

"I didn't think so."

Her fingers fumble with my belt, and I run my hands through her hair.

"Wow," she gasps as she frees my cock, ready and raging for her.

Her finger traces along the studs of my piercing, which goes straight through the head of my penis.

"Did it hurt?"

I let out a laugh. "Probably more than getting shot. Yes. But right now, it's so worth it."

She licks her lips and lifts herself off her heels to start licking around the head and the metal rod.

"Is it sensitive?"

"Hmm, yes," I groan, and she continues to tease the bar with her tongue. "Like that," I grit out.

Her hand grips the base, and she takes me in her mouth, her tongue swirling around my shaft as she bobs up and down.

"Holy shit, Rosa."

She looks up at me and it's perfect.

"You look so pretty sucking my cock."

As she goes deeper, I slam my eyes shut and start to thrust into her face.

"Holy shit," I mutter. Her hands grab my ass cheeks and her nails dig into the skin as she grips on while I fuck her hot mouth.

"I'm so close. Can I come on your tongue, baby?"

I look down and she nods.

"Hmm, my good fucking girl." I stroke her hair and hold on.

She stops sucking and starts licking up along the shaft, all the way to the tip, and latches onto the piercing before taking me back between her lips.

And I lose it.

Grabbing the back of her head, my fingers tangle into her soft hair. I explode, letting myself fill up her mouth.

"Rosa!" I roar, flinging my head back as she takes every last drop.

My chest heaves as, with one final suck, she sits back on her feet, and I watch as her throat bobs as she swallows.

I drop down onto my knees in front of her, framing her face with my hands.

"That was in-fucking-credible."

I plant my lips over hers, deepening the kiss as my tongue finds hers. My salty taste is still there in her mouth.

"You have no idea how much I needed that, Rosa. Thank you." I touch my forehead against hers.

"I think I need to do that to you more often." She licks her lips and I bite back the groan. I can't shake the dread in my stomach that we won't have many more moments like this. Not after today.

"I second that. Any time my cock is anywhere near any of your holes, I am a happy man."

I press a kiss on the tip of her nose, and she shakes her head and pulls back, her eyes searching mine. Then she grabs the back of my head and I slam my lips over hers. The kiss is enough to have me groaning in her mouth and my cock springing back to life.

"I really have to get to work. Once I'm done, I'm all yours again."

I don't know for how long. But, for as long as she's in this house, I am going to make sure there are enough memories to last us both a lifetime, because we need them.

I stare at this beautiful woman, a woman who was a shell of this version of Rosa a few weeks ago.

I cuddle her into me. She laughs as I start to press wet kisses all along her neck.

"That tickles!"

I rub my beard along her skin, her body vibrating against me. Her laugh makes me smile from ear to ear.

"Okay, time for a bath." I lift her up and carefully submerge her into the bath. She laughs as the bubbles tip over the edge and go all over my shoes.

"Oops." I glance down at the puddle I'm standing in before bending over. "One last kiss, then I have to go," I say, dropping to savor her swollen lips.

As I open the door, I stop as she asks, "Was it Uncle Frankie? Is he home?"

There's that sparkle in her eye, and for that second, it makes me hate him less. Knowing if he stays alive, he can help her.

All those times he's questioned Rosa's safety and my plans. He was never going to let me hurt her. She needs someone to help her fight. No matter how fucking angry I am at him right now, if Maddie is unharmed, alive and well, then maybe, just maybe, I will let him live. For her.

But what he's really up to, and his plans for me, are anyone's guess.

"I think so, baby."

She gives me a sad smile and nods. I forget she is the daughter of Marco sometimes; she grew up in this life. My own mafia princess.

My heart skips a beat when I realize, earlier, she knew what she was saying. She was allowing me to kill her family if it meant I would come back to her.

We are in deep. Far too deep.

Chapter Thirty
LUCA

Grayson yanks open the doors to Marco's Italian restaurant. Enzo confirmed both Marco and Frankie are in here. But he made no mention of Maddie.

With our guns pointed, we storm toward a relaxed-looking Frankie, who smiles at us. I look to my left and Marco is tied to the chair. *What in the fuck?*

"Welcome, come, take a seat." He gestures to the two chairs opposite him at the little wooden table.

"I don't think so, Frankie. How about I just shoot you instead?"

I walk past Grayson and head straight to Frankie, pressing my gun into the side of his head, and he laughs.

That asshole.

"I wouldn't do that if you want to see your precious Maddie again."

I relax my grip slightly at his reminder.

"Where the fuck is she?" Grayson roars.

"Where would be the fun in simply telling you? Come and sit." Frankie's voice drops into a serious tone, and he kicks one of the chairs free of the table.

Grayson nods to me and pulls out the chair. My eyes dart to Marco and a whole new wave of anger barrels through me as I think of the hurt he's caused Rosa, after everything he knows she's been through.

Today he will pay.

"Frankie, just shoot the asshole," Marco grits out.

Oh, fuck this.

I whip my pistol and point it straight at him. His eyes go wide. I smirk, my finger itching to pull the trigger.

"If anyone's killing my brother, it's me," Frankie announces and pulls out a gun from his suit jacket. He presses it right between Marco's eyes and pulls the trigger.

Marco slumps backward, blood spilling onto the table.

I take the opportunity to pull back my right fist and slam it into Frankie's jaw. "You motherfucker!"

He rubs his jaw. "I'll accept that one. Good shot." He looks at Grayson and nods. "I might need to get some sessions in with you."

"I don't fucking think so," Grayson snaps.

Frankie shrugs. "Please, just sit. I will explain everything first."

I pull out my chair. This I need to hear.

The fact that Romano was right, that his information will lead us to Maddie, sits heavily on my shoulders as I pull out a cigarette and sit. "Spit it out then."

"Maybe I'll start by formally introducing myself." He places his hand on his chest. "I'm Frankie Falcone. And this, next to me"—he nods to Marco's body—"was my older brother."

176 ~ LUNA MASON

I take a drag, thinking about Rosa. She's the only thing stopping me from killing this two-faced snake right now.

I listen as Frankie explains himself and puts forward his "peace offering." Blabbering about how he wants to take over the city with me. How he took Maddie because he needed Grayson angry enough to help with his efforts for taking out Marco and eliminating the Falcones that backed him.

I can't stand it any longer. Grayson is a ball of fury next to me. All I want is Maddie home safely and to get back to Rosa. After today, it all changes. I can't be hers anymore. I will be owned by the Capris.

"Release Maddie, and then we can talk," I interject.

Frankie leans back and interlaces his fingers behind his head. "I'm not releasing her until we reach a deal. I'm not stupid. As soon as she's free, one of you will more than likely try to kill me. Maddie has already warned me of my impending death."

I let out a laugh. That does sound like something she would say.

"We will discuss the deal in private. Grayson needs to get to Maddie. It will just be me and you once she's released. I'm interested in what you have to say."

Not for the reasons he thinks. I know he worked for Romano and that he's calculating. He could help me out of this and be the one to help me wipe them out next.

"But don't forget, I hold the upper hand here. So I suggest you start making amends for your errors if we ever consider trusting you again." I pin him with a glare, and he nods.

I put my gun on the table, and Frankie joins me. "Grayson, take both of our guns." I slide mine to him and Frankie follows suit.

Neither of us needs to die today. We need a new plan.

"Fucking let her go." Grayson points Frankie's own gun at him. Frankie throws up his hands in surrender and fixes his gray eyes on me.

There's not much I can do if Grayson wants to shoot him.

Frankie nods to his phone. "May I?" He slowly lowers his arms as he locks a stare with Grayson.

With a growl, Grayson drops his arm, and Frankie pulls out his phone.

"Loudspeaker," Grayson snaps.

The call connects and an Italian voice says, "Boss."

"She can go, Theo," Frankie says, then hangs up and tosses the phone on the table.

Frankie tells us she's in London, and as I'm sending Grayson off to get his girl, his pocket vibrates. Quickly digging his own cell out, he slides the accept button, and I can hear the tinny sound of Maddie's voice calling his name.

After all these weeks of searching, it's over.

I watch as Grayson sprints out of Marco's Italian restaurant. The same Marco who now has a bullet through his skull and is slumped over in his seat opposite me.

I glance over to a relaxed-looking Frankie, who stands and grabs a bottle of scotch from the bar and two glasses. The clever fucker knew how to play us, knew our values about family. He kept up his end of the bargain and released Maddie. Now, I keep my calm, for Rosa.

"Nice touch, killing your brother." I take a long drag on my cigarette.

"He had to die. Trust me. He deserved that. I've been waiting years to end him." His nostrils flare as he looks over to his dead brother's body. Not a single ounce of remorse on him. The guy is a psychopath.

"Now, what do you want with me? You've made your

point, you've released Maddie. You now run the Falcones. So what? A truce?"

He chuckles. "A truce?"

He leans forward, his elbows resting on the table. "No, I actually have a proposition for you."

"Go on . . ."

"We join forces. Create one unified group to go up against the Capris. We will run every line of smuggling into New York. They still have a foothold here, so we take their business and remove them from the equation. Stealing their guns was a brave move, but we can take them, especially with the army you've built."

I lean forward, flicking my cigarette over the ashtray. "You mean the family I'm marrying into?"

He slams his hand down on the table. "Marrying who?"

"Maria. Who do you think gave you up? I had to dance with the devil to lock you down." I grab the glass and swallow the contents in one gulp.

He lets out a ragged breath, his pale gray eyes narrowing.

"Shit. What is the exact deal you've made?" he asks, lighting up his own cigarette.

"They smuggle guns using my shipping ports. I marry Maria, my new watchdog, for her visa. If I don't, he will kill my entire family, starting with my one-year-old niece. Turns out he wasn't too happy with us stealing his imports."

"Jesus, fuck, Luca."

Smoke plumes into the air. We sit in silence with a corpse.

"I can help you," he finally says.

"How? You've been lying to me for over a year. I can't trust you." I toss down my cigarette into the ashtray.

"Look, I'm sorry about Maddie. I did it to protect them both. I needed him angry. I needed him to help me wipe my brother out. Maddie was getting in the way. I had to do something."

"You didn't have to fucking kidnap her, Frankie!"

"Well, I mean, I guess." He shrugs. "I looked after her, Luca. Honestly. Ask her when she comes home. She will tell you. I never intended to cause either of them any harm. But I had to end Marco. So, for that, I am truly sorry. I had to do what I thought was right for everyone here. I've been planning my revenge against him for years, and I couldn't let anyone get in the way."

In a way, I get it. I have no clue what Marco did to him, but it must have been fucking bad.

"But we have bigger problems. Romano is coming for our city. We need all the manpower we can get. Marriage or not, that won't protect you. Maria is a bitch, like a rottweiler. She will be waiting for, if not planning, your slip-up. That I can assure you."

I sit back, assessing him.

Over the last year, he's proven to be one of my top recruits. And after the stunt he's just pulled, I know he's smart. Too smart to have as my enemy. Today is a stark reminder: Rosa needs protecting. While I'm with Maria, I can't, but Frankie can.

She called him her protector once, so now he will have to do it again.

"Fine. On one condition. Until I can trust you again, I have the final call on every move we make. We take down the Capris together, we protect our families. That includes Rosa. You protect that woman with your life, Frankie."

He scratches his beard, his eyes darting over to his dead brother, and then his eyes go wide.

"Rosa? You said she was dead?"

"She's not dead, Frankie. I lied."

He runs his hand through his dark brown hair, relief washing over his features. Smacking his hands on his knees, he grins at me. "You fucking got me there."

"I mean it. She has to leave my place tomorrow. I want you to put her up somewhere with her sister. Look out for her, protect her like you used to."

He frowns. "How much do you know?"

"Enough to know she trusts you. That's one of the reasons I kept you alive."

Silence fills the room,

"Deal." He offers me his hand. I hesitate before grabbing it.

"Well, *partner*, what is our first move?"

If I didn't like this asshole so much, I'd punch him again in his perfectly sculpted jaw.

"Looks like I have a wedding to plan, to a rottweiler of a woman, plotting my death." I roll my eyes.

"We won't let them kill you. At least, we will make it hard for them."

I push back from the table. "Looks like we'll make a good team after all." I grab the door, the fresh air hitting me.

Frankie pours himself another drink. "Yeah, because we are both ruthless assholes."

I chuckle. He's right.

Chapter Thirty-One

LUCA

Dread weighs in my stomach as I push open the front door to my mansion. I know what I have to do, even if it's the last thing I *want* to do.

The war with the Falcones might be over, but this is the start of a whole new battlefront.

Luca Russo and Frankie Falcone, taking over the world. Step one, taking the power from the Capris and protecting my family. Which means I can't keep her.

I suck in a breath, quietly closing the door behind me.

This will be the last time I get to have her there.

I creep my way up the grand staircase and head toward the bedroom, shrugging off my Armani suit jacket and resting it over the banister. My door is ajar, so I peer through. A peaceful Rosa is snuggled up, her long jet-black curls fanning over the pillows.

I slip in through the door and remove my clothes, putting them on the black leather chair in the corner, and get into bed next to her. As soon as the mattress dips, she stirs next to me, making my cock twitch at the sweet little moans that escape her plump lips.

She nuzzles into my chest, so I wrap her tiny frame into mine, pulling her as close as I can.

"You're home," she whispers. I bury my nose in the top of her head, inhaling her vanilla scent and closing my eyes.

Home.

This is our home. For one more day.

"No matter what happens next, *my treasure*, you will always be my home," I say, meaning every single word.

She plants a soft kiss to my stubbly jaw. A single tear falls from my eye.

The day I kidnapped her, I never thought she would steal my heart in return. I believed she was a typical wild child, a spoiled mafia princess. How wrong I was.

I just pray to fucking God tomorrow won't send her spiraling back into the life I found her in. Where she masks her pain to stop the world from seeing her weakness.

After everything she's been through, I don't blame her for turning to the bottle to help ease the torture eating her up from the inside. If I could go back in time and stop that asshole from abusing her, I would do it in a heartbeat. I wish I could delve into her brain and erase the memories. I would gladly take on every single ounce of heartache for her.

She truly doesn't realize how special she is.

Her warm breath blows against my chest as I close my eyes and slip into what I know will be my last night of peaceful sleep.

DEVOTED ~ 183

THE SCENT OF fresh coffee stirs me from my sleep. As I blink open my eyes I am met with a sight of sheer beauty. I trail my gaze up her long slender legs, groaning as I take in the matching black lace lingerie that she's not even trying to hide with her open silky black robe. She gives me a bright smile, her big dark eyes gazing into mine.

"I thought you might need this," she says. She has a slight hint of an Italian accent there, hidden under the surface of her New Yorker tone.

I sit myself up and watch as she licks her lips, staring at my six-pack.

"Thank you, baby."

I lean over and grab the mug of coffee, letting it burn its way down my throat. All it does is intensify the sickness I'm feeling.

I pat the mattress to signal for her to sit. And she does, without any hesitation, like always. My little submissive. But instead of sitting next to me, she pulls back the comforter and straddles me, her perfect breasts now staring me right in the face.

I can't do this.

Squeezing my eyes shut, I take a breath.

"Rosa, baby. It's time."

She sits back, her ass now squashing my throbbing cock. A quizzical look is painted on her beautiful face.

"Time? For what? To tell me what's been bothering you?"

Bringing my palm to cup her face, I stroke her cheek with my thumb. "I have to let you go, tesoro. I don't fucking want to; it's the last thing I wanted to happen. When I said things got messy, I underestimated just how bad. I have to protect my family and you. To do that, I can't keep you."

She drops her gaze from mine. The seconds feel like a lifetime. My eyes start to sting.

"I-I don't understand? I thought you would keep me safe? That I could stay with you?"

I shake my head as the warm tears fall from her eyes onto my fingers. I'm doing everything I can to stop my own from breaking through.

"This is keeping you safe, it's protecting you. Frankie will look after you. The Capris—I'm in too deep, but your uncle is helping me. Right now, there is no way out for me, baby. If there was even a glimmer of hope, I wouldn't do this. You have to trust me."

She sniffles and backs away from me. My heart starts to split as the seconds pass.

"I need you to be strong, Rosa. I need you to be the real Rosa, the one you've shown me. The one who can take on the world and fucking own it. I can't have you. I wish more than anything I could. Trust me. But life has other plans for me, yet again. They are way out of my control."

She cuts me off. "What plans?"

Here we go.

"I'm engaged, Rosa."

Her body stiffens on top of me. I'm sure I can hear her heart shattering right before me.

"No. Luca, no. Please don't leave me. I can't do this without you. I need you," she chokes out.

I can't take it. Seeing her in pain is like being stabbed in the chest. It physically hurts. I wrap my arms around her shoulders and pull her into me, squeezing her tight.

"I'm so sorry," I repeat over and over, the sound of her sobbing filling the room.

Once the tears subside, she hiccups and pulls herself from

DEVOTED ~ 185

my hold, leaving me empty. I don't have the strength to tell her that I watched her uncle murder her father yesterday. Her whole world is falling apart and I can't stop it.

"You don't have to do this, Luca. Please don't do this. Can't we find another way?" Her voice is barely a whisper.

She stands and pulls her robe tight around her body.

"Trust me, right now, there isn't another way. I wish there was." I pull the comforter off my legs and stand, closing the distance between us. Tipping her chin up with my thumb, I bring her nose to mine and close my eyes.

"I want you to do all the things you've said you wanted to do. Don't let your demons pull you into the darkness. Promise me," I say, my voice quivering.

I need her to be strong without me.

"My demons will never leave me, Luca. You held them at bay. But the nightmares will return. He might be gone, but that doesn't stop the pain. I can never get what he took from me back. I will never find this"—she gestures between us—"again."

If I ever find out who did this to her, I will give them a slow and painful death.

"Tell me who did this to you, Rosa."

She shakes her head.

It's the one thing she will never reveal, his fucking name.

"Do you love her?" she asks.

I snap my eyes up to hers, pleading with her to believe me.

Chapter Thirty-Two

ROSA

"No. And I never will. This is a means to an end. I'm marrying Romano Capri's daughter. You are the one who owns my heart."

My chest hurts, but I'm too angry to acknowledge it. If I really did own his heart, like he does mine, he wouldn't be doing this to us.

"I don't own it, though, do I?" Pulling the robe snug around me, I step back out of his embrace.

He drops his arms limply, a frown growing on his face. "What do you mean?"

"If I did, would you be letting me go? You'd stay, you'd fight for me. So, no, Luca, your heart can't belong to me."

He tilts his head to the side, letting his dark hair fall over his eyes. "But it does."

"Well, I don't want it," I spit back.

I regret the words the moment they come out of my mouth as I watch his face flash with hurt.

His green eyes pierce me, and he chews on his lower lip. "You don't mean that."

My fists clench. I don't know who I'm mad at right now. Whether it's him for stealing my heart, the world for taking him away, or myself for being so damn naïve.

"Was I just a joke to you? Did you and your friends sit there laughing about you getting to sleep with poor, broken Rosa? Your enemy's daughter."

"Are you fucking kidding me?" His face reddens and I take a step back.

His eyes darken. "I spent days holding you while you threw up all over my goddamn floor. I cuddled you while you screamed in your sleep. I was so worried sick I stayed awake for days—days, Rosa—just watching to make sure you didn't die on me. You know me well enough to know I would never think you are a joke." He shakes his head. "Un-fucking-believable."

"I clearly don't know you, not really. You asked me to stay. You let me fall in love with you." My stomach rolls like it's threatening to revolt. "How long did you know you couldn't keep me?"

"It doesn't matter. A few days. I don't even know now. They threatened Darcy. What the hell else am I supposed to do?" He throws his arms up in the air. My fingers thread around my throat as I watch him start to fall apart.

"I-I don't know, Luca." My voice starts to break. He laces his fingers behind his head as he searches the ceiling for a moment before lowering his gaze back to me.

"Do you seriously believe this was all a lie? That I don't truly love you?" His chest heaves as he takes a deep breath. "Because I do, Rosa. I love you so much it hurts. This is the last thing I ever wanted to happen. I even bought a goddamn house in

Greece for us to go to. I wanted it all with you." The muscles in his arms flex as he crosses them over his broad chest.

He loves me. He just told me he loves me, and I want to burst into tears. "How else did you seriously expect this to go? Did you want me to go and sit like a good little mafia princess and wait for her prince to come back to her?" I'm sick of being on the end of everyone else's stupid decisions in this hell of a life in the mafia.

He rubs his beard. "I-I—"

"No. You don't know. I get it, you have to save your family. You don't have me to worry about. I'm sure I'll survive. I did before. I know how to cope."

His face pales as he takes in the meaning behind my words.

"Rosa, no. Don't go back there, promise me."

"How can I promise anything? Clearly, I have no control over my own life. Everyone has choices to make, right? You made yours, but didn't care how it affected me."

He rubs his hands over his face. "Fuck, Rosa. I'm so sorry."

His face is twisted in pain, which just shatters my heart even further. It would be so much easier to be mad at him if he were a thoughtless asshole. But he's not. He's hurting, too.

There's a knock at the door and my stomach sinks. "I'm going right now?"

He just stares at me, tears brimming his bloodshot eyes. He slowly nods.

This is really it.

It just hurts so much knowing he's fighting for the right reasons, but I'm not one of them. I never wanted this to end. I stupidly thought I could be happy for once.

Luca was my happy place. I'll never forget what he has

done for me, so for that, I wipe away a tear and step into him, hugging my arms around his waist.

He pauses before his arms envelop me, and he pulls me even tighter against him. I inhale his manly scent for the last time.

"I'm sorry for snapping at you. I will always be grateful to you for saving me. I shouldn't have said that," I whisper.

A fresh wave of tears threatens, but I won't break down. Not until I'm on my own again.

"I'm sorry, too. I'm sorry for breaking us. I'm going to miss you so fucking much, tesoro."

I nod against him. I fear if I speak, I will shatter.

"You're taking my heart with you, okay?"

I feel the words rumble from his chest, and I wish I could meld myself with him and remain living in this moment. This is the first place I've ever felt at home. The first time I've experienced love.

When I leave here, I will be leaving my heart here with him, too.

Chapter Thirty-Three
LUCA

"Why can't I ever just be happy, Luca?" I wipe away her tears with the pad of my thumb. I don't have the answers for her. I often think the same fucking thing.

Another loud knock comes from the door.

"You will be. Now is the start of a new life for you, baby. Take it with both hands." I swallow the lump forming in my throat at what her "happy" might look like. The fact that she could find a man, create a family, all without me.

"One last kiss?" My voice shakes.

She wraps her hands around me and squeezes. "No."

"Please, Rosa. Don't make me beg." I'm desperate to have one last taste of heaven before I get sent to hell.

She lifts her head and pouts. "Make it last a lifetime."

I cup her face and claim her lips for the last time. I kiss her until there is no air left in my lungs, hoping she understands

DEVOTED ~ 191

just how much she means to me. I know it's already fueling my resolve to get her back.

"You're perfect, tesoro."

I rest my forehead against hers, fighting my own tears. Never in my life has a woman stolen my heart.

She goes up on tiptoes, her soft hand stroking my cheek. I lean into her touch, savoring this moment.

"You are perfect, too, Mr. Russo. I'm going to miss you."

The door bangs again. Those three little words are on the tip of my tongue, but I hold them back. When I do say them again, I will do it properly, and there won't be a goodbye following it.

I sigh. "You'd better get going."

She offers me a sad smile as I step away.

She disappears into her room and quickly returns wearing a black sundress, tugging her pink suitcase behind her.

I dart after her and grab the bag to carry it down behind her, dropping it next to her as she slips on her sparkly sandals. I lean on the door frame and watch as she opens it to Frankie. It pisses me off that he can look that happy when I feel this shitty. He pushes up his aviators with a large smile. "Rosa!" He opens his arms to her, and she ducks underneath, dragging her suitcase.

"I just want to go," she huffs, not looking back at me.

I swallow down the pain.

Frankie watches as she throws her case into the back seat and follows it, pulling the door shut behind her.

"I take it I have making up to do on all fronts." Frankie shakes his head.

He hurt her. He will have to earn her trust again. The same as he will have to earn mine again.

"Look after her, Frankie."

I slam the door shut and lean against it. The house is too quiet to be here with my own thoughts. It's already empty without her.

I CAN'T HANDLE it. She's everywhere in my house. Every time I turn around, I'm reminded of her. Even by those stupid hair bands that get everywhere. Her perfume. Her favorite caramel syrup.

I need to remind myself why I'm putting myself through this torture.

So, here I am, knocking at my brother's front door at eight p.m. I can't shake the fact that I think I saw Antonio lurking in the shadows down the road as I drove in.

A reminder of the threat that looms over me.

The door swings open, and Keller greets me with little Darcy nestled in his arms. His face flashes with concern. "Everything okay?"

I step inside and find Sienna chasing Max around the house, his laughter filling the room.

"You need to brush your teeth, young man!" she admonishes once she catches him.

Keller and I both chuckle.

"Drink?" he shouts over his shoulder.

"Please, a fucking strong one." I follow him into the kitchen.

He bundles Darcy into my arms. I hold her tight against me and kiss the top of her black curls.

As Keller pours the Macallan, I pace around the kitchen,

bouncing Darcy up and down, and she giggles. For a moment, I don't hurt as bad.

"Uncle Luca will always protect you," I whisper.

Her big dark eyes look up at me, and she gives me a toothy smile.

"Here you go." He places the glass down on the island. "Let me take Darcy upstairs, then you can tell me what's going on."

"Night-night, beautiful." I scrunch my fingers in an exaggerated wave.

She babbles back, and I laugh. No one will ever lay a finger on her. I would rather die than let anything happen to any of them under this roof. They are my family and I will do everything I can to protect them.

Chapter Thirty-Four
LUCA

Three Months Later

"Are you coming to the party tonight, Mom?" I brace myself for her wrath. She wasn't exactly pleased with the wedding invitation.

"No." Her tone is harsh.

She doesn't look at me; she keeps reading the newspaper on the table.

I let out a sigh and drink my coffee while the clock ticks behind me. I know she's hurting.

She's always wanted me and Keller to find love, like she had with Dom, her late husband. He died before she started fostering me and Keller. From the stories, the love they shared was everything. That's why she never moved on. Her heart only belongs to him.

After everything she's done for us, I wanted to one day see

her smile at my wedding. Give her grandbabies to dote over like she does with Max and Darcy.

She looks up at me, her eyes flashing with anger. "Of all the things you've done, son, this is the stupidest. I can tell just by that look on your face, you know it, too."

A pain shoots through my chest as I see the disappointment on her face.

"Mom. I wouldn't do this if I didn't have to." I reach my hand out to hers and she pulls away.

"You always have a choice, Luca. Marriage isn't about power. It's about love. You might be the leader of the mafia, but to me, you're still that scrawny young boy I took in off the street. I expect more from you. Family first. Always."

"I am doing it for my family, Mom. I'm doing it to protect you all." She doesn't understand that Romano's threat is very much real. I am doing this for them; my own happiness is a small sacrifice.

"You always do everything to protect everyone else. What about yourself? What about your own heart? Do you think I'm blind?" As if to prove her point, she takes off her reading glasses and lays them on the paper in front of her.

"W-what?" The wrong end of her disappointment is not where I want to be.

"You have such a big heart, Luca. Wasted. I just want to see both of my boys happy. Your love lies with someone else, doesn't it?"

She gives me an accusing look. She's right. I pull out a cigarette and she slaps it out of my hand so hard it flies across the room.

"Ignore it all you want. It won't go away. Once someone steals the beating of your heart, that's it. You either fight for it or live a miserable life without her."

Rubbing the back of my neck, I realize she's got me there. I just wish I could fight for it. The house doesn't even smell like her anymore. Most nights I toss and turn, wondering if she's sleeping or if her nightmares are back. I even parked outside the house Frankie moved her and Eva into. I sat there for hours, in the pitch black. I couldn't go in. Knowing I have to let her move on doesn't mean I don't fucking miss her with every fiber of my being.

My home doesn't feel like one anymore.

I run a hand through my hair in frustration. "How did you know? Are you a witch?"

"Oh, Luca," she chuckles. "I have eyes. That is all. You think I didn't see the change in you with Rosa?"

We drink the rest of our coffee in silence, my mind spinning. All I can think about is dark hair twirling around my fingers, soft lips touching mine, and quivering thighs framing my ears. My heart is stuck on Rosa.

I stand and press a kiss to Mom's forehead.

She clasps her hand over mine on her cheek. "You do whatever you have to. You always do. But I won't have any part of this. I draw the line here. When you decide to marry Rosa, then I'll be there."

I nod and walk out of the kitchen. As I open the door, she wraps her hands around me and nuzzles her head into my back.

"Just because I'm angry doesn't mean I don't love you, Luca. You'll always be my son, no matter how stupid your choices are. I'm just asking you to really think about what you want."

I know exactly what I want, *who* I want.

"I love you, Mom. I wish it were that easy."

Chapter Thirty-Five
ROSA

Swirling around the champagne in my glass, I can't lift my gaze from the bubbles. I haven't touched a drop in almost six months now. In that time, I've lost my father, gained an uncle back, and lost my heart.

But I'm surviving. If being with Luca taught me anything, it was my own strength. Deep down in there somewhere, I am alive. He's the only reason I haven't taken a sip of this drink. I can hear his husky voice telling me I can do better.

"Rosa!" Eva flips her red hair as she walks in, breaking me from my trance.

As I my head up to meet her bright blue eyes, she looks to the glass in my hand and back to me with a frown forming. She might be my younger sister by two years, but right now, she's the one holding us both together.

"I thought you'd quit drinking, Rosa?" Her hands now on her hips, she is the spitting image of our mother. I, however, have my dad's Italian genes.

DEVOTED ~ 201

"I have." I shrug.

I don't have an excuse. It's the only way I know to stop the pain. The day after I left Luca, I opened a bottle of vodka. It's like he knew. Before I could even take a sip, Dr. Jenkins knocked on my door and we had a two-hour session.

Even when Luca's not with me, he's always watching out for me.

Eva gives me a sad smile and closes the distance between us, reaching for me on the barstool.

"We don't have to go tonight if it's too much?" She clasps my hand and squeezes, so I set the champagne flute down on the marble countertop.

"Uncle Frankie expects us there. He made it clear yesterday. Remember his whole speech about putting up a 'unified front'?" I huff. There are days I really hate being a part of the lifestyle.

"Well, I'm sure he would understand. He loves us like his own." She pushes the glass a little farther from my reach.

I raise my eyebrows. "Pfft, that's why he lodged a bullet between Dad's eyes?" I mutter.

"Seriously? We both couldn't stand him. You wanted to be as far away from him as possible, remember? Uncle Frankie was always there for us as kids. Well, until Dad sent him away. Give him a chance, sis." She bats her lashes. "For me."

"Fine." I can pretend all I like that I'm holding a grudge because he killed my dad. But it's not why I'm bitter. It's the fact he abandoned us all those years ago. He was the best uncle, the fun one. The uncle that would have burned down the world for me if he knew what Dante had done.

"I mean, he's paying for this pretty sweet mansion for us. And he's taken care of re-enrolling you at college. He wants to make amends."

202 ~ LUNA MASON

As she slides the champagne even further away from me, Eva's eyes light up as she flashes me a big smile. Every day, it's a choice whether I drink or fight. So far, even without Luca, I'm managing. I don't ever want to go through the torture of withdrawal again. She pats my hand. "I promise I won't leave your side. It's just one night, well, then the wedding to get through."

A pit forms in my stomach.

As if attending Luca's engagement party to the gorgeous Italian mafia princess, Maria Capri, wasn't enough, Uncle Frankie also insists on taking us to his wedding. I don't know what the date is; I threw that invitation straight in the trash.

"I'll be fine," I lie.

It's going to break my heart all over again. In the three months since I last saw him, he's been on my mind every single moment.

I can't shake the memory of his intense green eyes, or his deep voice as he calls me his treasure.

I miss him.

He was the first man to ever really hear me. I told him my deepest, darkest secrets and he just listened. He made me believe in myself again, just by being there.

His patience is the reason I'm turning my life around.

Now I have to sit there, plaster a fake smile on my face, as I watch the only man who's ever made me feel worthy parade his new fiancée around. When, deep down, I wanted that woman to be me one day.

But he let me go. He abandoned me, too.

"I'll go grab our jackets. Frankie will be here any minute," Eva calls out as she darts toward her bedroom down the hall.

Sliding off the barstool, I take the full glass of champagne over to the sink and watch as the contents pour down the drain.

Shit, do I want that drink. But I'm not the same Rosa anymore. I don't need that to numb myself. My destructive coping mechanisms will never fully leave me, but I can learn to curb them. I understand there is no right or wrong way to deal with trauma. But drinking myself to death probably isn't the answer.

Scanning my outfit in the full-length mirror in the hallway, I've dressed the way I feel—like I'm going to a funeral.

My tight black dress hugs my slim figure perfectly, resting just above my knees. I love how the low plunging neckline shows off my full breasts. And I'm wearing the highest pair of gold killer heels I could find. If I have to do this, I want to be able to look him in the eyes and make sure he sees me.

Eva comes barreling red-faced from the hall and shoves a black leather jacket and clutch in my hand.

"Come on, we have to go. He's outside!" she says, then disappears out the front door. God, I love her, but she is chaos.

"One sec!" I rifle through my clutch and dig out my signature deep red lipstick and swipe it across my full lips.

I might feel like crap on the inside, but I look damn good on the outside. A part of me wants Luca to see what he's missing.

He might not be mine anymore. But that doesn't mean I can't push his buttons from afar.

I sigh and head toward the front door. I bet he is dreading this as much as I am.

Chapter Thirty-Six

LUCA

"Here. You look like you need it, boss." Grayson slides a double scotch across the gilded table toward me with a frown, his freshly tattooed wedding ring on display. "Can you believe this? Last month, it was me and Maddie in a whirlwind wedding. I shit a brick when you dropped that invitation on my table. Never thought I'd see the day you'd settle down, too."

The ice clinks against the crystal. I grab it and don't even hesitate swallowing the whole thing, letting it burn its way down.

"Yeah, it's gone by too fast. I need a whole bottle to get through tonight." I say, tightening my grip on the glass.

"She can't be that bad." Grayson pushes another full drink across to me.

"Oh, trust me, she is. She's only been living with me for a month and I can't fucking stand it. She's already thrown out half my shit and replaced it with her tacky, glittery bullshit.

DEVOTED ~ 205

And made it quite clear that everything that was mine is now hers."

I leave out the part where she's become my full-time babysitter, reporting my dealings to her father. Or the way she flips out at the slightest thing, like me not having dinner with her. And not sharing a bed with her.

I can't do it. No way.

"How long have you got to stay married to her?" Grayson raises an eyebrow while leaning back into the leather seat.

"I didn't set an end date. Until I can wipe out her whole family?" If only I had access to a nuke. I'd save the world the misery of Maria.

"Fuck." He shakes his head. "Why are you doing this? We have Maddie back," he says softly.

Why am I marrying the she-devil? I can't have Grayson and Keller too close to the truth. I know they will come up with more drastic measures that will free me from this marriage, but in turn put them all at risk. I can't let that happen.

"It's not that simple anymore. Some things are out of my control."

My family. All of this is for them. I am doing what I need to protect them from Romano's threats. All while pining over a woman I can never have. At least I have the images ingrained in my mind of her spread out on my bed. I can still feel the way she shivered against my touch. The way she screamed my name when she came all over my cock.

The way every morning she would wake up smiling up at me, her big dark eyes flashing with desire.

She was perfect for me. My stolen treasure.

And now she's just a memory.

My fingers dig through my hair as I shake my head slowly back and forth.

206 ~ LUNA MASON

"What's going on, Luca?" Grayson questions. "It's her, isn't it?"

"Drop it," I say through gritted teeth.

I don't need another lecture on following my heart. I don't want to hear it. In keeping them all safe, I have to keep them in the dark. They think I'm only doing this as a deal for the Capris searching for Maddie. I want them far away from this.

"Boss, we've all said we will stick by you no matter what. We've got your back. You don't have to do this." His large palm smacks on the table emphatically, making my drink jump in front of me.

My hand flips in a circular wave. "It's too late to back out now, Grayson. The deal has been signed. She's probably moved on. I told her to."

It hurts, the fact that another man will get to call her his. Will get to treasure her like I only wished I could. I just want her to be happy.

Her pain runs deep, but I saw her strength. She's a fighter. As long as she stays clean. The moment she slips behind that mask, Rosa becomes a shell of herself. A woman hiding her scars from the world. Not that I can blame her.

A heavy hand clasps down on my shoulder. Turning around, I'm met with Keller's huge frame sporting a white shirt and black tie.

"Brother." He sticks his tattooed hand out for me to shake.

"Have you seen Mom?" I ask as my palm disappears within his.

He nods with a frown. "Yeah, she's looking after Max and Darcy. She's fine. Sienna and Maddie are just in the restroom. They'll be here in a minute. Hmm." Keller's chest rumbles as he looks at Grayson with a grin.

"What?" I snap at him.

He gestures around the decorated room. "I thought you'd have called this off by now."

"Not you, too. Look, I'm having some growing problems, sure. But having a she-devil invade your personal space and overhaul your life is a little bit of an adjustment."

That's one way to put it.

"You didn't seem to mind Rosa living with you." Keller smirks.

"Fuck off." This is already hard enough.

"Where's Maria then?" Grayson asks.

"I dunno, she was getting her horns cut off or something before the party." Her actual story was she needed lip filler. Like anyone here cared.

Grayson spits out his drink and laughs.

"She took my Amex and left. Told me she would meet me here." The longer she's gone, the better. I don't really give a shit how much it costs.

"Have you seen Frankie yet?" I ask. Grayson shrugs and knocks back his scotch. Those two still aren't on the best of terms. Even after Maddie assuring us Frankie didn't hurt her, Grayson can't forgive him. To be honest, I wouldn't either. If someone took Rosa from me like that, let alone with my baby, I'd have every right to be pissed. But if I am going to win this fight, I need them all. Including Frankie.

"Luca, darling." The high-pitched voice I've grown to hate echoes across the VIP area, and I cringe.

Her stilettos click against the floor as she gets closer.

She flits over, not even acknowledging me, heading straight for Keller. I'm not surprised; he is a local celebrity. I was sure she would sniff around him. Not that he would ever entertain another woman.

"You must be Keller," she purrs while holding out her left hand to him.

She's wearing a tight white dress that barely covers her ass. Her fake tits are filling it perfectly. Last year, I can't lie, I would have fucked her. That probably would have made this whole experience less painful.

But now, the thought disgusts me.

My heart lies with Rosa. I can't even picture myself with another woman. Marrying Maria and actually being in a relationship with her are two different things. I just can't bring myself to do it.

"Maria, nice to meet you." Keller shakes her hand with a tight-lipped smile. He drops it quickly and steps back to drape his arm around his wife, who is now by his side scowling at Maria.

They're on their best behavior tonight. As are Grayson and Maddie.

Grayson nudges himself to the edge of the booth as she turns to him.

"Grayson, pleasure to finally meet you." She holds out her hand for a moment, inviting the handshake that never happens.

He just nods to her, keeping his distance and pulling Maddie flush against his chest, his hands protectively placed on her bump.

"I've heard so much about you both." The way the lies roll off her tongue is almost impressive. I've never spoken about any of my family to her. I didn't even want to do this tonight, but Maria insisted on meeting them.

My men both glance at me and I roll my eyes.

"Luca, darling. Go fetch me a champagne, I'm dying of

thirst here. But I need a straw." She points to her extremely plump and shiny lips.

"Yep. Gladly." *Get me the fuck away from this.*

Sliding out of the booth, I head toward the bar and heave a sigh of relief. "Two bottles of champagne and a straw, please," I tell the bartender.

Crossing one ankle over the other, I lean on the bar, and I look out over the crowd as the End Zone starts to fill up. Like always, it's hopping. A credit to Keller's hard work. The bartender coughs behind me, and I turn to grab the bottles and glasses on the tray.

Why the fuck am I doing this?

As I turn to head back toward the VIP area, the air starts to fizzle around me and my heart starts hammering.

My Rosa. She's here.

I can't move; my eyes are locked on her. Her jet-black hair cascades down her slim frame all the way down to her waist. She is the most beautiful woman I've ever laid eyes on. That figure-hugging black dress rests just above her knees. She has that class about her, unlike my fiancée. Rosa is a natural beauty with her plump red lips and dark lashes.

With every sensuous step she takes toward me, my hands start to go clammy. She clasps her hands over her stomach with delicate grace, which makes my cock twitch, knowing those little breathy moans she would make when I'd suck on her nipples.

"Luca!" Frankie announces as they reach me. But I can't take my eyes off Rosa, who is doing anything to avoid looking at me.

"Frankie," I greet him and glance toward the other girl, who I'm assuming must be Eva. She's very similar to Rosa in facial features, just a bit taller and with deep auburn hair and blue eyes.

The three of them stand before me, and Frankie eyes the champagne. "Oh, we are celebrating tonight!" he chuckles.

"Something like that," I mutter, snapping my attention back to Rosa, who's now picking at her red nails.

"You already know Rosa." Frankie raises an eyebrow with a small smirk.

"This is Eva." He nods to Rosa's younger sister, who gives me a bright grin before nudging her sister.

"Nice to finally meet you, Eva." I smile before turning my attention back to the woman who owns my heart.

She tips her head up, and her dark eyes bore into mine. I've dreamed every night for months that she was happy and carefree without me. But that pain, that darkness, is still there resting behind them.

"Hello, Rosa." My throat feels as if it's on fire, and I'm choking the words out.

She gives me a tight-lipped smile. "Luca, good to see you." I can't help but notice the slight shake in her voice.

And it guts me.

"I need a drink. Let's go," Frankie says, turning on his heel and striding toward the VIP area. Leaving me with the sisters, both of whom probably hate me.

With the tray still in my hands, my eyes lock on Rosa.

"I'll meet you guys in there," Eva says before rushing after Frankie.

"Rosa, are you okay?" My chest hurts to see her. It takes everything in me to not pull her into my arms.

She pulls her lower lip between her teeth and stares pensively at the glasses between us. "I'm fine."

The nights we would spend staying up until dawn just

DEVOTED ~ 211

talking and watching movies. Well, and fucking. Now all I have is one-word answers, and she can barely look me in the eye.

"You promise?" Every day since she left, I've kept an eye on her from afar. I know how much she struggles, how much she hides until she can't take it anymore. I have to know she's okay, that I didn't break her. It would kill me.

"Yes, Luca. I promise. I don't think I'll ever truly be okay. Not anymore. I'll live." She casts her eyes to the floor.

The panic stirring around in my chest makes me feel like I'm about to have a heart attack. I can't take this. There aren't words that will fix this ache, and taking her into my arms isn't an option.

"Come on, let's go meet the others." I gesture toward the reserved area where everyone is gathering.

She lifts her eyes to mine and gives me a sad smile. Which basically is a knife through the heart. The last person on the planet I'd want her to meet is Maria.

I follow her lead. My eyes are pinned to her pert ass as we head toward the rest of the group. Maddie is now cuddled into Grayson's side, and Sienna has a protective Keller behind her with his hands firmly around her waist.

Both women watch me warily as I put the tray of drinks down on the table.

"Ladies." I smile at them both.

They give me *that* look. They've told me I'm an idiot for doing this. Their husbands clearly have no filter, because both women are now strongly on team Rosa.

"Fiancé." Maria waltzes toward me. If she sticks her chest out any farther, she's going to tip over.

Maddie and Sienna both scoff and look away. Maria snakes her arms around my neck; her intensely sweet perfume is nearly suffocating as it burns my nose.

I go stiff as she brings her mouth to my ear.

"Introduce me to my new friends," she hisses with venom in her tone.

Turning, I whisper back in her ear, "Get your fucking hands off me."

This was never part of the deal. Marriage on paper, nothing else.

She fake laughs and removes herself, tapping me on the chest and giving me a purposeful stare. I clench my jaw in response.

I glance up to see Rosa looking at me with the shine of tears in her eyes. Her lips are a quivering line. When she catches my gaze, she quickly turns away.

"Rosa, Eva, Frankie, this is my fiancée, Maria." Bile rises up my throat at the words. Rosa flinches in response. Her sister wraps a hand around her arm, squeezing her closer.

Running a hand over my face, I dig out the pack of cigarettes in my suit jacket. I'm itching to get away from this.

"So lovely to meet you all. Would you like some champagne?" Maria asks.

Rosa's eyes snap to mine as Frankie and Eva reply "yes" at the same time Rosa blurts out "no."

Maria's eyebrow flies up as she looks Rosa up and down.

"You don't drink? What are you, pregnant? Or just boring?"

Clenching my fists, I open my mouth to tell her to stop, but Rosa beats me to it.

"Maybe I just don't need a drink to have a personality anymore. Unlike some, clearly," she spits back.

I can't hide the smile that forms on my face. Damn, I'm proud of her.

Maria picks up a flute of champagne and holds her hand

out to Rosa. The table goes silent. "Oh, come on, let your hair down. You know you want to. You never know, one day you might get to marry a man like Luca. These kinds of men don't want boring women like you." With a twisted grin, she pushes the drink toward Rosa, who takes a faltering half step backward.

Fuck this.

I snatch the glass out of Maria's hand, and her eyes go wide. "Enough!" I snap. I hear Sienna gasp behind me.

As I slam it on the table, the stem shatters and the bubbly contents spill over the edge. I storm out of the VIP area and head toward the back exit.

Chapter Thirty-Seven
ROSA

My cheeks heat up. Everyone's staring at me. Maria scowls at me as Frankie steps in between us.

"Rosa, come on, I need another soda, anyway. Come with me?" Maddie says, sliding herself heavily out of the booth and approaching me with a smile, her green eyes searching mine. She knows. Grayson helps her up, and she holds on to her bump, stretching her back.

I nod, and she loops her arm through mine and leads me away from the VIP lounge.

"Thank you." I barely hold back the tears.

Instead of going to the bar, she diverts us to the left and taps a keycard against a scanner, opening a set of black double doors that lead into a hallway.

"Please ignore everything that vile woman said. I think she could tell right away how Luca feels about you. The way he looks at you, Rosa, it breaks my heart. Go talk to him. I'll wait here and cover you." She gives me a bright smile before wrapping me up in a hug.

I already like Maddie.

She's already shown me more kindness than any of my old friends. They didn't even notice I was missing for two months.

"Thank you, Maddie," I say, giving her a tight squeeze.

"Go. You two need to speak." She gives me a gentle pat on the back before she lets go.

I make a dart toward the back exit as best I can in these heels and push open the door. The waft of cigarette fills my nose as I walk into a cloud of smoke.

Luca takes a long, silent inhale, the red ember glowing in the darkness. Without a word, he digs around in his suit pocket, pulls out the white packet, and holds it out to me. I blink back the threatening tears as I remember our mornings together, sitting on his balcony puffing away, watching the sun rise.

Putting the filter between my lips, he flicks the Zippo. The flame dances in front of me as I lean in and light it. Closing my eyes and taking one long drag, I let it burn its way into my lungs.

I tip my head back and exhale. Luca lets out a low groan. "I miss you, tesoro."

Crossing my legs like I have to every time I'm around this man, I take another drag.

Sadness fills his eyes as he stares at me.

"I miss you too, Luca," I say softly. I just want to memorize him. This feels like a stolen moment.

He takes a step toward me and I take one away, my back now flush against the cool metal door. My blood is pounding in my ears. Tossing my cigarette to the floor, I suck in a breath. His familiar sandalwood cologne surrounds me. I drop my chin down to stare at the gray pavement, and electricity sparks through me as his thumb tips it back up. His deep green eyes search mine before settling on my lips.

I've craved this moment. When his hand wraps around my throat, desire pools in my core as his thumb gently caresses the column of my neck.

"I knew this tattoo would look gorgeous wrapped around your neck." His lips tickle over my ear.

I furrow my brows and pull his palm back enough to look. I gasp when I spot the dark rose spanning across the entire front of his hand. "W-why did you get that?"

His thumb traces my lower lip. "To remind me of my endgame."

"And what's that?" My heart is in my throat. Deep down, I know his answer.

"You. Rosa. You are my endgame. You always will be." His eyes sparkle as they gaze into mine.

"How can I be? You made your choice. You're marrying another woman."

Anger swells in me, and I push at his chest, but he doesn't move. He only takes a step closer so our bodies are flush. His other hand trails along my thigh, all the way down to the hem of my dress.

His long exhale pours heat down my chest. "I know, but that doesn't stop me wishing it was different."

"Then why marry her? Why let me go?" A knot of frustration churns in my stomach.

Disappointment clouds me when he removes his hand from my thigh.

"You know I don't have a choice," he groans while moving

a loose strand of hair away from my face. Even if it might be a good reason, it doesn't mean it doesn't hurt me.

"Do you know, every night I lay in bed, replaying our time together? It's like I can still feel you there with me." His finger traces across my collarbone, sending ripples of desire through me.

Does he do all of this with her? Does she sleep in our bed?

The agonizing thought of betrayal makes me flinch away from his touch.

"No, Rosa. I haven't, nor will I ever, go near her. I'm yours."

His fingers move down my arm, leaving a path of fire in their wake. "I remember every night we spent that you let me explore every inch of you. Giving yourself over to me. Trusting me to be the man to bring you back to life."

A gush of air leaves my lungs as the memories swim to the surface. And fuck, it hurts.

He brings his nose into my ear and takes a deep inhale.

"The way your back arches and your lips part at the slightest touch." His words feather against my neck and I clench my legs together. "Most of all, I think about the way you'd jump into my arms when I came home. You'd have the brightest smile before you kissed the life out of me. I miss the way you opened up to me, and only me."

He takes my hand in his and places it over his thumping heart. His eyes darken as they settle on mine.

"I will take everything you told me to the grave. You can trust me with your life. I will always be honored that you were brave enough to tell me. And I will always be there for you, no matter what."

A warm tear slides down my face.

"Thank you," I sniffle.

"One last kiss?" he whispers.

"I thought our last one was our last?" I bite the inside of my mouth.

"We will have as many last kisses as it takes to finally be back where we belong, tesoro."

I know we shouldn't. I don't want to be the other woman, but he has me under a spell. I'll never be able to resist this man. I crave him in ways I really shouldn't.

I nod slowly, biting down on my bottom lip.

One last kiss.

His palms cup my cheeks as he crashes his lips over mine. Closing my eyes, I let him take control. Deepening the kiss, his tongue invades my mouth. He's slow and gentle, like he doesn't want to break me.

With a quick peck, still cradling my cheeks, he pulls back and smiles at me with a flash of his perfect white teeth.

I run my hands through his hair, our noses touching.

"I want more." The words fall from my lips.

"I want it all," he counters, nipping my lip.

I crash my lips over his and he groans into my mouth. Hoisting myself up, I wrap my legs around his waist and he grabs hold of my ass with one hand, his other tattooed hand snaking to grab my neck again.

"Fuck, Rosa," he growls, his hard-on pushing against my panties.

"We can't do this, not here." He sighs, resting his forehead against mine.

I cup his stubbly jaw, bringing his eyes to me. This hurts him, too.

"Why don't we just run?"

He sucks in a breath. "Trust me, Rosa, I've spent the last three months debating every option to get out of this. Trying to find a way back to you, where I can whisk you away and we live our lives on the beach. There just isn't a way. Not right now, at least."

Tears brim in my eyes. I unwrap my legs from him and he helps me stand. Pulling down on my dress, I can't even look at him.

"I guess that was our last kiss, then."

I try to hide my bitter disappointment at his rejection. We stand there in silence, the air crackling around us. I clear my throat to break the spell.

"I best go back in before Uncle Frankie starts looking for me," I mutter, and he nods, taking a step back.

"If you ever need me, you know where I am. I mean it."

I scoff. "I don't think so. You have a new life to be planning. You don't need me pestering you. I'm a big girl now. I can cope on my own."

Maybe if I say the words out loud, he might believe them. I'm starting to, but it would have been a hell of a lot easier with him by my side, helping me fight.

Hurt flashes across his face and his brow furrows. Taking a step toward him, I brush my fingers along his dark stubble. I don't want him to hurt, either.

"Hey. It's okay, Luca. I promise you. We can still be friends?" I give him a sweet smile.

We both know that would never be an option. It would tear us apart. We can't resist each other.

"And I'll always be grateful for everything you've done for me, Luca. You changed my life, you brought me back to life. And for what it's worth, I'm proud of you. The way you protect your family. They don't know how lucky they are to have you in their corner. You deserve to find happiness, too."

He nods and nuzzles his face into my palm.

"The one person who brings me happiness is the only person I can't have."

"No, but sometimes you can't have it all." I lean forward and press a quick peck on his cheek, and he sucks in a breath as I do.

"I'll see you around, big shot," I whisper and push open the door.

My heels click along the wooden floors. Maddie is still waiting in the hallway for me. She gives me a bright smile and a wave as I make my way to her.

"All good?" she questions.

"I'll be okay," I say, holding back the tears.

"Oh, Rosa. Come here," she says before wrapping me up in a motherly embrace. Something I haven't experienced since my mom died. And I lose it. I break down, sobs racking my chest, and she holds me tight.

"I can't do this." I thought I could, I thought I could face him, the booze, everything. But it's too much. I'm scared I'm slipping right back to where he found me. I don't want that. Not anymore. I've been given a taste of a happier life, and I want to hold on to it.

She pulls back, holding my shoulders, her bright blonde hair shining in the lights.

"You can do this, Rosa. I promise you." She digs out her phone from her bag and hands it to me.

"Put your number in there. If you need anything, even just a friend, I'm here." She wipes the smudged mascara from under my eye.

I type in the number and hand it back to her.

"Let's get back in there." She loops her arm through mine and we work our way through the crowd back to the VIP lounge.

DEVOTED ~ 221

Grayson watches her like a hawk. Snatching her wrist, he pulls her onto his lap the second she reaches him.

Uncle Frankie raises an eyebrow at me, and I shrug my shoulders in response. We are not quite at the opening-up stage just yet. Maria is busy tapping away on her phone, sipping champagne.

"Has anyone seen Luca?" Keller asks.

Maria shoots me daggers just as Luca makes an appearance. My eyes go wide as I spot the dark red smudge of lipstick on the corner of his mouth. Keller must see the same thing, since he winks at me with a knowing grin before turning to Luca and miming wiping his mouth with his thumb. Luckily, Maria is too busy glaring at me to notice.

Luca smirks at me and rubs his thumb along his lips, and Keller covers his mouth, holding back a laugh.

"Rosa, really?" My sister hisses in my ear.

"What?" I give her my best innocent look.

"You know what!" She jabs me in the ribs discreetly.

"It's not what you think. Just leave it. Okay?" I shoot her a frown.

"Oh, there you are!" Maria pushes herself out of the booth and squeezes herself against Luca's tall, muscular frame.

I straighten my spine. It might kill me inside, but I can't let them see it. My hands start to tremble. The bottles of champagne are mocking me on the table.

I need to get the hell out of here.

"Frankie, I have to go. I'm meeting Jas and Olivia at Rush," I blurt out, a complete lie. A small shake of my head stops Eva's question before it leaves her mouth.

"Fine. Just be careful." He doesn't look my way, as he's flirting with the waitress who's serving another round of drinks.

"You coming?" I ask Eva.

"Yep." Her tone is harsh.

Great.

I say my goodbyes to the table, and give Luca and Maria my congratulations, faking the hell out of my smile, and dart toward the exit. I can still feel his touch on my skin and his kiss on my lips.

There's no way in hell I'm attending that wedding.

Chapter Thirty-Eight
LUCA

I open the door to Frankie's mansion. The place isn't anything I'd expect from him. It's filled with whites and creams, floor-to-ceiling windows. And absolutely spotless. Whereas I prefer to live in the darkness, surrounded by blacks and grays. I mean, he even has fucking plants.

"Luca, we're in the kitchen," Frankie's deep voice bellows through the foyer.

We?

I make my way through the living room and around the corner to the dining room. Frankie and another guy—some Neanderthal-looking motherfucker with a scar that runs along the left side of his cheek. His amber eyes greet me, but he doesn't say a word.

Frowning, I turn my attention to Frankie. Who, as usual, is leaning back in his chair grinning like he doesn't have a care in the world. But I can tell he doesn't trust this guy, despite his laid-back demeanor. His eyes stay narrowed on his guest.

"Everything okay?" I ask.

Frankie sits up and laughs.

"Oh, yes. Don't mind grumpy here." He nods to his angry-looking guest. "He's an old friend of Marco's."

The mention of his name makes my spine straighten.

"We were discussing some family issues. He was just leaving." Frankie gives his guest a pointed stare.

Scarface stands, pushing aside his chair.

"Well, I guess I will be seeing you around, Frankie," he says in a thick Italian accent.

Oh, he does speak.

"Hmm, let's see how long you stick around for this time." Frankie pins him with a glare.

"See ya," I say. I don't have the patience to deal with anyone else's shit today.

Once the other guy is gone, I step closer to the table. "We need to speed this up. I don't know how much more I can deal with her," I say, sitting myself down on the chair opposite Frankie.

"Why? She's no good in bed?" he smirks, wiggling his eyebrows.

"Who the fuck knows? I won't be sticking my dick anywhere near her," I scoff, which only makes him laugh.

He leans back, threading his hands behind his head. "A happy marriage in the making. Good job. We're making progress on our plans, then."

My jaw aches, I'm clenching it so hard. "The sooner the better."

If I have any chance of getting Rosa back, I have to deal with this. That kiss, I may have called it our last one. There is no way in hell it will be. There has to be a path back to her.

DEVOTED ~ 225

That's why I caved and texted her. Maddie gave me her number slyly, and now I can't stop.

"Right, coffee, then work." He slaps his palms on his navy Armani suit trousers and heads off to the coffee machine.

Digging out my phone from my suit jacket, I sigh, as there are no new messages. I've never checked my damn phone so much, obsessing over when Rosa's next reply might pop up. I'll do anything just to talk to her.

I miss her.

Frankie sets a steaming cup of coffee down in front of me and sits back down. "Okay, we have a call in ten minutes with Romano. He's arranging another two shipments with us for next week. Oh, and let's not forget his upcoming visit."

I roll my eyes.

Maria wanted her parents to fly from Sicily to New York for the weekend so she could go wedding dress shopping and look for a venue in a couple of weeks. Our wedding isn't for another three months at least.

"You can't keep pushing back the date of the wedding, Luca. We need your name on that marriage certificate. We earn back his trust, then we take him out. You signing on that dotted line shows your commitment to them. They're strange like that over there," he says, leaning back in his chair and downing the contents of his cup.

He's right.

I just need to bite the bullet and get this over with.

But something is stopping me—no—make that some*one*.

"I'm thinking of offering Dante a job with us. Something low grade to start until he can earn our trust. I remember him being one of Marco's best at one point, before it all went to shit. He can help with security on the shipments."

The mention of Marco's name has me clenching my fists. I can't deny Frankie is right—we need the best. If we are going up against the Capris, we need solid numbers and fighters.

"Fine. He's on trial. One fuckup and he's dead."

"Agreed."

Chapter Thirty-Nine

ROSA

"Done!" Eva announces, setting the curling iron down on the dressing table next to me.

"Thank you, sis."

My first Friday night out on the town in God knows how long. I've gone for a glittery gold eyeshadow that pops against my dark eyes and olive complexion and my favorite deep red lipstick.

Since Luca's engagement party, we've spoken a few times over text. I hashed it out with Dr. Jenkins. I even told her about the kiss. She said it was clear that although Luca and I have a deep emotional connection, holding on to it would only curb my progress. Which made me realize I need to start doing more things for myself, like focusing on my new career.

I just can't seem to let him go, though. He is my new addiction, and I fear he always will be.

I thought I was doing pretty good with moving on and distracting myself. But one look and I'm back to square one.

228 ~ LUNA MASON

Him invading my every thought. Between that and the texts, even if they are "friendly," I can't turn my brain off.

I want him, plain and simple. My heart craves him more than alcohol right now.

I look over my new hair and makeup in the mirror and, damn, it's the best I've looked in years. My skin is glowing, my hair is shining. I look less skinny and drawn and more fit. I think I have the long walk to the college campus and my evening yoga sessions to thank for that.

Eva gives me a sweet smile and hands me my Chanel perfume. "It's nice seeing you happy. I was worried about you after the engagement party. Are you ever going to tell me what happened with Luca outside?"

I shake my head. "It's done. Over. I need to move on. He's healed me in ways no one could ever fully understand. I need to use that to rebuild."

I brush her off with a half-truth. I have this funny feeling that he and I are way past being done.

"You never know. Looking this smokin', you'll have tons of men lining up for you tonight," she giggles.

"Maybe." I shrug, heading for the door.

Perhaps there is another Luca out there for me. I've found it once, maybe I can find it again.

"Text me when you're on your way home." She blows me a kiss as I make my way out of my bedroom and toward the front door.

"Will do, love you."

THE CLUB IS packed. Rock music is pounding through the speakers. I push my way through the jostling and grinding crowd. How did this used to be my life? I jump as my ass is groped and pick up the pace.

My two best friends, Jas and Liv, texted to say they had a booth at the back of the club. I hesitate before going over—they still don't know I'm not drinking. I can't help but worry that they will be disappointed that their "fun" friend is gone. I was always the wild one of the group, dancing on the bar and throwing shots down my throat.

But I can't let anyone take this away from me. My mind has never been clearer, my skin brighter. I don't even wake in the night with flashbacks of Dante.

Luca has replaced every kiss, every touch, every thrust, with a new memory. Now that's all that replays in my head rather than that traumatic night.

Shaking myself from my thoughts, I spot Jas and Liv in deep conversation at the table. Two guys I don't recognize, definitely of Italian descent, are sitting on either side of them. They're watching me intently as I make my way over.

Liv and Jas attract men wherever they go. They're rich and beautiful and the life of the party. Always. They were the perfect distraction for me.

My friends' eyes snap to mine and smiles light up their faces. "OMG, Rosa! You look stunning! We missed you so much!"

Liv ushers her new man friend out of the way. He stands, letting her slide past so she can barrel into me, wrapping me in a tight squeeze. Jas follows close behind and pulls us both together in a hug.

"Okay, okay! I can't breathe, guys!" I giggle. "I missed you both, too!"

They think that I went to Italy after I left Luca. I didn't reach out to tell them I was home. I didn't trust myself going back into their lifestyle. I wasn't ready.

"You have to meet our new friends, Rico and Danny." Liv excitedly points her manicured finger to the two guys sitting in the booth.

"They have a friend joining in a sec." Jas winks at me.

God, no. A shiver runs down my spine, and I laugh awkwardly as Liv grabs my hand and drags me toward the table. I slide into the booth behind her.

"Hi." I give the guys a wave.

"Hey," they both grunt back.

They look familiar, but I can't put my finger on why. It's probably the fact they look quite Italian. Most of my dad's guys did.

"Rosa, what are you having to drink? Vodka?" Jas asks.

"Just a soda and lime, please." I flash her a tight smile, hoping she leaves it.

"God, you're not pregnant, are you?" she gasps.

I spot the two guys shooting each other a look.

Shaking my head, I chuckle. "No, I'm just taking a break for a bit."

Jas raises a brow at my words. I brace myself for another *you're so boring* lecture. But it doesn't come.

"Oh my god, were you in rehab?"

I nod. It's a hell of a lot easier than explaining I was kidnapped and fell for my kidnapper and got clean in that time.

"We were worried about you. So, hell, if drinking is off the table, we will join you." She shoots a look at Liv. "Won't we?"

Liv splutters on her champagne, placing it down on the table. "Yep. Just after this one."

"It's fine. I can be around alcohol. I'm not that bad. I just need a time-out."

I want to be able to enjoy a drink without having to black out and forget. Until I fix my mind, that isn't happening.

"I'll go get them, it's okay! What are you all having?"

The group rattle off their orders, and I head to the bar. Tapping my Amex on the counter, I scan the room. Everyone is dancing and laughing. It's funny; when I'm drinking, it makes everyone look like they're having the time of their lives. When, deep down, I wonder how many are chasing away their own demons.

A man clearing his throat behind me catches my attention. I spin around. "Sorry, am I in your wa—"

All the oxygen is sucked from my lungs as I come face to face with *him*. His amber eyes eat me up, his lips turned up into a sleazy smirk. That scar that runs along his left cheek. The face that haunts me.

Dante. My abuser. My rapist. My nightmare.

My heart begins beating at a thunderous pace as I back up into the bar.

"No, no, no. This can't be happening." My voice quivers.

"Is that how you're going to greet me? After all these years, my Rosa." His deep Italian voice brings bile to my throat. Even now, after six years.

"Get away from me, Dante," I spit out while fighting back tears. I have to get away from him. Spotting an exit to my left, I make a run for it.

Pain radiates up my arm as he grabs hold of my wrist and squeezes. Pulling me roughly against his chest, he wraps me tightly with his muscular arms until I can barely breathe.

"Baby girl. There's no escaping me this time," he grits out with venom in his tone. "I missed you so much, Rosa."

This can't be happening. The room starts to spin as he brings his mouth to my ear. I hold my breath, too afraid to move.

"I can't wait to have you all to myself. God—" He sucks in a breath. "You smell just as pure as when I had you last."

Before I can respond, he grabs me by the waist and lifts me into his arms.

"HELP, SOMEBODY!" I scream, hitting his chest, which vibrates against me as he laughs.

"Ignore her. My fiancée is just drunk. I'm taking her home."

I hear another guy chuckle, and he swiftly carries me to the exit.

"Baby girl, everything is going to be okay. I came back for you, just like I always promised," he whispers as we get outside, the freezing air hitting my sensitive skin.

Hot tears stream down my face. I can't move. I can barely breathe.

I hear the clicking of the car unlocking and the door opening. He bends and slides me into the passenger seat. I squeeze my eyes closed as he leans over me and buckles me in.

"Don't you dare fucking move, Rosa. You know what happens if you disobey me." He smirks, and I'm back to being the naïve seventeen-year-old again. The one who was too scared to say no to him. I know what he's capable of. So I do as he says.

He doesn't take his dark eyes off me as he circles the front of the car and slips into the driver's seat.

"Time to take you to our new home, Rosa. We can finally have our forever."

My head whips around to face him.

"What do you mean?" I look down at my trembling hands as his huge fingers lace through mine.

"It's all been agreed with your uncle. We're getting married in two months. You'll finally be mine." A wide grin lights up his face.

"Uncle Frankie would never—"

I stop myself. Dad banished Frankie before it came to light about Dante. Which means Frankie doesn't know anything about what this monster did to me.

"I don't want to marry you." I don't know where my bravery comes from, but the words fly out of my mouth.

"It doesn't matter what you want. The deal's been made and I suggest you get on board. That is, unless you want me to take precious Eva instead. I hear she's still pure. I bet she would feel even better—"

"No!" I cut him off. I can't hear it.

He's not taking my baby sister. Not her. Terrifying images of him doing to her what he did to me flash through my mind. Fear surges through me. His malicious laugh fills the car. The same sound that plagued my sleep for the last six years.

"Always protecting her, aren't you? I stopped by your house earlier. She's definitely aged well—the perfect woman."

I swallow the bile rising up my throat, shaking my head.

"Well, it's settled, then. Here's to our forever, baby girl," he says, turning on the ignition.

His hand settles on my thigh, and he squeezes. His touch burns my flesh. Tears fall down my cheeks. I focus on my breathing, just like Dr. Jenkins taught me.

"I made Frankie a promise to protect you. I love you, Rosa. I've loved you since the day I started working for your dad. So, I want to win over your heart. I want to do this the right way this time. But, remember, if you don't catch on quickly, poor little baby Eva will pay the price."

I turn to face him, anger bubbling inside.

"And this is how you think you'll win me over?" I spit out, unsure where this confidence is coming from.

"In time, Rosa, you'll learn to love me. You have to if you

want to keep Eva alive. I'm prepared to wait. As long as you behave, that is."

He gives me a warning look and tightens his grip on my leg. Pain radiates from the bruising force of his fingers.

"You're hurting me," I whisper.

He releases his hand quickly. My eyes home in on the angry red marks now on my skin. The first of many, I assume. Men like him don't change. They can't.

Chapter Forty

LUCA

One Week Later

"Boss, we've had word there's been a hit on one of our containers down at the docks." Grayson's voice booms through the loudspeaker, and I clench my fists and stare down at my phone that's resting on my glass coffee table.

"For fuck's sake. Who the fuck is it this time?" We have drugs and guns arriving. Either one would be a huge loss.

"I've sent some of our recruits down there now. I'll have more information in a second."

Maria's heels click along the marble hallway, and I groan. She's the last person I need here right now.

The past week I've been walking on the edge. I can't get through to Rosa. She's missed her appointment with Dr. Jenkins, and it's driving me crazy.

I've waited outside her and Eva's house on multiple occasions and she's never there.

"Luca, we have some exciting mail!" she announces. I lift my head up to see her waving a small piece of paper at me with a devious smile on her face.

"One sec, Grays." I click the mute button.

"Got it."

"Well, what is it?" I hold my hand out to her.

"Oh, you are going to love this." Intrigue gets the better of me; I never see her this excited about anything. I snatch it from her bright red nails.

My eyes scan the invitation.

Fuck.

I can hear Maria's psychotic laugh next to me, but even that isn't louder than the sudden ringing in my ears. My hands shake as I read over the words again, hoping I had momentarily lost the ability to read.

Nope.

You are invited to the wedding of Dante and Rosa.

My heart hammers against my ribs, and I fight the urge to throw the contents of my stomach up all over Maria's new white fur rug underneath my feet.

What the hell?

"Luca, you've gone awfully pale. Shall I get you some water?" Her nasally voice drips with feigned sweetness.

"I'm fine," I croak out, my mouth now dry.

Throwing the invitation down onto the table, I snatch up my phone and bring it to my ear.

"Grayson, change of plan. I have somewhere I need to be. You go down to the docks, and I'll meet you there." I rush my words out, fumbling around in my suit to grab my cigarettes.

"Got it, boss. Everything okay?"

"I'll talk to you later," I say and cut the call.

Pacing over to the kitchen, I swipe up the keys to my Bentley from the black countertop. Maria watches me the whole time, her stare burning the back of my head. So, I turn to face her. Her fingers dig into her crossed arms, and I swear daggers are shooting from her eyes.

"What's your problem now?" I snap.

"I've told you once, and I'll tell you again. Do not embarrass my family." She storms over to me, her long fingernail jabbing into my chest.

"You have a weakness for that girl. I saw it at our engagement party. And do you know what weaknesses get you?" I can smell the wine on her breath as she raises her face closer to mine.

I stare at her blankly. I don't have time for this.

"Killed. Luca. So I suggest you go and blow off some steam. Get her the fuck out of your system. She's gone forever. She will never be yours. Because you, Luca, are mine. I won't let that little slut take everything I've worked so hard for," she seethes, darkness flashing through her eyes.

My jaw tics. Who does she think she is?

I lean in, my frame towering over her.

"And do you know what calling her a slut will get you?" I growl.

She squints her eyes at me, and I bend down so my lips brush against her ear. "Killed. Maria. With my bare hands. You are in *my* fucking home. You are marrying me. You will do and behave as I say from now on. If one more word comes out of your mouth about Rosa, I will end you. Do you understand?"

She sucks in a breath and takes a step back.

I'm done listening to her. For weeks now, I've let her walk

around my home like it's hers. Thinking she has one over on me because she is a Capri. Well, enough is enough.

Straightening myself, I pat down my suit jacket.

"Glad we cleared that up. I won't be home tonight," I say, heading toward the door, leaving her standing with her mouth hanging open.

"We'll see," I hear her mutter behind me.

As soon as I open the door, I light my cigarette and take a deep breath, letting the chemicals burn down my throat.

Rosa.

Digging my phone back out, I scroll and find her name in my contact list and click the dial button. It cuts off, telling me the number I called hasn't been recognized.

I find Frankie's number, and he answers on the first ring.

"Luca. To what do I owe this pleasure on a Sunday morning?"

"Two things. First, we've had a hit on one of our containers down at the docks. I'm heading there now."

"What?"

"Yep—you coming?" I ask.

He groans. "I'm just in the middle of a little fuck session with Lacy and Katrina—"

"Hey, my name is Cathy!" a woman shouts in the background.

The line muffles. "I don't give a fuck what your name is. If you don't shut up, I will gag you."

I clear my throat, hoping to remind him I'm still listening.

There's a shuffling sound before I hear his voice get closer to the receiver again. "Sorry about that, yes, I will meet you there."

"Fine. Grayson's on his way. Don't wind him up today." The last thing I need is those two at each other's throats.

"I'll try. I don't know when he's going to get over it. I

DEVOTED ~ 239

mean, even his wife likes me, for fuck's sake. Should I let him take a free ride at my face, get it out of his system? He's so emotional." I hear a smack come through the phone and a garbled woman's moan.

I raise my eyebrows. Now that isn't a bad idea. Stick them both in the boxing ring, let Grayson beat his ass.

"That could work. Anyway, I got Rosa's invitation." I try to keep my tone neutral.

"You remember Dante? Our new guy?" he grunts.

Anger bubbles within me.

"The asshole who didn't speak? Doesn't seem like Rosa's type, and isn't he older?"

"Who am I to stand in the way of love at first sight? Apparently that's what happened."

A bad feeling settles in my gut. Why wouldn't she have mentioned this at the party? Why did she kiss me? Is this why she's stopped texting me?

"Anyway, we're having a little dinner party tonight to celebrate. Not that Rosa knows; she's been very quiet about it all. I've barely seen her. Can you make it? Bring Maria?"

Running a hand down my face, I take a final drag of the cigarette and stub it out on the gravel. "I'll be there."

I need to see her with my own eyes.

If she is happy, it might break my heart, but I won't stop it. I could never do that to her. I swallow past the lump in my throat. I want her to be happy, but with me. Only ever me.

I can't let her go, not now, not ever.

And if anything is a kick in the ass, a wedding invitation will do it.

Chapter Forty-One

ROSA

I twiddle the massive engagement ring that rests on my finger, taunting me. He's making sure it's clear to everyone who I belong to. Even down to the engagement ring. Every time I look at it, I feel sick to my stomach.

He invited my sister to dinner last night so I could ask her to be a bridesmaid. She has no idea who he is. Dad made sure I told no one else to hide from the shame of it all. I, however, decided not to tell her to protect her. I don't know if I managed to convince her this is real. She has suspicions, I'm sure. I just hope she doesn't pry too much and bring Dante's attention back on her.

But I'm doing this to protect her. She has a life to live, one not consumed by nightmares. She is my only family. I know what this man can do, and I won't let him.

I just have to bide my time and find a way out of this. Somehow.

As the days have gone by, he's gotten more restrictive.

First, he made me stop seeing Dr. Jenkins. Then, he took my phone. It was my lifeline to Luca.

He drops me outside the doors to college and picks me up the second I walk out of the classroom. There is no escape from him.

Every damn day, I have to battle the urge to drink this away. I can't even count the amount of times I've poured a glass of chilled white wine. I've even sniffed it. I manage to pour it away. Holding on to the tiny shred of hope that I can find a way out of this hell.

After a scalding hot shower, I pick out an outfit, one I used to wear back in my partying days. I slip it on and look in the mirror. A deep red wrap dress that falls just above my knees, pinching me in at the waist. I swipe on a matching lipstick. I need to hide what I'm feeling.

I can do that on the outside.

I jump as the front door slams shut, vibrating throughout the house. I quietly shut my bedroom door.

"Rosa. Are you ready to go?" Dante shouts from the hallway.

"Two minutes," I call back.

I snatch my clutch off the dressing table. Not that I need it. I don't even have a phone right now. But I need something to put my sneaky pack of cigarettes in.

As I round the corner, he's resting on the door frame, holding his hands—smothered in gold rings—in front of him. His eyes roam my body up and down, settling on my breasts.

I pull down on the hem of my skirt uncomfortably as he assesses me.

"I like." He licks his lips and stalks toward me. I squeeze my purse into my chest.

When he reaches me, his boozy breath hits against my cheek.

"Let's go put on a show for Uncle Frankie. Seeing as I now work for him and Luca. You're looking at their newest recruit."

My eyes go wide.

"What?" Just him saying his name is like a kick to the chest. Not Luca.

"I'm weaving my way into your life in every way, baby girl. There is no escaping me." He laces his fingers through mine and drags me toward the door.

That must be why he hasn't been home much since he took me.

I need him to be as far away from Luca as possible.

Chapter Forty-Two
LUCA

"Where's wifey?" Frankie says, ushering me in the door.

I straighten my spine.

"Just me tonight. I nearly strangled the bitch to death earlier. So we need some time to cool down."

He chuckles and slaps me on the shoulder.

"I'll get you a scotch. Ideally, if you are going to kill her, do it after the wedding, like we planned."

I roll my eyes.

We make our way through Frankie's extravagant house. Chandeliers hang in the grand hallway, throwing ribbons of light on the floor in front of me as I walk through.

Frankie opens up the dining room doors. My breath hitches as my eyes connect with hers.

My treasure.

Her perfect, plump lips make that sexy O as I stride through, not taking my gaze from her.

She's all I want right now. I crave her.

The asshole, Dante, coughs, stealing her attention from me. She looks down to her hands on her lap, like she's just been told off at school. I take the available seat next to her. Electricity shoots through me as my hand brushes her smooth thigh.

And God, that dress. It's torturous being so close to her but not being able to have her.

The way she jolts next to me tells me she feels it, too. Not all hope is lost just yet.

Frankie takes a seat opposite me, his stern bodyguard, Theo, to his right, his hair slicked back into a topknot.

Rosa's sister, Eva, gives me a sweet smile, which I return. But I can't shake the way she's staring at Rosa. Something isn't right between those two.

Frankie's server hands me a glass of champagne. Taking a sip, I lean back in my seat, using this moment to scan my eyes over Rosa. She's lost weight again. Her fingers tap nervously against her thighs as she picks away at the skin around her nails. It takes every bit of strength I have not to lace her fingers through mine to calm her down.

"Well, to the happy couple!" Frankie beams and raises his drink for a toast.

"I'm a lucky man," Dante says, placing a kiss on her cheek, and I death grip my wine flute.

I watch as she squeezes the glass, and her hands tremble as she sets it back down without taking a sip.

As everyone continues chattering, she excuses herself from the table. Dante watches her like a hawk as she exits the room.

My phone vibrates in my suit jacket. Pulling it out, I see Grayson's name lighting up the screen.

"Excuse me for a second." I nod to Frankie.

I accept the call and leave the room.

"Gray. What's up?"

"I got the details on that missing shipment." I can hear Maddie's voice in the background.

Everyone has happy women with them except me. I have the devil in my house. "Good, what's the news?"

"It wasn't a hit. It was a reroute—" His voice grows muddled as he says something in the background. Can't they all not be getting laid when they're on the phone with me?

"What the hell do you mean?" My patience is running thin.

"The shipment was diverted to the Capris' warehouse. Maddie, stop for—" He lets out a small gasp.

Fucker.

"Okay. Is that all?" I can't handle much more of listening to them messing around.

There's a thump, like he dropped his phone. "Sorry, boss. You alright?"

"I'm just at Rosa's engagement dinner."

The line goes silent.

"Luca," he sighs.

"I don't want to hear it. Not today, Grayson. I can deal with this."

"Fine." He huffs.

"Keep me updated," I say and cut the call. As I stuff it back in my pocket, I can't help but notice the distinct sound of Rosa's sniffles. I head toward the sound and lightly tap on the bathroom door. "Rosa, baby, can you let me in?"

The lock clicks, and I breathe a sigh of relief that she still trusts me. Her puffy red eyes greet me. Instinctively, I wrap my arms around her tiny frame, my brow furrowing as I feel her ribs through her skin.

Resting my chin on the top of her head, I tip my face forward and inhale her sweet floral scent. Kicking the door open further, I walk us in, Rosa still attached to my torso. Her warm tears spill through my shirt.

I close the door and turn the lock, my back against the door. I tip her chin up, forcing her to look at me.

"Who is he? Why the sudden engagement?" My jaw tics.

I know I have no right to be angry; I'm engaged. But not out of choice.

She casts her gaze down and bites her lower lip.

"You will always be mine, tesoro. Always. Now, tell me. Why are you doing this?"

"Because I need to move on."

I take a step back. I know her well enough to know she's lying to me, the way her pupils dilate, the way she's now picking at the skin around her fingers.

"Do not lie to me, Rosa."

She closes the distance between us, and I close my eyes as she trails her finger along my jaw.

"You have your reasons for your engagement, I have my own. I have to do this." Her voice is stern, but she keeps stroking my face, skimming them south, down my shirt and stopping at my belt. I bite back the groan from her distraction tactics. All the blood is leaving my brain and heading straight for my dick.

"You love him?"

Her eyes go wide. I can't put my finger on it, but it's definitely not love her face is filled with. She shakes her head and relief floods me.

"Okay, better question. Do you still want me? Because I want you. I've never stopped," I rasp, brushing my nose against her jaw. She shivers against my touch, tipping her head back.

I trail my index finger along her arms, a tiny little moan escaping her lips.

"Yes. God, yes, Luca."

My fingers find the hem of her dress and hoist it up, cupping her ass. I lift her and sit her on the sink.

"Touch me, Luca. Please. Make me feel whole again. I want to feel alive. Only you can do that."

"I'll always make you feel good, Rosa. I was created for your pleasure. But I need something from you."

"Anything."

"I need you to go back to therapy. And I need to be able to contact you."

"Okay." I watch as her neck constricts as she swallows.

"I'll send you another phone. I can't not talk to you. It's killing me. I need you."

She nods. "We have to keep this a secret, though."

What is she hiding? Right now, I can't argue with her, not when I am doing the same thing as her.

"Agreed." I nuzzle my face into the crook of her neck and inhale. Fuck, I've missed her. I will take her any way I can. I can't live without her, so this will have to do, for now.

"Good girl. Now spread those legs wider for me."

I grin as she complies. Dipping my fingers under her dress, I hiss as I brush her lace panties, making my cock throb in my pants.

Hooking her thong to the side, I slide my finger along her slit, coating myself with her slick juices before slipping into her entrance. My other hand traces along her collarbone before wrapping around her throat, giving it a gentle squeeze.

The way she reacted at my engagement party, when my hand found her neck, tells me this is definitely something we need to explore.

"Mmm," she hums, closing her eyes.

I keep my grip gentle so she can still breathe. I don't want to leave a mark—this time. Claiming her lips for a ferocious kiss, I pump my fingers in and out of her.

"God, you are perfect, Rosa," I rasp. Her hips start to grind to my rhythm.

"More, Luca," she shouts. My eyes go wide, and I slam my palm over her mouth.

"Shh, Rosa. It's not a secret if you announce to the house who you really belong to."

Her eyes twinkle. There's my girl.

I replace my hand with my lips, and she moans into my mouth. God, she was always so vocal, screaming out my name. It's always so perfect.

I look down as her hands grip tightly onto the counter. That big diamond resting on her finger makes me murderous. But, as her walls begin to constrict around my fingers and her legs begin shaking against me, it distracts me from the garish rock.

Her moans get louder, from little breathy pants. Rolling up my sleeves, I offer her my tattooed forearm. "Bite down on my arm. No screaming today, Rosa."

I can't have this getting back to Maria. I have a free pass away from her tonight.

Her lips part as she bites down on my flesh. As I circle her clit with my thumb, pain radiates through my arm as her teeth sink into me, no doubt drawing blood.

"That's my good fucking girl, Rosa. Come all over my fingers for me," I growl, my cock painfully straining against my zipper.

Her body starts to convulse as I stroke her orgasm out of her, my hand smothered in her juices. She is perfect.

She releases her teeth from above my wrist. I watch as droplets of crimson drip down my arm and smile. I bring my arm up to my mouth, and her eyes go wide as I lick the blood off and roll my sleeve down.

Her chest rises and falls frantically. "Do you feel better now?" I ask.

She nods with a sly grin.

"Always, with you. You know that," she whispers, looking down to the ground.

"Hey." I call her beautiful big eyes back to me.

"One day, I'll be all yours. You keep my heart beating, Rosa. Just have hope. I'm not giving up on us. Or on you." And I mean every word. My mom is right. Rosa owns my soul, and I will find a way.

She bites her plump bottom lip. "I don't want to lose you. I need you, Luca."

Her dainty hands wrap around my blue tie and she yanks me toward her.

"One last kiss?" Her eyes sparkle as she throws my own words back at me.

I chuckle and shake my head. I love playful Rosa. The real Rosa.

"Baby, we can keep calling it that, but we both know it never will be. Those lips are mine, and I'll have them whenever I can," I mutter against her mouth, her warm breath hitting against me.

She takes my lips, offering me a slow, sweet kiss. She tastes like fresh mint and sin.

"I'll head out first. I need to get some fresh air to settle this—" I look down at my raging hard on tenting my pants.

Stealing one more kiss, I brush a stray strand of hair behind her ear and press my lips to her forehead.

"I'll get a phone to you tomorrow. Do you want to do this, Rosa? I will give you as much of me as I can. I promise."

"Like secret fuck buddies?" Her face crumples, and I shake my head.

"No. Rosa. We were never just a fuck. What we have is far more than that. We just have to be careful, for now. I promised myself, if you were happy with him, I'd leave you be. If you didn't want me anymore, I could stop this. I don't know why you're doing this; I trust you will tell me someday. But for now, I will be here for you. Until you're ready."

I can't risk Maria finding out. She's already on a Rosa warpath. She's calmed down since the little altercation we had about the engagement news. The plan is coming along nicely. We have regular gun shipments running alongside the cocaine. My family is safe.

The only thing that could ruin this is my infatuation with the woman in front of me.

Her lips part as if she's going to tell me something, then she snaps them shut.

"Why are you risking everything for me, Luca?"

"You will always be my first choice, Rosa. You are my endgame. These last few weeks have made that clear for me. I will fight for this."

I turn and slowly unlock the door. My heart is cracking as I turn away from her. Like it does every damn time.

Why did this have to be so goddamn complicated? At least I now have control over her fiancé. Frankie offering him a job was the best idea that man's ever had.

Chapter Forty-Three

ROSA

With trembling legs, I sit myself down on the toilet, catching my shaky breath.

Can I really risk seeing Luca more?

I can't let Dante know about him, not when Eva's safety is on the line.

But Luca isn't a man to give up, I know that. Maybe if he can get me through this, maybe one day he can help me. I was so close to telling Luca the truth, but he's protecting his family. He would kill Dante, just like that guy who tried to hurt me at his house.

That puts everyone in danger if his fiancé's family finds out.

I take a deep breath, wiping under my eyes. I'm not the weak little girl Dante once knew. I can push back. I can say no. I know what kind of monster he is now. I just have to find a way out that keeps me alive long enough for my new happily ever after.

Luca.

"Rosa, what the fuck are you doing?" Dante says, his heavy fists pounding against the bathroom door.

"Coming!" I shout back, shutting off the faucet.

Bracing for impact, I slowly inch open the door. He towers in front of me, his amber eyes squinting as he looks me up and down.

"Come on," he grunts, grabbing me tightly around the wrist and dragging me back into the dining area.

All eyes are on us. He plasters on a fake smile, and I do the same. My eyes search for Luca, but he's fixated on the hand grasping my forearm. I pull my arm back hard enough it forces Dante to let me go. He shoots me a scowl but releases me.

Fuck, it's sore. But I can't rub it. Luca will know he was hurting me.

As we take our seats, my body brushes against Luca's shoulder, sending sparks of desire straight to my core. I know he feels it, too, the way he stiffens. Luca keeps his gaze firmly on Frankie opposite him, but his thumb connects to my right hand under the table and he starts to gently rub my arm in small circles. The same spot Dante just had a hold of.

I try to subtly pull away from him. The fear of discovery has my heart racing like I'm about to have a heart attack. But Luca laces his fingers through mine, putting my hand back in its original position, and continues to massage my tender wrist.

"To us!" Dante announces, holding his flute of champagne in the air. My sister gives me a smile and joins him. I know I'm hurting her by hiding away from her, but it's the only way I can keep her safe.

I stiffen as Luca leans forward and offers his hand to Dante right in front of my face, giving me a subtle wink. With those same fingers that were just inside me, he's offering to shake my fiancé's hand. My body is on fire.

"Congratulations. You're a very lucky man." Luca's words tickle my ear as his hidden hand squeezes mine. Their handshake looks intense, like they're both vying for power. With white knuckles and bulging tendons, it's only after Dante grunts that they separate.

"Come on, give me a kiss, fiancée." Dante drapes his arm over my shoulder and tugs me to face him. It's like cold water being thrown over me.

I can feel the waves of anger rolling off Luca next to me, so I slip my hand from his and start to trace the square around his knee. Anything to relax him, to remind him of us.

With him by my side, I can do anything.

Taking in a breath, I shut my eyes and let Dante press his lips to mine. I don't kiss him back; I stay still, hoping this will be over quickly. I sigh in relief when he breaks away, but his jaw twitches as he leans close.

"I expect better from you next time," he whispers in my ear, his voice full of venom.

FRANKIE'S ITALIAN CHEF cooked us a delicious three-course meal. It was so tasty, I couldn't resist digging in. It's the first meal I've been able to devour in a long time.

Every time Luca brushed my thigh, I had to clench my legs together.

Luca stands from the table, nodding to Uncle Frankie.

"I have to go. Congratulations." He turns to me, his eyes then settling on my fiancé. A darkness clouds his features.

He stands and walks behind me, stopping at Dante's chair. Grasping his hand firmly on Dante's shoulder, he bends and whispers in his ear. I know it's nothing good. Dante's face goes red and his jaw clenches. He doesn't say a word back before Luca turns and strolls out the door.

He left me on my own with the monster. Eva shoots me a questioning look as Dante pushes himself up from the table.

"Well, thanks for a lovely meal, Frankie. But it's time I get Rosa back home." Dante waits as I slide my chair back.

I stand and give Frankie a tight-lipped smile. *Keep it together, Rosa.* Dante clasps my trembling hand, and I give my sister a wave as he all but drags me out of the room.

He walks us down the long hall in silence until we are near the end. Then he twists my arm up, bending my wrist uncomfortably.

"Ouch, let go!" I whisper.

"Who the fuck is Luca to you?" he spits as we step outside of the house.

"N-no one. He's just Frankie's business partner."

"I don't believe you. You little slut." He turns to face me and I back away. Fury flashes across his dark eyes as he stalks toward me.

I wince as he brings his muscular arm up, bracing for the impact. My eyes shoot open as he softly brushes my lips with his rough fingers.

"You're all mine. You'd do well to remember that. I promised you I wouldn't hurt you again. Don't push me to break that promise."

I let out a shaky breath. I've been waiting for him to snap. There is no way this man can be anything but a monster.

"Do you understand?" he says softly as he slides one of his heavy hands over my shoulder.

I bite the inside of my cheek and give him a small nod.

"Always so obedient," he mutters, cupping my jaw with his rough palms and bringing his lips to mine.

Squeezing my eyes shut, I freeze in his grasp. All I can concentrate on is not throwing up.

"I might as well be kissing a brick wall. Work on that," he grumbles, pushing me away roughly.

I keep my head down and he yanks my hand, dragging me to his car. He throws the door open and pushes me in. The slam of the door shutting echoes through the parking lot. Staring straight ahead, I blink back the tears. I wish my life was anything but this, that I was going home with the man my heart belongs to.

We pull up outside his home after a silent drive. His knuckles are white from squeezing the steering wheel. He cuts the engine and turns to me. "Get inside, and I want you naked on the bed waiting for me."

The blood drains from my face.

I shake my head, my hands now trembling, and I grab the handle. I could run, but it would only make the punishment worse.

"I'm not asking again, Rosa. I need to fuck that man out of your system. I've been nice to you up until this point. Now, you're going to be my wife, so that means you let me fuck you whenever I want," he grits out, his face expressionless.

"You said you wouldn't push me. You wouldn't do this!" I don't know if I can survive this again.

"You should think about that before you whore yourself off to other men. Now be a good little wife and get ready for me. I've been waiting six years to sink into that tight little cunt." He grins at me, and I want to puke.

Bowing my head, I open the door and get out of the

256 ~ LUNA MASON

car. His footsteps follow closely behind mine, like a hunter stalking his prey.

He unlocks the door and holds it open for me, and I make a beeline to the bathroom in my room.

"Why can't you follow a simple instruction, you stupid bitch!" he yells and I flinch, backing myself into the cabinet.

With fury in his eyes, he strides toward me. His hands clamp around my biceps, and I try to shake him off with no success.

"Dante, please," I croak, scratching at his forearms.

I thrash my body around to try to shrug him off, but he only tightens his hold, scowling at me the entire time.

"I like it when you fight," he mutters and begins sloppily kissing along my jawline.

Tears stream down my cheeks.

His thick fingers wrap around my neck. "God, Rosa. I can smell the fear seeping from your pores and your heart pounding against my fingers."

I yelp as he bites down on my earlobe. "Please, don't, I'm begging you."

He pulls back, his face searching mine. For a split second, I think he might stop this. But he throws me onto the marble floor, my side smashing against the ground. I roll over onto my back and he towers over me with an amused look.

I scoot myself away from him until my back hits the wall.

He walks toward me, unzipping his pants, and holds his hard dick in his hand. I fight the urge to spill the contents of my stomach all over the floor. My lungs start to burn. *This can't be happening.* I close my eyes, my chest heaving, and I think about Luca. I try to imagine him charging through the door and whisking me away. My savior.

But that won't happen.

I have to fight for myself for once.

I remember the words this psychopath told me.

"How could I ever love you if you do this to me?"

He stops dead in his tracks. My ears are ringing and my palms are sweaty as I muster the strength to stand and face him.

"I need time," I whisper while holding my arms across my belly.

I have to figure a way out of this life, and I think I've just found my ticket by playing along with his delusion.

"Fuck!" he roars, smashing his fist into the wall next to me, making me flinch.

I quickly recover and take a step toward him.

With fury in his eyes and his nostrils flaring, he pulls at his hair and starts pacing like an animal in a cage.

Despite the nausea and my trembling hand, I rub my fingers along his cheek. "I think we can get there, Dante. I really do."

His features soften, but doubt still clouds him. I swallow. He needs more to make this believable.

"I will give myself to you in time. I need you to understand that we need to build our relationship. If you truly want my love, that is."

"I can give you some time," he huffs, placing his hand over mine and pressing my palm against the scars that line his face. I resist the urge to snatch my hand away.

"Thank you," I whisper, smiling at him.

He leans forward, and I squeeze my eyes shut as he places a wet kiss to my forehead before storming off into the kitchen. I'm too frightened to move.

The fridge slams shut and I close my eyes. I'm desperately craving a drink right now, but I have a glimmer of a lifeline, and I need to think clearly if I'm going to tame the beast.

I suck in a breath as he comes back into view. My heart thuds erratically against my rib cage when he brings his hand to my face, and I fight the urge to flinch.

"I'm sorry, baby girl." His touch is gentle. "I'd never hurt you unless you deserved it."

I snap my face back to his, now full of concern. Visions of my sister flash in my head. Now I truly know the level of crazy I'm dealing with.

"Okay." It's all I can muster right now.

"I meant what I said. I want you to love me, Rosa. I'll be better. I promise. Just don't do anything stupid, for Eva's sake."

I nod and watch as a crocodile tear slips from his eye.

He sighs and backs away from me, leaving me speechless.

I survived another day. I know his delusional weakness.

Maybe there is a light somewhere for me.

Chapter Forty-Four
LUCA

The door edges open, and Rosa's face appears through the crack. "You going to let me in, baby?" I say, resting my hand on the door.

The locks click and I push my way through. I made sure Dante was put at King's Gym for a recruitment day this morning, so that will keep him occupied.

I stop just inside, taking in my beautiful girl. She's in a little pair of red satin shorts and a black cami with her curls bundled on the top of her head. I step toward her and watch as a big grin settles on her full lips.

She squeals as I pick her up at the waist. Her legs wrap around me, and I crash her into the wall behind us.

"This is a nice surprise." She runs her hands through my hair as I lean forward and capture her lips.

"I wanted you all to myself," I mutter between hot kisses.

I scan the old-style apartment. There isn't much here—just a little kitchen, a dining table set for two, and a shabby black leather couch in front of a TV. Is this really how she's been living?

My cock strains against my pants as her pussy rubs against me. This is risky, but she's always worth it.

She starts to undo the buttons of my shirt and pulls my tie off. Her light touch along my abs sends electric jolts through me.

"I need you, Rosa. I need to be inside you. I need to feel you." I swear to fucking God, I've dreamed about this for weeks now. Being back where I belong.

"Do it." Her hungry eyes meet mine, begging me. I bite down on her lip.

"Bedroom," I pant out. Her hips grind against me as I carry her. She might just make me come in my pants.

"My bedroom is the second door on the left." The words haven't left her lips before her teeth nibble on my neck.

I keep her safely wrapped around me and kick open *her* door. Not *theirs*. I lay her down on a double bed with white sheets. Shrugging off my jacket and shirt, I scan the room. It's like the rest of the apartment, basic.

"Strip for me," I command.

I grab her new phone and a little box out of my jacket and place it on her bedside table. She doesn't even notice; she's too busy shuffling her shorts off with her hips in the air.

The perfect sight.

I push down my pants and boxers, holding my raging hard-on in my hand, and watch in pure delight as she peels her top over her head, revealing her little black bra. I lick my lips and kneel on the edge of the bed, pushing her to her back with my ravenous kisses. I settle between her thighs, resting on my forearm. I slide down each strap over her shoulders, following it with delicate kisses.

She drags her arms free, and I slide my hand under her back and unclasp it, ripping it away to reveal the real treasure. Her nipples are already standing at attention, and I can't resist. I take one in my mouth and suck, making her back arch, which pushes her wet, hot pussy against the tip of my cock.

Her skin flushes beneath me and her fingers burn into my arms as she tugs me closer.

I kiss all the way down her quivering belly, planting kisses on each thigh before burying my lips between her legs.

"Luca!" she whines, her fingers finding my hair and shoving my face into her pussy.

I chuckle. "You're that desperate for my mouth?"

I take one slow taste along her slit and she cries out.

"You love fucking my face, don't you? My perfect dirty girl. Mine, only ever mine." Her hips buck, and I continue to lick in long, slow movements.

I want her on the edge before I sink inside of her. I need her to explode around my cock.

I grit my teeth, realizing I can't mark her, to claim her in every possible way.

I slide two fingers inside, and her wetness coats them and drips down my fingers. As I suck on her clit, she lifts her hips, giving me access to push a finger against her tight, puckered hole.

"You going to let me in, baby?"

"Fuck, yes," she all but screams as I slide that finger in, her muscles clamping around it.

I groan against her pussy. "Jesus, Rosa, I can't wait for your tight asshole to strangle my cock."

"Mmm, yes." Her breathing is heavy as she soaks my face. She's more than ready for my cock now.

"Soon." I plant one final kiss on her pubic bone and remove my fingers, leaving her body sagging. Her face flashes with annoyance and she whines. I can't help but laugh. "Baby, I'm about to fuck you within an inch of your life."

Chapter Forty-Five
ROSA

I scream out his name as he pushes his piercing inside of me, all the way until his hips hit against me. I stretch around him, the pain balancing against the pleasure.

He bends both of my knees into my chest, his tattooed hand finding its way to my throat.

"You want to try this a bit tighter this time, baby?" His thumb tilts my chin.

I look up at his hooded eyes. "Yes."

A grin dances on his lips. "Good answer. Take a deep breath in for me."

I do as he says, closing my eyes.

"Eyes on me, Rosa. I need to be able to read your reactions with this."

I furrow my brows, my heart rate picking up. Excitement bundles with nerves in my stomach. I trust him.

There is something about having his fingers squeezing around my neck, letting him control me, letting me focus only on him that thrills me. I need him to take my mind off everything else right now.

Tipping my head back, he arches my throat against his palm.

He bends down and kisses me, slowly tightening his grip. "Deep breath in."

And as I do, he crashes his lips back over mine. His mouth claims me while his hand restricts my airflow.

I claw at his back as he starts to fuck me, as he promised, within an inch of my life.

The only thing I can feel is his cock pounding into me. I keep my eyes focused on Luca as he pulls away. His steady gaze never leaves mine.

My lungs burn. Blood thumps in my ears as my orgasm starts to build.

"Good girl," he grunts, releasing his grip a tiny bit, allowing me to take in a small breath.

He starts to circle my clit. "You are perfect, mine."

My eyes go wide, and he releases his grip immediately. Leaning down on his forearms, he kisses along my neck where his hands were. Stars fill my vision as I explode. My now croaky voice shouts his name, filling the room.

After a few more pumps, he joins me with his own climax spilling into me.

He keeps kissing my neck, his fingers lacing through mine, pushing my hands above my head.

Jesus Christ.

That was the most intense feeling I've ever experienced.

I flutter my eyes closed, focusing on my breath. In for four, out for four.

"Now, that was amazing, Rosa. Can we add choking to our keep list?"

I nod. "Definitely." My heart flutters. *Our list.*

His breathing evens, and he frees my hands. "Let me clean you up."

Cold air breezes against my sensitive skin. He kneels and opens my legs wide, settling his head between my legs. I sit up, resting on my forearms, and watch as he starts to lick down my thighs.

His tongue brushes against my heat, and my head flies back.

"Oh, Luca." I fall back onto the soft mattress.

"Shh, cleaning."

It only takes a few swirls of his tongue to have me on the edge again.

"Lucaaa," I moan out.

I jump as the door slams shut, shaking the thin walls.

Luca's face snaps up and he jumps off of me. "Fuck," he mutters, shaking his head.

"ROSA!" Dante's deep voice booms, making my heart rate accelerate.

Shit, I'm breathing so fast I'm going to pass out.

Luca places my top and shorts in my hands and drops a soft kiss to my forehead.

"Calm down," he whispers.

I look up at him in horror. "You need to hide." I frantically dress myself. Luca bundles his suit in his arms, quickly putting on his boxers.

Dante shouts my name again. "Two seconds, I'm just getting changed," I call out.

"I'll see you soon, okay?" Luca drops a quick kiss to my swollen lips and darts toward the small window opposite my bed.

I watch in shock. "Luca, what are you—"

He tosses his clothes out and climbs over, dangling his feet out. I gasp as he falls out of sight. I rush toward the window, just after I hear the thud.

Oh my God.

My hands fly over my mouth. I can't look. It's the second floor. That fall would hurt. To my relief, when I look out, I find Luca picking up his clothes. "Fuck off." He glares at the men walking past, staring at him.

I look back at my crumpled sheets and smooth them out quickly.

"I'm coming in," Dante yells angrily.

My door flings open just as I snatch a hoodie out of the wardrobe. I need to cover the red marks on my neck. I pull it on and turn to him.

He eyes me suspiciously. "What were you doing?"

"I had a nap, read a book, and I got a bit chilly, so I put on a hoodie. I was going to make a salad for lunch if you feel like joining me?" I smile sweetly at him.

He frowns, and I start to panic.

"Close the fucking window next time. I need to shower, then I'll eat." I follow his gaze to the dried blood coating his knuckles and swallow. The stark reminder of what he's capable of.

He shuts the door, and I hold myself up against the wardrobe. That was too close.

A phone lights up on the nightstand, next to a little black box. *What the hell is that?*

I snatch the mysterious new cell up from the table.

A text from "L" is on the screen.

L

Hide that box, it's a little present for you.

> Remind me not to jump out of the window
> next time, my ankle is busted.

Intrigue getting the better of me, I open the lid, revealing a little black-and-gold vibrator. My cheeks instantly flush, and I snap the lid closed, tucking it safely away under my bed.

> **ROSA**
> I can kiss it better next time.

A text pops up immediately.

> **L**
> I'm counting on it.
> **L**
> I've missed us.

There's a pang in my chest. We shouldn't be doing this. I just don't know if I can stop. Not now. I can't lose him again.

> **ROSA**
> I missed you far too much.

Chapter Forty-Six

LUCA

I sit across the table from my soon to be father-in-law, Romano, and his wife, Celeste. He is the epitome of suave, with his gray slicked-back hair and Ray-Bans covering his eyes. Even through them, I can feel him assessing me.

The waitress delivers our espressos. "Thank you." I nod to the waitress as the rest of the table ignores her.

Maria looks at her like she's dirt on her Jimmy Choos.

"Business is going well, son." Romano breaks his silence.

I nearly cough out my coffee at the word *son*. Nobody other than my mother calls me that.

"Yes, very. We're ready for new shipments. We have warehouses lined up for storage. Buyers from all around the country want in."

"Good." A heavy ring on his hand reflects the light as he reaches for his drink. After a long sip, he looks at me over his glasses.

DEVOTED ~ 269

"And your commissioner—he's still on board?"

"Of course." The real crux of the problem. The commissioner is the only thing keeping me alive right now. I've failed to mention to Romano the fact that Commissioner O'Reilly will only work for me.

"I have a business partner I'd like you to meet in Italy. It would be nice to have my daughter home for a few days. Why don't you come? Bring all your family for the weekend? Little Darcy would love the beaches, I'm sure."

The bastard. Reminding me of his threat, disguised as a big, happy vacation.

My family won't be going anywhere near him. Keeping my anger at bay, despite it threatening to boil over, I manage to say, "Sure. Just let me know when."

"I'll be picking up my wedding dress this Saturday. So it will have to be in two weeks," Maria chimes in, and I have to physically stop myself from rolling my eyes.

"Of course, darling." I draw out the last word and give her a cheesy grin.

"It's a date, then." Romano slams his palms on the table, and suddenly the eyes of the entire café are on us.

"Only six more weeks till the big day! I can't wait!" her mom excitedly says. "I've got your brothers' suits already."

Maria stiffens next to me, and I raise a brow. Her father remains expressionless.

"Brothers? I thought it was just Antonio?"

Maria leans into me. "I have a half-brother," she hisses.

Interesting. Another to add to the hit list.

My phone starts vibrating in my pocket. Maria wrinkles her nose at me, but I ignore her. Rosa's name is flashing up on the screen.

"I have to take this." My chest feels tight with excitement.

"Hello." I try to sound professional as I leave, pulling out a cigarette and heading to the outside seating. "How are you, tesoro?"

"I'm fine. Are you busy?" Her soft voice is like music to my ears.

"For you, Rosa? Never."

I light my cigarette, looking at the couples sitting in front of me, all deep in conversation. As I glance through the window to the café, I can see Romano and Maria having a heated conversation. As her mother locks eyes with me, I look away.

"I'm on my own." Her voice is so quiet I can barely hear her.

"Then why are you whispering?"

"I don't know," she giggles, and I remember how much I miss that sound.

"I'm in a meeting at the moment. I can come over after that?"

"W-what, here? What if Dante comes home?"

I know he won't be. I have him out on runs all day.

"Don't worry about him, baby."

As she goes to reply, Maria storms out. "Luca, your lunch is here."

I hold up my cigarette to her and excuse her. The line is silent.

"Rosa, are you still there?"

"Huh—yes. Just forget about it. We can see each other another time, maybe. Sorry."

Before I can get a word in, she cuts the call, and I shake my head.

Fuck.

I limp back to our table and as I approach, Maria flicks me a look.

"Why the hell are you limping?" she hisses in my ear as I sit.

"Jumped off a bridge trying to kill myself to get away from you."

She huffs and carries on picking at her salad. I sit there, unable to get Rosa's voice out of my head.

I need to see her.

Chapter Forty-Seven

ROSA

As I push open the front door, I toss my bag down on the floor. After my session with Dr. Jenkins, I need a cigarette and a coffee.

Today we discussed another coping mechanism. Journaling. So on the way home, I stopped and picked up a little notepad with my Capricorn star sign on the front.

I'm going to start with five things I want out of life.

I stop when I spot Dante's worn-out black boots. He's home.

"Rosa?" he calls out.

I tug on the sleeves of my cardigan and try to form a fake smile.

Stepping around the corner, I freeze in my tracks. The dining table is scattered with red roses, with two pillar candles flickering on the table and two place mats set out.

I take a step back as he appears from the kitchen.

"Come have a seat. I've made us lunch." He looms over

DEVOTED ~ 273

the back of one of the chairs and pulls it away from the table. A forced smile twists the scar on the side of his face.

"I—uh, just need to freshen up," I lie and dart out of the room, slamming my bathroom door shut.

Gripping the sink, I take a deep breath. In and out. Luca's voice replays in my brain, soothing me. Telling me to keep focused. Remember why I'm doing this.

I flush the toilet and pull down my dress so it's at my knees. In a moment of panic, I scramble out my phone from my purse.

ROSA
He's home. I won't be able to talk tonight.
L
It's all taken care of. Don't worry, baby.
I'm all yours for the night.

My heart flutters as I reread his text. The whole night?
I bite back a smile.

"Rosa!" Dante yells, the sharpness in his tone making me hurry. Making sure my forbidden phone is on silent, I throw open the bathroom cabinet and place it behind a bottle of bleach.

As I reenter the room, he's still holding out the chair for me.

"You look lovely, Rosa."

I nod and take a seat.

"Thank you."

This whole charade of being nice to him is starting to wear thin.

He sets down a plate of chicken with a variety of vegetables and potatoes. I try to stop the slight tremble in my hands

274 ~ LUNA MASON

as I pick up the cutlery. I'm about as comfortable right now as I would be with a gun to my head.

He watches intently as I take a bite. The salt on the chicken makes my mouth dry up.

"Could you pass me the water?" I croak out.

"I have wine?" He grins.

"No." I hold my hand up, hoping he doesn't press any further.

He starts shoveling in his food like the pig he is. I sit and watch him in disgust, keeping my facial expression sweet and loving like he wants.

"So, I've hired a wedding planner. I've set the date for the last weekend in July. I've already had her pick out a dress for you, too. So, no need to worry your pretty little head about a thing." He looks up and grins at me, like he's impressed by his efforts.

"Why so soon?" I watch his knuckles turn white as he grips his knife. My leg starts to bounce erratically under the table.

"Why wait? I've waited six years to claim you, Rosa."

I gulp down my water, my throat feeling like it's closing in on me.

"Is that a problem?" He waves the knife as he asks, and I shake my head.

"Good. See, we can get along. You'll have the best life with me, Rosa."

I almost scoff at his words. I manage to stop myself just as his phone rings.

"Hello?" He stares at me intently, his face reddening. "For how long?"

"Two fucking days?" His hand starts to shake. "Yes, no, I do want to keep my job. I just don't like leaving my fiancée."

My heart rate picks up. It's Luca.

"I'll be there in half an hour. I'm just finishing—" His knuckles pop as he squeezes his fist.

"Fine."

He stares at the blank screen before he launches his phone across the room. His nostrils flare. "Don't even think about leaving the house while I'm away," he spits out as he stands.

"Where are you going?" I try to keep my voice neutral and not betray the excitement building inside of me.

"Work." He slams the chair against the table, making it jolt into my stomach.

"Shit," I hiss out in pain.

"I'll be gone until tomorrow evening."

He downs the last of his wine in one swallow and storms out of the apartment. I feel like I can finally breathe again.

Chapter Forty-Eight

LUCA

After cutting the call with Dante, I can't even hide the smile on my face. One whole night with Rosa.

I pour myself a scotch and sit on the far end of the couch. As I pick up the remote, Maria looks up from her phone.

"I'm watching that, leave it on." Her nasally voice makes my skin crawl.

I pause the program, *How to Get Away with Murder*, and smirk at her. "Planning something, are we?"

She cackles. "I wouldn't have any problem getting away with it."

I exit Netflix and she grumbles under her breath. I flick over to boxing. One of our up-and-coming guys, Jax, the King of Chaos, is fighting tonight. We managed to get him the pre-fight card. The next one, he'll be the main event. He has a pure hunger for blood.

I check the time on my Rolex. Nine p.m. I sent Dante to

DEVOTED ~ 277

the fight with Jax as part of security and to deal with the underground gambling side tonight. Before now, I would never have dreamed of giving someone new this kind of job.

But it keeps him away from Rosa.

Which means I get to see her.

She's my addiction. I can't go weeks without seeing her, without tasting her. I need her. But with each time I see her, I fall harder and deeper in love with her. I can't help it. Not that I'd even want to try to stop this.

Mom is right. She was meant for me.

I rub my palms against my pants.

Fuck it. I'm done waiting.

I stand and toss the remote at Maria.

"Where are you going?" she snaps.

I look back as she stands up, hand on her hips, glaring at me with hatred.

"What makes you think I'm going anywhere?" I slip my car keys into my pocket.

"You have been acting weird all day. Like an excited kid."

She frowns at me, and I laugh. "Must be all the wedding talk. Got me all giddy."

I push myself away from the counter and brush past her. Her hand grabs my forearm, and I grit my teeth and turn to her, looming over her.

I flick my gaze up and down her and her ridiculously short little nightdress and those lips that look like they're about to explode off her face.

"Can I help you?" I keep my stare pinned on her hand, with my diamond glaring back at me on her finger.

She bats her lashes and sadistically grins at me. I swear she's possessed sometimes.

"You know . . ." She runs a long fingernail up my arm.

It makes the little hairs on the back of my neck stand up. "Spit it out."

"We are going to have to consummate our marriage." She pouts her already ridiculous lips until they look like two balloon animals fucking under her nose.

I keep my face straight. We won't, because the Capris will be six feet under by my wedding night. But the thought makes me shiver. I don't think I've ever slept with anyone this vile.

She unwraps her hand and brings her pointy nail to my chest, biting down on her bottom lip as she trails it down my shirt.

"What in the fuck are you doing?" I snatch her hand before she can reach my belt.

There's only one woman on this planet who can touch me. And I'm on my way to show her.

"We should practice. We've barely even kissed. I have needs, Luca."

I physically shiver in disgust.

I bring my lips to her cheek and brush along her jaw. She lets out a shaky breath as I whisper, "I'd rather cut my own cock off. Find someone else."

Shaking off her hand, I back away. She stares at me open-mouthed.

"Fuck you." Her eyes narrow into pinpoints of darkness.

"Still pass," I call out as I slam my door shut.

Her dad might hold the ultimate card to keeping me in line, but this woman doesn't. I'm doing everything he asked, so he's happy with business. I have built an entire army ready for war. I just have one more fight to deal with to have it all. And Maria won't stop me. No one will.

Chapter Forty-Nine

ROSA

After drying my hair and taming my curls, I put on a knitted black cardigan over my black cami and leggings. Now I have to tidy the house before Luca arrives; I can't have him seeing the state this place is in.

I start going around the house, picking up all Dante's empty beer bottles and shoving them in the trash bag. I don't even want to look in his room.

Sliding on my sneakers, I head down the stairs with the heavy bag of garbage. The glass bottles smash against each other with each step.

Wiping the sweat from my forehead, I open the garbage cans outside the main entrance to the building and toss the heavy bags into the empty bins.

"Jesus, I'm unfit," I mutter to myself.

"You're the fittest girl I've ever seen." A deep, familiar voice makes me jump.

I gasp and turn toward the voice, the one that makes my stomach erupt into butterflies and melts my panties off.

"Luca," I whisper.

He's leaning against the door, one leg crossed over the other, biting his lip as his eyes scan my body.

"What are you doing here?" I hold back my smile.

Pushing himself off the wall, he takes two steps toward me. "I'm here to take my girl on a date."

"A date? With me? Looking like this?" I point down at my plain clothes and shoes. Not a scrap of makeup on and half-damp hair.

"You look beautiful to me, tesoro."

My breath hitches as he crowds into my space while looking down at me. Wrapping a strand of my hair around his finger, he rubs the lock as he fixes me in his gaze.

"You are the most gorgeous woman I have ever laid eyes on, Rosa. You don't need to hide your natural beauty. My cock gets hard at the sight of you, whatever you wear."

"We can't let people see us together." I cast my eyes down.

He shakes his head with a sly grin. "For what I have planned, it isn't an issue." He tips my chin up, his green eyes flashing with desire.

"Where are we going? For a quickie in the car?"

Not that I'd mind. I'd take anything from Luca. My body craves his touch, no matter how fleeting.

He chuckles and strokes my cheek. "You really think a quickie would be enough? Have I not proven to you yet that I have to worship you—every single part of you? I want you coming apart on my tongue, my fingers, and my cock. Tonight, I want to show you what life will be like for us one day."

I go up on my tiptoes and kiss him. My hands skim

through his soft hair, and he lifts me into his strong arms, making my back crash against the brick wall.

"Baby, if we don't stop this, I will fuck you right here, right now," he rasps between kisses.

I lick my lips and look around; it's pretty dark out already, and the stupid streetlights barely light up anything. I see the corner of his mouth twitch, his gaze burning into me.

"I don't need dates, flowers, anything like that. I just want my Luca," I whisper.

His lips brush against my jaw, and I tip my head back, squeezing my legs around his waist, pushing his hard dick against my seam.

"Rosa, I want to show you love. True, unconditional love. All the dates, the extravagant gifts." He pauses, bringing my left hand to his cheek, pulling off my engagement ring with his teeth. "A real diamond, the wedding of our dreams, the family. Every. Single. Damn. Thing. That will bring a smile to those beautiful lips. I want to give you that. No, I *will* give you that. It's the only thing keeping me going, tesoro."

I choke on a sob as he presses his lips to my forehead. In his arms, I am safe. I am loved, cherished, and everything in between. He is mine and I am his.

He is my forever.

True love, I've never had, but I would bet my life that it's this. It has to be.

"I want all of it, Luca. I want this, forever. Vita mia. *My life*."

"You will forever be my always, Rosa," he whispers.

There is a sadness that creeps into his tone, and I cup his face.

"You are happy, aren't you?"

He casts his gaze down and shakes his head. "No, but I will be."

"I want you to be happy."

Guilt fills me. In all of this, I've been so stuck in my own head, my own worries and problems. I forgot about him. I know, despite his hard exterior, that mafia boss brutality, he carries his emotions. He hides behind that funny, cheeky guy.

In all of this, he is struggling, too.

"When I wake up with you in my arms every day, that's when my life will truly begin."

I crash my lips over his.

He slips my engagement ring inside his suit jacket. I hide the panic—I need that back, I don't want to poke Dante the bear when he's home. I need to pick my fights carefully. I don't want Luca pressing the subject.

He pulls back and pushes a stray lock of hair behind my ear. "We have all night, and trust me, we will make use of every single second. But I'd like to take you on a date. Is that okay?"

I squeeze my legs together to try to relieve the building pressure. This is the sweetest thing; he just wants to spend time with me.

"I'd love that, Luca. Thank you."

With a gentle hand behind my waist, he leads me to his car, where he tucks me into the passenger seat before sliding behind the wheel.

"So, where are we going?"

He shoots me a grin with a twinkle in his eye as we pull up outside the movie theater.

"A movie night?" I beam.

"Just like we used to." He winks, making my heart flutter.

Chapter Fifty
LUCA

I tug her into my side, nodding past the cinema attendant. I've booked out the entire building for the next four hours. She points to the marquee in the lobby. "It has our names over the door!" she says, full of excitement, grabbing another handful of popcorn.

I don't know what spies Romano has on me, so I booked the entire place for us. No one will see us. I paid well to make sure.

"What are we watching?" she asks, looking up at me with wide eyes.

"Whatever the hell you want to, baby."

She purses her lips, deep in thought, and then a mischievous look passes across her face.

"Do you like horror films?"

I don't know the last time I watched one. My life right now is pretty much one.

"I guess." I shrug my shoulders.

"You guess? Are you sure you're not scared of ghosts?" She grabs the popcorn from my hands, not taking her eyes off of me.

"There is only one thing that truly scares me, Rosa."

She raises an eyebrow. "Hmm?" she says through a mouthful of food.

"Losing the people I love."

She nods in agreement. I shake my head. It clearly hasn't registered what I mean.

I take a step forward. "Losing you scares the hell out of me, Rosa."

Her mouth falls open, then snaps closed as the theater attendant steps up to us.

"Have you decided on a film?" he asks while he straightens his bright blue hat.

I swing my head around in annoyance. "Whatever new horror film you have." I dismiss him and turn my attention back to her.

"It's okay. I'll hold your hand through it." She winks at me and wanders down the aisle between the rows of chairs. I jog behind her and snatch her fingers, needing the contact.

"You'll be doing more than holding my hand, baby," I whisper and watch in amusement as her cheeks flush a deep red.

Once we settle in our seats, the lights dim.

She places the popcorn on her lap and turns to me. "I'm still soaked from earlier," she purrs into my ear.

I want to tease her to her limit tonight. I have that little list she wrote still in my wallet. I've memorized the damn thing. She wants to be edged—well, this is her first little taste. Although, I'm not sure how long I can hold off myself.

"Patience."

Keeping my eyes on the screen, I lean over her, purposely brushing my fingers along her thigh as I grab the popcorn.

I don't particularly like the stuff, but I need something to take the edge off.

I tense as her fingers trail along my thigh toward my dick, which has been painfully aching for her since we got out of the car.

"Not yet," I hiss. I take her hand and place it on her lap, then drape my own around her neck letting my fingers idly stroke up and down beneath her ear. She rewards me by letting out a little moan.

By the time we hit the thirty-minute mark in the film, she's shifting uncomfortably in her seat, and I can smell her arousal from here. Just how I want her.

Screams fill the room from the screen, but I don't even know what's going on anymore. I take the opportunity to gather her arm and lightly stroke that sweet, sensitive spot just on the inside of her elbow. Her little secret place that will have her soaking for me.

"Please, Luca." She wiggles in her chair, trying to claim back her limb. I hold on to her bicep and taste all the way down to her hand, taking each of her salty fingers in my mouth, licking them clean.

I lean over, nibbling on her earlobe. "You're going to be a good girl for me and sit through the rest of this film. I'm staying with you tonight. I want you ready to explode the second we walk through the front door. Can you do that for me?"

She shakes her head, and I chuckle. "Tough."

I sit back in my seat and snatch the popcorn and stuff a handful in my mouth, pretending to watch the film. When, in fact, I spend the whole movie watching Rosa squirm next to me.

I'll reward her for it when we get home.

286 ~ LUNA MASON

WITH ROSA WRAPPED tightly around my body, I kick closed the door. As I ravage her mouth with mine, I rip off her top.

She gasps, and I slam my lips over hers. She's pent up and ready to combust.

She pulls on my tie, and we tumble through her bedroom door. I shake my head as she tugs at my shirt. "Do you want to have some fun?"

"How much fun?"

I bend down and throw her over my shoulder and carry her into the kitchen. I swipe the two sets of cutlery off the table, and I lay her out.

"Stay still." I open the fridge only to be met with bottles of beer and wine. My fists clench.

The asshole doesn't even have the decency to not drink around her. Instead, he lines it up under her nose for her to battle every day.

I look past the milk carton and spot the whipped cream. Perfect.

I slowly pull down her leggings, brushing the smooth skin all the way down her thigh. Those toned legs almost make me salivate. I yank the leggings off and let out a ragged breath.

"Rosa. I don't tell you this nearly enough. But I plan to. You are simply beautiful."

I hook my fingers under her black thong; she lifts her hips in the air, and I rip the material off her.

"Hey! Those were my favorite!" she whines, but that glint in her eye tells me she couldn't care less.

Pushing her leg open, I slide a finger inside of her.

"It seems to have gotten you nice and wet for me, though. Do you like me ripping off your panties, Rosa?"

I slide in a second finger, and she bucks her hips, her legs falling open as far as they go, leaving her exposed to me.

"I wish we didn't have to hide. I want this every day," she pants out, and my heart fucking constricts in my chest.

She has no idea how much I want that, too. How I've obsessed over this woman.

Bending down, I lick small circles on her clit with the tip of my tongue while stretching her with a third finger. "My girl loves being stretched, doesn't she?"

"Y-yes," she all but screams.

Her juices coat my hand as I suck on her clit. The second her walls start to clamp around my fingers, her legs twitching next to my head, I remove my fingers and stand.

"What, Luca. No."

She drops her head back on the table, spilling her dark hair over the edge, and lets out an annoyed sigh.

"I want to bring you right to the edge, tesoro. I want you writhing in pleasure and ready to explode, over and over again. Until finally, when I sink inside you, you come apart all over my dick, letting me fill you up with all of me."

Taking the whipped cream, I squirt it all over her stomach. "The bra. Off."

She does as I say and tosses it to the floor. I circle her nipples with the cream, the coolness turning them to peaks.

I shrug off my jacket and roll up my sleeves, loosening my tie.

She licks her lips, looking down at my muscular forearms.

"Jesus, Luca. Those arms should be illegal. Like I could get myself off just thinking about them and those veins."

I chuckle and shake my head. Women get horny over the strangest of things.

"So, not my massive cock that you love so much?" I raise a brow.

I bend down and lick the sweet white fluff off her stomach, running from her pubic bone all the way up to her breast and sucking on that rosy bud.

"Or what about my tongue?" I whisper.

"Mmm, yes, I love your tongue," she pants while tipping her head back to expose her slender neck.

I continue my pursuit of licking her clean. Every single inch of her. Leaning down, I run my mouth all the way up her throat, and she cranes it the other way so I can bite down on her sensitive skin.

"On all fours, tesoro," I murmur against her skin with a grin.

I rub my dick through my pants as she turns over on top of the dining table. Walking around her, I get a full view of my dinner.

"Spread them wider for me." Obediently, her knees widen, lowering her hips within reach.

I kick the chair out of the way so I can get closer. With my palms, I spread her cheeks, opening up her ass for me.

"Luca," she whines as I start to blow little breaths of air against her pussy and licking up her come that's starting to drip down the inside of her thighs.

She jolts forward as my tongue connects with her clit, and I nibble all the way to her entrance. Wrapping my hands around her thighs, I pull her back to me and start to fuck her with my tongue.

"Oh my God!" she moans, letting out little breaths that are making my cock throb.

"You're doing so well, baby." I pepper kisses all the way up. "Still trust me?" I question as my mouth hovers above her ass.

"Yes, Luca. I trust you."

With that, I slide two fingers into her pussy and start to lick the rim of her puckered hole, my thumb finding her clit. Her hips start to roll against me, her breathing quickens, and I let her ride me, taking everything I can give her. Slipping out my fingers, I trail them toward her back entrance and tease her there.

"Luca, please, do it." There is desperation in her voice.

"Fuck," I mutter as she wiggles her hips and pushes back on my soaked index finger, screaming as it slowly slides inside. "You're so damn tight, Rosa."

With my other hand, I hold on to her hip, slide my middle and ring finger inside her pussy, and start to slowly up the tempo of all three.

"I c-can't." She drops her head to her hands.

"You can. After this, I'm sinking my cock so deep inside your pretty little pussy that you'll feel me for days. You'll walk around knowing you are mine and only mine."

I snake my hand around her petite, naked frame and pinch her nipple, kissing along her shoulder and letting her ride my hand.

"Such a good girl for me, Rosa. Come all over my fingers."

And she does, completely, her body writhing, her fists clenched, screaming out my name on the top of her lungs.

It's fucking perfect.

"You're incredible, Rosa," I whisper as she comes down from her high, her body going limp against mine.

As her labored breathing starts to settle, I remove my fingers and sit her up to face me. She looks up with a glint in her eye. Her fingers loop around my belt and she tugs me toward her.

"Your turn," she begs, and I nearly explode on the spot.

Chapter Fifty-One
ROSA

I fumble with his belt, and he leans back to give me better access so I can free his erection, already glistening with pre-cum. I look up at him through my lashes. "Tell me how you like it?"

He's the only one I've ever done this to, but I want to give him the earth-shattering climaxes like he gives me. I want to know every possible way to turn him on.

"Just your mouth around my cock," he grunts as I wrap my fingers around him.

I drop myself off the table and get on my knees in front of him. I grab the base in my hand and start to stroke, licking up the white liquid from the tip, letting his salty taste swirl around my tongue.

He lets out a low rumble, which drenches my thighs.

"I know, but I want to make it incredible for you, Luca. Do you like it when I lick it? Do you want me to use my hands, too?" I'm rambling.

"You really want to know?" He looks down at me, cupping my cheek.

I nod, using my tongue to run along his piercing.

He groans, which spurs me on more. His hands lace through my hair. "Okay, do more of that.

"I want you almost suffocating on my cock, letting me fuck your mouth until my come slips down your throat, and you'll swallow every last drop."

I squeeze my thighs together, a burning need now throbbing between my legs again.

"And extra points if you slide your hands between your legs and play with yourself at the same time. The only way I can enjoy myself is if you are, too."

I lift my head just slightly, his dirty words causing all kinds of havoc inside of me. I spy the can of whipped cream on the counter and grab it, squirting a line along his shaft.

I take my time licking him clean, and his hands knot in my hair, pushing on the back of my head, coaxing me to open my mouth and take him.

I close my eyes and take him as far back as I can go. "You're not even halfway, baby."

What?

As I use my saliva to get him as wet as I can, the metal of his piercing hits the back of my mouth, making me gag.

I bob up and down a few times, his grip on my hair getting tighter and tighter. I jolt as his fingers find my nipple and squeeze.

He bucks his hips, holding me firmly in place with his hand. "Make yourself nice and wet, Rosa. Let me hear how soaked you are from sucking my cock."

I can't moan with my mouth stuffed full enough to have tears pooling in my eyes.

His thumb wipes a drop away. "These are the only tears that are ever acceptable."

He takes his finger and licks it from the tip.

His hips stop thrusting, and I pick up the pace with my fingers. His phone starts ringing in his pocket. "Ignore it," he groans.

As soon as it stops, it starts again, so I pull it out, and I freeze when I see the name on the screen.

Dante.

"What? Who is it?" He frowns.

"It's him," I stutter.

He rolls his eyes and takes the phone from my hand.

"Y-you aren't going to answer that, are you?"

My body is on high alert. I don't feel bad for doing this with Luca. I don't even consider this cheating. Our situation is difficult, but we are only marrying for our families, not for love. But the implications for us both if we get caught—that is the reason I feel this panic.

Luca is the only person keeping me going, keeping me sane. Making me feel loved and cherished. If Dante had come back for me before Luca, I have no doubt I would be dead right now. I would have overdosed or drunk myself to death to escape him.

He pouts, looking between the screen and me, until a smirk dances on his lips.

"I am, and you're going to be a good girl and make me come before the call ends."

He pushes my head forward, sliding his cock back into my mouth and letting out a deep moan.

I guide my hand toward my throbbing pussy. I need to be distracted in every possible way right now.

"Dante. I'm a little busy. What do you want?" he gruffs out.

With pressure on the back of my head, Luca pounds into my mouth with short, shallow strokes. I suck on his cock, using my tongue to swirl around the tip, just how he likes it.

A panicked Dante comes through the speaker. "I can't find Jax. He slipped out of the hotel."

"Well, go fucking find him."

Dante's voice becomes background noise. I can barely hear him over the thumping in my ears.

"It's Vegas, he is probably—" Luca stops midsentence, his thighs tensing under my fingers. I slide up his shaft, sucking hard on the tip.

"—in a casino," he coughs out eventually.

His head tips back and his eyes shut. "I have to go," he says through gritted teeth.

"But—" Dante protests.

Luca cuts the call and steps back, tugging his boxers back over his dick.

"Luca, what? You were about to—" My fingers quiver over my clit. I was so close myself.

"I have a better idea." He winks and throws his phone on the table next to me.

My cheeks heat as he picks me up and strides us to my bedroom.

"One second." I kiss his cheek, and I wiggle free to dart for the bathroom, locking the door behind me.

I need to pee.

"Rosa! I just licked your asshole. Are you really locking the damn bathroom door on me?" he shouts.

I giggle to myself, flushing the toilet.

"Baby, please." He puts on a whiny voice for me.

My face is flushed in the mirror while washing my hands. When I'm with him, I forget the constant threat I am living with. I push it out of my thoughts and focus on the feral man, desperate for me, who is now banging on the door.

I don't know how long we can keep doing this, so I need to savor him, enough to last me a lifetime.

I open the door and he pushes it further, his hungry eyes ablaze. He sets me right back on fire again with the heat going straight to my core.

"Don't shut me out," he growls.

"Care to join me in the shower?" I tug on his tie and back onto the cool tiled floor. He follows me like a puppy.

"There is quite honestly nothing more I've ever wanted in my life, Rosa. Shower me."

His deep, gravelly voice has my pussy throbbing for him. The room fills with steam as the hot water turns on. I pull him down to me and kiss him.

"Do you want to take charge, Rosa?"

I look up at him. *I can do this.*

I nod.

He rewards me with another kiss.

"You better get me undressed then, gorgeous." He winks.

Hmm. I tilt my head, biting my lip.

"I thought I was in charge. I find you so fucking sexy in these suits. It gets me absolutely soaked, especially when you roll the sleeves up."

I look down at his tattooed hands and exposed arms. "Take off your watch."

He quickly sets his watch and phone on the counter as I drag him, fully clothed, with me under the spray of water.

He lifts me up by the hips and slides my back up the tiled wall.

"Tell me where you want me, baby."

"I want what you said earlier—fuck me so I can feel you for days."

"As you wish."

I wrap my legs tighter around his waist, and he holds me up with one hand against my ribs, my back flush against the slippery wall. His hand finds its way, leaving a wake of goose-bumps under his touch. I have to bite back a moan when he finally starts circling my clit.

"God, Rosa. You are soaking for me."

He slides a finger in, but I can't hold in the erupting giggles. He shoots me a questioning look, but I can't stop laughing. "No shit, Luca. We're in the shower."

He thrusts another finger in response, which has me gasping rather than laughing. He bites on the inside of his cheek.

"Your mouth will get you in trouble." His breath is hot against my neck.

"Yeah?" I lean forward and take his bottom lip in my mouth, sucking hard.

"Oh my God, Luca, you're so wet for me," I tease and lick the moisture from his jaw.

"You are a menace." He drops his lips to mine, as if to shut me up. "And I love it."

I moan against his mouth as he ups the pace, losing myself to the sensation of the hot water splashing over my skin, and Luca sucking on my nipples.

His teeth tighten, sending a pleasant shock through me. "I wish I could mark you. Claim you as mine for the world to know."

"One day, maybe." I want that. I want to be his in every way possible.

"No 'maybe' about it." His stubble tickles my chest.

My fingers work their way down, and I cup his hard-on through his pants. "For now, I just need you inside me."

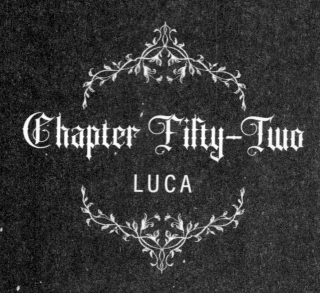

Chapter Fifty-Two
LUCA

Pressing her hand harder, I can't fight the thrust of my hips. "That's how much I want you. I'm desperate now. I have never, ever in my life been more turned on than I am right now."

I lean down and take her rosy bud in my mouth. She arches her back, grinding herself against me. "I want to ride you."

"Rosa, you can ride me like a fucking horse. I need to be inside you. I'm about to come in my pants, and I have never done that before."

She starts to roll her body, her bare pussy rubbing against my clothes. Her hands grab both sides of my face.

"Well, I think you need to do just that," she says hoarsely, upping the momentum.

Holy shit.

Her hot center rubs against the taut fabric covering my cock. When she moans, her breath beating against my lips has my thighs twitching.

"Oh my God, Luca," she pants, gripping my face tighter. "I'm so close and you're not even inside of me."

She crashes her lips over mine, her tongue invading my mouth as she ferociously kisses me, grinding her sweet heat against my pants, rubbing against my piercing, which sends tingles through my whole body.

Blood pounds in my ears as her nails dig into my back. "Come for me, Luca. Give me everything," she whispers against my lips before claiming them again.

And I lose it.

I squeeze her breast in my hand and jerk my hips forward, pushing my dick against her. The pressure from the stud through my tip as it hits against her sends me crashing over the edge.

"Fuck!" I shout, and she joins me.

She screams out my name as I explode in my boxers. I can barely breathe. I kiss her like it is the last kiss I'll ever have.

My cock twitching, my chest heaving, and my body drenched.

Holy shit. That was incredible.

As I regain my breath, she looks at me, and my heart palpitates. I love this woman with my entire being.

"Thank you," she whispers.

She goes to move her legs, and I hold her in place.

"Can we just stay like this for a second?"

My head is fucked.

She cuddles tightly into me, and I rest my forehead against the tiled wall over her shoulder, letting the beads of water drip down my face.

"Come on, boss man. You really do need a shower now."

I chuckle against her. "Are you going to wash me off, then?"

She shakes her head and instead nips at my earlobe. "I'm

going to dry off and get ready for you. I need you inside of me as soon as you're ready. So, clean up and meet me in the bedroom."

"Fuck, yes."

I put her down on the ground, and as she goes to step out of the shower, I pull her into me and press a soft kiss to her temple.

She gives me a sweet smile, and I slap her ass as she leaves. She snatches a towel from the rack and shuts the door.

I let out a heavy breath as I tear off my suit.

I OPEN THE bathroom door and find Rosa sitting on the end of the bed with her back to me. She has a towel wrapped around her body and is tying her hair up into a bun on the top of her head.

My dick starts to get hard again just at the sight of her.

She is humming away, brushing her hair up. I stand and watch her. She fascinates me.

She hasn't even noticed me yet, so I quietly close the door behind me. On tiptoes, I creep toward her, crawl up on the bed, and tug her backward against me.

"Luca?" she sighs as I pull her tight into my chest.

"Yes, baby?"

I slowly undo her towel and let it fall open, and she settles between my legs.

She tips her head back, revealing her neck to me. I can't help but lick the remaining drops of moisture from her silky skin.

"I wish we could do this every day." She rests her head back on my shoulder, batting her thick lashes at me.

"I know, baby, me too."

One day, this will be our life.

I brush my fingertips along her collarbones, settling my hand loosely around her throat before dropping a kiss to those plump lips.

She smiles against my lips, and it makes my chest tight. I am completely and utterly, head over heels, in love with this woman. I have been since the moment I held her in my arms, watching her battle her addiction. The strength she showed only made me fall deeper for her.

And now, the woman cuddled up to me is the best version of herself. I am so damn proud of her. I just wish she'd tell me why she's marrying that oaf.

But it doesn't change the fact she is everything to me. She stole my heart.

She adjusts herself in my lap, her naked ass brushing against my cock, turning to straddle me. Her arms dangle over my shoulders and our faces are just a whisper apart.

"I love you, Rosa."

Her breath hitches, and I hold my own, a sudden doubt clouding over me. We said it before, in the midst of one of the worst days of my life. I meant it then, but now, even more so.

She runs her hands through my hair, looking into my eyes, my soul, even.

"I love you, Luca. I love you so much." My heart beats twice as fast. "More than anything. Now let me hear you say those words again."

"I will love you. Forever." Unshed tears shine in her eyes.

I press my lips against hers, holding her tight, never wanting to let go.

I can't shake the sadness that consumes me. What if we can't have our forever? If I can't find a way out that keeps her and my family out of danger? I can get her out of her wedding easily. I'll simply lodge a bullet in his brain. I've been itching to do that since her engagement dinner. I saw how hard he grabbed her wrist, and in normal circumstances, that would be enough for me to warrant his murder.

The only reason I haven't is because I don't truly know the extent of Rosa's mess. I've explored every possible scenario. Does she owe him money from her addiction? Is she paying her dad's debts? I've had Enzo run his details and nothing— the man is a fucking ghost.

I will find out the truth, one way or another. I'm hoping it's straight from her mouth.

"I promise you, I will find us a way out of this, Rosa," I whisper against her hair.

"We both will, Luca. We will fight for this."

Damn right. I pull back, letting my fingers wrap around my favorite place, her neck.

"Can you tell me why you're marrying him?"

She closes her eyes and shakes her head.

"I promise you, when our moment appears, when you're free of Maria, when no one is in danger, I will tell you the truth. I just need you to trust me. I have it covered. I just need you to be patient."

"Patience isn't really my thing, baby."

She scrunches up her nose. "I know. Can you try, for me?"

I crack my neck to the side, trying to relieve some of the pressure building. Every time I see his face, I want to slam my fist into his jaw. I don't know how much longer I can keep calm.

"Has he touched you?"

Her throat bobs against my palm. "No. I promise, only ever you."

She acts like she wants to say more, but snaps her mouth shut.

"Rosa."

I fear she's holding back because she doesn't know how I'll react.

"Can we drop it, please? We have a whole night together, and I really want to make the most of it." She pouts, batting her lashes at me.

She's clever; she knows my weakness.

I lay her down and cover her body with my own.

"You want this?" I nudge the tip of my cock against her pussy.

She nods frantically, biting down on her lip.

"All of it?" I tease, sliding the head inside.

"Yes, all of it," she hisses, as I inch in deeper.

With one thrust, I completely fill her, causing her to cry out, and I let her.

"That's right baby, scream my name."

Chapter Fifty-Three
LUCA

As I loosen my tie and shut the front door, the exhaustion takes over. I'm ready to get into bed. A whole night with Rosa was perfect; it was everything. But we didn't sleep, not one second.

I come to a standstill at the raised voices coming from a back room.

"This is my home, now get the fuck out, you old bitch!" Maria's screeching voice reverberates off the walls.

"This is my son's home. You are the one who is not welcome in our lives. You think I don't know what your family is up to?"

My mom's voice has me running to the kitchen. As I round the corner, I find her—sixty years old, five foot nothing—squaring up to Maria.

I rush over and wrap my arms around Mom's shoulders. I don't need the Capris having an excuse to hurt her.

"What the fuck is going on?"

My mom whips her head to glare at me. "Language."

I hold her stare in warning, turning my attention back to my fiancée. Her dark hair is pulled back in a bun and her huge lips are painted bright pink.

"You don't speak to my mother like that. This is my home, and she's more welcome here than you are." I step toward her. "What did I tell you, Maria? I told you, you behave how I tell you to in my home."

She tips her chin up in defiance and laughs. "You have no idea. Why don't you tell your mom what you were up to last night?" She lets out a sadistic chuckle, looking at my mom.

"Working." I keep my voice stern.

"You will both regret this." She jabs her finger into my chest. "You'll do well to remember that I come first now. I made that clear, my father made that clear. So, you won't be having any family over anymore. This is my house now."

She pushes herself off my chest and storms up the stairs. Running a hand through my hair, I turn to Mom, who's looking at me with concern on her face.

"You need to call this off." She points up the stairs where Maria just exited.

"I can't. There's too much on the line."

Grabbing two tumblers out of the cupboard, I pour in the Macallan and slide one to Mom.

"What about that girl? Rosa?" she asks quietly.

"She's engaged." I cast my eyes down and swallow the contents of my glass, letting it burn its way down.

"I told you not to let her go, and look what's happened." She smacks me on the back of the head.

"There's still a glimmer of hope for us, I think," I say, rubbing where she hit me.

"Luca Russo. An affair? Really?!" She slams her palm on the counter next to her glass.

"Shh." I flick my eyes toward the stairs.

"I put up with a lot from you. I turn a blind eye at your antics. But this, watching you throw away your chance at love, is breaking my heart, son."

"I can't find a way to have it all, Mom." Shrugging my shoulders, I take another long drink of the biting liquor.

She steps toward me and her wrinkly hand grabs mine.

"Then you choose what will make you happy. That's all you can ask for out of life: love and happiness." Her eyes brim with tears, and a lump forms in my throat as I watch.

"Just think about it, really think about what or who you want. I want more grandbabies, preferably. All I want is to see my sons living the lives they always dreamed of, the lives they never imagined when they were fighting to survive on the streets."

I wrap my arms around her frail frame, my emotions getting the better of me.

"I love you, Mom."

"I love you too, son." She squeezes me.

And I know what I have to do.

I have to pick my heart.

"Come on, let's get you away from the bitch. Do you have some of that garlic chicken at home?"

She chuckles and pulls back.

"No, but you can help me make it today." She pins me with a stare.

"Fine, if I must."

"You know, Dom and I used to cook together every night. His cooking was far better than mine. I learned everything you love from that man."

I smile down at her and wrap my arms around her shoulders as we walk to my car, thinking about how Rosa and I would cook together in my kitchen. That damn smile on her face when she finally nailed that carbonara recipe. When I came home, the kitchen was a complete whirlwind, oil splattered up the tiles. Rosa's cheeks were flushed with pure concentration on her face and her lips pursed as she grated the parmesan on the top.

It was perfect.

"What are you smiling like an idiot about?" she asks before I shut her door.

"Nothing." I shake my head.

I ROLL UP to the warehouse and check the time. I'm only half an hour late to meet the commissioner. It took longer than expected at Mom's. She only had half the ingredients, so we had to go shopping first. All she talked about was Rosa. And her pure hatred for Maria. According to my mom, she has a bad aura.

The door squeaks as I push it open. Stacks of wooden pallets line the sides of the warehouse as I walk through toward the office.

Commissioner O'Reilly is sitting at the desk, tapping his pen against his whiskey glass, watching the clock tick up on the wall.

"Sorry I'm late." I salute him.

"You're lucky I have a day off today, boy. This had better be important. My daughter is taking me to the shooting range soon." He isn't in his formal blues today, but a pair of khakis and a dark polo. He almost looks like a regular person.

"Can your daughter out-shoot you?" She must be good. I know some of those ribbons he wears on his uniform are for marksmanship.

"Almost." He flashes a smug smile as he leans back.

I take a seat opposite him, and he motions for me to spit it out.

"I need to take Romano out sooner than planned," I say bluntly.

He looks down his hawkish nose at me. "No."

"It wasn't really a question. I've set it in motion. I can do it in Italy, away from here."

He stands, his chair scraping against the concrete. He walks around the table and clasps my shoulder.

"Have you lost your damn mind? In his territory, you really think they won't slaughter your whole family in retaliation? It has to be done here."

Fuck. I shake my head. He's right.

"Get your head out of the clouds, Russo. You're a mafia boss, not some normal guy who wants a wife and kids and a nine-to-five. You'll never be able to have that. You need to do this here, and quietly, where we can get rid of any trace of them."

He pats me a little too hard on the back, and I drop my head, squeezing the bridge of my nose.

A life I never asked for.

"I'll see you for the next payment. You need to see the plan through, boy."

I don't have time. I need them gone, out of the way. I don't want to wait another day to have Rosa. But then I think about Keller and little Darcy. And the calm and collected way Romano threatened a baby.

"Fine."

He slams the door behind him, and I pick up the tumbler from the table and smash it against the wall.

"Motherfucker!"

Everyone else around me can have it all. I have sacrificed my life for their happiness, for what? To be used as a hitman for the cops. Taking out the leaders they don't have the balls to.

Gripping the sides of the table, I steady my breath.

There's only one thing I want.

Only one person I want.

My tesoro.

But the commissioner is right about one thing: I'm Luca motherfucking Russo, and I'll take what I want.

I have to find a way.

Chapter Fifty-Four
ROSA

I'm expecting Dante home any time now. I've cleaned every inch of the apartment. The smell of sex and Luca is gone. Now I'm sitting here eating pancakes with whipped cream and strawberries, blushing to myself, remembering how incredible it felt all over my body.

My phone rings. Shoving another mouthful of pancakes, I dig it out of my purse. I expect it to be Luca since I sent him a picture of the pancakes, telling him it doesn't taste as good as he did. But it's not the secret cell he got me that's ringing, it's the one Dante contacts me on.

"Hello." It's so hard not to sound upset when I talk to him.

"Hey, baby girl, what are you doing?" His voice has a lighthearted tone. Even when he's being nice, it sets my teeth on edge.

"Just eating pancakes. Where are you?" *Please be gone longer.*

"I'll be home tonight. Do you miss me?"

"Yes," I lie, swallowing the lump in my throat.

"I've arranged for your first dress fitting this afternoon."

Suddenly my appetite dies. "What dress fitting? I haven't even picked one?"

"I picked for you, remember?"

"But—"

"But, nothing, Rosa. I've told you you're going, so you do as I say. Take your sister. She looks like she's been bored without you."

I massage the back of my neck, taking a calming breath in.

"You've seen Eva? I thought you were away?"

He chuckles, raising the hairs on my arms.

"I have eyes on her all the time. The second you slip out of line, you know what happens to your innocent little sister." He emphasizes the last few words, and it makes my stomach tighten.

Panic starts to grip me. If he has eyes on Eva, is he watching me? Has he seen Luca?

I lean back in my seat, rubbing at my temple. No, he can't. Because he wouldn't be able to control his anger; he would punish me.

"Okay, fine. I'll be at the dress fitting. Text me the time and address."

"God, you're learning fast. See how much easier it is when you don't fight me?"

I want to fight; I just need time to work out a plan.

I hear loud voices in the background. "I have to go. I'll see you later. Say hi to Eva for me."

He cuts the call, and my tears erupt. That little glimmer of happiness that remained from my time with Luca shatters.

MADDIE CATCHES MY hand before we walk through the doors to the bridal shop. Luca must have given her my new number. She texted me a few days ago, telling me she's also coming on the Italy trip.

"You don't have to do all of this, Rosa," she whispers.

I turn to face her and nearly bump into her expanding stomach. A chill runs down my spine. *Have we been too careless? Who else knows?*

"What do you mean?" Throwing up my eyebrows, I try to give her the best innocent look I can muster.

"Rosa, I know you're in love with Luca. There's still time. Call it off and have your real fairytale. With the man that loves you." She offers me a sad smile.

I wish I could.

"I do. I will always love him. But it's not meant to be. I'm marrying Dante. You know how this life works, Maddie."

Even saying the words brings bile up to my throat. I swallow it down and straighten my back.

A smiley blonde woman thrusts a champagne flute into my hand. Without a word, I hand it to my sister.

"Welcome, we're so excited for you to try on your gown. Although, it's very unusual for the groom to pick the dress without the bride knowing. What a fun change." She gives me a practiced pat on the arm.

I fake a smile, and Maddie furrows her brow at me.

"Yep, that's Dante. He's very particular about this wedding."

Suddenly, that champagne doesn't seem like a bad idea, but I can't. I won't.

"Well, you are going to look absolutely stunning in

this number." The woman stands back, looking me up and down with her index finger at her lip, assessing my body. "Hmmm. It may need taking up. It's quite the dress and you are petite."

If I were to pick my dress, it would be Grecian style. With a plunging neckline, maybe even backless, with diamanté chains across.

Something elegant with a pop of sparkle.

She ushers us through to the fitting rooms. A whole room is filled with floor-to-ceiling mirrors and a stand in the center surrounded by plush blue velvet seats.

I don't want to do this.

"Come on, it's okay to be nervous. A wedding can be scary. But just try it on." With a flourish of her own long pink skirt, she leads me through to the cubicle.

My hands fly to my mouth, and I gasp as she pulls back the curtain to reveal the monstrosity that is my wedding dress. *How could he?*

A corset style embedded with thousands of crystals that then puffs out into a massive Cinderella-style skirt.

I would drown in this dress. It's not elegant or classy.

"Wow. That's, uh, something." Eva gestures with the wine glass, both arms waving to encompass the billowing size. "What? It's just not very, I don't know, you." She shrugs and takes a sip of the champagne.

Maddie wraps her arm around my shoulder. "Maybe try it on. You'll look stunning in anything."

I laugh and shake my head. Yeah, right. I let out a sigh of defeat.

"Okay, get me in this thing."

"If you'd like to get undressed, step into the middle and pull it up. Give me a call when you're ready, and I'll fasten

312 ~ LUNA MASON

the back." Her giant blonde hair doesn't move as she turns to leave.

I nod hollowly, not taking my eyes off this sparkly disaster in front of me.

She closes the curtain, and I run my fingers along the rough material. Slipping off my black dress and heels, I slide it off the hanger and it drops to the floor.

How the hell am I meant to even walk in this?!

I step in and pull it up, my heart in my throat as I look at myself in the mirror. I feel like I'm drowning in this material. My heart sinks as I realize I'm never going to have a real wedding. I'm never going to have those butterflies of excitement picking out a wedding dress. I'm never going to have that moment where I look at my groom at the end of the aisle and my world stops for a moment.

Dante's taken that away from me.

He's taken everything from me. And I'm not sure how much is left to give.

I might be stronger now, but I'll never be strong enough to fight him.

He will always hold this power over me. This control. The threats.

"All okay in there?" the saleswoman's voice calls through the curtain.

"Ready." As I'll ever be.

Her face is frozen in an overexaggerated smile. "Wow. Rosa. You look just like a princess fit for her prince."

"Yep." Except I'm not marrying my prince. I'm marrying the monster.

As she begins tightening the corset, I stumble as she pulls the ribbons tight. Fuck, I can barely breathe in this. Maybe this is how he wants to finally kill me.

"Perfect, all done. Fits like a glove." Clapping her hands softly, she steps out of the way so I can leave the changing room.

Grabbing a bunch of the skirt, I hike it up and stomp over to the viewing area and stand up on the display.

Throwing my hands up to Maddie and Eva, I do a little spin. "Well, what do you think?"

They both stay silent.

"Wow, it must be good, to keep you two quiet." I cross my arms and stick out my lower lip in feigned annoyance.

My sister is the first to break out into a fit of laughter.

"I'm sorry!" she wheezes. "You look like you're drowning in a sea of sparkles."

She's carefree and laughing at me. This is all for her, I remind myself.

I turn to the wedding dress lady. "Can I have any taken off the length? I can't walk in this."

"Of course!" She rushes over and gets on her knees and starts fussing over the hem of the dress, stabbing little needles in it.

I jump as an alarm pierces through my ears. It's so loud I have to shut my eyes. I let out a scream as water beats down on me from the ceiling.

"Okay, girls, stay calm. There must be a mistake. Follow me." The woman gets off the floor and leaves.

What the hell is happening?

Maddie and Eva follow her through the door. I carefully get down from the stand and as I reach for the handle, something slams behind me. I turn and a smile creeps up on my face as a dripping-wet Luca stalks toward me with his index finger at his lips and a devilish smirk.

Chapter Fifty-Five
LUCA

"What are you doing here?" she hisses.

The water dripping down my face doesn't distract me from the sparkly puffball she's wearing. She bites her bottom lip as I approach. I reach around her and click the lock into place.

I somehow got Maddie to agree to my plan. I played it off as one last-ditch attempt to get her to call off the wedding.

I mean, it wasn't a complete lie. Grayson let slip about this little trip and it hurt that Rosa didn't tell me. I thought, after saying we're going to fight for each other, she would give me something to work with. But instead, I stand here, staring at the woman I love, in a wedding dress that isn't meant for me. I know she loves me, but this is a punch to the gut.

She is mine. She should be wearing a dress for our wedding. This shouldn't be happening. My jaw tics as I scan the outfit.

"I came to see my girl." I band my hands around her waist

and pull her to me. "Only you could make something so ugly become so beautiful."

She blinks a few times and wipes the water from her face. Black makeup smudges under her eyes. "Shut up. This dress is beautiful."

I lean back to look down my nose at her, and she bursts out into laughter.

She looks down at the damp fabric ballooning around her. "It's horrendous, isn't it?"

I grip her chin and tip her big, dark eyes up to mine. "You could wear anything, or preferably nothing, and be the most beautiful woman that walks this earth."

Before she can respond, I take her lips with mine, and she moans into my mouth.

"Why are you doing this, Rosa? I thought I was your future?" I can't hide the disappointment in my voice. This hurts.

"I didn't want to make him suspicious, Luca. You want to protect your family? This coming out will put them in danger, won't it?"

I bow my head. She's right, and she knows it. My throat burns as she looks up at me with pain in her eyes. She doesn't believe we can do this, that we can fight this.

I shake my head in defeat. This is how she wants to play it. If she isn't prepared to fight for me, to risk it all for me, then so be it. I lean down, and goosebumps erupt on her tanned skin. I trail my index finger along her bare forearm, all the way up to that little spot on the inside of her elbow, and as always, a little moan escapes her.

"You're right. But when you put this dress on, I want you to only think of me. I want to invade your mind as much as you do mine. Even on your wedding day." I almost choke on the last words. I hope there's something I can do to keep that from happening.

She wraps her arms around my neck as I scoop her up, and I place her gently on the stand in the middle of the room. Taking a step back, I rub my stubble as I take in the full image of her.

This is the last kind of dress I'd imagine her picking. It's not her.

"Luca, please, do something. I need to touch you."

"Patience." I hold my finger up.

With the size of that dress, I'm trying to figure out how to fuck her.

"Put one foot on the ground and leave the other up on the stand for me," I command.

She shuffles around and does as I say. I drop to my knees and crawl toward her, lifting up the hem of the dress and getting underneath.

"Oh fuck, you've got heels on," I groan.

I pepper kisses along her calf and work my way up her thigh. "Spread wider for me, gorgeous."

She opens her hips and moves her leg back slightly, giving me the perfect view of her silky red thong.

Using two fingers, I hook the panties to the side and suck on her clit.

Knowing I'm the only person to ever do this to her makes me want to keep doing it. Forever. The way she responds so perfectly. The way she shatters against my tongue. It's beautiful.

I grip her leg that's on the stand to steady myself as I ferociously lick and suck.

"Luca, oh my God. Your mouth is going to give me a heart attack one day." The dress shakes around us as her knees quiver.

I nip her clit then push two fingers in her entrance, sucking up all the juices as I start to fuck her.

God, the sounds she makes.

"I need more," she moans.

So do I.

I need to be inside of her. I need her out of this awful dress.

A knock at the door has her startling against me. I push back open her thigh and continue licking.

"Guys, you've got five minutes max. I've got her on the phone to the fire alarm company."

"Got it, thanks Maddie," I shout before Rosa can reply.

I hear her giggle from outside the room.

Five short minutes.

She spreads her knees wider, and I reward her with another finger.

"Shit," she hisses.

I up the pace until she shakes like a leaf above me. I lick her all the way up her slit and slide my thumb into her ass. Her moans fill my ears as I pump in and out. I groan against her, my dick threatening to explode as she rocks her hips against my mouth.

"Take what you need, baby," I say before diving back in.

It doesn't take long before her walls clamp around my fingers, her pussy throbs against my tongue and she comes apart. I ease up and slide my fingers out with one last lick. I press a kiss on the inside of her thigh.

Sitting back on my heels, I try to regain my breath and rub my pulsating cock that's strained against my pants.

Fuck.

As I get out from under her dress, I'm met with a flushed, yet soaked, Rosa. She has a twinkle in her eye and a grin on her full lips.

"Now, are you going to tell me why you're really doing this? We are running out of time." I look down at her dress.

"Luca," she sighs, reaching out for my hand. I pull away, rubbing the water from my face.

Why won't she just tell me the truth? I've been pretty open with her. I'm trying to find a way. I can't stand back and watch her marry him. It will kill me.

I grip the back of her head and pull her face toward mine.

My lips hover over hers. She tries to kiss me, but I hold back.

"Please just tell me, baby," I whisper.

Fear dances in her dark eyes. I hate this. Anger starts to bubble through me. The more I look at her in that dress, the more obvious it is she is hiding something from me. Fury rolls beneath my skin at the thought of another man touching her. She is mine.

I drag myself from her and pace the room like a wild animal. I take some deep breaths, pulling my fingers through my soaked hair. I can taste her on my tongue, but I can't look at her right now.

"Luca, please." She's so quiet I can barely hear her.

My eyes snap up. "How can we do this if you can't even let me in? I thought we were better than that?" My voice is raised. I kick the chair in frustration and she flinches.

She actually fucking flinches.

My hands ball into fists. *What the hell is going on?*

"You don't trust me?"

Hurt flashes across her face. "You know I do." Her lower lip quivers.

"Then why?" I throw my arms up in the air.

Silence. She doesn't even answer that now.

"Do you know what, I can't do this. All I want is you, Rosa. Do you know how difficult it is to function when I have you constantly invading every single thought? When I'm trying to find a way out of my engagement, keep everyone alive, and orchestrate every moment so we can see each other? Do you?" I shout.

"I'm sorry." It's barely a whisper, but it tips me over the edge.

I step toward her. "I don't want sorry, I just want you. I am so madly in love with you. You know I will do anything for you. You say the word, it's done. I would lay down my whole life for you."

I shake my head, letting out a laugh.

She tips her head down to the ground, so I lift her chin back up.

"I can't do this all by myself. So I am asking you one more time, why the fuck are you marrying Dante? If you're expecting me to find us a way out, with less than two weeks, I need the truth." I spit out.

"No."

"No?" I blink at her. "Are you fucking ser—"

I step past her and launch my fist into the wall, rage burning through me. I stop when I hear the word leave her lips.

"Treasure."

I blink a few times, my heart now in my throat. I turn to see Rosa trembling in front of me, her bottom lip quivering. I have just spent the last few minutes shouting at the woman I love. Pressuring her into telling me something I have no right to know.

She asked me to trust her.

I take a step away from her. I have no clue what to do.

"I'm sorry." My heart rips in two. I am her protector. I should never make her feel anything but safe. If she could tell me, she would.

I fucked up.

Pacing in front of her, I tug at my hair until my scalp

burns. "Rosa, I am so sorry. I shouldn't have shouted; I shouldn't push you. I just, I don't know what to do anymore. Seeing you in that dress, thinking of you marrying someone else, it makes me crazy. I'm so desperate for you, I just—fuck!" Burying my face in my hands won't hide the shame I feel for losing control. "I'm truly so sorry."

She closes the distance between us, her shaky hands hold on to my shirt.

"I'm sorry, too. This is so hard for both of us. Never, ever doubt my love for you, Luca. But do you see why I can't tell you right now? That angry streak of yours. I know you'd never hurt me, but what if your actions end up hurting the people we love? I need you to trust me. I am handling my situation, and you are handling yours. One day, we will be together. But right now, there is too much at risk for both of us."

"I hate this. So much."

"I love you. You are the only man who will ever own my heart, my soul, my entire being. Now I need you to remember that in the future. No matter what." She grabs my hand and places it against her chest. "Yours. Only yours."

A tear slips down my cheek. I rest my forehead against hers and close my eyes, letting her sweet coconut scent soothe me.

"Breathe for me, Luca. Get your head back." Her hand slides down my body, she bends slightly and starts tracing that square around my kneecap with her nail. I do as she says, breathing in and out, focusing only on her touch.

"I love you so damn much, Rosa," I whisper.

"I know you do, and I love you just as much. Now, go. I'll see you this weekend for the trip."

Fuck, how did I forget? I have to spend the whole weekend with Dante parading Rosa around like a prized possession.

But, if I plan this right, I will have as much of her as possible.

Chapter Fifty-Six

ROSA

The last time I was on a plane, we flew back to Italy to have mom buried. In hindsight, I think I was in a better mood then. My calves are bruised from Dante bouncing his heavy duffel against me as we walk. The dread of being cooped up in a room with him for the duration of our trip makes my stomach roll.

We take our seats on the private jet. I squeeze in next to the window, and Dante thuds down next to me.

Luca walks down the aisle with his mirrored shades on. I can tell he's looking dead at me, just by that little grin on his face. He stops at the row in front and takes the seat right in front of mine.

Maria's irritating voice booms through as she enters, and I watch as Luca visibly cringes at her entrance.

"Luca, baby. I want the window seat."

He pushes the glasses back on top of his head and shoots her a look, not moving from the window seat. I bite back a snicker.

Dante leans in, and I pull away. "All that arguing they do I bet makes for some great sex," he says loud enough for Luca to hear.

I swallow the lump in my throat, ignoring him.

I know he's wrong. But that doesn't stop the clawing jealousy that rips through me that she might be the one that gets to keep him. If we can't figure this out in time, he probably will sleep with his own wife.

"Dante, Maddie is insisting on sitting with Rosa, some girly talk or some shit. You're up front with me. Leave them to it." Grayson points to the chair in the front.

Maria's head whips around to me and shoots me eye daggers through the center of the seats.

With a huff, Dante moves, and I can finally breathe again.

Maddie strolls back and plops down next to me, groaning as she tries to get comfortable with her swollen baby belly.

Thank you, I mouth to her.

"Anytime." She smiles. "Plus, it means I get to read my smut in peace without Grayson wanting to put his dick inside me. I mean, I love it, but it's hard work when you're pregnant!"

I can't help but giggle.

"I thought you get super horny when you're pregnant," I whisper.

"I was, before I became the size of a beached whale. Turns out, that just made my husband even harder for me." She nods to Grayson's blond head, biting back a smile.

"Don't make me drag your ass into that bathroom, sunshine. You know I will," he calls out from the front of the plane.

"Oh, I dare you," Maddie shouts back, her cheeks as red as an apple.

"You want it just as badly as he does." I nudge her shoulder.

"Shh. Don't tell him that. Because he will barge over here. And I want to spend some time with you."

"Aww, that's nice. Since I stopped partying so much, I barely hear from my 'friends' anymore."

"Well, you don't need those assholes anymore. You've got me and Sienna now."

"I appreciate that."

She leans in and whispers, "I can see all of our kids, including yours and"—she widens her eyes and gestures toward Luca sitting in front of me—"well, you-know-who's kids running loops around us while we sit and sunbathe. Having afternoon tea, as Sienna calls it." She winks exaggeratedly and smiles.

"I don't know if that will ever happen." I round my shoulders. It's true, and it hurts.

Maddie raises an eyebrow and looks at the wall next to me. I frown and turn to find Luca's hand, slotted through the gap between the seat and the wall. He starts motioning me with his finger.

I grab his hand, and he puts something in mine. I take it back and unravel the crumpled receipt he placed there and read the scribbled handwriting.

You will have my babies. All five of them.

My cheeks start to heat as I shove the note down my bra.

Maddie chuckles next to me, flicking open her Kindle. "What did I tell you?"

I STAND AND wait for my luggage to appear from the hole in the wall. Dante has already retrieved his and headed to the car waiting outside. Everyone else has gone, except for me.

324 ~ LUNA MASON

I jump out of my skin as arms wrap around my waist. As soon as that musky smell hits my nostrils, I know it's Luca.

He nuzzles his face into the crook of my neck and tickles me with his lips.

"That note. I meant it," he murmurs into my cheek.

"Hmm hmm," I hum, biting back the grin on my face.

"What are you doing back here?" I turn to face him.

"Wanted to steal a quick kiss from my girl." He leans forward and presses his lips to mine.

"Much better. I can't stand being in the same room as you and not being able to touch you. We're going to have to find a way to be together on this trip. It's been so long. I need to be inside you."

I know what he means.

No matter how much sexting or phone sex we do, it will never, ever beat the real deal. I'm just hoping after what happened at my dress fitting, he will stop backing me into a corner about why I'm marrying Dante. It's to protect everyone. I can't have him flipping out, murdering everyone, and risking their lives. His fiancée's family threatened a baby. I can't have that on my conscience. I'm protecting him, whether he likes it or not.

Leaning my forehead on his shoulder, I let myself enjoy the heat of his body pressing against mine. "I'm sure we can figure it out."

"I spent the entire flight on Google Maps pinpointing fuckable locations. I'm ready to go."

"No, you did not!" I hit his chest, and he pins my hand over his heart.

"You bet your ass I did. I'm desperate for my next Rosa fix. I'm even debating dragging you into those disabled toilets over there." Cupping my ass, he turns my body to the wall of bathroom doors.

"Eww. No thanks."

"Fine. Just be ready, gorgeous. I'm coming for you. Then I'll be coming inside you." He rolls his hips and presses his hard bulge against my side, proving how urgent he is already.

I clench my legs together, my body on fire for him.

"Just tell me the time and place." I push up to whisper in his ear, "I'm always wet for you. Even now, from one kiss, I'm soaked."

He pulls back and shakes his head.

"Fucking hell, Rosa," he groans.

The carousel beeps and starts moving, and my pink bag is hurled out.

Luca grabs it before it passes.

"Let's go, before I bend you over right now."

I let out a breath and look over to the bathrooms.

"You said no." He grins and shrugs at me, walking toward the exit.

I run after him and pull him back before he reaches the security door. We're safe in here. Everyone else has left through customs and they can't get back in.

I crash my lips over his. People complain behind us as we block the door, but I don't care. He deepens the kiss, I lean back, and he moans into my mouth. My arms encircle his neck as he cups my ass and squeezes.

We don't get many moments where we can pretend we're really just a couple in love.

Chapter Fifty-Seven
LUCA

Romano decided to inform me today of a last-minute shipment to New York, but the only guys I would trust to oversee the delivery are here, in Italy.

"Good morning, Luca. Is your fiancée waking you up at seven in the morning now?" Frankie's voice is filled with gravel. I'm pretty sure I just woke him up.

"Frankie, is Jax trained up enough to handle cargo?" I don't even say hello. Romano has my head all messed up with these surprise demands.

All I want to focus on is how to get some time alone with Rosa.

He groans. "I wouldn't recommend sending him in alone. He's still learning the ropes and can be a bit, well, heavy-handed."

Shit.

A woman's voice comes through from his end with a soft lilt of Italian. "Can't the boat be delayed? We're heading back stateside in just a few days." His words get muffled, like he's covering the phone.

"No, it can't be delayed. Romano said this was an important delivery. Nevermind. I'll take care of it." I hit end and stare at my phone.

Asshole. He's always getting laid.

I dial the only other person in the world I would trust, my brother.

"Luca, is everything okay?" Recently, every time we speak, Keller's voice is filled with concern.

"Yes, everything is good. But—"

He chuckles, cutting me off. "I knew something was coming."

"I need you to oversee a shipment tomorrow. Romano surprised me with it this morning."

I wouldn't drag him into this if I didn't have to. I let him dip his toes back in when it came to finding Maddie.

"Uhh, yeah, sure. How long are we talking? Sienna isn't feeling well again."

Shit. I pinch the bridge of my nose.

"No, don't worry, Frankie has Jax up to speed. I'm sure he will be fine."

He growls. "Don't be so fucking stupid, brother. I'll do it. You know I will do anything for you. Stop trying to do everything on your own."

I'm trying to keep him out of this mess.

"Plus, you know I'm good at my job."

That is true.

"Fine. I'll send Jax and my best recruits with you. Let me know when it's done. Just keep your eyes peeled. We can't trust Romano." It pisses me off he scheduled this when he knew I'd be out of the city.

"Anything else you need to tell me?"

"No," I reply quickly.

"I'll let you know when it's done. I had best go and sweet-talk my wife."

As soon as we cut the call, I lay on the bed, hands behind my head, and stare up at the ceiling fan, the warm breeze blowing through the sliding doors. My brother has it all—the wife, the kids—he's just so happy.

I want that.

Chapter Fifty-Eight
ROSA

Dante snores next to me and I lay there staring at the ceiling fan, sweating from the three layers of clothes I'm wearing. At least at home, I don't have to share a bed with him. But here, he said it would look odd to everyone if we did that, especially to Uncle Frankie. If he thinks I'm actually sleeping, letting myself be vulnerable near him, he has another thing coming. I'll just sleep on a couch during the day.

I've been desperate for more time with Luca. With every subtle hand brush, with every little grin he gives me, I need more.

I slowly roll onto my side and lean under the bed to grab my secret phone and hover over Luca's name.

> R
> Are you awake?

It's three a.m. I doubt it.

L

Do you want to play, tesoro?

Scooting myself to the edge of the bed, I tiptoe into the en suite, leaving it dark.

R

You know I do.

L

How far do you want to go?

L

Touch yourself, Rosa. Get yourself soaking and ready for me.

I bite my lip and slide my hand under my panties. Circling my clit nice and slow, just how Luca does it.

L

Good girl. I'm stroking my cock, imagining you spread out on the bed for me, dripping down your thighs.

R

I missed you today.

He's been locked away in the office overlooking the pool all day with Uncle Frankie, Grayson, and Dante. Despite not being *with* him, just being near him, even with Dante in the same building, makes it all more tolerable.

I slide a finger in and bite the inside of my cheek to stop the moan.

L

I swear I can hear your breathing. Fuck, Rosa.

God, all I want is this man.

L

This isn't enough. I need you, Rosa. I
want to fill you up and watch you come
apart under the stars. Meet me?

Shit, yes. I start shedding layers of clothes until I'm just in my bra and panties.

R

By the pool?

I quietly peer out of the bathroom. My heart is in my throat as Dante rolls onto his back. It stops me in my tracks as I watch his breathing return to normal.

God, I'd love to smother him with a pillow. It's crossed my mind.

Grabbing my black silk robe from the back of the door, I slip it on.

I tiptoe out of the room and rush down the stairs to the back door.

As my hand connects with the handle, I'm pulled backward. I squeeze my eyes shut and hope it's Luca.

My back connects with his body, his rock-hard cock presses against my ass. His warm breath beats against my sensitive neck.

"How have we waited this long? It's been killing me, watching you flit around through the window, flaunting that perfect body in those barely-there swimsuits," he whispers.

His fingers trail to the front of my robe and he unties it. Goosebumps erupt all over my skin as he skims down my stomach, reaching the hem of my thong.

"Are you ready for me, baby?"

I hum in response and nod, resting my head back against his chest.

332 ~ LUNA MASON

I feel empty the second he removes himself from me. He grabs my hand and opens the door to the courtyard.

The stars twinkle in the dark sky and the infinity pool in front of us lights up the gardens. They cast a soft glow behind him, creating a halo around his muscular body. He's like my very own dark angel.

He stops in his tracks and turns to face me. His eyes roam my body and he licks his lips.

"Swim shorts?" I say, raising a brow at him.

"You can't go for a middle of the night dip without them." His full lips turn up in one corner in a mischievous grin as he darts toward me, picking me up by the waist.

I giggle as he throws me over his shoulder, his hand slapping my bare ass cheek in time with every step closer to the pool's edge.

My hands brush over his chiseled abs as he slides me down his body.

Before I have time to register my feet being back on the ground, he laces his hand in my hair and pulls my face into his. Claiming my lips, he kisses me with pure passion. I wrap my hands around his neck and he moans into my mouth.

He breaks the kiss, cupping my cheeks.

He pulls down his swim trunks, his hard cock springing free. I take a step forward and wrap my fingers around his shaft, using my thumb to rub the piercing at the tip.

He throws his head back as I start to pump up and down. "You kill me, woman."

I drop to my knees on the damp ground, shrugging off the robe, giving him the view I know he wants.

I lick around the tip and pay special attention to the metal bar. His hands grip the back of my head, pushing his cock deeper down my throat.

"Take it all, Rosa."

He reaches the back of my throat, making tears pool in my eyes.

"My good girl," he grunts out above me.

I bob up and down, cupping his balls. His hips thrust, and he pounds in and out of my mouth.

"Fuck. Fuck, Rosa!" He erupts in my mouth. I dig my fingers into his thigh, but I don't swallow.

I suck all the way to the tip and release him and stand. He grins and bites his bottom lip, bringing his thumb to my lips and swiping across.

"You don't want to swallow today?" His eyebrows rise, and I shake my head.

His salty cum still swirls around in my mouth as he nods and drops to his knees before me. His hands band around my waist and he pulls me in.

"Go on, then, give it to me. My dirty girl." He tips his head back and opens his mouth. I lean over and spill the contents of him back into his mouth. His hands tighten around me as I do.

He pulls me down to my knees and then clambers over me until I'm lying on my back on the wet tiled floor.

I lift my hips as he rips off my thong and spreads me open. His mouth connects to my pussy. His hands cup my ass and raise me further in the air. The warm liquid from his mouth smothers my pussy. As I rest my legs on his shoulders, it takes everything I have not to scream out as his tongue fucks me.

"Shit, Luca."

He sucks on my clit in response.

"My come only goes in one place, baby. You've had your fun. Now it's my turn."

He pushes my legs apart and settles on top of me, resting

his forearms next to my head. Brushing his fingers along my throat, bringing his lips to mine.

The salty taste of his come lingers in my mouth.

"God, you have no idea how much I love you," he whispers between kisses.

I do, because I love him just as much.

He tenderly traces my jaw, bringing me back to those dazzling emerald eyes filled with love.

"Soon. I promise you. No more hiding. I will fix this. I will give you everything you've ever dreamed of."

I nod and hold back the tears.

Unless my fiancé drops dead, this will never happen. It's a dream, a fantasy. But Luca's the only thing that keeps me alive.

"Want to get in the water?" He flashes his teeth, giving me one of his delicious grins.

He clambers off me and holds out his hand. I accept, and he pulls me up and wraps me in his arms.

Tugging me behind him, he races us to the stairs. I follow him up to my waist in the warm water. He stops and turns, his eyes scanning my body with pure hunger.

He pulls me closer, taking my nipple in his mouth and sucking. "Can you be quiet, little one?"

I smile at my old nickname. "Only if you make me."

His teeth tighten on my breast in a playful nip. "That smart mouth of yours will get you in trouble."

I bite my lower lip; it's impossible to ignore my pussy throbbing, begging for attention.

"How much trouble?"

"If you want a spanking, all you have to do is ask. Is that next up on our list? What do you want to try today?"

DEVOTED ~ 335

After him slapping my ass earlier, I want it, but not as much as I want him inside of me.

"I've never done it in a pool," I say, taking his hand and kissing his palm before lowering his fingers to my neck.

"Woman. I'll choke you anywhere."

His hands lace around my throat lightly and my eyes go wide.

"Harder," I whisper. I avert my gaze to his arm and his eyes light up.

With that, he lifts me by the waist and submerges my body into the water. Wrapping my legs around him, I'm surprised to feel he's ready to go again.

He walks us over to the edge of the infinity pool, and he presses my back against the glass. I arch my body toward him, urging him to touch me.

His fingers connect to my clit and he rubs slowly before he slams himself into me. I can't scream past the firm grip he has on my throat.

"Oh God, Luca," I hiss.

He sticks out his lower lip in an exaggerated pout. "What did I say about your mouth?"

"More. Please, Luca." I rake my fingers down his sides, trying desperately to pull him into me.

"Fuck, I love it when you moan my name. I can't wait to hear you scream it again."

The water swishes around us as he thrusts in and out of me. I do everything in my power not to cry out.

His thumb curves under my jaw as his lips move over my shoulder. "Too much, you squeeze my arm. Okay?"

I nod.

"You know how this works, say it."

I bring my chin down to rest on his knuckle and bite my lower lip. "I understand, sir."

"Jesus," he grits out, thrusting harder into me.

His hand tightens, and I suck in a breath and close my eyes. Letting the splashing of the water take over as he fucks me.

He's all I can feel. Taking over every single one of my senses. My brain completely focuses on him and the pleasure he brings me. Taking my nipple in his mouth, he sucks, his fingers now wrapped so tightly around my throat I can't breathe. It's euphoric—the sensation that normally causes me panic has the complete opposite effect.

My legs tremble around him, and I arch my back, needing more pressure, making his dick hit that spot that sends me barreling over the edge.

"Baby, come for me," he growls into my ear.

Stars fill my vision as I explode around him.

"Fuck, fuck, fuck," he curses in my ear, spilling himself into me.

He unlaces his fingers and starts to pepper kisses on my neck. His cock is still twitching inside of me.

"You are so perfect, tesoro," he whispers.

And I smile, looking down as he continues his assault of delicate kisses that tingle my sensitive skin.

This is where I want to be, every day.

When I'm with him, nothing else matters. Not even the demons in my head.

With him I am free. "I love you, Luca."

He cups my jaw. "I love you, Rosa. I didn't believe it was possible to find a love like this. Unconditional, passionate, all-consuming. I can't live my life without you by my side.

Soon, we won't have to sneak around. I want you to wear my ring and be proud of me."

"Hey—I am proud of you." I cut him off and stroke his smooth chest.

"Rosa, I can't find any way out of this that doesn't start a war. I can't put my whole family in danger."

I sigh, resting my head against his sticky chest.

"But you are now my family, too. Once I end the Capris, we leave this life and start a new one."

If he can pull this off, I can wait. I will do what it takes. Once they are out of the picture, I can tell him the truth, and he will finally end Dante. My nightmare will be over.

There is hope.

Chapter Fifty-Nine
LUCA

A calm and collected Romano sits opposite me. With Frankie to my right, he pours us all a brandy. I pull my phone out and set it on the table, waiting for Keller's message. He left a couple of hours ago for the shipment.

My leg bobs up and down. I hate being stuck so far away just waiting on a call.

"Nice courtyard," I say, looking over at the sea view.

"You seem distracted." His voice is low as he lights up a cigar.

"Just overseeing your shipment. Hard to do in a different time zone, with little warning," I reply.

Frankie clears his throat next to me.

"Been a while since you've been in Italy, Franks."

"Franks," what the hell is that? I bite back a laugh.

Frankie crosses his leg casually. "No need to come back here. I got my revenge. I'm home now."

"How did you do it?" Romano asks. A tendril of smoke works its way around Romano's head. It almost looks like two horns erupting from his hair. Fitting, considering his daughter is a she-devil.

"Bullet between the eyes."

Romano scoffs, banging his hand on the table. "Boring. I tortured my brother for five whole days before he begged me to end his life, with a knife straight through the heart."

Romano turns to me. "You'd never kill your brother?" he asks.

"No." I'm not giving him more than that.

Our attention turns to my buzzing cell on the table. Romano smirks. "You might want to get that. And make sure we can all hear."

Shit.

I snatch it up. Relief floods through me when I see Keller's name.

"What the fuck was that, Luca?" he yells into the phone so loudly my speaker crackles.

"What?"

I stand, and Romano points at me. "Sit, boy. I want to listen."

My heart hammers. "Keller, what's going on?"

"What's going on? I just nearly had all my limbs blown off."

My eyes narrow at Romano, who's laughing.

"Is everyone okay? Are you okay?"

"I will be when I get on a plane to Italy and come fucking slit his throat." His tone drips with violence.

"Calm down, I'll straighten this out. Just go home."

"Go home? I have two dead bodies to take care of. O-fucking-kay?"

340 ~ LUNA MASON

I flick Frankie a look—he's giving Romano a death glare.

"Who?" I'm trying to remember who I assigned to help him.

Keller's voice gets quieter. "Jax, do a headcount. Who are we missing?" I can't hear the names, but at least Jax is well enough to help.

"Keller. Let Jax take care of this. I trust him. You just get home." I need him back with his family.

"We're having serious words when you get back, brother."

"We will." I slide my phone back into my pocket. "Fuck you," I spit out at Romano.

He sips on his brandy. "Maria doesn't share very well, Luca. You'll do well to remember that," he says calmly.

My heart stops. *Rosa.*

Frankie looks at me, confused, and I shake my head. Not now. I rack my brains. How would he even know? Maria hasn't been at the villa—there's no way.

"Frankie, we're leaving."

I storm out of the pavilion with Frankie hot on my tail.

"Maria is waiting for you by the front door, she's coming back with you," Romano calls out.

"Jesus Christ," I whisper. As if this day couldn't get any worse.

———

BY THE TIME we arrive back, it's dark. The villa is lit up; it's romantic, really. It makes me just want to find Rosa and sneak off again. My blood boils and I storm up the stairs.

"Where's our room?" Maria asks.

"Your room is down the hall." I point. "Last on the left." I can't even look at her.

DEVOTED ~ 341

Her door slams shut, and I jog down the stairs. I have to see Rosa.

I come to a halt at the landing when I hear shouting.

"You're going out dressed like a fucking whore, Rosa. That's why I'm pissed!" Dante roars.

Glass shatters, and I run to the kitchen, my hand resting on my gun. I have had enough of today, and I need to release some of this anger. Dante the douche just gave me my outlet.

"I'll go change." Her voice trembles.

Like hell she will.

When I come around the corner, I see a pale Rosa standing there, shaking, as he looms over with his fists clenched and half raised.

I clear my throat and as he spots me, his eyes go wide.

"Rosa, I need you to go upstairs for me."

She looks at me in horror and shakes her head. When she doesn't move, I ask again.

"Please." The word *baby* nearly slips from my tongue.

She sighs and drops her head. The back of my hand brushes hers as she walks past.

I can feel the heat of anger rush through me when I hear her bedroom door close.

"You think that's how we speak to women?" Not just any woman, my whole world.

I stalk toward him, and when he doesn't respond, I shout, "I'm your boss, and I'm asking you a question. Is that how you speak to women?"

"N-no. But she was—"

I hold up a finger.

"She was nothing." I cut him off. "That will be the last time you speak to her like that. Otherwise, you're done."

His jaw tics.

"The slut needs to be put in her place, boss."

No one talks about my Rosa like that.

I launch myself at him, pulling back my right fist and punching him square in the jaw.

He retracts his arm and throws a sloppy right hook that I easily duck away from. I lay into him until his nose cracks under my fist and blood splatters up my shirt.

Grabbing him by the scruff of the neck, I throw his head down onto the marble counter. Hefting the glass bottle next to me, I smash it next to his head.

Pinning him down, I hiss into his ear. "If I ever hear you call her that again, I will rip out your tongue."

"Luca!" Grayson shouts.

Holding Dante down, I look up at a shocked Grayson. And hold my hand with the broken bottle up to wave at him.

"All fine in here, just teaching him some rules."

He looks down at Dante with a frown. "I think he gets the message."

"Aw, don't ruin my fun, Dad."

Dante starts to say something, and I lift his head and slam it back on the counter. "Did I say you could speak?"

"Luca, just let him go." Grayson's eyes flick upstairs.

Rosa.

With an exasperated sigh, I toss Dante on the floor like the piece of trash he is.

"I suggest you stay away from me," I spit out in disgust and storm outside, grabbing a cigarette and lighting it.

"What the fuck happened?" Grayson asks.

"He smashed a glass at Rosa and called her a slut."

He leans back against the wall and crosses his arms. "You're in deep, aren't you?"

I laugh as I exhale the smoke.

"Whatever gave you that idea?" Taking a drag, I stare into the dark sky. "I love that woman so damn much I don't know what to do with myself anymore."

"Shit."

"Hmm. Shit, indeed. The worst part is, she loves me just as much. Yet here we are, both engaged to two of the worst creatures on the planet."

He grunts as he rubs his fingers over his wedding band. "Why don't you run?"

I pin him with a stare. "Oh, trust me. Every time I'm with her, I debate packing a bag and running as far away as I can."

"Well, what's stopping you?"

The fact that I make one slip-up, Romano has my family killed. I can't protect them if I run.

But I can't tell him that. So, instead, I raise a brow. "Am I that bad of a boss?"

He will know my plans soon enough, but right now isn't the time.

"What? No. I don't mean it like that." Grayson waves his hand and pushes from the wall. "I just know how it feels to want someone so bad you'd sacrifice everything for them."

"I can't leave, not yet. I have to finish what I started. I don't want this to all backfire on you, Keller, or your families. Sometimes, you have to sacrifice some of your own happiness for everyone else."

I take in another drag. I have to find a way to fix this before next weekend. I need the commissioner to agree to work with Frankie, to let him take the reins on removing the Capris. He's more than capable.

"Luca, you've given up your life for this mafia. Isn't it about time you take what's yours?"

344 ~ LUNA MASON

I laugh and toss the cigarette butt to the floor and stub it out with my Oxford.

"I can wish in one hand, shit in the other, and see which one fills up first. I'm going to go check on Rosa."

"You two are making it obvious." He gives me one of those concerned-father looks.

"Seriously? How? Was it her screaming my name in the pool last night that gave it away? Or the session we had outside of the villa earlier?"

His eyes go wide, replaced with an approving grin. "I'm impressed."

I shrug. "What can I say, we've spent the last few months sneaking around. We've gotten pretty damn good at it. A far sight better than you and Maddie ever were."

"Fuck off."

The door slides open, and Frankie storms through and slams it shut.

"Why the fuck did you nearly glass Dante to death?" he angrily whispers.

"I was protecting your niece, Frankie." I walk toward him, my nose inches from his face. "I suggest you stop questioning my actions, especially since I'm looking out for your family. I'm not in the mood." I barge past his shoulder and slip back inside.

"Don't. Not now, Frankie," Grayson warns.

Okay, progress. At least Grayson didn't punch him this time.

I breeze past Dante, who's still in the kitchen. He's holding an ice pack up to his swollen nose.

I don't give a shit what any of them think right now. I need to get to Rosa. I need to know what is going on.

After double-stepping up the stairs, I tap on the door.

DEVOTED ~ 345

Nothing. "Rosa, can I speak to you?" I keep my voice stern, in case anyone's listening.

Maria is in the room next door. The last thing I need is that vile creature coming out of her lair.

The door cracks open and relief washes over her features. I wrap her up in my arms, kicking the door shut.

If Dante does come back up, I need to know, so I leave my back against the door as I hold her.

I press a kiss to her glossy red lips and brush the stray strand of hair out of her face.

"Rosa, baby. What happened back there?"

Her face scrunches and she tries to look away, but I don't let her. "Come on, you can talk to me. Has he hurt you? Has he done this before?"

Her eyes go wide and she quickly recovers her expression. "N-no. I don't know what happened tonight. He's never behaved like this around me before."

Hmm.

"You swear?"

She nods, but it's not enough.

"Words, Rosa. Because I swear to God, if he has touched you, or even spoken to you like that before, I will go down there and stab him to death and let him bleed out in the pool."

She opens her mouth and snaps it back shut. She dips her head and nuzzles it into my chest.

"No. Luca, I swear. He's never done anything like this before."

So why did her voice just break?

"Hmm" is all I can say, my mind reeling.

"He loves me, Luca. He would never hurt me."

I tip her chin up so we're nose to nose. I don't see a way

out; that little glimmer of hope I had was wiped away today. It was that easy for Romano to get to Keller.

"No, baby. I love you. I am the only man who truly loves you. That piece of shit doesn't even deserve to breathe the same air as you. Today I realized something—no matter what I do, until the Capris are gone, I can't keep everyone safe. So I am speeding up my plans. Soon, this will be over."

"Really?" Her hands clasp together over my chest.

I nod. Once I land back in New York, I will put an end to this. I pull her tight, dropping a kiss to the top of her head. I will get her away from Dante. I will make sure my family is safe.

And then we are leaving.

Chapter Sixty
ROSA

I haven't seen Luca since we landed in New York. He said he had a plan, that soon we could leave. That's all the hope I need to get me through my time left with Dante.

"Rosa, get your ass out here!" His deep Italian voice sends shivers down my spine.

I jump off my bed and head to the living room.

"Is everything okay?" I fiddle with the rings on my fingers.

He stomps around the corner from the kitchen, his left eye completely swollen and purple.

"Dante?" Fear prickles the back of my neck.

A grin appears on his face as he towers over me. His nose brushes against my cheek, and I freeze.

His breath is laced with scotch. As it hits my nose, it makes me want to gag.

"Don't worry. Do you really think I want to touch Luca's sloppy seconds? You fucking whore!" he whispers with pure venom, and my heart stops.

He knows.

"Nothing to say for yourself?" He steps back, glancing at his watch. "Any second now—"

My ears ring. What has he done?

He winks at me as his phone rings.

He doesn't even say hello. "Do you have her?"

Everything crashes around me.

Eva.

He nods, cutting the call. "You did this to her."

"What have you done?" I scream. I lunge at him, whacking his hard abs with my fists.

He grabs hold of them so tightly the bones grind together. "I'm just keeping her safe for now. Until you marry me, then I might let her go. If you go anywhere near Luca again, I will kill her and then him. I might even film them both for you. There is no one to save you now. I might never have gotten to kill your dad, but I'd say my revenge is a lot sweeter this way."

He licks his lips and pushes me away so my back slams into the wall behind me. I watch in horror as he walks away, sits on the couch, his legs propped up on the coffee table, and turns on the TV.

As I tiptoe back to my room, tears fall freely down my cheeks. His words echo after me. "I wouldn't even bother texting Luca. If you so much as breathe a word of this to him, I'll make that call. Don't test me."

<hr />

HE WENT TO bed an hour ago, so it's safe to start my plan. I want to know who called. I need to find Eva before it's too late.

The last thing he would ever expect from me is to actually fight him.

I tiptoe out of my room, keeping all the lights off, and stand outside his door. Pressing my ear against the smooth wood, I listen for any movement.

As soon as I know he's asleep, I carefully sneak in. My heart is almost coming out of my chest.

You can do this, Rosa—for Eva and Luca.

It's dark, so I use the wall as a guide, heading for where his nightstand should be. I creep toward it until my foot connects with the wooden table.

I hold my breath and lightly brush my hands over the top, hunting for anything that resembles a phone. My fingers touch the glass of a screen, and I flick the silent button on the side and then remove the cable, bringing it to my chest before I pull so the light from the screen doesn't disturb him.

Once safely back in my room, I punch in the code I think I saw him use in Italy: one one one four five nine.

Nope.

One one one seven five nine.

It unlocks, and I gasp.

Now, with shaky hands, I pull up his call log.

Luca's name is there; so is Frankie's. The last two calls are from "M." Who the hell is M?

The time of the calls are eight thirty p.m. and then nine thirty p.m. The first time would be it.

I scroll over to his messages, clicking straight on the ones from M.

D

Keep her tied up. I have R where I want her. Our plan is still on.

M

Good work, D. Not long now. They will
suffer, don't worry.

I can barely see. I don't understand. I never did anything
to Dante. He is the one who should be suffering.

I pull up my phone and enter M's contact details. I can't
risk waking Dante. Before I swipe up the apps, I go to his
map app.

There is one recent search, an address only a block away. I
take a picture with my phone and then lock his.

He hasn't moved this whole time. I plug it back in, switch
it back on loud, and leave.

My head is spinning as I sink down on my bed.

I need Luca. I can't do this on my own. Maybe if I explain
everything, he and Frankie can fix this and find Eva.

No. That means starting a war, risking everyone.

It might just save my sister.

I leap from the bed, grabbing my overnight bag, and start
throwing in the contents of my wardrobe. Rifling through the
drawer, I look for my passport and my secret phone.

The door flies open. I turn and Dante stands with arms
crossed, watching me.

My phone clatters to the floor.

"Going somewhere?" His deep voice makes me want to
vomit.

I have no words. I can't speak as fear grips me.

He holds out his hand. "Give me that damn phone. You
can't be trusted, can you?"

I shake my head. It's my one lifeline.

"Rosa!" he roars, lunging at me.

He grabs me by the waist, throwing me up in the air, and I
bounce off the bed, crashing onto the floor.

"You won't be leaving this room until our wedding. One more wrong move, Eva dies," he spits out, snatching the phone from the floor and kicking my bag on his way out.

The door slams shut, making me jump.

I curl up into a ball on the floor, sobs erupting through me.

I've lost everything.

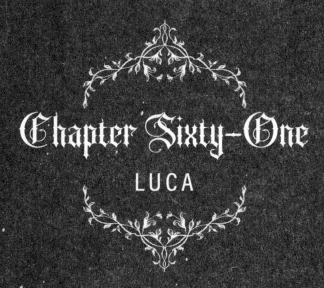

Chapter Sixty-One

LUCA

I hit dial on Rosa's number for the twentieth time. It cuts off on the second ring.

"Everything okay?" Frankie asks. I look up and he raises a brow.

"Fine," I lie.

"You said you wanted to speak to me?" He sits down heavily in the chair across from my desk.

I drop my forehead against my hand, propping myself up as I stare at the silent phone in front of me. "We need to kill Romano."

"Yes, we established that, Luca. In time, we will."

"I don't have time. I need it done before Rosa's wedding."

"I mean now."

He leans back and hooks his arm behind the corner of his seat. "And how do we plan on that? Fly out to Italy? Start a war over there? The commissioner made it clear it has to be done here."

"How do we get them here?" I knock back the scotch, hitting dial on Rosa's number again.

Frankie's lips thin. "Who the fuck do you keep calling?"

I swallow, unable to tell him.

"What is going on with you?" His eyes narrow.

"Just leave it. How do we get Romano here? You know him well enough. Kidnap Maria?" I'd love to have her gone.

He throws his head back and laughs. "No. We want him and his family on their own with minimal protection. Not an entire army."

"Okay, so the plan is—"

He cuts me off with an exasperated sigh.

"After Rosa's wedding. I invited the whole family, and they accepted. I also arranged a meeting at one of our units the next day. That will be when we make the hit, if you really can't wait any longer. We just have to hope he doesn't bring his whole organization. It depends on how much he trusts us."

My jaw tics. *Rosa's wedding.*

I need to do this before the wedding. So I have all of three days.

"When do they fly in?"

"Friday night. I've made it clear that the wedding will have high security. No one will be ruining Rosa's big day. If you want him gone, it's the night before or at the meeting."

"The night before it is, then." Only two more days. I can do that.

I hit dial on her number again. If I kill Romano before her wedding, she won't need to marry him. Everything will be out in the open. I'll deal with the consequences with Dante and Maria.

"I'll get everything arranged. This is one big fucking headache, Luca." The crisp lines of his suit twitch as he bounces his knee. A frown forms on his face as he looks at a text on his screen.

"I know. Once it's done, we have it all." I'll have everything I need: Rosa.

"Or, we start an all-out war in New York." He shrugs, clearly not giving a shit about that option.

The phone rings in my hand. My heart races until I see the caller ID. Dante.

"Hello," I greet him.

"Luca, I'm throwing a little pre-wedding party tomorrow night at Trance, the club where me and Rosa fell in love. Will you be there?"

I mute the call, mainly to get a hold on the seething anger that his words raise. "Did you know about a wedding party for Rosa tonight?"

He shakes his head. "No, I just had a text from Eva. She said she's gone to Italy to visit her aunt? I'm trying to get hold of my sister. She's not talking to me at the moment, though."

Why would Eva up and leave before her sister's wedding?

I hit unmute. "Yes, I'll be there. We all will."

"Great. See you then." Dante sounds particularly happy with my answer.

He cuts the call. That's the most he's ever said to me, let alone with such a cheery tone.

A bad feeling settles in my gut.

"Have you spoken to Rosa?" I question, swallowing past the lump in my throat.

"Not since Italy. I've been a bit preoccupied. Why?"

He leans forward, resting his elbows on his knees, studying me. "Please don't tell me you're doing all this to stop her wedding, Luca?"

I open my mouth to answer and can't. "And what if I say yes?"

He stands, shaking his head with disappointment. "Love is a weakness, Luca. You need to let her go, keep her out of this mess."

With that, he slams the door to my office.

Come on, Rosa, answer your phone.

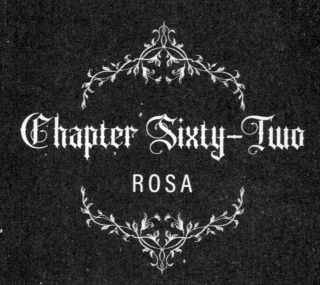

Chapter Sixty-Two
ROSA

We arrive at Trance, the club Dante originally stole me from, and head through the back exit. The bouncers nod at us to go into the VIP area. The whole area is filled with black and gold balloons, and the gold tables have black runners. Bottles of expensive champagne adorn every table.

I stare at the sign right in front of me. "Congratulations Rosa and Dante." And it makes me feel sick to my stomach.

The room is buzzing with people. It's just a swarm of them, all sipping their drinks and laughing away. Celebrating the end of my life.

He yanks my elbow. "Smile. Be the good fucking liar I know you are."

The clicking of stilettos overshadows the chatter, followed by an irritating voice, one I recognize. Maria.

"Dante, lovely to see you."

I watch as she wraps her arms around him for a friendly hug.

She turns to me, looking me up and down and turning back to Dante. *Oh my god, is she M?*

I scan the room, searching for the one person who can get me through this. Luca.

My eyes lock with his as he leans against the bar. He nods at me, and I blush. I watch as he gives his order to the bartender, not taking his gaze off me as he does.

Anger flashes over his face as he looks past me.

"Rosa," Dante hisses behind me. He bends down so his head rests on my shoulder, his hands locked on my hips. I stand still, not even breathing.

I push myself out of his hold and he drags me back into him, my back hitting against his hard chest. He laughs.

"Silly, silly girl."

He thrusts a phone into my hand. "Press play, baby girl."

The room starts to spin as I hit the little triangle.

A flash of white and copper is all I see at first. The view pulls back and focuses, making my stomach drop.

The bare body of my sister, mottled with marks and bruises. Her red hair is a wild mess down her back as she sits reversed on a wooden chair. Naked and tied.

She begins thrashing against her ropes, turning her face to reveal her mouth covered with white fabric. I can't take my eyes off the blood dripping from her forehead and the tears streaming down her face. Bile burns in my throat as Dante's face fills the screen. "Say hi to your big sis, Eva." He grins into the camera, yanking off her gag.

"Rosa!" Her voice is hoarse and cracks as she screams.

I suck in a breath as the camera zooms closer. Her face is

full of pure fear as Dante swipes his fingers across her swollen lips.

"I'll be back for you later, gorgeous."

"Fuck you," she spits back at him.

I gasp as he slaps her across the face, making me drop the phone to the floor.

"You monster!" I turn to him. "What have you done? Why are you doing this?"

He chuckles, bending down and collecting his phone.

I hit my fists against his chest, which vibrates as he laughs at me.

I can barely see straight. My heart beats at a hundred miles an hour and my chest is heaving.

"You asshole. I hate you."

He wraps his rough hands around my wrist and holds them up to restrain me.

"This is no way to speak to your fiancé." He pulls me into him. "Calm the fuck down."

I push against him, and he holds me to him, my face squashed against his black shirt, blocking my airway.

"I warned you, Rosa. I told you what I would do. This is all your fault; everything that has happened to you has always been the consequences of your own actions."

"Why did you rape me?" I barely manage to get my words out.

"Let's just say your father took something from me. It was only fair I took something from him. You. You enjoyed it. I remember. I still have the claw marks on my chest from your nails. Once I've had you checked over and clean, I'll be taking you again. Every day until the day you die."

"I can't breathe." I struggle to even choke the words out.

He releases me, and I stumble backward, hitting the leather booth behind me.

My lungs burn as I claw at my chest, pulling at my dress, trying to loosen the constricting fabric. "I hate you. I will never love you."

He towers over me, a darkness consuming his eyes. "And I'm here to torment you for the rest of your life."

Clutching onto the seat, I stumble around the front of it, away from him.

My throat is closing in on me, my ears are pounding, and as I look up, everyone starts to swirl into one blur.

The room tips as I fall back onto the cool bench, gasping as stars burst behind my eyes.

Chapter Sixty-Three
LUCA

The bartender slides over my scotch. I lean on the bar and watch Rosa and Dante's interaction.

My blood boils when his hand wraps around her waist. I grip my glass, imagining it's his neck. It takes everything in me to stop myself from going over and doing it for real. Maria reappears at my side, but I don't take my eyes off Rosa.

"What's going on over there?" Maria's voice makes me squeeze harder on the glass.

I glance at her, but by the time I look back, Rosa is holding on to the booth and her face is deathly pale.

When I step toward Rosa, Maria's hand wraps around my arm. "It's just a little lover's tiff, darling. She's a big girl. Let her handle it."

Rosa's rubbing along her neck and chest. She looks like she's going to be sick.

I can't see what she's saying.

DEVOTED ~ 361

I take a step forward, and Maria's hand tugs on my wrist.

"Don't you dare," I growl.

"You don't want to do this, Luca. Just stand here like a good boy and watch. I think it's time you show your alliance to our family." Her nails dig into my arm.

Shaking off her claw, I stride closer to eavesdrop more easily.

I watch as Maddie waddles over to Rosa and wraps her arms around her shoulders. Sienna follows closely behind. Rosa doesn't move. Her legs are spasming up and down on the seat, and I can't see her face anymore.

"Rosa, do you need me to call an ambulance?" Maddie asks in a soft voice, stroking her shoulder.

Ambulance.

"I-I can't—" She can barely speak.

Romano's threat looms over me. I can feel Maria's gaze burning into the back of my head.

If I do this, that will be the final nail in the coffin.

People start to crowd around her. Dante wades through to tower over her.

"Get up and stop fucking embarrassing me, Rosa," Dante spits out as he leans over and smacks her outstretched foot.

I see red. My decision is made.

That asshole never deserved her.

"Get the fuck out. Everyone. Now!" I shout, my nostrils flaring as I push through bodies. The room goes silent except for the sounds of Rosa's sobs, stabbing me in the heart.

I zero in on Dante.

"Everyone. Including you. Out!" I point at him, and he steps in front of Rosa, blocking my view.

The room turns into panic as people rush out of the exit. I look up and spot Maria watching my every move.

362 ~ LUNA MASON

Ignoring her, I turn to the three women huddling in the seat. "Maddie, Sienna, I've got this." As they get out of the way, I start to reach for Rosa.

Dante steps in front of me.

"She's my fiancée, my problem. Just because you've been fucking her doesn't mean you own her. She belongs to me, Luca."

He tugs her up by the wrist and she stumbles.

Red swims into my vision. I pull the gun from my waistband and press it firmly into his chest.

"Get your hands off her. Now. If you don't remove them, I'll happily do it for you, right before lodging this bullet into your chest. She's mine and always has been. Do you understand me?"

Dante doesn't move. He holds her arm up like she's a marionette, and she weakly hangs from him. Her eyes roll in her head and her rapid breathing is a snare drum beat in my ears.

A slow smile curves up the side of his scarred lips before he tosses her at me.

I barely catch her as she falls limply against me.

"I will always own her. She'll come back to me. You just watch." He straightens out his jacket and walks away.

As I slide to the floor with Rosa cradled across my lap, I glance up in time to see Maria shake her head, an evil grin on her face as she saunters behind Dante.

Rosa's wheezing brings me back to her.

My gun clatters against the wooden floor as I pull her into me.

Gently caressing her face, I turn her so I can look closely. "Rosa, baby. It's me, Luca."

Nothing.

"You're okay, tesoro. I promise. Can you do some breathing with me?"

DEVOTED ~ 363

She nods and relief fills me. I lift her a little higher so she's sitting on my thigh, wrapping her firmly with my arm. With my other hand, I start tracing a square lightly around her kneecap.

"Okay, let's do a breath in for four and out for four. Slowly. Ready?"

Taking a deep inhale, I do the same.

"One, two, three, four. Hold, two three, four. Now keep doing that for me baby, you're doing great."

I feel her chest expand against my hand.

"Good girl."

I pull back slightly and cup her cheeks in my hands. Her bloodshot eyes are streaming with tears, but she's still as beautiful as ever.

Chasing away the droplets with the pads of my thumbs, she nuzzles against my hand.

"Do you feel better?" I whisper.

She bites her lip.

"Can you just hold me?" Her voice quivers.

"You know I'll do anything for you."

Including sacrificing my own family. A sliver of ice runs up my spine. I'll deal with the consequences of this later.

Resting my chin on the top of her head, I let that sweet coconut scent fill my senses.

"Tell me what's going on, Rosa. Please, let me in."

I'm hesitant to push her, but something is terribly wrong, and I need to know.

She pauses, her hand rests against my heart as she looks up at me. "Luca, what about Maria?"

I clench my jaw. "She knows, everyone knows, Rosa."

Fear takes over her face. "But—"

I wipe away another tear from her cheek. "We have it covered."

Well, we have a plan. One very much reliant on Rosa's wedding. Right now, I don't care. We will kill Romano, and she will be safe.

"No, Luca, it's okay. I can tell Dante it was a mistake, that I still want to marry him. You don't understand. I have to marry him." Her words come out so fast it takes me a moment to comprehend.

"Not happening."

"Luca, it has to. You can't protect me." She hiccups.

I can feel the tension rolling off her, so I hug her and hold her tight.

"I will lay down my life for you."

She stiffens in my arms. I stroke my fingers along her back in small circles.

"Luca, I need to—"

"I love you, Rosa. I promised you we would fight, and now we have to. We are going to have to fight with everything."

I bring my nose to touch hers. "Rosa, you are mine. I will protect you and your family with everything I have. I love you. I need you to fight with me. Can you do that for me?"

My breath sticks in my lungs, waiting for her to reply.

In a tiny voice, she says the words I was hoping for. "I will fight."

I press my lips against hers and she kisses me back as she wraps her arms around my neck.

"I love you, Luca." She smiles.

I know I've made the right choice.

That's why I'm doing this, to see that goddamn smile, every day.

Chapter Sixty-Four
ROSA

The silence in the room is deafening. I take his tattooed hand, mine still shaking like a leaf. He pulls me to my feet, grabbing my hips to steady me.

"Endgame time," he whispers in my ear.

I slide my hand from under his and take off the engagement ring that's been weighing me down for weeks to hurl it onto the floor.

"Our endgame."

Butterflies erupt in my stomach as the pad of his thumb circles my wrist. We walk over to his friends, and he pulls me possessively to his side. Maddie wipes away her tears as Grayson cuddles her into him. Keller's holding Sienna to his left, both friends not taking their eyes off Luca.

"Well, that was quite the performance, brother," Keller chuckles, and Sienna elbows him in the ribs. I can't help but laugh.

"He means, welcome to the family." Sienna beams.

Maddie rushes over, wrapping me up in a bear hug as best she can with her belly bump. "Everything will be okay, Rosa. We will do everything we can for you two."

"Thank you." The comfort she shares brings fresh tears to my eyes.

"When this all dies down, we will do that movie night, I promise."

I sniffle. "I'd love that."

Grayson clears his throat. "Luca, what is the plan now?"

I stiffen, completely forgetting about Maria and the danger we've just put everyone in. Luca squeezes my hand, offering a calm support as I lean against him. It's as if the man can read my every thought.

"Keller, I need you to take the girls and kids to the safehouse. Do not leave there until I tell you. I need to tell you all the truth about what is going on.

"I was marrying Maria to protect you. Romano threatened Darcy—well, all of you, actually. He wants my ports to distribute them out in the States. Marrying Maria solidified the alliance, tying me to them. The explosion at the docks, that was because she was upset about Rosa. So now, you're all in danger. I'm so sorry."

I wrap my arms around his waist, burying my face into his chest. Sienna gasps, and Keller pulls her into him.

"I'm going to fucking kill him," he seethes, his fists clench.

"No." Luca cuts him off. "I will fix this. You are going to look after our family. Protect them. I'm not risking you, and it's not up for discussion. I have a plan. Well, had. We take out Romano tomorrow."

"Why didn't you tell me?" Grayson runs a hand over his face, pressing a kiss to Maddie's head. Her eyes brim with tears as she folds her arms over her protruding belly. My heart breaks for her. This whole mess means she's going to be in a safehouse while her husband is out fighting, because of me. When she could give birth at any moment.

I'm sorry, I mouth to her.

She shakes her head. "Don't be silly."

Luca sighs. "I thought I could protect you if I married Maria. Frankie and I planned to take Romano down after the wedding and take his guns with us."

"Frankie?" Grayson's face turns red as anger shadows his features. "You trusted Frankie?" he spits.

Luca steps forward and I release my hold. He squares up to Grayson until there are only inches separating their noses.

"Yes. I trusted Frankie. I did what I thought was best. I sacrificed my happiness to try and protect all of you. Now can you get out of your head, forget about Frankie, and help me end this?" Luca sets his arms on Grayson's shoulders. The blond giant relaxes as he squeezes his eyes shut.

"Fuck." He looks over to his wife and she smiles at him, not hiding the pain on her face.

What have I done?

Panic threatens to close my throat off. I have to get to my sister. I remember the words Dante threatened me with. That he would kill Luca and Eva.

I suck in a breath. "If I go back to Dante and explain. I could lie? Say that you just knew how to help me from before? If I still marry him, Maria might not be as mad?"

Luca's head snaps around with fury as he takes my face in both of his hands. "Not happening, Rosa. I won't let you near that man again. I need you to fight, goddammit. Please, Rosa, I need you to fight for us. That strength I know is in there, I've seen it. We are so close to our forever, tesoro." He kisses the top of my head.

"I need to get my sister," I whisper.

He pulls back. "She's in Italy?"

"Oh, uhh—she's home. She's staying with a friend," I stammer. My nails dig into my palm. I almost told him. Dante would kill us all if he found out.

"We'll get her." He pulls me tight against his muscular frame. "Grayson, with me. We're taking Rosa to Eva. We will get her and drop them off at the safehouse. Then, we get Frankie, and we come up with a plan. We end this."

Grayson nods, his face stern as he turns to Maddie. "I'll be back soon, sunshine. I promise you. I love you and you—" He bends and places a kiss on her stomach. Her cheeks go bright red. She bites down on her lip, mascara running down her cheeks.

"Luca?" I look up at him, watching his friends, expressionless. "I'm scared. I don't want you to leave me at the safehouse. I want to come with you."

He smiles down at me. "It shouldn't be for long. I'll check in on you every day. Once this is over, we're free, Rosa. Just remember that." He brings my hand up to his mouth and kisses my ring finger.

His eyes sparkle. "And then I will deliver you to our new world, tesoro. I just have to burn it down first."

"I need my phone so I can get a hold of Eva." Once we get out of here and everyone is at the safehouse, I will tell him everything. I have the address on that phone, I just need to find it.

Chapter Sixty-Five

LUCA

We sit in the car outside Rosa's after I checked to make sure it was empty. She said she needed a few minutes to gather her things. I hand Grayson a cigarette and take a drag off of mine.

"What's the plan, boss?" Grayson asks, looking out the window.

"I take out Romano." I lean my head back, the pressure in my temples almost unbearable.

"Commissioner O'Reilly is on board. He's taking care of the cleanup. It will be like the Capri family never existed. They're all staying a few blocks away; they came for Rosa's wedding. I say we blow the fucking house up." The thought of a giant fireball ending their reign makes me a little giddy.

"Now that, I can get behind," he chuckles.

This whole thing has turned to shit. "I'm sorry, Grayson."

"It's fine, Luca. I understand."

370 ~ LUNA MASON

"Once this is over, I'm out. I can't do this anymore. I just want to sail away with Rosa. Far enough away I won't hurt my family anymore."

"Luca, I'm a big boy. It's the mafia. I knew what I was signing up for. As long as Maddie and my kids never end up in the firing line, it's okay. You aren't going anywhere."

I couldn't think of anything better than a quiet life with my girl.

I just hope I can pull this off. If I do, then we're out of here, or I will die trying.

My phone starts ringing in my jacket, and I frown at the name that pops up on the screen.

"Enzo?"

"Luca. There's been a police report of a disturbance at your mom's. Scanners are suggesting a break-in. Cops haven't arrived at the scene yet. Want me to wipe it and send my guys?" I can hear him typing in the background.

Fuck. The blood drains from my face.

"I'm heading there now. Yeah, clear it."

"On it." He doesn't say goodbye before the line clicks.

"What happened?" Grayson asks.

"My mom. There's been a break-in." Cold dread fills me.

"Shit," Grayson hisses.

Rosa. Shit. I run up the stairs to her apartment and find her throwing clothes around her room, the drawers hanging open and empty.

"Baby, I need to go to my mom's. There's been a break-in. Are you ready?" Panic throws my words out in a jumble.

"Oh God, is she okay?" Her hand flies to her neck and her face pales.

"I don't know." I swallow down the bile in my throat.

"I can't find my phone. I need it to call Eva. Go check on

DEVOTED ~ 371

your mom then come back here. I'll be fine." She digs into her closet, pulling dresses from the hangars.

"I'm not leaving you."

Grayson clears his throat behind me. "I can't get hold of your mom."

Shit.

"Okay. Rosa. Lock the doors. If you need me, you call Grayson from this one." I hand her my phone. "The password spells out *Rosa*—7072. I won't be long. I love you, baby."

"I love you, too, Luca." She rushes to me and wraps her arms around my waist.

I drop her a kiss and sprint back to the car, Grayson at my side. This can't be happening. I speed off into traffic, running red lights and gripping the steering wheel until my knuckles turn white.

I'm praying to God it's just a break-in. That she's at Zumba or whatever it is she goes to all the time.

I pull up outside her house, unholstering my gun. I kick open the little gate and head to the side entrance. I motion to Grayson to go check the back.

He nods and heads off around the side of the house.

My feet crunch on the glass of broken picture frames. I bend down and pick up the photo that's face down on the floor. My heart is in my throat as I turn it around. It's me, Keller, and Mom on the day of Keller's wedding in Vegas.

I creep toward the living room. Spotting the steaming cup of coffee placed on her little table in the kitchen, I know she was just here.

When I step around the corner, my gun clatters to the floor.

No.

No. No. No.

Bending over, I violently throw up at the sight. It feels like every internal organ is trying to tear loose and flee my body.

I can't look. I smash my fists into the nearest wall, my vision blurring from the pain.

"Fuck!" I scream at the top of my lungs.

I rush toward her and slide to a stop on my knees into a pool of blood smeared across her wooden floor. Her shirt is split and a dark hollow is opened in the center of her chest. My trembling hands pick up the red mass resting on top.

Her fucking heart. The monsters ripped it right out of her. I slump over her, grabbing at my shirt. I can't breathe; the metallic smell is suffocating me.

The clock on the wall ticks, and I sit there, staring. Her mouth is open, her gray hair covered in blood. Sobs sear painfully through me.

"Mom, no. Not you."

I pull her lifeless body onto my lap.

Resting my head against hers, I hurt so badly, I can't even see.

"I'm so sorry," I repeat over and over again. Squeezing her against me, I rock back and forth.

What have I done?

The front door crashes open, and I don't even flinch. I'm too numb. I don't care who walks through.

"Luca." Grayson's voice echoes through the room until he steps through the kitchen. "Shit," he mutters when he sees me.

I can't even look at him.

"Luca. We need to go," he says quietly.

"No. I can't leave her. Not like this." I clutch her tighter against me, her cold skin pressing against my cheek.

"Luca. Look at me." He grabs my shoulder, but I refuse to turn.

She's still a little bit warm. There is still some life there before she leaves me completely.

"We can't stay here. Luca, it's not safe. I'm so fucking sorry." Tears brim in his eyes.

"No. Just leave me here." I look back at Mom, uncontrollable tears pouring from me. "I love you, Mom," I sob.

"Luca. Please." He snatches my gun from the floor.

He crouches back down and takes her body from my lap.

My hands lay on my knees helplessly, covered in her blood. "I-I did this. I killed my own mom."

"No, you didn't. These assholes will pay, I promise you. Right now, we need to leave. The police are on their way, and we have to get back for Rosa." He pulls me up, and I stumble. Nausea washes over me in waves.

Grayson grabs me. "I've got you."

I follow blindly. I can't even find the strength to look up. There is only one person I need right now.

"Take me to Rosa."

Chapter Sixty-Six
ROSA

Grayson's number goes to voicemail again. My phone that was hidden in Dante's room now sits in my hands. I stare at the map of the address I found on Dante's phone.

My leg bounces up and down. It's less than a ten-minute walk. Panic rises as I wonder if something happened to Luca. What if Eva is already dead?

I can't just sit here.

I put Luca's cell back on the table next to my passport, slip on my sneakers, and head out.

It's a normal, middle-class-looking house with a little gate at the front. The address matches. I was expecting a warehouse or something creepy-looking. All the lights are out and the blinds are down.

The bolt on the gate slips easily, and I walk hastily to the front door. My hand wraps around the handle. *Please don't be locked.*

I pull down and the door swings in.

There is a staircase in front of me and a door to my left. I ignore the fear building inside of me and open it. I let out a sigh of relief as I turn on the lights and discover an empty room stacked with moving boxes.

Down the hallway, I come across the next white door. I open this and, again, click the light on.

"Hello, baby girl."

I'm frozen with fear. I can't even bring myself to scream. Shaking from the shock, I turn and run as fast as I can, my lungs burning as I reach the front door.

His heavy footsteps get louder as he chases me.

"You can't run from me," he laughs.

I launch myself down the steps and sprint out of the gate, keeping my eyes focused in front of me. The dim streetlights are the only source of light as I race down the street.

My scalp burns as my ponytail is nearly jerked from my head. As I smash into him, he wraps his arms around my torso. I kick and flail in his grip. "Get off me! Someone help!" I scream as loud as I can.

His hand clamps over my nose and mouth.

"Shut the fuck up, you stupid bitch," he whispers.

He drags me back toward the house even as I fight him with everything I have. He grasps my elbows painfully and pushes my back onto the metal of the car.

"Luca can't save you. He will be a little busy right about now. He won't have time for poor little Rosa."

"What have you done, Dante?" Agony rips through me at the thought that he may be hurt.

He lets out a malicious laugh before tossing me into the back seat. It's only then, when he slides into the driver's seat and the lights are on in the car, I see the dried crimson stains on his shirt and hands.

I muffle my cries with the back of my hand.

"Time to go home. We have a wedding tomorrow, and you had best get your beauty sleep."

The forever that was just in my grasp slips away into a nightmare.

Chapter Sixty-Seven
ROSA

"Someone is here for you," Dante calls out from the living room. I peer out of my bedroom and find him grinning by my door.

"Who?"

Please don't be Luca.

"The soon to be dead ex-boyfriend of my wife. Now go out there, break his heart, and tell him to come to the wedding tomorrow. I want to feel his pain. I want to watch him suffer before he dies."

"No."

"No? Okay, instead, I'll give you the location of Eva's dead body as a wedding present tomorrow. Up to you." He shrugs with a smug grin.

He holds his phone up so I can see the screen. "Make your choice."

He presses the call button on "M." The blood drains from me. A familiar high-pitched female voice answers the call.

"Oh, hello, big brother."

My mouth falls open—Maria. Hearing her voice is a kick to the gut.

The knocking at the door gets louder. How the hell am I going to do this to Luca? I have to get him to believe me.

I snatch the phone out of Dante's hand and end the connection. "I'll do it."

"Off you go, then. If anything happens to me, Eva dies, too. Remember that."

His deep laugh follows me as I approach the front door. I have to do this to save Luca.

I pull open the door and gasp, taking in the broken man before me. His unbuttoned white shirt is smothered in blood, his eyes are bloodshot. I lean forward and swipe a stray tear from his cheek.

"Luca," I whisper.

"Mom's gone, Rosa."

I wrap my arms around him. Screw Dante, he won't see in the hallway, anyway. I'm devastated for Luca. I know how much he loves his mom and the lengths he will go to protect his family. I fight back my own tears, threatening to explode. This proves just how dangerous Dante is. No matter how much I want to tell Luca the truth, I can't.

There is no way out.

"I'm so sorry, Luca." My fiancé murdered his mom. Because of me.

His brows furrow. "We need to go, Rosa. Grab your bags."

He reaches his fingers to lace through mine, but I pull my hand back.

"Rosa?"

"I can't." I suck in a breath, ready to perform like my life depends on it.

"Tonight proves exactly why we can't leave. It was your *mom*, Luca. What if it's Darcy next? We will never forgive ourselves. So I will be marrying Dante tomorrow—"

"No—"

I hold up my finger to cut him off, fighting every urge to break down.

"This stops, now. Before anyone else gets hurt. Where are we going, Luca? Jetting off into the sun and leaving everyone else here to deal with our mess? That isn't you. You fight. Well, right now, I need you to do just that. Just not for me anymore." My voice breaks, and I try to pull myself together. I don't have any fight left in me.

His jaw clenches as he searches my face. "I'm not leaving without you, Rosa. It's not happening."

I grab his hands, holding them in mine.

"You have to." My stomach rolls, knowing I'm holding back the truth from him. "You need to go out there, get your revenge. Maria, Romano, all of them, need to pay. You are going to come to my wedding tomorrow—"

His head comes up. "No."

"You said you would always do anything for me, right?"

"Not this," he whispers.

"Luca, look at me." Warm tears roll down my face; I plead with him without saying the words. "Please, Luca."

His hands rub up my arms, and I flinch when he reaches my tender biceps.

"If you can't do this, we have no future. I need you to trust me for one last time to protect our family. Leave, go and be with your brother, with Frankie."

I nod slowly, trying to get the message across. I drop his name in. If anyone can save us, it's Frankie.

Dante will no doubt be listening to my every word, waiting to make that call.

"I can't just leave you here, Rosa." His nostrils flare.

I go up on my tiptoes, pressing a soft kiss to his stubble. I close my eyes, hating the final blow I am about to make. I will make this believable to Dante—I have to.

"I belong to Dante, Luca. I always have. I need you to witness our marriage, to prove to everyone we are over, that it never meant anything. You have to let me go."

"Like fuck I do," he growls, looking past me into the house.

I place his hand over my erratic heart.

"I'm sorry, Luca." I release his hands and step back, propping myself up against the door for support.

"Well, well, well, who do we have here?"

I go stiff as Dante snakes his hand around my waist, pulling me into his side.

"Go to hell," Luca snarls.

His arm goes behind his back. Shit, his gun. Remembering Dante's threat, I jump out of his hold and grab Luca's elbow tight. He frowns at me.

"Don't, Luca." I keep my tone firm. "Go." I point at the stairs and nod toward them.

Dante laughs behind us. I swear, once Eva is free, once everyone knows the truth, he is going to have a painful death. That in itself keeps me going.

"Rosa, move," Luca growls.

I stay firmly in place between the two of them.

"No. It's over. We are done, Luca."

His green eyes stare into my soul. This man knows me

better than anyone. He knows how much I love him. I have to trust he will know something is wrong. At least, I hope so.

"Endgame, Rosa," he whispers.

That one word offers me hope as I watch him walk away from me.

Chapter Sixty-Eight
LUCA

"Luca. Speak to me." I can hear Grayson talking; I just don't have it in me to respond. I'm dead on the inside. What was that?

"I am going to rip every single one of those assholes limb from limb for this. We have to get Rosa out of there. Call Frankie, get him to meet us," I say through gritted teeth.

"Already done. He's on his way. We have to be clever here."

He's right. But I don't care. First up, I want to slice Maria's throat. And watch as the life drains from her body, followed swiftly by Dante. I can't face Keller. I can't be the one to tear his heart out, too.

"Fuck!" I slam my fist on the console in front of me.

"Luca. Rosa is alive, the wedding is going ahead, right? He has a motive for this wedding, we know this. So we go back to the house, fill Frankie in, plan our next move. You've seen what they're capable of. Rosa played the game, Luca. She did you proud. She didn't mean anything she said. Get your head back."

She might not have, but it hurt, that's for sure.

"I want to kill him, Grayson." My hands shake with rage. What if he's hurting her? What if I can't save her?

"You will. Doing anything right now puts her in even more danger. Trust me, I dealt with my fair share of hostage situations." Grayson glances over as he turns the car into the driveway of the safe house.

My throat starts to close up. I can't breathe.

He reaches out and puts his hand on my shoulder. "Luca. Calm down."

I can barely hear him. I keep pulling at the door and swivel in my seat to start kicking at it.

"Fuck," Grayson shouts.

I jolt forward as the car comes to an abrupt stop. He disappears out of the driver's side. My door flies open, and Grayson grips my arm and pulls me out of the car.

"Come on, let's get you cleaned up and a glass of scotch."

He releases me and I look down at my shaking, bloodstained hands.

Mom.

The contents of my stomach rise up into my throat. I'm so dizzy. I turn away from Grayson and throw up all over the pavement.

He pats me on the back. "It's okay, Luca."

"This is not okay," I croak out.

My world is crumbling.

He grabs my arm. "Come on."

He guides me past the armed guards outside the safe house. Leading us into the kitchen, he pulls out a white leather seat at the dining table. The house is eerily quiet. Everyone must be asleep.

Sitting heavily, I lean forward. My head falls into my

hands and my fingers knot at my hair. The memory of her lying there in a pool of blood is on repeat in my mind.

"Grayson? Is that you?" Maddie whispers.

"In here, sunshine," he calls back.

She stops dead in her tracks, "Luca, oh my God. What happened?" she cries, rushing toward me.

I shake my head soundlessly. I can't say the words. If I do, that means she's truly gone.

Grayson places a large glass of scotch in front of me, and I tip my head, downing the contents in one burning swallow.

Grayson touches her hip gently. "Baby, can you go get Keller for me?"

It's like I'm living in someone else's body. I'm here. But I'm not.

Maddie leaves the room and Grayson sits next to me, bringing the bottle of scotch. I hold my glass out to him and he pours me another.

I don't know how many I get through. But it still hurts, so I clearly need more.

"Grayson, what's going on?" Keller's deep voice echoes through the house. "Fuck. Luca. Tell me."

He takes the seat next to me as I take a deep breath. "Mom is dead, Keller. She's gone." My voice cracks.

"No," he says bluntly.

Keller looks between Grayson and me. The realization hits when he spots the blood on my shirt.

My heart fractures as he screams, throwing the bottle of scotch against the wall.

"I'm going to kill them!" He kicks the chair back and paces behind me.

I laugh. I actually laugh.

I'm breaking everyone around me, and I can't stop it.

DEVOTED ~ 385

"Keller. Sit," Grayson warns in his military tone, running a hand through his hair.

"Grab another bottle of scotch, Grayson." Resting my elbows on the table, my head in my hands, I let the tears erupt.

All I can see is her.

Grayson pours another drink.

"The bottle, not a glass." I put my hand out.

"No. We don't have time right now. Frankie will be here any second. Getting drunk isn't the answer. I'm sorry to both of you. But if you mess this up, you could lose Rosa. I'm not letting that happen." Grayson stands like a statue, the scotch firmly in his hand.

Keller firmly grips my shoulder. I can see the tears brimming in his eyes, but he holds them back. "I don't care what I have to do, brother. I will help you get her back and avenge Mom's death."

How is he even still looking at me right now? Why hasn't he beaten the shit out of me? This is all my fault.

"If you even say what I think you're going to, Luca, I will knock you the fuck out. You didn't do this." Keller pats my back and downs his scotch.

I look down at the crusty blood on my hands. "I'm going to shower."

———————◆———————

FRANKIE REACTED AS well as expected. Grayson filled him in while I cleaned up. By the time I get downstairs, glass shards cover the kitchen floor. That second bottle of scotch is nowhere to be seen.

Frankie's head snaps up as I step into the room, a darkness flashing across his features.

"You should have told me, Luca. A long time ago. If any-thing happens to Rosa—" He storms toward me with his fists balled in front of him.

I hold up my hand. "If anything happens to Rosa, I give you full permission to kill me, Frankie. Now, sit down and help us figure this out. We only have a few hours before the wedding. Dante is holding something pretty big over her head, I'm assuming, so we have to play this the right way."

I take my seat next to Keller. Frankie sits opposite me. "Tell me everything Rosa said to you. She's a smart girl, she always has been."

She is, but she is also vulnerable, haunted by her past. I tell him word for word. He leans back and I can see his master-mind working.

"She needs you at that wedding for a reason, Luca. And we need Romano and Maria there."

He rests his elbows on the table. I light up another cigarette.

"I'll speak to Romano. I'll beg him to get Maria to take you back—one more shot. I can play this off, especially if Rosa goes through with this wedding. She isn't a threat to Maria if she's married to Dante. They will think they have the upper hand. Then we follow through with our plan. We get them to that warehouse. You get the commissioner filled in. We need their men stopped, so let Jax and the crew deal with them. We end Romano, we end Dante, we take back Rosa."

I scratch at my stubble. "You are an evil genius, Frankie."

"I worked with Romano long enough, I can get him eat-ing out of the palm of my hand if I need to. I just need you to play along with Maria for another twenty-four hours. Can you do that?"

Grayson pins me with a look.

"Yes." I don't know how, but for Rosa, I'll do anything.

He pushes himself up to stand. "I'll go make the calls. Grayson, ready that army."

"On it." He pulls out his phone.

Frankie looks at Keller. "Look after your brother and make sure he doesn't do any stupid shit in the next half hour."

Keller cracks his knuckles and winks at me. "Handled."

Time seems to crawl by as we wait for Frankie. Every second I'm without Rosa is a lifetime. I don't know how many times I've tried that breathing technique, but it turns out there is no cure for this level of pure rage, grief, and heartbreak.

Frankie waltzes back into the room. "Luca, go take a nap, then get your ass back home. Maria is waiting for you. They will all be attending Rosa's wedding. You will put on the fucking show of your life. Don't let them see your weakness. If they do, this is over."

My weakness is my love for Rosa.

I have to watch her marry another man.

"Remember why you are doing this, Luca. For all of us, for Rosa, for our empire, for revenge. She won't be married for long."

"I've got this." I pull up the commissioner's contact on my phone, my knuckles turning white as I grip the phone.

He answers on the second ring.

"Luca. This better be good, it's the middle of the night!" His croaky voice echoes through the room.

At least he can sleep at night.

"Change of plans. Romano dies tomorrow. I'll send you the details. We need all the help we can get."

"What, why?" He suddenly sounds wide awake.

"Because if I don't, I lose everything."

Chapter Sixty-Nine
ROSA

The day every girl dreams of is, instead, my nightmare. Trapped in a tiny room in the church, I can hear the chattering of the guests outside, all waiting to come in to watch the end of my life.

I wrap the shawl tighter around my arms, hissing as the soft fabric brushes against the bruises. The marks he left me with.

I am numb at this stage. My eyes are dry from crying myself to the point of exhaustion after watching Luca walk away from me. That is the only shred of hope I am clinging onto. That he is working on a plan, that he realizes something is seriously wrong. It's my only chance now.

If anyone can save Eva and me, it's Luca. I just need to keep her alive for now. But, after what I've seen, I'm losing hope.

My heart is in my throat as the door swings open, Dante's presence taking up the doorway. He steps toward me and my legs start to shake. Fresh red scratch marks span his other cheek and my heart sinks. I know that was her.

"Only a few more minutes until you will officially be mine. The new Mrs. Capri."

Shivers run down my spine. Tears well in my eyes.

"Don't cry, baby girl. This is a good thing. You get to be my personal slave, and in return, your sister gets to live her life."

"What have you done to my sister?"

He laughs, tipping his head back, clutching at his stomach. Once he stops, he storms toward me and grabs my arms.

I try to jerk free. "Get off me! I'll scream. You think they won't hear me out there?"

He steps back and scratches his stubble. "Your sister fights harder than you. Especially when I took her virginity."

He rubs the red marks on his face, and I double over, heaving.

He yanks me back up by my shoulder, grabbing my chin, forcing me to face him. No matter what I do, I lose. Rage burns through me. This monster has taken everything from me. I've been silent, I've played into his game.

With all the strength I can muster, I push at his chest, and he takes a step back with a smirk.

"Is that it? All you've got?"

I look to my left on the desk, picking up the candlestick, and I launch myself at him, hitting him as hard as I can in the head. Pain sears from my wrist as he grabs it. We lock eyes, his now completely black.

"You know I love a fight, baby girl. Keep going; it will only make me fuck you harder later."

"You won't." I draw back my knee and slam it straight into his balls as hard as I can.

He doubles over, clutching his groin, letting out a guttural scream.

"You fucking bitch," he growls. I sprint past him, my lungs on fire when I reach for my escape.

"I don't think so." He snakes his hand out and grabs me.

I battle in his arms, trying to free myself.

"Get the fuck off me!" I scream as loud as I can.

He clamps his hand over my mouth and nose, muffling my cries for help.

"If you don't calm down, I'll have your sister and your little boyfriend out there killed with one phone call. I suggest you behave." Venom drips from his tone.

Just like it did that night.

I squeeze my eyes shut. He licks along the side of my face, tightening his hand over my mouth. "So delicious, Rosa. You taste better than your sister."

I feel sick to my stomach. He releases me and I gasp for air. He laughs at me while straightening his tux.

"I-I'm not marrying you," I splutter.

"You are." He leans forward, his breath hitting against my neck. "Because if you don't, your boyfriend will die. Is that what you want? Two deaths on your conscience? I know you can't handle that. Poor little broken Rosa."

I swallow the bile in my throat.

"You can't kill Luca."

"You know now that I am a Capri. You know the resources I have available. My family is in that room, and an army is waiting outside. Trust me, we can kill Luca.

"You try to run again, you utter a word to anyone out there, you will stand there and watch Luca die. It's over, Rosa. I don't know what you thought you were doing with him, but there is no going back now." He steps toward me and tips my chin up, a darkness covering his eyes. "You are mine."

"No. I'll never be yours." My bottom lip quivers.

"You know he's back with Maria? They're coming here together. He doesn't give a fuck about you. No one does."

He abruptly releases his hold on me, and my back crashes into the stone wall behind me.

He snatches up my bouquet from the little wooden table and shoves it into my hands.

"Well, what's your choice? Marry me and let Luca and Eva live? Or run, and they both die." He crosses his arms across his chest.

There isn't a choice. I lower my head to the ground. "Okay."

"There's my little obedient slave." He leans down, his eyes locked on my lips. I turn my head so he kisses my cheek. He grabs my face and tugs me to face him. His lips crash over mine with the sour taste of whiskey. His rough hands hold my cheeks.

I push at his chest, and he laughs at me.

"You better get used to it. I'll be claiming every hole of yours tonight. Both sisters on the same day. How perfect is that?" He blows me a kiss and backs away, locking the door behind him.

Chapter Seventy

LUCA

We pull up outside the quaint church; the parking lot is filled with guests. I tug on the neck of my collar with nervous energy. My Rosa is in there.

"Are we all set?" I ask Frankie.

We've planned for two outcomes, the latter ending in a bloodbath. We are, however, trying to avoid that option. I won't risk Rosa. He tugs at his sleeve, and I catch the briefest glimpse of the handle of his pistol poking under his arm.

"Jax and Keller are parked down the road. We have backup arriving now. It looks like Romano has five SUVs with his men outside. Enzo is ready and waiting for the security footage to give them their orders. A few of our men will be inside the church with us."

I spark up a cigarette. "And Maria?"

"She's waiting for you. I wouldn't expect a warm welcome, but she's under her dad's orders that the wedding is still on.

Watching you sit through Rosa's wedding should be enough to keep her where we need her for now."

I can't wait to end that bitch.

My jaw tics, the anxiety building within me. I could walk in there with my army and take them all out.

I can't, no matter how much I want to. That risks Rosa. She wants me here for a reason. She needs me. Dante has a hold over her, which I very much intend on finding out today. Even if it means he has to think he's won.

Discarding my cigarette on the ground, I turn to Grayson getting out of the back seat, his stern face scanning the area. Even a man who has come face to face with terrorists doesn't have complete confidence in our plan. None of us do. But, right now, it's all we have.

An army and a group of men who would die for their family.

"Are you good, Grayson?"

He drags his gaze away from the line of cars parked along the road. "Let's do this."

MARIA IS THE easiest to spot in the crowd in a short white dress and a diamanté headband. Her bloated lips turn into a scowl when she spots me.

"Oh, Luca. You decided to come." Maria's high-pitched voice has me balling my fists.

Don't fucking kill her—not yet.

Her ridiculously high heels click against the pavement. I bite down on my tongue.

"Of course. We have a deal, right?"

She tuts and closes the distance between us. I step back. I don't trust myself not to wrap my hands around her throat and strangle the life out of her.

"We're giving you one last chance, Luca. You've embarrassed me, you've embarrassed my family. You've lost our trust. I don't know why, but Daddy has let it slide this time. I like New York. I want my own empire here. Once that little slut is out of the way with Dante, we should be good. I expect better from you." Her long fingernail trails down my crumpled shirt, and my blood boils.

"Plus, I really can't wait to watch you fall to pieces on little Rosa's big day," she cackles, and my hands shake with pure rage. "Luca, it has to stop—this fantasy you're living in. Look at you. You reek of booze. Man up. Otherwise, you'll be planning at least ten more funerals this month."

Chills run down my spine, the image of Mom tormenting me again.

"Today is a test. You're going to show my family you can be trusted and that you're not swayed elsewhere. You are mine."

I swallow past the lump in my throat. I don't think I can do it. She tugs my tie, and I hiss.

"Just because they're in a safe house doesn't mean we won't find them." She grins at me like the sadistic bitch she is. I simply nod and she releases me.

"I can't wait to watch you squirm, Luca."

"Fuck y—"

"Luca!" Antonio puffs on a cigar, flicking his gaze between me and Maria. Where is Romano?

I lock eyes with Frankie across the parked cars, and he shakes his head.

Fuck.

"If all the guests would like to make their way inside, we

are almost ready to begin," the priest announces from the double doors into the church.

My spine goes stiff as my eyes lock with Antonio's. The guests flood the church, but I stand my ground.

He sticks out his hand to me. I hesitate, gritting my teeth. Maria narrows her eyes at me, so I force myself to clasp his hand, tighter than he does mine.

"How are you coping?" His eyes are hidden behind his mirrored sunglasses.

"Fucking fine," I say through my teeth, holding on to the little ounce of self-restraint I have. The gun in my waistband is itching to be pulled out and pressed into his forehead.

"Are you going to behave today, Luca? My father is very concerned that your intentions are not sincere," Antonio says.

I'm seething, imagining wedging my bullet into his brain and it splattering across the stones beneath our feet.

Where is the old asshole, anyway?

"He's made his point, loud and clear. Don't worry." I can still feel my mom's warm heart against my fingers.

I turn on my heel and head to the church.

"You have plenty more family members to pick from, Luca. Quite the family man, aren't you? Mrs. Russo was us being kind to you. Little Darcy, however, now that's a different story." His smooth Italian accent hits like a brick.

I stop, bile rising up my throat at Darcy's mention. My two-year-old niece. I wish I'd had another drink this morning. Rubbing my jaw, I try to relieve some tension.

I turn and hold my hand out, nodding to Maria. She smiles up at her brother, like the cat who got the canary, and saunters over to me, lacing her fingers through mine.

"Good choice. We aren't joking." Flashing me an exaggerated smile, she swings her hips next to me.

I take a step into the church, the weight of the world on my shoulders nearly crippling me. I look up at the array of colors shining through the stained-glass window.

The room is filled to the brim with guests, white roses lining the ends of each aisle. A gold cross sits at the head of the church, and I laugh to myself.

If there is a fucking god, he hates my guts.

With what I have planned, I won't be getting welcomed into heaven anytime soon.

I have a one-way ticket to hell.

Chapter Seventy-One

ROSA

I hear a click and face the door.
 "It's time to go, Rosa." I turn to face the man standing there. He's similar-looking to Dante with jet-black hair, just a smaller build.

I clutch my bouquet as if it will offer me some sort of protection. My feet are rooted to the spot.

I toss the shawl onto the chair, and the man's eyes go wide as he spots the marks scattered on my arms.

"Put that back on," he says gruffly.

I shake my head. "It will ruin my dress. Dante won't want that. He picked this out for me. He put these marks here; it must mean he wants me to show them off."

He narrows his eyes. "Fine, just pull your hair over or something. We can't have the priest seeing these."

I do as he says, letting my curls fall over my shoulders and down my arms.

As he holds open the door, his suit jacket falls open, and I catch the silver glimmer from his gun My mouth goes dry.

Giving me a knowing glare, he says, "Move."

I shuffle past him, the cold air beating against my skin. The parking lot is nearly empty. I don't know why I expected Luca to bring an army. It was the hope I was clutching onto. Disappointment consumes me. Maybe I was wrong. I'm not his *family*. He made clear he would do anything to keep them out of harm's way.

I was grasping onto the idea that our love might come close.

Not that it matters now. I've failed them all.

He walks me toward the entrance, my heels clicking against the floor as we reach the double doors.

They open, but I can't move. Every single person turns in their seat to gawk at me, like some sort of animal in the zoo. The crowd is a haze, a blur of color. All I can focus on is the monster grinning at me in his black tux, his hands in his pockets.

My heart rate spikes as the violins play. My body is screaming at me to turn around, to run away. There isn't a way out of this. I don't have a choice. I chose Luca's life over mine, and I will never regret that decision.

I take my first step through the threshold, my massive dress weighing me down. I hold my head up high, shoving my emotions deep down, keeping my eyes fixed on the gold cross, every step a stab in the chest.

Electricity fizzles in my body, and adrenaline takes over. It's fight or flight, and this time, I can't let my body win. I have to fight.

I peer to my left and my feet almost stop as I see the back

of Luca's head, next to his fiancée. I do everything I can to hold in the sob that threatens to erupt from my throat.

I can't look at him, not when I basically have a gun to my back. I have to do this to save us all.

But he will always own my heart. He is my forever.

A forever I will never have.

I know I won't survive this marriage.

I keep my gaze on that cross, Dante's big frame in my peripheral. My arms tense as I grip the flowers, trying to stop the tremble, which only makes it worse; my legs feel heavier with every step.

The tiniest whimper leaves my throat as I pass Luca, leaving him behind me. My past. My eyes lock with Dante's evil ones.

He grins at me and blows me a kiss.

Chapter Seventy-Two
LUCA

"You're doing well so far. No one would know your heart is breaking inside," Maria leans over and whispers.

I ignore her, shooting daggers at Dante.

My fingers dig into the chair in front of me so deeply the wood splinters. Frankie coughs from his seat in the aisle next to mine and gives me a tiny shake of his head when I glance at him.

My leg bounces up and down erratically as the violins start playing.

"If we could stand for the bride," the priest announces.

I stand, holding my hands in front of my body.

The room goes silent and everyone turns to the entrance.

I can't. I can't look at her.

I fear if I do, Maria will be right. My heart will shatter.

My body is on high alert as she approaches me from behind. Everyone is muttering about how beautiful Rosa looks.

I squeeze my eyes shut as if I'm in physical agony.

I've failed her. I promised I would never abandon her, yet here we are.

Her heels clicking against the wooden floor get closer to me. I take a deep breath and open my eyes, turning my head to the right.

All the air is sucked from my lungs, tears stinging in my eyes as she draws level with me. For some kind of punishment, my eyes roam her body. Her dark hair is curled, cascading down her back.

That horrid fucking dress.

My gaze stops on her left arm. There are small bruises scattered on the outside of her bicep. She keeps her eyes forward and continues walking down the aisle.

I lean forward, getting a better look as she passes me.

Distinct fingerprint bruises mark her skin. He marked her. No one touches my Rosa.

As I take a step toward her, Maria's nails dig into my arm and she pulls me back. She leans into me. "Unless you want the next funeral to be Rosa's, I suggest you stay where you are, Luca. We are ready for war. Are you?"

My heart pounds, sweat beading on my forehead.

I look over at Frankie, who shakes his head at me.

The violins come to a stop and the room falls silent. Everyone takes their seats and watches as Rosa approaches Dante. He turns to the crowd and smiles straight at me, fresh scratch marks on his cheeks, leaving me shaking with rage.

The priest welcomes us and who knows what else he says. My ears are ringing so loud I can't concentrate. I can barely remember how to breathe. Every ounce of willpower is being used not to get up and shoot him between the eyes.

And slit the throat of the bitch who has her claws digging into my thigh.

Chapter Seventy-Three

ROSA

I take my final steps toward him.
    My abuser.
    My husband.

"Welcome, you look beautiful. Are you both ready?" the gray-haired priest asks with a beaming smile.

I nod, and Dante takes my trembling hands. My throat is closing in on me.

"You made the right choice," Dante whispers. He leans closer. "I told you that first time. You'll be mine forever."

Bile rises up my throat, and I swallow it back down.

I go up on tiptoes and whisper in his ear, "You mean when you raped me?"

He squeezes my hands tighter.

"You'll never escape me, Rosa. Never."

He releases me and takes a step back, smiling to the crowd.

The priest raises his arms and begins his speech.

"Welcome to the wedding of Rosa Francesca Falcone and Dante Pierre Capri."

I hear rustling coming from the guests. My eyes meet Frankie's ice-cold ones. His chest rises and falls rapidly, and his nostrils flare.

"Rosa?" the priest says, handing me my vow card.

I shake my head and take the notes. "Sorry."

"Would you like to start with your vows?" He gives me a small gesture, beckoning me to begin.

I take a breath. Dante coughs and nods his head to the left. I follow his eyeline straight to Luca. His face is expressionless. And that hurts more than anything right now.

"I, Rosa Francesca Falcone, take Dante Capri—" I say the last word as loud and clear as I can.

"—to be my lawfully wedded husband. I promise to worship you in every way—"

I pause and look up from the card to Dante, who's smirking at me. He nods back down to the card.

"Carry on, it's good. I wrote these just for you, sweetheart." He winks.

"I promise to serve you. To give myself entirely to y—"

My eyes scan the rest of the vows. "To give myself entirely to you. In every sense of the word. I will be your slave. You will be my master. I give my life to you, and every—"

Blood thumps in my ears, my vision blurry through my tears.

I drop the paper to the floor.

He bends down and picks it up and thrusts it into my hands again. He laces his fingers around my wrist and squeezes. I try to pull it back, and he won't let me.

We stare at each other. A silent battle.

The garish red marks on his cheek make everything

obvious. No matter what I do, Eva pays the price. Shit, it might be too late for her already. I have to fight for myself now.

"I'm not doing this." My throat starts to close up.

"You better take one last look at Luca, if that's what you really want to do," he taunts with anger in his eyes as he looms over me.

The same way he did that night.

I bring my hand up to my throat, snatching my wrist back.

He tips my chin up with his thumb. To the people watching it would look sweet.

My eyes meet his.

I choose to fight with Luca.

I scan the crowd—Frankie, Grayson, and Luca are all here. He's not on his own. I suck in a breath. This is my last chance.

"Treasure."

Dante's eyebrow raises in confusion. "What the fuck are you talking about? Are you high again?" he hisses.

I turn to the crowd, my eyes landing on a red-faced Luca.

His mouth falls open, stunned. At that moment, the guests all turn to a haze.

All I see is him.

I just hope it's enough.

I can't do this on my own anymore. I can't save Eva, I can't save myself.

I need him.

Chapter Seventy-Four

LUCA

Rage consumes me as the word *Capri* falls from the priest's lips. Rosa's bottom lip quivers. Frankie, in the row opposite me, mutters, "Fucker."

I turn to Maria, who's facing straight forward, not hiding the grin on her big lips.

"Surprise," she whispers.

My heart races. I rip my hand from Maria's and rub my sweaty palms along my suit trousers.

This can't be happening. This whole damn time, the assholes set us up. I raise my head and Rosa's watery eyes lock on mine, pleading with me for help.

My heart stops for a second as her lips open, and her voice cracks as she says the one word on this planet that changes everything for us.

"Treasure."

My heart is in my throat as I stand. The eyes of the crowd

are completely on me. They gasp as I snake my hand around my back, resting it on the handle of my weapon.

"Treasure," she repeats, this time louder, laced with pure hopelessness.

My whole world stops. Everything fades around me. Fuck the consequences. I'll fight a war to keep her safe. I'll give up my own life if I have to.

Nothing comes close.

I hope Enzo is watching this closely, because our army needs to arrive any second.

I unholster my gun and point it straight at Dante.

"You piece of shit!" I shout.

He holds up his hands in surrender.

"Sir, you need to—" The priest raises his palms, stepping between Dante and Rosa.

Swinging the barrel at him, I drop it to gesture at his chest. "I suggest you back up. This isn't a time for God and forgiveness. I am the devil, and I'm here for revenge."

His lips thin into a straight line, but he backs slowly away from the podium.

Keeping my gun aimed at Dante's head, I take a step toward Rosa, cupping her face in my palm. She flinches as the sound of gunfire outside the church erupts. I look into the crowd as our men all stand and scatter around the room. It's us against them.

Thank you, Enzo.

"Baby, it's going to be okay," I whisper, bringing my forehead down against hers. "I love you. I promise, he will *never* get a chance to hurt you ever again." I pull her into me and hold her tight, then turn my attention to Dante. "On your knees."

"Luca. Don't do this. Not for her. You saw what I did to your mom."

My nostrils flare.

Fury builds until I explode.

"You fucking cunt," I grit through my teeth, taking a step toward him. He doesn't show a single shred of fear.

"Don't make me repeat myself, Antonio," Frankie bellows from behind me. I glance up to see that he and Grayson have their guns pointed at Antonio.

Dante takes a half a step away and crosses his arms. "That little slut asked for it. She even whored herself out to me years ago when I was working with her dad. She was obsessed with m—"

"Shut up!" Rosa releases herself from my hold and kicks her heel straight into his crotch, hard enough to make me wince.

"I hate you! Give me back my sister!" she screams at him, clawing for his face.

I keep my gun aimed at him, holding her by the waist. "Baby, I will handle all of this. I need you to focus for me."

Rosa turns to me, her tears seeping through my shirt.

My mind is still reeling from his last words.

"Say that again," I command.

"What? That I took her virginity?" He gives me a crooked smile.

I look at a now-pale Rosa; her bloodshot eyes meet mine, and she nods.

"It was him, Luca," she whispers.

I stumble backward as the realization hits me.

This whole time she's been trapped with her rapist. And I've let this happen to her.

"Took. Not given." Every piece of me is shaking as I tower over him.

His eyes go wide as I press the gun against his forehead, itching to pull the trigger. Rosa grabs hold of my arm and tugs. "Luca, he has my sister," she whispers.

Dante grins at me. "Well, I've already *had* her."

So this is what he had over her. Her sister.

"Where is she?" Rosa's screams rip through me.

"We will find her, I promise you." I kiss the top of her head, pulling her flush against my side again. I won't let him anywhere near her.

"A single bullet isn't enough justice for what you've done to her. Right now, I really have to fucking shoot you."

I smirk at him, switch my aim to his right kneecap, and pull the trigger.

It feels so good watching him fall to the floor, clutching his leg as he cries out in agony.

The room erupts into screams.

The gunshots outside get louder as the guests and our guys work their way from the church. Frankie appears by my side.

He puts his hand over my arm, which is still shaking with my need to shoot Dante over and over. "Your car is out back. Take her. We've got this."

The entrance door opens and in walk Jax and Keller, an army of men filtering through the door behind them.

Frankie grabs Dante by the collar. "You, Capri piece of shit, are coming with me."

"Take him to the basement. Find out where he's keeping Eva," I spit out.

"He has Eva?" Frankie's tone turns into a growl of pure anger. "I'm going to make you regret even being born, you prick," he seethes.

DEVOTED ~ 409

"Let's go." I keep Rosa in front of me and head toward the back exit.

I help her fold the hideous dress into the passenger seat and speed off. Once we're free of the church, I put a call in to Enzo.

"Boss? You're good?" I can hear the chatter in the background of all of his radios.

"Yeah. Did the commissioner come through?" There hasn't been a sign of police yet, but that doesn't mean anything.

"I haven't heard anything yet on their scanner. So far it's hush-hush."

Good. Cops make shit messy. "What's the status?"

"Maria slipped out. Antonio is dead. An armored SUV is waiting outside for extraction. Frankie has Dante in there already." His voice gets muffled as he talks on another line.

I let out a huff of air. "Any injuries? Do we know where Romano is?"

"One dead, boss. No updates yet on Romano."

"Who?" My heart races.

"Rico."

As bad as it is, relief washes over me at the fact that it's not any of my family. "I'll send a payment to his family. Recover the body when this is over."

"Will do."

"I'm taking Rosa to the safe house now. Thank you." After tossing my phone into the center console, I gather her hand back in mine.

We have guys stationed there twenty-four seven. They understand they die before anyone touches our women, our families.

I turn to Rosa, who's staring blankly out of the window, shaking like a leaf.

"You saved me," she whispers.

"I will always be there to save you, tesoro mio." I squeeze her hand tighter. "And I will always be there to love you."

As soon as we are in the clear, I pull over on the gravel shoulder and take her face in my hands.

I drop a kiss to her lips. "I hope you know how brave you are."

I thought I knew her strength. But today, she showed me how truly powerful she is. How big her heart is. The fact that she would sacrifice herself to save her sister makes me love her even more.

"W-we need to find Eva. He said he'd kill her. Maria is in on it with him, and she knows where Eva is!"

"So that is what he had over you this whole time?"

She nods. "And then he threatened you, Luca. But I couldn't do it. I couldn't marry him. Even if I did, he would never stop. He's already raped Eva."

Her face pales. I squeeze her hand tighter.

"He would have killed us all, eventually. I'm so sorry. I've messed up, haven't I?" she sobs. Her head lowers, and she hides her face in her hands.

"Rosa. Look at me." I pull her hands away. "You should have told me a long time ago. I will do anything for you, Rosa. You are my whole fucking world. My entire soul is yours. If that means I tear down a whole city to keep you safe, then that is what I will do. I swear to you, from this moment on, no more pain."

"I wanted to tell you. I tried to keep him away, to protect everyone. I had no idea until last night who he really was. My dad killed his mom, Luca. That's why he's haunted me."

I stroke her face, holding back my own tears. "Did he—"
Acid rises up into my throat.

My stomach rolls, thinking about him touching her, forcing her all this time.

I brace myself, waiting for her response.

A look of disgust flashes over her. "No."

I close my eyes and tip my head back. "I love you, Rosa. After today, he won't be able to terrorize you again. I promise."

"Can we go home now, Luca? I just want to go home."

I press a kiss to the tip of her nose. "We will be at a safe house for now; everyone is there. Until we work out a plan and find Eva, we won't be going home for a little while, baby."

"But you'll be with me, right?" Her fingers wrap around mine tightly.

"Yes, I'll try to be there as much as I can. Once we find Eva, you and I are out of here."

Her smile breaks out with a flash of her white teeth. "I want that."

"Me too, baby. Me too."

Chapter Seventy-Five

ROSA

Luca nods to the armed guards stationed outside the house. He steps forward and stops in front of the door, his fingers on the handle. He turns and scoops me up into his arms.

"Luca!" I shout.

"I've dreamed of this moment, Rosa. Well, not quite *this* moment. But finally having you to myself." His strong arms hold me easily as he carries me down the hall.

I bury my face against his chest, the emotions are overwhelming.

He leads us into his bedroom and places me down on my heels. We stand there, staring into each other's eyes. Neither of us knows quite what to say. He brushes his hands along my arm and I flinch.

His jaw clenches.

"Why didn't you tell me it was him?" His voice is soft, but I hear the hurt there.

"He threatened to—" I can't bring myself to say the words.

"Eva." He lets out a long sigh.

"But he did it, anyway. He tortured and raped her, Luca."

"The bruises?"

I watch his Adam's apple bob. "Last night. I went looking for her—"

"Fuck," he hisses.

"I rifled through his stuff a couple of days ago. I found an address. I thought maybe that might be where Eva was. So I went there."

"You what?" he groans.

I sniffle and nod.

"He was there. I didn't find her. I tried to run, but he caught me and dragged me back to the car."

The words are rolling out of me. I need to tell him everything.

"When you came to the door, he was on the phone with Maria. He had blood all over him. He told me to make you come to the wedding. He wanted to break you, they both did."

"You did an amazing job, Rosa. You did the right thing, you kept yourself safe. That's all that matters." A tear slips down his cheek.

"No, Luca. I'm not all that matters. Are you okay?"

"I don't matter, Rosa."

I wipe the drop from his cheek. He must be breaking inside. He lost his mom, and he's started a war for me. Yet he thinks he let me down.

"Yes. Yes, you do. To me, you are everything. Without you, I am nothing. Never say that again."

I wish I could show him just how I see him through my eyes. The most powerful man in the world.

"I'm so sorry, Rosa. I'm sorry I didn't see this happening. I would have taken you away sooner."

"You saved me, not just today, but all those months ago when you took me. I would never have survived any of this without you."

He drops his head to rest against mine.

I place my hand over his chest; his frantic heart hammers against my palm. "Vita mia, Luca. I love you."

He runs a hand through his hair. "I found her, Rosa. I can't get the image out of my head."

Guilt creeps over me. If I had been stronger and stayed away from Luca, his mom could still be alive. I shake my head. I can't think like that now, not when he needs me.

His tattooed hand covers mine. "But all that matters now is that we are here, together. Nothing can keep us apart."

"No more last kisses?"

He looks down at my hand on his chest and frowns. I almost sag in relief as he slides off that disgusting engagement ring that has branded me for months. I'm free.

He pockets it. I don't question it. I never want to see it again.

"They never were going to be our last kisses. There isn't a single thing on this earth that would have kept me from you."

I pull back. "I need you to get me out of this monstrosity, Luca."

He places me down and starts unlacing the corset. Every time his fingers brush my skin, I shiver in anticipation.

As soon as it's loose, I push it down and step out of it.

"Burn it."

He bundles it up in his arms, walks toward the balcony, and tosses it over the side, wiping his hands with dramatic flair when he's done.

He doesn't realize the pain he's taken away from me with that simple act. When he reaches me, I cover my bruised arms with my hands. They're a purple testament to my failures.

"Please don't hide from me, baby. I love every inch of you." He tips my chin up to face him. "And that also means don't keep your feelings or your demons from me. I'm here to battle them with you. Always."

"And the same goes for you. We fight together, remember?"

He nods. I push myself up on my tiptoes and press my lips to his.

"I love you, Luca."

"My heart beats for you and only you, tesoro."

A knock at the door interrupts us from falling farther into each other's arms.

"What?" Luca shouts in annoyance.

The door creeps open. Grayson peers around the edge and Luca spins me behind him. "I don't know how much longer I can hold off Frankie. If you want to do this, Luca, you need to take over."

Dante.

He's down in the basement.

"Go. Finish this." I tap Luca's back.

His hand tightens on my hip. "I'll be down in a minute."

He turns back to me as Grayson closes the door. "I'll make him pay for everything, Rosa. I might have let you down, but never again, starting right now."

"It's really going to be over?" My voice cracks. After all of those years of nightmares and looking over my shoulder, it feels as if a weight is being lifted.

He nods as he tucks a stray strand of hair behind my ear.

"And then our lives finally begin, tesoro."

Chapter Seventy-Six
LUCA

Frankie slams the basement door shut while wiping a bloodied hand across his forehead. "He's ready for you."

I pull back my fist and launch it into his cheek. He stumbles backward, a look of shock on his face.

"You brought him back here. You allowed their wedding, you fucking asshole!" I roar, grabbing him by the throat and slamming my knee into his groin.

He shouts in pain. "What the hell, Luca?" he hisses.

I shove him back against the wall and pull my knife, pressing the the tip of the blade into his neck. "Is that why you really killed your brother? You knew he let his man rape his daughter and then let him get away with it?"

His mouth falls open. "What? I-I had no idea."

"Bullshit. You're just like your brother," I spit, pressing the tip of the knife in further. Blood trickles down the blade.

"Don't you dare." His eyes flash with anger.

"Give me one good reason why I shouldn't end you. You're no use to Rosa, anyway. You abandoned her. You let her get engaged to her rapist."

"Marco was responsible for the death of my girlfriend. And my unborn child. That's why I killed him, okay? That's why I worked for Romano. I have been plotting his end for a long time."

Shit.

He rubs his neck as I remove the knife.

"That's why I left. The explosion that killed Rosa's mom also killed Leila. Marco killed Romano's first wife, and that was the retaliation. I had to leave. I couldn't leave Rosa and Eva as orphans, so I let him live until the time was right. I didn't know, Luca. I swear to God." His fists ball at his sides.

"Jesus, Frankie."

He takes a stride toward me, and his finger taps hard against my chest. "I'll let this one go, since you're protecting my niece. But you try that again, I'll end you. Never speak of my past again. Do you hear me?"

My eyes narrow. "I think you need to explain that to Rosa."

I know it eats her up, thinking Frankie abandoned her. Even if, in his own messed-up way, he loves her.

He grips my shoulders, and his gray eyes darken. "I will. Now, let's go and unleash hell on that piece of shit down there. I need to find Eva."

I descend the stairs to the basement and my mood lifts in anticipation.

Dante's guttural screams are like music to my ears. The metallic scent of blood lingers in the air.

Red is smeared across his forehead, and his nose has a new bend to the left. He tugs at the unrelenting chains on his wrists.

I look over at the metal bench, the smell of burning flesh filling my nostrils. Five of his toes and two fingers are laid out in a line.

Dante's eyes go wide when he spots me. Lighting a cigarette, I make my way toward him.

Sweat beads on his forehead, mingling with the crimson.

"Nothing to say?" I let a plume of smoke waft into his face.

"Fuck you and that fucking whore upstairs," he yells.

I draw back my right hand and crack it into his mouth. Blood splatters, followed by a couple of teeth bouncing on the floor.

"You don't get to speak about her, or ever say her name again," I say through my clenched jaw.

He hisses as I stub the cigarette out on his forehead.

A fresh wave of hatred washes over me thinking about what he did to my girl. I push my thumb into the corner of his eye and push, hard enough for it to pop under my thumb and out of its socket. I grab the soft ball and pull, relishing his screams as I jerk it free. "That's for even looking at her." I promised Rosa pain, and that's exactly what I'll deliver.

"No more. Please, just get it over with." A stream of fresh blood streams from his sunken eyelid.

The room erupts into laughter. "You're pleading with the wrong men, Dante. We show no mercy."

I clutch Rosa's engagement ring, the thing that trapped her for months.

"Open your mouth," I command.

He shakes his head.

Grabbing his jaw, I pry open his mouth and shove the massive diamond in. "Now swallow."

He clenches his teeth, fighting to shake my hands free.

Pinning his head, I pinch his nose shut and cover his mouth with my hand.

"I said, fucking swallow."

Leaning in, I whisper. "If you don't, I'll cut your dick off and make you eat that instead."

He tries to thrash under my suffocating grasp, but finally does a dramatic swallow.

He's not nearly in enough pain yet. "Keller, pass me the hammer."

Keller steps out of the shadows and drops the heavy weight of a small sledge into my palm. I take a step back, swinging my arm up, and with an angry load of force, smash the hammer straight onto his kneecap.

The bone crunches as his lower leg juts limply out in front of him. He tips back his head and lets out a bloodcurdling scream.

I clench my teeth. I bet that hurt like a son of a bitch.

I prop the mallet on my shoulder. "Now, where the fuck is Eva?"

Tears stream down his sweaty face, dripping from his split lips.

He lets out a wheezing laugh. "Why does it matter? She's probably dead by now."

My heart sinks for Rosa. In all honesty, I don't believe Eva is alive. Not now that I know Maria was in on it.

"What limb next?" Frankie calls over, holding up the hacksaw.

"Hands." I toss the hammer on the table next to the severed digits.

Dante's mouth opens with a low moan, and he frantically begins shaking his head. Frankie hands me the saw.

"What's your preference, left or right?" I touch each one with the tip of the tool as I ask.

"Fuck off." He sucks in saliva and spits it at my shoe. I kick it off.

"Both, then." I shrug, and Grayson laughs behind me.

Shedding my jacket, I roll up my sleeves and slide out my tie. Amputations can be messy. "Frankie, hold him back, then you can do the other one." It's the least I can do for pulling a knife on him earlier.

A sadistic grin creeps up on his lips.

"Gladly." Frankie's eyes are dark as he wraps his arm under Dante's chin.

"This is for touching her," I hiss. Dante shakes against the metal chains. I hold down his clenched fist and put all my pressure onto the hacksaw as the teeth start to tear through his flesh.

By the time I hit bone, he slumps in his chair.

"Hit him up with some adrenaline. He needs to feel everything," I call out. Grayson jabs a needle into his neck and pushes the liquid in.

"He'll be right as rain in a minute."

I slap his cheeks. "Wakey! Wakey! We still have a little while left."

He groans, his one eye flickering open.

"You don't get to die yet. You've tortured Rosa for years. It's only fair you feel her pain." I drag the serrated edge over the last flap of skin. The lifeless hand lands with a soft thud.

Yellow liquid pools next to my feet.

I look at him with disgust. "Really? I expected better from Romano's firstborn."

"My dad will kill you."

"Well, he can join you and your brother down in hell. A little family reunion."

Grayson works on patching up his hand, burning the stump and wrapping it. The cooking meat stench has me cringing.

"Why do I suddenly want a hot dog?" Grayson chuckles, wrapping the stub left of Dante's arm.

I rip open his shirt, revealing his hairy chest, and pull the small blade out from my pocket.

"This is for her nightmares."

I scatter deep cuts across his chest and abdomen. His muscles tense as I slice away, creating a pattern of fissures.

He gasps for breath between each pass of my blade, barely able to keep his head up. I glance over to Frankie. He's itching to get to him. If anyone can get Dante to speak, it's Frankie.

I step back and beckon to him with the tip of my knife. "You're up."

Frankie grabs Dante by the throat, forcing him to look at him. "One last chance before I cut your dick clean off. Where the fuck is Eva?"

"Get fucked, Frankie," Dante coughs.

Frankie stands back, lifts his foot, and kicks him in the chest, toppling over his chair.

"You think he'll really cut his dick off?" Grayson appears beside me, his arms crossed, watching Frankie. I swear there is a glimmer of approval from Grayson.

"I'm banking on it."

Frankie's wild eyes look over to us. "Keller, unchain him and hold him down."

Keller unlocks Dante's bonds, lays him flat on the ground, and pins his legs.

"Grayson. Grab his arms."

Frankie unbuckles Dante's belt, yanking down his pants and revealing his shriveled dick. We all burst into laughter. Dante's pleas are garbled through his swelling lips.

I hand Frankie my blade. He yanks the flaccid organ and starts cutting. Keller and Grayson look away. I've never heard a man scream like this—loud enough my ears are ringing.

Frankie kneels back, Dante's chunk of tissue barely filling his hand. "First time I've cut a dick off," he grunts.

He shoves the detached cock into Dante's mouth to muffle the screams. He's bleeding all over the concrete; I doubt he has much longer to live.

"He's not going to tell us where Eva is." Frankie stands with a resigned sigh and tosses Dante's little snippet into the growing puddle.

But it isn't over yet. We won't stop searching for her. Dante, however, is done. I just want to get back to my Rosa.

I lock eyes with Grayson. "Burn him."

"You got it, boss."

The four of us, we are sadistic fucks. Each of us has lived a life of pain. We aren't good men. We never will be. But we will always be the best for our women and our children. Everything we do is for them.

And right now, I want mine wrapped tightly in my arms.

Keller and Frankie drag the bloody, unconscious man out the small door leading to the van. There's a walled-off area at the other end of the property for just this kind of barbeque. In our line of work, these places become second nature.

Grayson douses Dante in gasoline, the stench clouding the air. I suppose it's better than piss and sweat. Dante's eyelids flutter; he's conscious enough to know what's going on.

I walk over with a cigarette in my mouth. The men back away.

"This is for Rosa."

I light the end, take a drag, and throw it onto his chest. The four of us stand back, watching as the flames take over his body. He flails on the charred ground, leaking screams of despair that fade to the crackling sound of inferno.

"I'm going back to my woman."

They all nod, the flames dancing in their eyes. I've seen enough. He's gone.

Chapter Seventy-Seven

ROSA

The house is deathly silent. Sienna, Maddie, and the kids went to bed. It was a good distraction for a little while. It is nice to finally feel like part of a family. I can't help but feel bad that Maddie is forced into a safe house when it's her due date tomorrow.

She tried to make me feel better, telling me she was having a home birth, anyway. Grayson won't let her in a hospital unless absolutely necessary. Not after Frankie kidnapped her from one.

I should be surprised, shocked, even. But I'm not. Not in this life.

Not when my boyfriend is torturing my ex-fiancé in a basement.

I lay in darkness, replaying today over in my head.

Did I make the right choice? What if I messed it up?

I muffle a cry with my hand. What if Eva is dead?

Guilt shreds through me. No matter what choice I made, I couldn't win.

I hear the door slam downstairs. I'm worried about Luca. I know what it's like to chase away nightmares, to live life numb.

He's carried the weight of the world on his back for too long. The man who sacrifices everything for everyone else, never himself.

For once, he deserves to have the weight lifted from him. I want to share the burden with him. I want to fight for him.

I throw off the covers and put on one of his black T-shirts, letting it hang on me like a dress, and head down to find him.

Chapter Seventy-Eight

LUCA

The rain hammers down, and I take a drag and exhale the smoke, tipping my head back against the seat of my patio furniture.

My body reacts the second that door slides open, her big brown eyes meeting mine as she holds on to the side of the door. My cock immediately hardens at the sight of her in my shirt.

"Are you okay?" Her sweet voice makes my heart pound.

I nod and tap on my lap. She warily looks at the rain and darts under the canopy. I groan as she shuffles her ass on my thigh, trying to find her comfy spot.

She tips her head back and rests it on my shoulder, exposing that slender neck.

"Want a drag?" I rasp, trailing my other hand along her neck to watch the goosebumps erupt on her skin.

"Please."

I inhale a deep drag and grip her cheeks. I bend over, so

DEVOTED ~ 427

my mouth hovers above hers. Her full lips open for me and I exhale into her mouth, watching as her chest rises. She tips her head back, releasing the smoke into the air that surrounds us in a haze.

She switches positions and straddles me. "Baby," I groan out as her pussy grinds against my cock.

I don't have the restraint I need right now.

Plucking the cigarette from my hand, she takes one last drag, desire flashing in her eyes. She flicks it from between her fingers out into the rain. Her hands frame my face. "I want you, Luca."

I squeeze my eyes shut. "I can't be the man you need me to be tonight, tesoro. I don't trust myself."

I'm fueled with rage and adrenaline. I'm covered in the blood of her fiancé.

"You might not trust yourself, but I trust you, Luca. You need this, so use me. Let me be the one to take care of you."

I shake my head. I can't risk hurting her. She forces me to look at her.

"I'm not a fragile princess anymore, Luca. I know what I crave, and it's you." She looks down at the red stains on my shirt.

She leans forward, her breasts pressing into me, and her plump lips brush along my stubble, sending a rush to my dick.

"I'm all yours now, yours to claim."

Oh, she knows how to get to me. My eyes lock on her neck, and I bite my lip. I can't help but think how beautiful she would look with red marks along her throat.

Running her hands through my messy hair, her nails scratch my scalp, pushing a groan from me.

"And I'm yours, all of me," I pant.

428 ~ LUNA MASON

Our eyes lock, the hunger in hers matching my own. I could never deny this woman. She can take my heart out of my chest and keep it if she wants.

"Make me yours, Luca. We've waited long enough for this moment. Take it."

My hand laces around her neck, my mouth just above hers as she sucks in a breath.

She lifts her hips and gives me a teasing smile as she seductively runs her hand down her stomach to disappear under the hem of her top.

She slips those fingers up to reveal their glisten. I'm salivating at the scent of her sweetness.

"This is how ready for you I am, Luca." Her eyes sparkle under the lights.

I take her fingers in my mouth and suck them clean. My dick nearly explodes as my taste buds erupt to her wetness.

"You're a goddamn angel."

Chapter Seventy-Nine
ROSA

I gasp as he hoists me up, my back crashing against the brick wall behind me. His grip on my throat tightens, and he pushes up my top and rips off my panties.

The cold rain beats against my skin, but it doesn't make a shred of difference because I am on fire.

His feral gaze meets mine, and it only sends pleasure to my core.

I want to give him everything he needs. I want to be the one he can turn to, just as he is for me.

"Open up for me." His tone is gruff.

I do as he says. His fingers run along my pussy before he thrusts two fingers in. I let out a scream and bite down on his shoulder, muffling my cry.

"No more hiding." He latches on my neck and sucks. "I want to hear every whimper, every moan. I want you to scream my name at the top of your lungs. Let the fucking world know that we won."

"Oh God, Luca," I cry out as he slides in another finger.

"My dirty girl likes being filled up, doesn't she?"

I nod, biting down on my lip.

"Kiss me," I moan.

I tug at his wet hair as his lips slam over mine, taking all my breath from my lungs. My body sags against the wall as he removes his fingers.

"Do you want my cock now, tesoro?"

"God, yes."

"Yes, what?"

"Please, Luca." I tug at his arms, begging him with my nails to fill me.

All I can think about is the relief I'll feel when that piercing hits inside me. He thrusts inside in one swift movement, and I scream as I stretch around him.

"Fuck, baby," he grits out. "I won't last long. You're so tight, so perfect."

I can barely breathe; all I can focus on is the ecstasy building within me.

He pushes up my T-shirt and squeezes my breast, pinching my nipple and sending my eyes rolling to the back of my head.

"I love you." His deep voice is almost sending me over the edge.

"I-I'm so close," I all but shout.

"Good girl, come all over my cock, beautiful," he whispers between sucking and nipping at my throat.

But he doesn't let up. He keeps pounding into me relentlessly. That metal bar hitting the spot that has my body trembling. He tightens his grip around me until I can't move.

He is doing exactly what I asked him to do.

I bite down on his neck and he shouts out my name, my back hitting against the brick wall with every hard thrust.

DEVOTED ~ 431

He pulls out of me, his nostrils flaring, and he spins me around, my shaky legs barely holding me up.

"Bend over the chair." His voice is gruff.

I do as he says, placing my hands on the wet plastic arms. He twists my hair around his fist and yanks my head back, at the same time thrusting into me from behind as his fingers dig into my ass.

His hips drive into me so hard our thighs slap, knocking me off balance. Losing my grip on the chair, we tumble forward and my mouth bounces off the arm of the chair.

"Fuck!" he cries, and my body sags when he pulls out, leaving me panting as I push myself up.

I turn and find him staring at me. A metallic taste hits my tongue, and I realize I've split my lip. He backs away with a horrified look as his hands pull at his hair.

"You didn't want that, Rosa! I hurt you!"

He pulls up his pants and goes to storm past me. I step in front of the door to block him, my palm hitting against his chest.

"I need to take a minute." He rubs his hands over his face.

"Nope. That's not how we're doing this, Luca."

He tips his head to the side.

"You didn't hurt me. I was close; you stopping is what hurt me. So go and sit back down and let me take care of *my* man."

I stand on my tiptoes, my puffy lips grazing his jaw. "Please?"

I push him back and saunter over to the metal chair. "Sit."

He blinks a few times before doing as I say.

A wild idea creeps into my mind when I spot a coil of rope on the floor.

I see the conflict on his face. I know what he needs, but he's so worried about breaking me. I want to show him I'm not that girl anymore. I can take control, I can look after us both.

I hate seeing him like this. I want him to forget, even just for a few minutes.

"Can I?" I hold up the rope between us. "You can't take it too far if you're tied to a chair." I wink at him.

He groans, tipping his head back. "Tie me, baby."

A thrill runs through me. I quickly get to work, tying his wrists together behind the chair. Once I'm satisfied he's not wriggling free, I pull my top over my head and walk around to face him.

"Jesus," he hisses, already tugging at his binds.

I straddle him and start working at the buttons of his shirt until it falls open, giving me the perfect view of his abs.

"That's better." I start peppering kisses along his chest, all the way up to his neck, occasionally biting down, causing him to groan.

I pull back and trail my finger down his stomach and pull his dick out of his boxers, stroking his shaft.

"Rosa, please."

I lift up, so the tip just teases my entrance. I lace my hands around his throat as I sink down.

"Shit," I hiss, sliding down to the base.

I start to ride him, nice and slow, rolling my hips so my clit rubs against him.

"You feel so good, Luca."

He bucks his thighs, and I press my weight back down to stop him. He leans forward and takes a nipple in his mouth.

I move back, removing my hands, and I start to circle my clit while riding him slowly.

"I need to touch you, Rosa." His gaze is fixed on my fingers.

"No."

His hooded eyes meet mine. I can see this is driving him crazy.

He tugs harder on his wrists.

"I swear to God, Rosa," he growls.

I lean forward and kiss him. He moans into my mouth, and I up the tempo, slamming myself on his cock.

I gasp when his hands wrap around me, pressing me closer into his chest. I don't care that he's free. I was only doing this to make him feel safer, not me. I trust him.

"Not even you can stop me from getting to you, tesoro." He grins.

His fingers run through my hair. When his hand grabs my ass, he guides me to fuck him how he needs.

I cry out when his hand slaps my ass.

"That was so fucking hot, Rosa."

"God, Luca. Yes."

He caresses my sore skin before his hand smacks there again. I crash my lips over his and ride him until I explode. He follows behind me, spilling into me.

The rain is still pouring down on us, dripping off our skin. He rests his wet forehead against mine, both of us fighting for air.

"Thank you," he whispers.

I stroke his cheek. "We look after each other, remember? I've got you."

I've never felt more alive. This morning, I thought my life was over. Now, I've never been stronger. With Luca by my side, with him inside me, I can take on the world.

He presses his lips gently over mine.

"Let's go get cleaned up for bed."

My heart jumps. Finally, I'm back where I belong.

Chapter Eighty
LUCA

I left Rosa sleeping soundly. As amazing as it was having her in my arms all night, I couldn't relax, but stared at the ceiling, debating our next move.

There is only one way out. I watch as the room starts to fill. Every single man that is part of our organization is filtering through the door of King's Gym until it's standing room only.

Frankie, Keller, and Jax stand behind me in the ring.

I can't help the pride that fills my chest. We built an army of loyal soldiers. We've come a long way in the last year.

I hold myself up on the ropes and look over the crowd as the last man shuts the door.

I hope I have this many when the war is over.

The room goes silent, all eyes on me, their leader.

"We have a two-part mission." I throw up my hand, index finger raised. "First, find Eva." I toss up another finger. "And second, kill Romano and Maria."

DEVOTED ~ 435

Enzo works his way through the masses, passing out a picture of each target.

"They're bringing their army over for war. We show no mercy. We have the commissioner on our side. They die. No questions, no hostages."

"Frankie and Keller will be splitting you into groups, giving you locations and targets to hit. It's going to be carnage out there."

The room erupts into cheers, and I smile. "You bunch of sick fucks."

"Where's Grayson, boss?" A ruddy-faced new recruit asks from the front.

"Having a baby as we speak."

Maddie is in labor. We've flown in the best doctors. They've gone to a second safe house with a small army of men to protect them.

I'm eagerly waiting for the call. I just hope it goes smoothly for them and that their beautiful baby girl arrives into this chaos safely. That's all I can ask for.

"Don't worry, he will be back soon to whip you all into shape. For now, though, you've got Keller the Killer himself." I smirk at my brother. "Now, let's go! Whoever has the highest kill count gets a hundred grand. Happy hunting."

I turn from the eager mob to Frankie. "I need you guys to meet me in my office tonight. I have something I need to discuss with you."

Keller and Frankie exchange a questioning look.

I duck under the ropes and push through the sea of our soldiers.

The war has started.

Now, I just need to let Rosa in on my crazy plan for us.

436 ~ LUNA MASON

BY THE TIME I get back, Rosa is still snuggled in bed. I stand in the doorway and watch her. She looks peaceful.

I shrug off my clothes and slip back into bed next to her. She sighs and cuddles up against my body, her soft skin brushing against mine. Even when my eyes threaten to close from exhaustion, I want her.

"Morning, boss man." Her voice is croaky. She rubs her eyes and smiles up at me.

I roll on top of her, pinning her hands above her head.

"I didn't have breakfast." I nuzzle my nose into the sensitive spot behind her ear.

She looks up at me through her long, dark lashes. "Is that so?"

My jaw tics when I spot those little purple bruises scattered on her bicep.

"Hey, back with me, Luca. I'm here with you."

I shake my head, taking in my woman.

"I'm so sorry I didn't save you sooner, that I didn't see what that monster was doing to you. I will make up for it every day for the rest of our lives. I'm so fucking proud of you, tesoro. The strength you've shown, you've fought harder than anyone."

Her eyes glisten with tears. As one starts to fall, I bend down and lick the salty drop from her cheek.

"I'm the luckiest guy in the world, getting to love you forever."

I just have to get us both out of here in one piece tomorrow. I don't know why my gut is screaming at me. Nothing in my life has ever been simple. Just a few more hours.

"No, I think I'm the luckiest woman. I've got myself a real-life book boyfriend who would burn down the world for me."

"I think we can do better than boyfriend." I nip at her bottom lip.

I will make this woman my wife.

"Now, get on your knees and grab that damn headboard. Time to feed your man." I wink, releasing my hold on her wrists. "Chop chop." I grin and sit on my heels, the blood rushing in my ears as she gets into position.

Taunting me with her curves and that fine ass, she wiggles her hips, gripping the black headboard.

I admire the view, the wetness already dripping down the inside of her thigh.

"You might want to hold on tight, baby."

She flicks her dark hair over her bare shoulders and fixes me with her big chocolate eyes. Grabbing her ass cheeks, I spread them open and blow on her pussy, which sends her bolting forward with a moan.

"I haven't even started yet, baby." I pat the curve of her butt. "Bring that back to me, and I'll put you out of your misery."

She drops her chest, pushing her hips back into my reach. "Good girl."

I feast on her like a man starved.

"So sweet, Rosa. All mine," I rasp.

"Oh my God, yes, all yours," she cries out.

I trace my finger along her spine. Mine to love and cherish and absolutely worship.

I grip her thighs, pushing her further into my face.

I want to suffocate. To take in so much of her, I forget my own name.

"Come on, baby, fuck my face." I slap her ass to spur her on.

She grinds against me, her legs shaking every time I lick her clit. Every time she twitches, it just makes me press harder, flick my tongue faster, and bury my nose deeper. She erupts when I suck. I let her ride her orgasm out, leaving her panting and her head collapsing onto the pillow.

Resting back on my knees, I line my cock up to her entrance, her ass still high in the air for me. Her body still twitches from her climax. "Are you ready to give me another one?" I'm desperate to be inside of her.

She pushes herself back, piercing herself on the tip, causing a moan to rip through my chest.

"I'll take that as a yes?"

"Always a yes," she pants against the pillow. I slide myself in, watching as her pussy stretches around me. My finger slides between her ass cheeks.

She cranes her neck, a sparkle in her eyes. "I want you there."

I stop pumping into her, registering her words. "Now?"

"Yes. Now. I want you to claim every single part of me, Luca."

I blow out a breath, rocking in and out of her.

"Please, Luca."

There isn't a chance in hell I could ever deny her anything. Let alone this.

"We will take it slow." I don't know if I'm saying that for her benefit, or mine.

I slip my cock out of her and thrust two fingers inside. "Get them nice and wet for me."

I bend over her back and pepper kisses along her spine, pushing a finger into her ass, causing her to gasp.

"You like that?"

"Hmm, yes."

I follow with a second; even with just two, it's so fucking tight.

I position myself behind her and spit in my hand, grabbing the base of my cock, making it soaking before nudging at her entrance. Her shoulders are up by her ears and her body is tense as she holds her breath.

"I'm going to need you to relax, tesoro. Trust me and breathe."

I inch further into her and hiss at the sensation. I won't last long, not with that tight hole suffocating my dick.

"Such a perfect girl, letting me claim your ass like this." I slowly press further into her.

"Oh, Luca," she cries. I nudge her legs open a bit further, bending down to kiss her shoulders. My finger finds her clit and starts to circle.

I hold her by the throat and pull her top half up, so her back is flush against my chest. I suck on her neck while my hand tightens around her neck, thrusting my finger inside her pussy. My cock is firmly in her ass.

Her eyes flutter closed, and little breathy moans escape her plump lips. "Ride me, baby. Let me fuck your ass how you want it."

Her legs spread over my thighs. She's perfectly open and exposed now, bouncing on my dick.

"I love you," I mutter into her neck before sucking on her tender skin.

Mine.

"Do you like being completely filled by me? Do you want this forever?"

"I do," she cries.

After a few more thrusts, my balls tighten, almost going back into my stomach. I empty myself into her ass, her name burning my throat as I erupt. Our sweaty skin slides against each other. She follows me shortly after. My chest swells, watching her come apart in my arms. I hold her tight, listening to my name leave her lips like a chant.

She turns in my arms, pulling me into her, her breasts squashing into my chest, and she kisses the air out of my lungs.

"Never let me go again, Luca."

"Not a chance. Never."

Once we settle in bed with her naked back resting against me, I cuddle into her until her breathing steadies. I hold on to her like she is the most precious thing in the world. I never want to let her go.

"How do you feel about running away with me?"

I look up at the ceiling and hold my breath. I know she wants to stay to find Eva.

She sits up. "Where are we going?"

"Greece?" I trace her arm with my fingertip, watching the row of goosebumps form behind it.

"All of our men are out searching for Eva, Romano, and Maria. Frankie is going to take the lead on this. I need you away from this, Rosa. And I swore I'd never abandon you, so we leave, together."

My fight is for her now. I will do anything to keep her safe.

"What about your family?"

"I'm going to speak to them. Keller and Grayson know how to look after their families, just like I will look after my own now."

"As long as you're sure, Luca. If they need you, we stay."

I shake my head and pull her into me. "Rosa, you are my life."

Chapter Eighty-One
ROSA

Sienna hands me a steaming mug of decaf. I helped her put Darcy and Max to bed. She has been on edge all day, waiting to hear from Maddie. Finally, at three p.m. we got the call. Maddie has a little baby girl, Hope. She is beautiful, with pouty lips and bright blonde, fluffy hair. My favorite pictures were the ones with Grayson holding Hope, next to a smiling Maddie.

All of these men are complete softies for their wives and babies.

I know Luca will be the same one day.

The men arrive home from the hospital and head straight to the office. Luca stops and gives me a kiss before heading up. A kiss that leaves me wanting more.

"Do you think they would want coffee?" I ask Sienna. I can't stop thinking of them sitting up there planning everything out.

She pulls her hair up into a bun and chuckles. "Scotch or brandy, maybe. Coffee, no."

"Oh."

Not once in all of this madness have I even touched a drop of booze. Not that I am anywhere near *cured*. I know I never will be. This, though, is a massive win for me.

And I only have one person to thank for that.

Luca.

"What are you smiling about? It looks good on you," Sienna says and sits next to me on the couch.

"Just that it's been a long time since I craved a drink, despite all of this. I think I'm getting somewhere."

She wraps an arm around me. "I'm happy for you. I'm glad you turned it around. Trust me, I've seen what that can do to a person."

"Yeah, it was rough. Luca is the one who pushed me through this."

"That's one thing about Luca. When he loves, he loves so fiercely. Even if it breaks him," she sighs.

"I won't break him. I'll try my best to heal him."

On my way to bed, I stop as I walk closer to the office, hearing Luca's voice.

"I'm not staying in this city with her, and I'm never letting her leave my side again."

Uncle Frankie raises his voice. "So you're going to leave us here to deal with this? Fucking bullshit. You can't just run from your problems. Rosa is safe here. I need your help to find Eva."

As the room comes into view, I can see that the men all sit around a large table.

Their heads turn to me. They probably hate me. I swallow the lump in my throat and back away.

"I-I'm sorry. I'll go."

"Rosa. Wait." Luca stands, but not before staring daggers at Uncle Frankie.

I suck in a breath as he throws his chair out of the way and beelines for me, wrapping his strong arms around me and pulling me tight.

I look up at him and smile, the first time I've genuinely smiled in a while. When he's holding me, nothing else matters. I slip my left hand from around his waist and press it against his chest.

He drops a kiss to my lips. "Come with me. You need to hear this. No more secrets between us. I won't hide anything from you. Ever."

I bite my lip to hide the smile, my heart fluttering. He's mine. No hiding, no sneaking around, no Dante.

He laces his fingers through mine and walks us over to his spot at the head of the table. Pulling out his seat, he drops down and motions for me to sit on his lap.

Nerves churn in my stomach as everyone stares at me. Guilt rips through me—I caused this.

"I'm so sorry," I blurt out. "I've put you all in danger because I couldn't take it anymore. I couldn't do it."

My hands cover my face, and Luca pulls me in.

Frankie slides his chair back and walks over to us.

"Rosa, don't you dare apologize for this. We are all sorry we couldn't save you sooner. It will eat me up every day. I should never have left you with your father. I should have protected you then, like I promised. But I will fight with my life to protect you now. I swear."

He shoots a glare at Luca behind me.

"This might be a good time to tell her," Luca says behind me.

My brows furrow in confusion. "Tell me what?"

Frankie huffs, his eyes narrowing at Luca. "Why I left after your mother's death."

"Okay?" I'm still confused.

"That explosion was in retaliation for your father's actions. He killed Dante's mom, Romano's first wife."

"Yeah, I know that. But why did that mean you had to leave? And then come back to kill him? I don't get it? Why didn't you even say goodbye?"

Luca squeezes me tighter.

Frankie balls his fist and looks away. "That explosion also killed Leila. My pregnant girlfriend."

My mouth falls open. I remember a pretty blonde woman there. I had no idea who she was. We always had guests, so it wasn't unusual.

"I killed your father as revenge. His stupidity ruined my life. I left because I didn't want to leave you and Eva without parents. But, now—" He runs a hand over his beard.

"—now, I wish I did. You should have been with me. I didn't realize my brother would fuck up so badly with his own kids."

"He changed after Mom died. I hated you, Frankie." I sigh.

He holds out his hands, palms up. "I know. I'm sorry."

"I was so angry. I knew that if you stayed, Dante would have never hurt me. And you would have never let him live like Dad did. I became an addict because I was petrified he would come back for me."

"Do you still need help?"

I shake my head. "I have it. Luca had me in counseling. He helped me through my withdrawals. I haven't touched a thing since. I mean, I came close."

Luca releases his tight grip on me, and I leap off his lap to hug my uncle. He was my best friend growing up. The one who would take me to school, listen to me moan about my bitchy friends, and take me for ice cream. A man whose life my father ruined, too.

"You saved me. That's all that matters. I'm just glad to have my uncle Frankie back." I hiccup. His chest vibrates against my face as he chuckles.

He hugs me tightly. "I'm sorry."

I pull away, wiping away my tears. "I forgive you."

I hop back on a smiling Luca's lap. I shiver as he brushes my hair away from my neck, his breath beating against my skin.

Grayson and Keller sit opposite Frankie and Theo with their arms crossed, looking at me and Luca.

Luca clears his throat. "The only way I can keep Rosa safe is leaving. I want Frankie to run this while I'm away. You want to take down Romano—he's yours."

I can feel heat flush my cheeks. "I can't let you do this; this is all my fault. I have to be here for Eva. You have to be here for your family."

"Rosa." He pins me with a stern glare. "I think I've made it pretty clear. My world revolves around you. Keeping you safe is my priority. I should never have agreed to marry Maria in the first place. I knew my heart belonged to you. I just thought I could one day have it all. And it turns out, I can. Because you are 'having it all,' Rosa. We can finally have the life we dreamed about."

Grayson clears his throat. "We'll make sure it's safe here, so you can both come home."

Frankie cracks his knuckles. "And Romano's mine to kill. I've been waiting ten long years for this. That fucker is going to pay."

446 ~ LUNA MASON

Luca gives him a sad smile, but quickly recovers himself. "I mean, I'm going to be lounging on a white beach in Greece with the love of my life. No rush."

I can't help but feel sorry for Keller, who's sitting there with a face like thunder looking on.

"Keller?" Luca's voice is soft. I look at Frankie and signal to the door. These two need a minute. They've just lost their mom, and now Luca is leaving.

Keller's tattooed hand runs over his face. I slink off Luca's lap, and he catches my hands. Turning to him, I give him a soft smile. "You need to speak to your brother, Luca."

He nods and sits back as Frankie, Theo, and Grayson stand to make their way to the door.

"I'm going back to my girls." Grayson salutes Luca and leaves.

I drop a kiss to Luca's lips.

"I'll see you back in bed, vita mia."

Chapter Eighty-Two
LUCA

I don't take my eyes off her as she walks out of the door. I want her by my side always. Grabbing a bottle of scotch tucked away in the safe, I pour two glasses.

"Are you okay?" I ask as Keller knocks back the drink.

He shakes his head and grunts.

"Are you?" he asks.

"Not even close, but getting there. I have my girl back."

"I don't understand why you have to leave."

I stand and walk to him, clasping my hand down on his shoulder.

"Frankie and Grayson can hold down the fort. We have our army. I don't want her anywhere near this."

He nods. "I'm proud of you, brother."

I tilt my head. *Proud?* I had our mom killed, and he was nearly blown up.

"You shouldn't be." I shake my head, the sudden need to drown my feelings creeping back up.

448 ~ LUNA MASON

"I'll miss you," he says.

"I know you will, I'm a fucking delight." I bite back a smile.

He spits out his scotch all over the table. "No, you're a pain in the ass, Luca."

I'm going to miss him.

"I never thought I'd see the day a woman nails Luca Russo down."

"She's special. I knew right from the start. I always joked about you and Grayson being pussy-whipped, but damn, I get it. That woman can tie me up and spank my ass and I won't argue."

She did rope me down, and I loved every second of it.

"Yeah, it happens, but I prefer to be the one doing the spanking," he chuckles.

A seriousness flashes across his face. "Why didn't you tell us? We could have helped. You didn't have to do this all on your own. If they threatened my daughter, you know I would have hunted every single one of those fuckers down."

His hand tightens around the glass.

"That's exactly why, Keller. You have a family. I'm not letting you risk it all to deal with my screw-ups. I stole the guns, I made the deal. I wouldn't let anything happen to my niece. I still couldn't save Mom though." My throat feels like it's closing in.

"You didn't kill Mom, Luca. Dante did. Romano did. And now we will get our revenge. You can't live your life blaming yourself. You'll go mad."

I scratch the back of my neck, the image of Mom lifeless on the floor still burning in my mind.

"I'll take you to the airstrip tomorrow. I'll call them to get the jet ready. I've heard Greece is nice this time of year."

We both stand, and he pulls me into his frame.

"I love you, brother. Never forget that. We might not have had the family growing up, but I'm glad we made our own." His voice breaks as he speaks.

"I wouldn't change it for the world."

Chapter Eighty-Three
LUCA

Rosa's head rests on my shoulder as Keller drives us to the airport. I let mine roll against the seat and let out a breath. "A few more minutes and we start our new life."

She sits up, beaming. "It's going to be everything we ever dreamed of."

I nod. "And more." I pull her back against me.

Keller looks at me through the rearview mirror and smiles.

I stroke her silky hair, finally feeling complete. I have everything I've ever dreamed of right here.

Our hangar comes into view. We did it.

"I love you, Ro——"

My body jolts and crashes into the metal door. Glass shatters around me. I instinctively wrap Rosa closer to me to protect her.

"Stay down," I shout. I rub my forehead and blood covers my fingers.

"Rosa." Panic laces my voice. I turn to her, and her worried eyes stare back at me.

The door slams, making her jump in my arms. Keller rushes out of the vehicle and rounds the front of the car, aiming his gun at the blacked-out SUV that's impaled into the passenger side of our car.

My Bentley.

Grabbing Rosa's face in my hand, I let out a ragged breath. I check her over, relieved when there isn't a mark on her.

She flinches and squeezes her eyes shut as the gun goes off. I squash her face into my chest and hold her tight, my other hand wrapping around my pistol.

Keller storms back to the car, opening my door. "We gotta go."

He puts his aviators up on the top of his head, fury in his eyes. I hesitate until I hear the rumbling of engines in the distance. I knew it was too good to be true.

And I know exactly who they want. But they aren't having her.

"Rosa, look at me."

Tears stream down her cheeks.

"I need you to be strong for me," I whisper, doing everything to keep my voice from breaking. "I need you to be brave."

She shakes her head. "Luca, no. I know what you're thinking. Please don't leave me. Not again."

I stroke my thumb under her eyes and wipe her tears. I turn to my brother, his face stoic. "Take her. Keep her safe."

He shakes his head. "Luca, don't do this. We can find a way. We need to run."

I gesture behind him at the convoy of blacked-out SUVs.

"There's too many. Take her. Get to Frankie as soon as you

can. Tell him to do whatever he has to, to keep Rosa safe. Don't worry about me." I rush my words out.

"Luca, I swear to God. I'm not letting you do this." She clambers onto my lap, wrapping her arms tightly around my neck.

Tears burn in my eyes as her sweet vanilla scent invades me.

I bury my face in her neck. "I love you, Rosa. I'll be yours forever. One day we will have it all, whether it's in this life or the next. My heart only beats for you. Now, please, go with Keller. Let me finish this."

Before she can reply, I yank her head up and crash my lips over hers. *One last kiss.*

I turn to Keller. "Please, just take her."

"No!" she screams, tightening her grip around my neck, but I don't move. I release my hands from her and hold them in the air and look to Keller, who leans in and grabs her by the waist. Her body hangs on to mine as he pulls her off me, taking my heart with him.

Her body flails against Keller's.

"Get off me!" she screams.

I can't look at her. I can't have this be the last memory of her.

Keller holds her up in one arm, his fingers tightly wrapped around his gun in the other. "Just hold them down. Don't give them anything. We will get to you. I swear to God. There isn't anywhere in this city we won't be able to find you. I'll burn the whole fucking place down if I have to. Just keep yourself alive."

I'm likely walking into my own death. I know this. It's strange, but I'm okay with that so long as Rosa lives.

"Make sure you tell my nieces and nephews how legendary their uncle was."

"Luca. Stop it," he warns.

I slide out of the car and hand him my gun.

"What—"

I hold up my hand to cut him off and shake my head. "You protect her. With everything. Now go."

He doesn't move.

"Fucking go!" I scream.

"Shit," he mutters.

I watch as he sprints away, Rosa's wails ringing in my ears. She will be safe with him. At least I know that. I watch until he turns the corner and they're out of sight.

Tugging my suit jacket, I straighten my tie. Then I twirl the ring on my finger and wait.

The engines of five SUVs roar toward me.

I hold up my hands and walk toward them, dropping to my knees on the ground.

I keep my eyes pinned on the car in the center. I know that bitch is in there, so I give her my best grin.

The car door slams and three masked men run toward me, training their barrels to my head.

"Is this really necessary?" I mock. "You want an empire, Maria? I'll give you mine if you ask nicely," I shout in the direction of the middle vehicle.

That will get her. She might want revenge, but she's also greedy. I'm betting on the fact she's trying to get power and prove to her dad that she's worthy. It's the only thing I can use to my advantage. I lived with her long enough to know her weakness.

One of the men puts his hand to his earpiece, and he nods.

He grabs me by the collar, his gun now pressed against my temple as he drags me to the SUV.

"We're going to have so much fun, Luca," Maria purrs, making my skin crawl.

"I can't wait," I mutter.

Something sharp jabs into my neck. "What the hell?" I squeeze my eyes shut. Of course she's drugging me.

"You bitch," I hiss as everything starts to blur. Her cackle is the only thing I can hear before the world goes black.

Chapter Eighty-Four
ROSA

My rib cage burns as Keller's massive arm crushes me against him, racing us through the streets. I jolt as he comes to a sudden stop, and I peek out of one eye. All I see is dull brick walls on either side of me.

He bends and puts me down on my shaky legs. "I need to make a call."

"Is Luca going to be okay, Keller? Are they going to kill him?"

My chest starts to heave. I can't lose him.

His strong hands clamp down on my biceps. I stare up into his dark eyes. He might think he hides it, but he's scared.

"Honestly, Rosa, I don't know. All I know is, I promised him I'd keep you safe. We focus on that first. We will do everything we can to bring him back to you. I just need you to keep it together."

"He can't die, Keller. I-I—" As I choke on my words, he pulls me into his side.

"Shh, Rosa. Luca is a clever guy. And tough as nails. He grew up fighting for his life. He won't stop now. Especially not now that he has everything to lose."

He slips out his phone and brings it to his ear, still wrapping me tight. Enough to keep my rising panic at bay for now.

"Frankie. We have a big problem. They've taken Luca."

I can't make out the words, but I can hear the shouting on the other end.

"She's with me. She's safe. I need you and Grayson to come get us. Get Enzo to source my location. I'll keep us moving, bring the armored truck." He cuts the call.

"Rosa, we gotta move."

Before I can agree, he bends and scoops me up again.

"I can walk. I'm not that fragile."

"Luca tells me you're the strongest woman he knows. But that's not why I'm carrying you. I can't have you lagging behind. You could be an open target."

"Oh. Thank you."

My body vibrates as he carries me. With my face nuzzled in his neck, tears stream down my cheeks. The only thing I can think about is being ripped away from the love of my life.

Car tires screech against the road, and I barely look up at the truck before I'm being plonked in the back seat and pulled into Frankie's chest.

Keller gets in the passenger seat and we take off.

Over the roar of the engine, I can barely hear the men whisper-shouting in the front. I don't want to hear how bad this is. I just want my Luca back.

"It will be okay, Rosa," Frankie whispers.

He might normally have the best poker face, but even he isn't hiding his worry.

"What's the plan? We have to act fast." The anger in Grayson's tone makes me flinch.

"I'm waiting on a phone call. Enzo is on standby, as are our men. I put out the call to every single one of them. We have hundreds ready. I just need his location."

"Romano?" Keller turns in his seat to face us.

Frankie shakes his head. "Even better, Maria. I can wrap that vile bitch around my little finger."

I push myself back from my uncle. "You speak to Maria?"

"I worked with them for six years, Rosa. They know what I'm capable of, and they don't want me as their enemy. I said I'll do what it takes, didn't I? I suspect, finding Luca, we should find Eva. They don't have many options in this city."

"Y-you haven't found her yet, though?" Doubt starts to creep up. If we haven't got Eva yet, how can we get to Luca quick enough to save him?

"Now that they have Luca, they'll think they've outdone us. They knew Eva wasn't enough to go for control. Luca is. I may have to forge a deal, though."

Frankie shakes back his sleeve and checks his watch. "Any minute now. Keep driving, Grayson."

"What deal?"

Frankie looks at me but doesn't speak.

"What deal, Frankie?" Keller repeats my words.

"It doesn't matter. They won't get it, they just need to think they will for long enough."

Keller's dark eyes flick to mine, and he shakes his head. We all know he's talking about me. I'm who Maria wants.

My fingers clutch at his arm. "Just give me over. If that

saves Luca, just give me to her. You guys need him more than me."

Frankie scoffs. "Not happening. If Luca loses you, Rosa, we'll essentially lose you both. He won't survive that."

Luca is strong. He'll be fine without me. "But—"

"Enough, Rosa. I've got this, okay?" Frankie pins me with a glare, the same as he used on me when I was growing up, to let me know when he was serious. I sit back, defeated.

His phone rings. "And here she is."

The car is silent, and Frankie brings the phone to his ear.

"Maria. Nice of you to finally return my call."

Even from here, I can hear her screechy voice faintly.

"You have something of mine. So, I'm listening."

Frankie taps his fingers on his thigh, his face expressionless. My hands instinctively wrap around my throat. God, I can't breathe.

"Hmm. What makes you think I'd do that? You have Luca, now I run the city, so I get to decide what happens next. You've done me a favor, really." He glances at me and shakes his head.

"And why would I want to work with you? You have my fucking niece. Although, I did enjoy cutting your brother's dick off."

I gasp. Keller and Grayson laugh up front. Frankie brings his finger to his lips. I gulp, backing away to the other side of the car until my back hits the door.

Frankie takes the phone away from his ear and rolls his eyes at Maria's screaming.

"Have you quite finished, Maria? I get it—you're trying to impress Daddy. Now release Eva back to me, we have a deal. We don't even need to let your father know about the mess you've caused here. Why isn't he here, anyway?"

What about Luca? The only thing calming my nerves is the calmness from Keller and Grayson. If they believed anything Frankie was saying, they wouldn't hesitate to kill Frankie, especially Grayson.

"Interesting. It will take quite a while for him to bring his army over from Italy. He's left you here to die, Maria."

He cuts the call.

I can't take much more of this. I run my hands through my hair. I just want him back.

Frankie holds up his cell, watching the screen. "We should have his location in five, four, three—"

His phone pings.

"Gotcha."

Ringing fills the car.

Another husky voice comes through the speaker. "I've programmed the location into your truck navigation, Grayson. Everyone is on their way now. They've been briefed to clear the building for your arrival to get you safely to Luca. Depending on how many men there are, you may have to join the fight. It's a big unit, so I'm expecting a small army to greet you."

"Don't worry, Enzo, we have that covered. Truck is loaded," Grayson says.

My palms start to sweat. "We need to get Rosa back to the safe house, is it on the way? We can divert," Keller says, looking to Grayson.

"No time. We protect her with our lives. This truck is armored." Frankie shrugs off his navy jacket, and his white shirt follows. He unfastens his black vest at the shoulder and sides.

He shoves it onto my lap and redresses. I stare down at the bulletproof vest.

"You need that more than me! You're walking into a war

zone, Uncle Frankie!" Panic rises. I just got him back. I can't lose him. Tears start to run down my face.

His voice is calm as he pats my knee. "I don't need it. I failed you once, never again. Now put it on."

We park down a side street, still in broad daylight. "Keller, protect her. Enzo is sending more men as backup. Just stay here; don't move unless you have to."

Grayson and Frankie jump out of the car and open up the trunk, arming themselves with guns, knives, and grenades as I look on in horror.

I pull my legs up to my chest and hug them tight.

Keller turns around to look at me. "Rosa, this will be over soon. Just hang in there for him."

Of all the things I've endured in my life, this moment right here is the worst. There is nothing I can do to save the man who gave me the world. Soon, I could lose everything that has ever mattered to me. I won't survive that.

I refuse to live without him.

The trunk slams shut. My phone starts ringing in my purse on the floor. I rifle through it and my heart stops when Eva's name flashes up on the screen.

"K-Keller. It's Eva calling."

"Shit. Frankie, Grayson, get over here!" he shouts before turning to me. "Answer it, put it on speaker."

Chapter Eighty-Five
LUCA

I gasp for air as the freezing-cold water sears my bare flesh. I hiss and bite down, shaking the droplets off my head.

"Oh, look who's finally awake, darling."

My vision may be hazy, but I'd know that irritating noise anywhere.

I sit up on my knees, yanking at the chains on my wrists that keep my arms out like I'm on the cross. Turning my head, I can see they're attached to the cinder-block wall behind me.

Her laugh echoes through the dingy warehouse. "Not so tough now, are you?"

Her heels click against the concrete. I bring my head up to face her. Despite her immaculate appearance, those bloodshot eyes don't hide her pain.

Good.

"I'm doing just fine. Never better," I croak out.

462 ~ LUNA MASON

As she steps closer, my anger spikes. Armed men follow behind her. She drops down to meet my eyes. My stomach churns as she trails one of her pointy fingers along my abs.

"It's a shame, really; you would have been a good fuck. We could have ruled this empire together."

"I'd rather die than fuck you," I hiss.

Her finger brushes down toward my belt.

"Don't you dare."

A sadistic grin takes over her face before she leans in and licks slowly along my jaw.

"Don't worry, your death will come in time, darling. We just have to get through the final show. I'm going to enjoy watching your heart truly shatter as I slice up your little girlfriend right before your eyes." She bites down on my earlobe.

I just keep telling myself Rosa is safe. My men will protect her with their lives. Maria can't get to her. I don't give two shits what they do to me. I can cope. Grayson's trained me to endure a decent amount of pain, and when the time comes, I'll lay down my life for Rosa without a second thought.

"You won't touch her," I sneer.

Her hands frame my face. "Oh, Luca, Luca, Luca. You really think I can't sweet-talk my dear friend Frankie into bringing her to me? I'm quite convincing when I need to be. That man only wants one thing: power."

I suck in a breath. My lungs are on fire as her sickly sweet perfume suffocates me.

"Enrique, bring her in."

No. Frankie wouldn't. Not his own niece. Would he? He shot his own brother.

I yank at the bindings on my wrists like a man possessed.

The door opens, and Eva is pushed through. She can

barely walk. The heavyset guy escorting her is having to hold her upright. Blood trickles down the side of her face.

Her eyes lock with mine and go wide.

"Just let her go; you have me now. That's enough," I say.

Maria grips my chin harshly. "You aren't in any position to make demands, Luca. Will this hurt your precious Rosa? Seeing her sister's dead body?"

Pain radiates in my chest. It won't just hurt her, it will kill her. She's risked herself for months to protect her sister.

Maria stands, and one of her men hands her a silver handgun. She presses it against my temple.

I look her dead in the eye, "Do you honestly believe I fear death, Maria?"

Her lips creep up into a smile and she bites down on her lip "Oh, don't worry, you aren't going until you watch Rosa die in front of your eyes. In the meantime, I am going to break you to within an inch of your life for the embarrassment you've brought me. You ruined everything for me, Luca. All because you couldn't keep your dick out of that little slut."

I scream out in pain as she grabs a hold of my crotch. Her nails dig into my shaft and she squeezes. My whole body erupts in pain, and I can barely see through the stars that cloud my vision.

She twists, and I gasp for air, tears pooling in my eyes. I go limp when she releases her grip. "I hear Frankie cut off my brother's dick. I might have to do the same to you later."

She stands back, her attention now on Eva, who is wavering weakly beside her. She aims her gun at Eva's head.

Eva tries to hold up her hands, which are handcuffed at her waist. "M-Maria, please don't. I can help you. I can take you to Rosa. I know I can."

"Don't you fucking dare, Eva," I spit out.

Anger replaces my pain. How dare she? "After everything your sister has endured to protect you, this is how you repay her? Keep your mouth shut."

Eva can't look at me. "I can. Rosa always looks out for me. Dante told me she almost found me herself. If you let me call her, she will come."

"Eva, think about what you're doing. Rosa is your sister. She loves you. She would never do that to you. Don't do this." I try to keep my tone soft, not to startle her.

Inside, I want to kill her myself. I don't care if she's Rosa's sister. She's putting my girl at risk, she dies.

Maria winks at me. "Looks like you gave yourself a few minutes to prove your worth, little Eva."

I pull against the wall holding my wrists. "Eva, please don't do this to her."

She hands Eva a phone. "Time to speak to big sis."

I close my eyes. Rosa only has one phone on her, but I don't know which one it is. I hope to God it's not the number Eva has.

My heart almost beats out of its chest as the call dials on the speaker. I want to throw up. I know Rosa will come running; I just hope my men don't let her.

"Eva." Rosa's soft voice comes through the speaker. As I go to scream at her to hang up, a hand clamps over my mouth. The more I struggle, the tighter it gets. I can't breathe. I try to fight him off. I have to stop her.

"Rosa, they're letting me go, but I need you to pick me up, alone. Can you do that for me?"

"Are you okay, Eva? I've been so worried about you. I'm so sorry I couldn't protect you. I tried so hard, I'll explain everything later. We never gave up on you." Rosa's panic comes through and my heart breaks.

Eva looks up at Maria, who nudges her to carry on.

"I'm okay."

"Oh, thank God."

"So, can you come?" Eva shifts nervously.

"I'll need to slip out somehow, but yeah, I'll be there."

"I'll text you the address. Thank you, Rosa."

"I love you, Eva."

The hand is removed from my mouth, and I suck in a lungful of air.

"Well, thank you. You're no use to me now, though."

Maria brings her arm up to point her gun in Eva's face.

She pulls the trigger. I avert my gaze as Eva's body drops to the floor.

I shake my head, the pain I feel only for Rosa.

I keep my expression unaffected as Maria drops down to one knee next to me. Blood pools on the floor from the hole in Eva's skull.

"I can't wait for Rosa to see that." She smiles excitedly.

Her warm breath hits against my lips, making me want to throw up the contents of my stomach. She licks her shiny lips, her gaze roaming my face, and swipes the moisture from my forehead.

With the bloodstained water on her fingertips, she tips her head back slightly and licks her finger clean.

I screw my face up in disgust.

"Mmm." She licks her lips and brings her nose to mine. My heartbeat hammers in my ears with the frustration of being so close to her and not being able to kill her.

As she leans in to kiss me, I tip my head back and smash it forward, hitting her square in the nose.

She gasps, blood gushing from her nose. I can't help but smile as her hands cover her face, the crimson seeping through.

The men all rush to her side as she stands.

"I think it's broken," she shrieks.

A big bald guy storms toward me. I brace myself as he pulls back his fist and sends my head bouncing off the wall behind me. Pain sears through my cheekbone. I do my best to shake the pain away, blinking back the stars in my vision.

The metallic twinge of blood swirls around my tongue, and I spit it straight onto his black, shiny boot.

He grunts and kicks me in the ribs, slamming my body against the concrete. I grunt out in pain as he does it again. My ribs crack under the force of his boot.

"Fuck you," I choke out. Clenching my fists and tugging on my chains doesn't relieve the stabbing agony in my side.

"Where is Dante?" he grunts in a husky Italian accent.

The asshole behind him with the slick black ponytail watches as Maria gets patched up in the corner.

"Difficult to say. I guess, in a way, he's everywhere."

Maria looks over, blood still dripping from her nose. She storms close and grabs my throat, her nails sinking beneath my skin. "Give me my brother's body, you monster."

She drags her nails deep into my flesh, all the way down the column of my throat. I tip my head back and quash the urge to scream at her.

When she gets to the base of my neck, she stops, keeping her claws in me.

"There is no body, Maria."

Hurt flashes across her face before she quickly rights herself. With a murderous glint, she pulls a flick knife from her bra and brings the blade up.

I gulp as she plunges the blade into the side of my abdomen. "Fuck!" I roar out.

She rips the knife out and my body sags. Holy shit, it

hurts. I look down at the blood trickling out from my side and breathe through the pain, just like Rosa taught me.

"Stitch him up. I need to get hold of Daddy."

Sweat beads on my forehead. The physical pain is one thing, but the panic I'm feeling by being chained here and not being able to protect Rosa is all I can think about.

A loud explosion shakes the walls. I bite back a grin. They took their damn time. I already have a stab wound, an injured dick, and a dead sister-in-law.

The familiar sound of gunfire has Maria's eyes going wide.

"What is going on?" Panic is clear in her voice.

They truly had no idea of the size of our organization. They might hold the power in Italy, but here, we rule.

Ponytail and crew head out of the door.

"Like that's going to stop them. It's over, Maria," I mutter.

Her eyes flash with anger and she storms toward me. "It isn't. Your men can't compete with ours."

"Let's see shall we, *darling*?" I mock.

Adrenaline floods through my body, dulling the pain from my stab wound and fucked-up ribs. Although, with the amount of blood still trickling out, they need to move quickly. She swipes up her blade from the floor, and I let out an agonized cry as she plunges it into my stomach. The pain sears like fire as she rips it back out.

She stands, her eyes fixing on the blood pouring from me, and shrugs. "I think that means I win."

Chapter Eighty-Six
FRANKIE

I crouch behind Grayson as we approach the parking lot of the warehouse. My ears ring from the gunfire.

He doesn't turn. "You ready? You cover behind, we take it straight through the middle. Our guys will hold them back. We have to get in there as quickly as we can."

"I've got you," I say, gripping the gun in my hand tighter.

He nods and motions to move forward.

We stay low and work our way around the wall.

Bodies are dropping to the ground. I follow behind Grayson, who's firing out shots left, right, and center with complete precision each time.

A guy launches himself at me from my left. I swing my arm across and shoot him in the stomach, kick him in the chest, and put a second round in his head.

Just another day at work.

Grayson beats open the warehouse door while I cover him. Our guys are doing a good job of keeping them back.

"Let's go," Grayson calls out behind me. I walk into the warehouse and close the door shut behind me.

As Grayson is scoping out the first row, I keep my sights aimed in front of me. He points to my right and I nod. Keeping my feet light, I check between each aisle of wooden crates stacked until I reach the end, where Grayson is waiting for me.

A door swings open behind him, catching my attention. Two guys burst through. "Behind you," I shout. I've already aimed and am pulling the trigger at the first guy. Grayson wipes the second out with a clean head shot.

Damn, he's fucking good.

My guy doubles over, clutching at his chest.

I pull the blade from my boot and grab him by the hair, tipping his head back to expose his throat. I slash across from one side to the other, watching as his life drains out of him.

I can't explain the pleasure I get from watching someone pathetically gasp for their last breath.

I let go, and he thuds to the ground. Grayson is already smashing down another door with his foot.

"It's blocked."

"They're in there, then. Come on, put your back into it, Grayson." Excitement dances through my veins. Everything is falling into place.

Maria will get me to Romano. I don't care how—that motherfucker is going to die.

We both turn as the warehouse shakes with more explosions coming from outside.

Grayson shrugs. "I taught them everything I know," he says before turning his attention back to the door.

Two more kicks, and Grayson gets it open enough to barge through.

Grayson starts shooting. A bullet flies past my head. I duck to the left, firing back. His gun clicks as a greasy, ponytailed guy runs toward Grayson with a blade in his hand.

I don't hesitate; I shoot him.

Scanning the room, I do a quick tally. We've killed three guys.

I smell her sweet perfume before I see her. The sound of her heels gradually gets louder until she comes around the corner.

"I see you made it, Frankie," she purrs.

She slinks toward me. My stomach churns, and I repress the memories of fucking her to the back of my mind. It was a long time ago, before she got all crazy.

"Maria."

She sashays up to me, and her hands start running up my shirt.

I look down. "You can't tempt me with your pussy today, sweetheart."

"Of course," Grayson mutters, shaking his head.

I run my fingers through her hair, and she fake smiles up at me. I grip it hard and yank her head back, bringing my lips to her cheek. "Take me to Eva and Luca."

"As you wish." She widens her puffy lips.

Oh shit, the confidence in her tone. This isn't good.

I nod to Grayson to follow us. This woman can't be trusted.

She leads us to another door. Her fingers wrap around the handle and she pushes it open.

Grayson is first in. "Fuck, Luca."

Maria tries to brush past me, but I grab her forearm and yank her into me. "You're not going anywhere."

She bats her lashes and puts her hand over mine. "You won't hurt me, Frankie. You know what Daddy will do."

That makes me genuinely smile. "I'm counting on it."

She frowns before her eyes go wide. She's catching on. I want them all dead.

"Frankie, get the fuck in here," Grayson yells.

"What have you done?" I growl.

She giggles. "Only what you would have in my shoes."

Well, shit.

They're both dead, then.

I drag her behind me. I spot Eva first. I squeeze Maria's arm so tight she screams out in pain. I barely notice it over the sound of blood hammering in my ears. Romano's death will now be ten times more painful than what I had planned.

Despite how I feel inside right now, I make sure no one on the outside can see that. Least of all Maria.

That's how I thrive in this world.

Grayson is yanking the chains from the wall when I glance over. Luca groans, and I notice blood is pouring from his gut. He's barely moving.

"Come on, Luca, stay with me, for fuck's sake." There is a hint of panic in Grayson's voice as he presses down on Luca's stomach to stop the bleeding.

"Where is Rosa?" he coughs out weakly.

Grayson glances at me before answering. "She's safe, Luca."

A stark reminder why, in this life, you don't have anyone close enough to rip you apart.

Never again.

"Can you get him out of here?" I call to Grayson.

He taps on his earpiece to Enzo. "Yes. Doc is on the way, too."

He helps Luca to his feet, holding him up. The color drains from Luca's face as the seconds pass.

I turn to Maria with fury. She tries to take a step back, but then she pulls her knee back and smashes it straight into my balls.

"Jesus fucking Christ." I double over and let her wrist go, my gun clattering to the floor.

I see her red fingernails through my blurry vision, and she picks up the gun. I force myself upright and groan.

She trembles slightly as she points the gun at Grayson.

Everything seems to stop; her finger twitches over the trigger.

I launch myself at her, snatching her wrist and pulling it toward me.

I hear the gun go off first, then I feel the pain splintering through me.

"Shit."

Chapter Eighty-Seven
LUCA

I blink a few times, waiting for the pain from the bullet to explode through me, but it doesn't.

"Frankie, are you okay?" Grayson yells from my side.

Frankie shrugs off his jacket, revealing red soaking through his shirt at his shoulder.

He looks down at the blood, and his sights firmly set on Maria. She backs away, throwing her hands in the air as he lifts her up by the throat.

"Get Romano on the phone." His voice is deep with anger.

She claws at his hands. He laughs in her face and manhandles her to dig into the back pocket of her black, skintight jeans to retrieve her cell.

"Code?"

She snaps her lips together, her face reddening as he increases the pressure.

"Code?"

He releases her momentarily and then flicks open a blade, pressing it against her throat.

"123193."

"Maria, is everything okay?" Romano's voice has me grinding my teeth.

"Daddy, help!" she screams. Frankie nudges the knife in further, enough for blood to start to trickle down the steel.

"Romano." His voice is calm.

There's a pause. "Frankie. What's going on?"

"I'm about to rip your world apart, Romano. Just like you did to me."

"I don't understand. You worked for me for years."

Frankie's deep laugh booms through the room.

"You really are clueless. I never came to you to pay Marco's debts. I was planning my revenge."

"For what?"

"That explosion didn't just kill Carla and Rita. No, it also killed my girlfriend and unborn child."

Maria's eyes go wide as the line goes silent.

"Nothing to say?" Frankie yells into the line.

"I didn't know." Romano's reply is so quiet I can barely hear him.

"Well, now you do, and now you're going to fucking pay. Starting with Maria's life. And then I'm coming for you. I won't stop until your whole world explodes around you. Now say one last goodbye to your precious daughter."

"Frankie, no, please don't do this. We can figure something out. I've already lost both sons," Romano pleads.

"Daddy!" Tears roll down her face. I feel no sympathy for her. She did this to herself.

"You wasted your last chance of saying goodbye. I'll see you very soon, Romano."

Frankie cuts the call, throwing the phone across the room before turning his attention back to Maria.

"I'll see you in hell, sweetheart."

He slides the knife across her neck from one side to the other in a swift motion. Her face pales as she splutters her final breaths. He holds her up until all the life is drained from her. Then he smiles.

He tosses the body to the ground. I follow his eyeline to Eva, face down on the floor in a pool of blood.

"Grayson, I'm going to need you to get this bullet out of me." Frankie doesn't look up from his niece, his face completely neutral.

"Let's get back to the truck. I'll do it there."

My legs are heavy as we walk through the warehouse. It takes every remaining bit of strength I have to lift my feet off the ground.

"Where is Rosa?" I manage to choke out, just three words leaving my lungs on fire.

"She's in the truck with Keller," Grayson grunts with my arm around his shoulders.

She's here?

The light burns my eyes. A sea of red covers the parking lot. The bodies of men are everywhere.

"Is the boss okay?" I see a blurry figure; I recognize the voice. I just can't see shit.

"I need to get to Rosa." I need to say goodbye.

I fall to a heap on the ground. I physically can't fight anymore.

I just need to get to my Rosa.

To tell her how much I love her.

To kiss her one last time.

I try to speak, but my body won't let me.

It's giving up on me.

Chapter Eighty-Eight
ROSA

"Keller, what's taking them so long?" My knee bounces on the floor mat as I try to watch out the windows.

He keeps his head straight, his knuckles turning white as he grips the steering wheel. "Enzo said they were coming out."

It seems like a lifetime ago Frankie and Grayson left. I hug my knees tighter. I haven't stopped crying, to the point that my eyes are burning.

"Oh, fuck." Keller opens his door and jumps out. My heart stops when I see them.

A red-faced Grayson is carrying Luca in his arms. Frankie comes into view, holding his shoulder, covered in blood.

I open the car door and step out, my legs barely holding me up. I grab the handle to steady myself.

"Get back in the truck," Frankie shouts, wincing while pointing at the van and storming toward me.

I clamber back in. Keller rushes over and opens the back

passenger door. Grayson lays Luca down on the seat next to me and I gasp. I want to be sick.

There is so much blood.

He's so pale.

"Put his head on your lap. I'll move him back so I can get in and keep pressure on his wounds."

I lift my hands from my lap, and Grayson lays Luca's limp head on me.

I can barely see through my tears.

"Luca," I whisper. "Is he—?"

I can't say the words.

"No." Grayson pushes in and slams the door behind him.

My hands cup his face; he's freezing cold. His breathing is shallow. The truck rumbles to life, and Keller erratically drives us.

I can't stop looking at Luca's face. Why does he look so peaceful? Why does he look dead?

I bend down and kiss his forehead. "Please don't leave me, Luca," I beg, hoping he can hear my voice. My tears drip onto his cheek.

"What the hell happened in there?" Keller shouts, making me jump.

"I got shot, Maria is dead, and Luca's not in great shape. The doc is meeting us at the safe house," Frankie gruffs out, clearly in pain himself.

Keller tosses his phone at Frankie. "Call Sienna. Make sure they're in their rooms. I don't want them seeing this," he growls.

I turn to Grayson. "He needs a hospital, not just a doctor."

"It's not safe there, not now. We need to know Romano's whereabouts. Our doc is the best, don't worry. We even have a setup for surgery in the basement." He keeps the pressure on Luca's wounds.

I can't bring myself to look at them. As soon as Frankie cuts the call, I swallow the bile in my throat and ask the question I don't know if I want to hear the answer to.

"What about Eva?"

The car falls silent and I know.

I look up and Frankie turns in his seat, the pain obvious on his face. He opens his mouth, and I cut him off, stroking my hand through Luca's hair for some sort of comfort.

"Don't say it, Frankie."

"I'm so sorry." He balls his jacket and presses it against his shoulder.

I look down at Luca.

My whole body starts to shake violently, and I let it all out. My sister's gone, Luca is dying on my lap, and it's all my fault.

I should have taken her place.

"I'm sorry, Luca. I'm so sorry." I hug his head.

We pull up outside our new home, and I can't move. Not even when Grayson takes Luca from me. They're talking, but I can't concentrate.

Frankie opens my door. "Come on. Luca needs you."

I take his hand, and he helps me out of the truck. I look at his bleeding shoulder and a fresh wave of pain hits me.

"You've been shot," I sob.

He pulls me into his hard chest, wrapping his good arm around me.

"I need you to listen to me. You're a fucking Falcone. We are strong. We are powerful. You, Rosa, are the strongest of us all. After everything you've been through, you amaze me. We need to go in there and be strong for Luca. We can never bring back the people we've lost, Rosa. It's life. We can't let it kill us. You did everything you possibly could for Eva. You always have. Don't let this break you."

I press my face harder into his chest. I can't bear it.

"What if he dies, Frankie? I can't sit in there and watch. I can't do it, Frankie."

He strokes my back. "Rosa, if the worst really does happen, don't you want to be by his side? I'd give anything to have been there to hold Leila's hand when she took her last breath. Don't let him down. Not now."

I release my arms and step back, wiping away my tears with the back of my hand. "Take me to him."

He nods, his hand quickly putting pressure back on his shoulder.

"Hey, isn't that really painful?"

"Extremely. I'm waiting for Grayson to fix me up."

I roll my eyes. Of course.

I follow him to the door, past a crowd of armed guards.

I WATCH THE seconds tick by on the clock on the wall. Frankie clears his throat opposite me. Two hours, forty-five minutes, and thirty seconds since Keller and Grayson took Luca into the operating room.

I tear my stare from the minute hand to my uncle, who is now in fresh clothing and has one less bullet in his body.

"How are you so calm?" I ask, the silence becoming deafening.

"A lot of practice over the years."

"Oh." I take another small sip of my coffee.

"I will avenge her death, Rosa," he says quietly.

I nod and look at the coffee swirling around in my mug. I can't even comprehend that she is really gone. I'll never get to see my sister again. I'll never get to hug her, to hear her laugh.

He can avenge her death all he likes. It doesn't change the fact that she's never coming home.

I don't have words or energy right now. "How did she die?"

"It was quick. That's all you need to know." He rubs a hand over his face, pulling out a packet of cigarettes from his pocket, sliding one across the table to me.

"I could do with something else, but I guess this will do." I shrug and pick it up.

"Rosa." His voice is stern.

"What?"

"You aren't going back there. Don't even consider it."

"I said I could do with it, not that I am," I snap back.

We head outside. I plonk myself down on the seat and tip my head back to look up at the stars. I inhale deeply, and tears pool in my eyes as I remember the nights with Luca, doing just this.

"This is such a mess. I should have just told Luca at the start. They killed Eva, anyway. It was all for nothing." I take another shaky drag.

"You did the right thing, Rosa. You protected your family. You were looking out for Luca, for us. You lived with that monster for weeks. The blame is all on Romano, not you. You have to stop thinking like that. I saw the fearless Rosa you became, the girl I watched grow up. Be that woman. Don't lose your fight. Not now."

Frankie is right: I have a choice. I can either let this break me, or fight for what I do have left. Luca needs me to be strong. And, deep down, I think I knew I wasn't going to see Eva again. Since the night before the wedding.

My life has been surrounded by death.

The door slides open and Grayson walks out, a somber look on his face.

I sit upright in my chair, rubbing my hands on my knees.

"Is he okay?" Frankie asks, offering Grayson his pack.

"Yes. He's going to be fine." Grayson pulls a cigarette out, then digs a lighter from his pocket.

I exhale a gush of air, covering my face with my hands as relief washes over me.

The flame illuminates his face. "He managed to stop the internal bleeding and stitch up the stab wounds. We will need to keep an eye on infections. Other than that, he will make a full recovery."

"Can I go and see him?" I throw my cigarette in the ashtray and jump off my seat.

Grayson nods, then looks at Frankie. "We need to talk."

Frankie stands, dusting off his pants. "Let's go."

"He's in the first bedroom on the left for now," Grayson says to me, his arm resting up on the door.

I duck under him and sprint up the stairs as fast as I can, pushing open his door. A warm light glows from the nightstand. I muffle my sobs with my hands, approaching the side of the bed.

He's hooked up to God knows what on an IV. His face is swollen and bruised. There are bandages around both of his wrists. I inch closer, placing my hand softly over his. I slip under the covers next to him and prop myself up on my elbow to face him, watching the steady rise and fall of his chest. With my other hand resting over his heart, I lay there, keeping vigilant for as long as I can, making sure it keeps beating against my palm.

It's not until I can't physically keep my eyes open any longer that I drop a kiss to his temple. "I love you so much," I whisper before shuffling back onto my own side of the bed and falling into a restless sleep.

Chapter Eighty-Nine

LUCA

I wake with a start and try to sit myself up. But a burning, stabbing pain radiates from my abdomen, quickly bringing me back to reality.

"Fuck," I hiss, laying myself back down.

I squint, looking up at the IV bags above my head. "What the hell?"

A warm feeling sends goosebumps along my bicep, and I glance down at the dainty hand wrapped around my arm. I follow it to the sleeping goddess next to me.

Her hair is fanned over the pillow, her lips parted as she lets out little breaths while she sleeps.

I try to roll over to face her, but I can't. Every single muscle is aching. Shit, I need some painkillers.

"Rosa, baby." I have to cough after two words, which only brings agony.

"Hmm." She smiles in her sleep.

Memories of her sister, Maria, even Frankie being shot flash into my mind. Does she know?

"Rosa."

This time, she blinks a few times and rubs her eyes. Suddenly, she throws herself upright, causing the bed to jolt, and I groan out in pain.

"Luca! Oh my God." She throws her legs over the side of the bed to get up.

"No, wait—" I try to raise my hand.

She cranes her neck and twists to face me.

I don't care how much pain I'm in right now. I want her. "Come here."

Her bottom lip starts to tremble, and she scoots over, stopping just a few inches from me. Her eyes scan my body.

"It's okay, Rosa. You won't hurt me. I just need you."

She snuggles her head into my shoulder, placing her hand on my chest. I rest my cheek against her hair and close my eyes.

"I was so scared, Luca. I thought I was going to lose you."

"Baby, I'm fine. I'm back here with you, and I'm never leaving your side again. There isn't a single power on this earth that could take you from me now."

"You think I'm ever letting you out of my sight again, Mr. Russo?" she hiccups, and I smile.

"I don't ever want you to, tesoro. It's just me and you now. Forever."

An eternity wouldn't seem long enough for me to love this woman. She is and will always be my greatest gift in life.

She props herself up slightly so I can see her beautiful face, those gorgeous chocolate eyes staring into my soul.

"I love you," she whispers.

"Louder." I want to hear her yell it from the rooftops.

"I love you, more than anything you could ever dream of."

"And I love you. I have loved you from the moment I took you, and I will love you until the moment I die."

A tear rolls down her cheek.

"Baby, don't cry."

She wipes it away before it reaches her chin. "I can't deal with more deaths."

I nod in understanding. My mom's still fresh in my own mind. That can haunt me another day.

"I'm sorry I couldn't save her."

She shakes her head. "It's okay."

I wince and bring my hand to her face, stroking her jaw. "You don't have to pretend with me, baby. Talk to me."

"I don't know what to say, how to feel right now. I'll have to deal with it all, eventually. We both will. But right now, I just want to be here with you. To be grateful that even after all of this chaos, we found our way back to each other."

"That I can do, Rosa. I promise you, we are going to have the best life. Anything you dream of, I'm making it happen."

She leans into my touch. "This was my dream. Being yours."

"You never stopped being mine, not for one second."

"And the same goes for you. You are completely and utterly all mine." She bites her bottom lip and I almost forget the pain.

"Give me a kiss, then. Show me that I'm yours, tesoro."

Her eyes shimmer, and she brings her face to mine, her lips delicately kissing me. "That doesn't feel like I'm being claimed," I whisper, earning me a smile.

"I can't get you excited, Luca. You've just had a major operation, you've been stabbed, you must be in so much pain." She traces my jaw.

"I am, but none of that matters."

"What am I going to have to do to show you that you do matter?"

"What do you mean?" My bandage crinkles as I lay back.

Her hands stroke my stubble. "You have a room full of people downstairs who would risk their lives for you. You have a woman sitting right next to you whose heart you own. You have nieces and nephews who love you. You have an army of men who respect you, who are willing to go to war for you. You matter, Luca. You spend your life sacrificing yourself for others, but I'm not letting you anymore. You come first now."

I can't argue with her. I know this has to stop. I have to make big decisions about my life soon. But one thing will remain the same. Rosa will always be top of that list.

"I know, baby. I will never ever stop putting you first, but I promise I will keep myself a close second. How is that?"

"Hmm," she fake pouts. "Well, looks like I'll just have to make sure I put you first on my list, too."

She drops a quick kiss and leaves me groaning as she retreats out of my hold and clambers off the bed.

"Where are you going?" The pillow feels colder without her.

"Like I said, putting you first. You need to be checked over by the doctor, and I imagine you need some painkillers? You've been too busy putting me first, you've most likely been laying there in absolute agony."

I bite the inside of my mouth to hold back my grin. The woman knows me better than I know myself.

"I'm right, aren't I?" She stands next to me now, hand on hip and an eyebrow raised.

"You might be." I'm in absolute agony.

"Honestly." She throws up her hands. "I'll be right back."

486 ~ LUNA MASON

"How about one last kiss before you go?" I offer her a smile and she stomps back toward me.

"Please, can we never say those words again?" She sniffles and I want to throw myself out of bed and wrap her in my arms. I can't, and it irritates the fuck out of me.

"Never again."

She bends and gives me another kiss, but this time, despite the searing pain, I grab the back of her head and deepen it.

"I love you," I whisper against her lips, closing my eyes as she rests her forehead against mine.

"And I love you."

***

THE NEXT FEW days go by in a blur of deep sleeping, to the point I might as well be waking up in an alternative universe and snuggling with Rosa.

She hasn't left my side. My perfect little nurse.

But today is the day I put into place the plans for our future.

Frankie has been busy rounding up our men, waiting for Romano to touch back down in New York.

The war isn't over quite yet. But my fight is.

Dread pits in my stomach. I'm meeting Grayson and Keller in the office in ten minutes. Deep down, they knew this was coming.

"Rosa, baby."

Her hand brushes down my chest, and she stops when she touches my bandages; I wince in response. They might be healing well, but it hurts.

"Could you give me a hand getting dressed?"

I pull back the cover to reveal her naked form pressed against my side and groan, contemplating if I can postpone the meeting another five minutes so I can have her sit on my face.

She pushes herself up, her tits now lined up with my lips, so I lean forward and take one of her rosy buds in my mouth.

"I thought you wanted to get dressed?" She tries to suppress the need in her voice, but she can't.

"I do, maybe just after breakfast?" I flash her my best smile.

"You go and do your thing, then you can have me for the rest of the day. How's that?"

"Hmm." I tap my chin, pretending to debate my decision.

"There is no 'hmm' about it." She backs away from me with a grin, knowing I can't chase her right now.

"Try that when I've recovered, Rosa. You won't be able to get rid of me."

"Good." She winks and throws on one of my black tops that hangs on her like a dress.

"Do you have to wear one of mine? It's not fair when I can't rip it back off you."

She rolls her eyes and grabs my gray sweatpants and a T-shirt to match hers.

She holds her hand out to me to pull me up. She carefully puts the T-shirt on me. As she pulls the top over my chest, I snatch her wrist and look up at her.

"Thank you, tesoro."

I can't lie, this hurts my pride a little. Having her dress me, helping me to the bathroom. It kills me that she witnessed the state I was in. She's taken it in stride, for now. I've scheduled a call with Dr. Jenkins tomorrow for her; she will need an outlet somewhere. I'm here for her, I always will be, but she also has to find the strength inside, especially when it finally hits her that her sister is gone.

"You don't need to thank me. I love you, no matter what. You've seen me at my worst and still loved me, remember?" She kisses me on the nose.

I will never forget that time. The pain she went through is far worse than a few stab wounds.

"You're far stronger than me."

She shakes her head and laughs. "Can you really say that when you spent a week holding back my hair while I threw up? Or when you cuddled me through my nightmares? God, I was so broken, wasn't I?"

She bows her head. I hold her hand, placing it on my cheek.

"I loved you then, I love you now. It doesn't matter how we got here. You were never *broken*, Rosa. You are my perfect little treasure. Only ever mine."

"I'm yours. Forever."

Forever doesn't seem long enough when I'm with her.

***

I STAND OUTSIDE the office door with Rosa still by my side. I can hear them all chatting in there already.

"You've got this. I'll go make us some lunch. Maybe we can sit outside and eat when you're done." Rosa goes up on tiptoes and kisses my cheek.

"Sounds perfect, baby."

I hobble my way slowly into the office, and Grayson and Keller are grinning at me.

"What?"

"You're milking this a bit, aren't you?" Grayson slides me a glass of scotch across the table.

"No, thanks." The last thing Rosa needs is me stinking of booze. "Are you guys just here to give me shit?"

They burst into laughter. "Sorry, boss," Grayson says while catching his breath.

"About that, I won't be anyone's boss anymore. I'm done. Out. For good."

That shuts them all up.

"So, which one of you is taking me to the airstrip this time?"

"I think it's best if we both go, in the armored SUV this time," Grayson chuckles.

"When?" Keller asks.

"A few more days. I have some things to take care of and ideally, I'd like to be able to get myself dressed."

"Fuck, things are going to be boring around here without you." Grayson shakes his head, throwing back his scotch.

"I'm sure Frankie will keep you busy in my absence."

"You trust him?"

"I do. Just don't ever fuck him over, Grayson. He might be slightly unhinged, but if anyone can ever run New York, it's him. It's up to you what role you want to take. You can be his right-hand man, you can run the recruitment process at King's Gym. Whatever you want, or if you want to take a step back, be with Maddie and Hope. Choice is yours."

He clenches his jaw and looks down at his glass. "I'll speak to Maddie."

Both of them will never completely be able to give this life up. It's in their blood. The chaos, the violence, the thrill.

We are all the same in that way.

Our women provide us with a calm in the crazy. They bring us back to reality when we need it. Yet each one of us will burn down the world to protect what's ours.

Chapter Ninety

ROSA

I climb into bed and slip in next to Luca, sliding my bare leg up his, and he groans.

"Where does it hurt?" I whisper, trailing my fingers along his chest.

He winces and tries to sit himself up.

"It would be easier if I told you where it didn't." He gives me a sly grin and my cheeks blush.

His cock twitches against my thigh.

"Really?" I fake an eye roll at him.

"I mean, you'll have to do all the legwork for a little while, baby. And my cock is really sore. I think you need to kiss it better for me."

He rests his hands behind his head, the angry red marks still wrapping around his wrists.

"I don't want to hurt you."

His eyes flash with hunger, and he pulls back the blanket, taking in my naked body.

"Trust me, the last thing you will do is hurt me." He bites down on his bottom lip. "Kiss me."

He doesn't have to ask twice. I lean over, crashing my lips against his. He moans in my mouth.

"Can you get my wallet in the drawer?" He fights a grin, which piques my interest.

I straddle him, his hard cock brushing against my panties, to get the black wallet.

"Open it."

I look at him, confused. "It's empty?"

He chuckles. "Inside—the note."

I open it up and slip out the paper, unfolding it to reveal my handwritten kink list. Something falls out and lands on his abs.

"What—"

My eyes go wide, and I gasp as I realize what I'm staring at.

A beautiful diamond ring, the band encrusted with tiny sparkling diamonds and one big rock in the center.

"Luca?" I whisper.

He picks the ring up and holds it out in front of me.

"I want forever with you, Rosa. I want to be yours. You own my every thought, my heart, and my future. Will you marry me, tesoro? Make me the happiest man to ever walk this earth."

"Yes, yes, yes," I squeal, dropping my body forward, cuddling into him and peppering kisses all over his face.

I quickly push myself off, remembering his injuries.

His eyes are shining, looking at me with pure devotion. He brushes my hair away from my face.

"We finally made it here, Rosa."

He grins and my panties melt. His cock throbs against my pussy, the desperation for him to be inside me taking over.

He pushes the back of my head, finding my lips, and that kiss itself is almost enough to get me off.

"Can I ride my fiancé now?" I bat my lashes at him.

"Fuck yes. But first, give me that hand."

He slides the ring on my finger. I hold it up, letting it sparkle in the sunrise beaming through the bedroom windows.

"It's perfect, Luca."

"Just like you."

Tears cascade down my face. Even in all of this mess, we will get our forever.

This time, I will wear his ring with pride.

"When do we leave?"

"As soon as I can physically manage it."

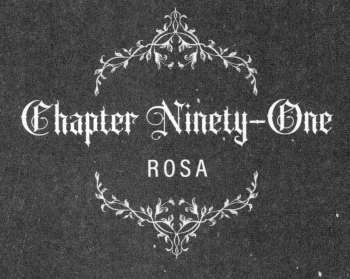

Chapter Ninety-One

ROSA

Luca clings onto my hand, leading me into his mom's home. The coffee mug she always drank from is in the center of the table, and the kitchen is filled with a whole florist's worth of vibrant flowers.

We take our seats, and Luca starts to bounce his knee, his pants brushing against my thigh.

"You've got this, Luca." I squeeze his hand under the table.

"Do you want to hold her?" Maddie asks Luca. She looks magnificent. Her bright green eyes are filled with love as she looks down at her little baby girl, Hope.

"Give her to Uncle Luca." He pushes his chair back from the table.

Grayson carefully places the sleeping baby in his arms. Luca's face softens as he looks at the sleeping infant.

He leans over to me. "I wasn't joking about wanting five of these," he whispers in my ear, making my cheeks burn.

494 ~ LUNA MASON

Having our own little family one day will be perfect. We have a lot of time to make up for just the two of us. I'd give him a whole herd of babies; I'd give this man anything he wants. He deserves it.

"I'm counting on it. We can practice on our travels," I whisper back and watch as his eyes light up.

"So, where is your first stop?" Maddie asks as Grayson pulls her onto his lap.

"Greece. Luca's bought a villa in Crete we're using as our base in Europe. From there, we can just do weekend trips wherever we want."

"We have a list," Luca announces. If my face wasn't red before, it is now.

"Not that list." He winks at me.

"We're going to miss you guys," Sienna pouts, wiping away a stray tear with a hiccup.

"We can FaceTime. You guys can even come out to visit?"

Maddie bursts out in tears. "Sorry, I've been an emotional mess since giving birth."

Grayson laughs, pulling her back flush against him. "You're perfect. Hence why I want to keep knocking you up."

She giggles and smacks a kiss on his cheek.

"Uncle Luca," Max says from his perch on his chair.

"Yes, Max."

"Did it hurt being stabbed?"

Sienna gasps. Keller and Luca both laugh.

"Yes, Max. It hurt a lot. But nothing your legendary uncle can't handle."

Max nods, deep in thought, before looking at Keller. "Dad?"

"Yes, son?"

"Have you ever been stabbed?"

"No. I'm too well behaved."

Grayson erupts into laughter and the whole table joins. All of these men are far from angels.

The doorbell rings. Max rushes to get it, and in strolls Frankie.

"Going to miss you." Frankie pulls me into his side; tears sting my eyes.

"You'll be plenty busy here without us."

Frankie's taking Luca's spot leading the mafia, with Grayson and Theo by his side. Luca is adamant that when we come home, whenever that may be, he doesn't want that life back. I don't know, that man is a natural leader. I can't imagine him being happy running a club or helping at the gym. I guess we will see what our future holds.

Whatever makes him happy, that's all that matters.

Frankie puts the bags of Chinese food down on the counter, shaking Luca's hand before reaching Grayson.

Everyone watches, holding their breath as Frankie extends his hand to Grayson. Maddie smiles sweetly at Frankie.

"Truce?" Frankie asks.

A few seconds that feel like hours pass before Grayson sighs and shakes his hand firmly.

"Yes, boss. You took a bullet for me. I can hardly say no, can I?" Grayson grins.

Maddie spins to face him and gasps. "He did what?"

Grayson plants a kiss on Maddie's neck. "You can punish me later, sunshine."

"Do you two ever stop?" Luca laughs and scrunches up his napkin and chucks it at them.

I lean back and watch Luca, taking it all in with a smile on his face. All of his family in one room, all back together and safe.

Luca drapes his hand around my chair, pulling me next to him. I look down at his tattooed hand splayed out on my shoulder, dropping a kiss on the dark rose covering the back.

I haven't shown him the tattoo I got this morning, when I told him Maddie and I were going clothes shopping for our trip.

I clench my thighs together just imagining how he's going to react. I think I'm going to be in for one hell of a reward.

"What's got you squirming in your seat, tesoro?" Luca's husky voice has my body reacting.

"Nothing," I lie.

He stands, holding Hope out to Maddie.

"If you'll just excuse us, we—" He pauses, scratching his stubble.

He clamps his hands over Max's ears.

"I need to fuck an answer out of my fiancé," he says with a completely straight face.

Sienna and Maddie both wink at me at the same time. I want the floor to swallow me up.

I scowl at Luca as he bends and picks me up off my seat, throwing me over his shoulder.

The cool air causes my skin to erupt into goosebumps as he slides me down his rock-hard body and my back crashes against the brick wall.

"I'll ask you again. What had you squirming in your seat?" He laces his hand around my throat and his finger delicately strokes my thigh. My dress is getting hoisted up my hips by his searching hand.

"I got a tattoo for you."

His hand stops moving. "Where?"

"I'm waiting for you to find it."

He growls. I bite my bottom lip.

"Don't make me drag you home, strip you off, and tie you to the bed so I can investigate every single inch of you," he whispers.

I give him my best innocent look. "Can't, we'll miss our flight."

"My private jet goes when I tell them to."

Oh.

"It's a surprise."

He pulls my lace panties to the side, exposing me. The hedges behind us around the side of the house provide our only coverage.

"Is that right?"

I hold in a moan as his finger slides along my pussy.

"Where is it?" he asks while sinking a finger inside me. He bites my earlobe at the same time.

"Arm," I pant out.

"Can I see?" His heavy breathing tickles my neck.

"Y-yes. If you add another finger."

"You drive a hard bargain, Rosa."

My eyes roll back as he fills me up further.

Tingles erupt through my body as he runs a finger along the inside of my left arm, all the way down my bicep until he hits *that* sensitive spot on the inside of my elbow he found all that time ago.

I look down at where his gaze is fixed on the fine-line initials "LR" inside a cute heart inked into my skin for him.

His eyes glisten as he stares at me. "I-I don't know what to say."

"Do you like it?"

"I fucking love it." He kisses me deeply, pushing his fingers in harder, causing me to moan into his mouth.

"It's still pretty red, but I love it, too."

"It's beautiful. I love you, Rosa. That is the one certain in my life, my undying love for you."

"Can you finish me off so we can go back in there?"

He growls in response, rewarding me with another finger.

Chapter Ninety-Two
LUCA

By the time I finish Rosa on my fingers on the side of the house, they've already eaten half of the food.

I twirl the ring on her hand around, watching as her, Maddie, and Sienna laugh and joke.

We've fought our way through hell, but we made it out the other side.

That's not without some losses.

My mom, Eva, and Nico.

I clear my throat at the head of the table. The last time I'll be doing this for a long time, if ever. With their attention on me, I smile as Rosa begins to trace around my knee.

"Before we go, I want to tell you guys how much I love every single one of you. I hope Mom is looking down on us, with Dom by her side, and smiling. Well, after the scowl for my behavior recently. She was truly one in a million. She saved us. Without her, we wouldn't be a family like we are today. So, to Mom, I miss you. I'm so sorry."

My voice starts to break. Rosa stands and wraps her arms around my waist from behind.

"You've got this, Luca," she whispers, and I take a deep breath.

"I hope we made you proud, Mom. I will do everything in my power to have the life you wanted me to. I'm finally happy." I turn back to Rosa, who beams back at me.

I love you, I mouth to her.

I turn to my family and raise my glass of soda. "To Mom, Eva, and Nico."

Rosa nuzzles her face into my neck, her warm tears spilling onto my shirt.

This is why we are leaving. We both need to heal, together. We need to see the world, to live a normal life for a while. To just enjoy each other. To be free and in love.

And when we're ready, we will come back, maybe even with a line of kids following us.

"And to the next Russo baby," Keller announces, and Sienna blushes.

"You're pregnant!" Maddie shrieks, jumping off her chair and throwing herself at Sienna.

"Yes, only a few weeks, though."

"Congratulations." I nod to my brother, who's bouncing Darcy on his knee.

Seeing them all thriving makes everything worth it.

"It better be a boy this time!" Max says, and I chuckle.

"Fuck, we're going to have to open a damn nursery soon," Frankie mutters, sipping his scotch.

"Might be a good idea. You never know, you might still have time to add a couple." I wink at him, and he looks truly horrified at the idea.

"Absolutely fucking not."

DEVOTED ~ 501

The sirens wailing outside catch my attention. Rosa turns to the window, poking me in the arm.

Frankie straightens his tie.

"I'll get it!" Max announces. Keller jumps up and grabs him, pulling him into his side.

I pull Rosa firmly onto my lap.

"What's going on, Luca?" she asks, the blue lights flashing through the window illuminating her cheek.

"I'll go," Grayson says. He tosses back the remainder of his scotch, gulping it down.

We sit in calm silence, mainly for the kids.

An officer walks in, followed by five armed guards. His eyes zero in on Frankie.

"Mr. Francis Falcone."

He stands with a shit-eating grin, putting his hands up to surrender.

"We're arresting you for the murder of Maria Capri."

The men behind him put their hands on their holsters as Frankie strides toward him.

Keller cuddles Max into his chest, and I pull Rosa against me.

"Go on, let's get it over with." He holds out his wrists, like he's done this before.

The handcuffs click shut. "Just how I like it," he mutters.

I slam my hand over my mouth to muffle my laugh.

"I've got this." I hold my hand up to him.

"I'll see you guys soon. Safe travels. Get me out in time to come for the wedding." He winks before being hauled away.

It's the stark reminder of why we're leaving this life behind. The one I want involves spending every waking second with Rosa. It'd be hard to do that from jail.

"I need to make a phone call." I tap Rosa's knee and she slides off my lap. I head out into the living room. I hit dial on Commissioner O'Reilly's name, and he answers on the first ring.

"We have a problem, George."

He laughs. "Does it involve a certain Falcone?"

"If you want Romano gone, he's your man. I'm out. I'm leaving tonight, and I don't know when I'll be back, so he is taking over. Trust me when I tell you, he will take down the Capris."

I can hear him clicking his pen; he doesn't have a choice.

"I'll get my daughter, Zara, to go down to the station. She can lead the case. He'll be out by the morning."

"Good."

"He better not fuck this up for me," he sighs.

"He won't."

"Well, I guess this is goodbye."

I swallow. "Thanks for everything, George. Keep an eye on my family for me."

"I will."

I cut the call. Rosa steps around the corner, her big eyes full of worry as she approaches and cuddles into me.

"Everything okay? We can stay for longer if you want?"

I shake my head. "It's done. Your uncle will be a free man by the morning. Nothing is stopping us, tesoro. Never again."

"Shall we go and say our goodbyes, then?" She looks up at me through her fluffy lashes.

"Is someone excited to join the mile-high club?" I wink and she blushes instantly.

"That, among other things." She bites her bottom lip, and my dick twitches.

"Well, you now have a lifetime of being worshiped like the absolute queen that you are, Rosa."

That is what I was put on this earth for, to worship this woman until the day I die.

And what a life that will be, devoting myself entirely to my stolen treasure.

Epilogue

ROSA

I watch in the mirror as he leans on the doorframe, his piercing green eyes eating me up. I pop a deep-red gloss onto my lips, but I can't take my eyes off him. His hair is perfectly styled, and his black tux hugs his muscular frame.

He'd make my panties wet if I was wearing any.

He stalks toward me, and I clench my thighs together. His tattooed hand trails along my collarbone, softly moving my curls over one shoulder, exposing my neck to him.

"Mmm," I mumble as he kisses along the column of my throat. His fingers lace around my neck, and my eyes flutter closed, and I lose myself to the sensation of his soft lips.

"You look spectacular, tesoro."

My eyes meet his in the mirror, and he grins.

"That hand tattoo finishes off the outfit. My own custom necklace." I giggle, and he squeezes tighter.

"The only hand that ever goes around your neck is mine. Wife," he growls.

My stomach flutters: *wife*.

"Not yet."

"In about forty-five minutes, you will be. Regardless, every breath, every beat of your heart, every smile is mine, and only mine."

"It always has been. Forever and always, remember."

The warm breeze flows through our balcony door. The only sound is that of the waves crashing against the shore. Greece is our tranquility. The past month, all we've done is swim, sunbathe, and explore each other and our list that seems to grow by the day.

We have our own little private beach; we spend our evenings watching the sun set and the stars appear over the white sand.

When I wake up cuddled into him, I am home. I'm no longer running from my demons, I'm no longer fighting. I am finally living for me. I'm so deeply in love with this man, and I will forever be grateful that he took me.

He stole the broken version of myself; he helped put me back together and now he just simply loves me.

I can never forget what I went through. Every day, I have this battle in my mind, but the choice is easy when I look at him. I choose him, us, and myself.

"Shall we go down there and make this official?" he whispers against my neck.

He brushes the tip of his finger over my tattoo on my collarbone and down to the one I had for him.

"I have a little present for you first."

His hand slips under my silky lingerie. "Would that be that you have no panties on?"

I laugh. "No, I can't wear any with my wedding dress." It fits so snug on my figure. This time, we picked my dress together from a little boutique store in town. It's a mermaid-style gown with lace and pearls and a beautiful open back that ties up into a bow.

He lifts me up in the air, and I shriek as he spins us around.

He slides me down the front of his body. "Today is going to be the best day of my life. I don't think anything will ever come close to this moment."

His face scrunches for a second, so I run my fingers along his perfectly trimmed stubble.

"Nothing ever comes close to being loved by you, Luca."

His lips crash over mine, and I squeeze my arms around him.

"Now, help me get into my dress."

"Rosa Russo has quite the ring to it."

What he doesn't know is that I've arranged for Keller, Sienna, Maddie, and Grayson, and their kids, to come to our wedding. Frankie couldn't. He's too busy hunting down Romano by the sounds of it, so he will be there on FaceTime.

I couldn't let Luca get married without his family here.

It's safe here.

And without them, we wouldn't be standing here today.

"You'll have to get us down to that beach to find out." I wink.

"You tease." He kisses all along my jaw and down my neck to the point that it tickles.

LUCA

THE WAVES CRASH against the shore behind us.

"I do."

Tears well in my eyes as she utters those two words.

She's now officially mine.

"You may now kiss the—" I don't let him finish before claiming my wife.

Keller and Grayson cheer in the crowd. Rosa smiles against my lips.

"How does it feel to be a Russo, baby?"

"Perfect."

"How does it feel being married, Mr. Russo?" She has a mischievous glint in her eye.

"Like everything in my life has finally pieced back together," I answer honestly.

I look back at my family, sitting on white chairs in the sand, smiling at us. Sienna dabs her eye and Maddie is in full-blown tears.

Even Keller and Grayson are smiling like idiots.

"Well, that's all of us married," Grayson says, snaking his arm around Maddie's seat.

"Except one, actually." Frankie's voice comes through Grayson's phone. Grayson turns it to face us so we can see him on the screen.

"Congratulations. Sorry I couldn't be there." The

unmistakable sound of gunshots goes off in the background. "I better go. I'll call you when I'm home. Jax, get the fuck over here!"

The call cuts off. "Do I want to know?" I ask Grayson.

He laughs and shakes his head. "No, no, you don't, boss."

I look down at my wife in her beautiful ivory dress. A dress that is perfect for her. Her red lips tease me.

"Are you happy?" she asks.

"I don't think there is any possible way I could be happier than I am right this second, tesoro. Truly."

"Me too, Luca."

"So, what's the plan now?"

"Well, we've arranged for some caterers to come down to the beach. We've got a fire being set up for later with marsh-mallows, popcorn, and some music. And then, I was kind of hoping we could try something off the list."

I press a kiss to the top of her head, my dick stirring to life just at the thought of it. "Mmm, and what item would that be?"

She goes up on her toes, her lips against my ear, and whis-pers, "It's about time you tied me up, don't you think?"

I let out a groan, tipping my head back.

"Okay, now I am officially the happiest man on the planet."

Bonus Scene

THE BIRTHDAY BOY

Seven Years Later

LUCA

"You think you can handle another club?" Frankie asks from across the table.

My phone buzzes in my pocket. Again. I fish it out, half listening.

"Yeah," I grumble.

Rosa's text lights up the screen—and just like that, I'm fucked.

A picture of her in soft, baby-pink lingerie, bent over in front of a mirror. That ass. That body. My wife.

The message? It steals the breath from my lungs.

TESORO

I've checked us in. Penthouse suite.
Meet me here as soon as you can. I'll be
waiting patiently for you, sir.

My hand twitches, desperate to grab her. To feel that soft skin under my grip.

"Luca?" Frankie's voice cuts in, tinged with irritation.

I clear my throat and force myself to look away from my wife's perfect body.

"I can handle it. What's this club bringing in?" I ask, my voice steadier than I feel.

He's probably already told me—hell, I haven't heard a damn word this morning. Rosa's been pulling my attention since sunrise. Her revenge for me working on my birthday.

"Guns. Luca. I literally just said that," Frankie mutters, knocking back his scotch.

"Sorry, man. It's my birthday. I'm a little . . . preoccupied. You know I split my time—business and family. Today? My wife wins."

A smirk crawls across his face. If anyone gets it, it's Frankie. He's head-over-fucking-heels for Zara the way I am for Rosa.

"Why the fuck didn't you tell me it was your birthday? I would've cracked open the good scotch."

I shrug, brushing it off. Birthdays never meant much when it was just me and Keller, scraping by, trying not to count the years we lost.

That changed when we found the women who turned everything around. Who made us want to live.

And tonight? I have one hell of a surprise waiting.

A hotel. A penthouse. A night without interruptions. No kids. Just Rosa. Just us.

Hell, my cock's already straining at the thought.

"Nah, it's good. I don't drink much now anyway."

Frankie nods like he gets it.

"So . . . next week?"

"Go," he says, waving me off, laughing.

And I don't hesitate. I fucking run. Straight into my BMW, then I'm tearing down the street toward the hotel. I practically trip getting out, tossing my keys to the valet like I'm on fire.

"I'm Mr. Russo. I need a key for the penthouse."

The receptionist nods. I fire off a text:

ME

I'm here. Be on your knees and ready for me, baby.

She slides the keycard across the counter with a tight smile. I thank her, then make a beeline for the elevator, swiping the card and hitting the top button.

As the doors shut, I loosen my tie, roll up my sleeves, and exhale.

Rosa. All mine tonight. No distractions. No limits.

Best. Birthday. Ever.

When the elevator dings open, I step into the suite—and stop.

Balloons fill the ceiling, a kaleidoscope of light and color. I smile. She did this. For me.

I move deeper inside, finding the bedroom.

And there she is.

My tesoro.

Kneeling. Head bowed. Hair cascading over her chest like silk.

That lingerie hugs every perfect curve. Not that it'll be on for long.

"Such a good fucking girl for me, aren't you?" I close the door behind me.

My eyes catch the mirror—her ass on full display. Goddamn.

She nods as I approach, my fingers threading into her hair.

"This . . . this is how a birthday should be celebrated," I murmur, tilting her chin so she's looking at me.

Her eyes—dark, gleaming—meet mine, and I forget how to breathe.

No matter how much time passes, she still knocks the air out of my lungs.

Above her, the bedposts shimmer with silver cuffs. I grin.

"I get to chain you up and have my way with you?"

She nods, lips curling in that wicked little smile that ruins me.

"But I was also thinking . . ." she purrs. "Maybe you get tied up. Let me take control. You relax while I enjoy you."

I groan, head tipping back.

Perfect.

So fucking perfect.

I wrap my hand—inked and possessive—around her throat, guiding her to her feet, my lips a breath away from hers.

"One hour. I'll give you complete control. Then it's my turn. Deal?"

"Two," she counters, bold as ever.

I growl, hand slipping to her ass, yanking her tight against my aching cock.

"Two. Agreed. Now tell me—where do you want me first?"

She taps her lips, eyes dancing with mischief.

"Naked. On the bed. Arms above your head."

"You got it, tesoro." I crash my mouth over hers, taking one last taste of control before surrendering it all.

She's confident. Fearless. Mine.

And I've never wanted her more.

"Best birthday ever," I breathe.

"I love you, Luca. Happy birthday. Now get naked."

I laugh, but her face stays serious.

I'm in for a hell of a night.

ROSA

I CUFF HIS wrist, then take a step back—just to admire the view.

My husband. Gloriously naked. Power handed to me without question.

He licks his lips, eyes dark, hungry. Still devouring me after two babies—I've never been more confident within my own body. And that's thanks to him.

"Hmm. What am I going to do with you, Mr. Russo? Shall I tease you until you beg?"

He shakes his head.

"Aww, but I owe you for all those times you edged me," I tease, sliding a hand over my breast.

I straddle his chest, giving him the perfect view.

"Crotchless panties. You're trying to kill me, tesoro."

I giggle, dragging my nails along his chest.

"You approve?"

He grunts, throat thick with lust.

"I love you in anything."

God. That man.

514 ~ LUNA MASON

I lean back, fingers sliding between my legs, parting for him.

"Mmmm, Luca . . ." I moan, circling my clit, his breath hitching beneath me.

"Get yourself nice and soaked for me, baby."

His words tighten my core. My fingers plunge deep. I cry out, lost in the sound of his voice, the feel of his gaze.

"Damn, baby. Such a good fucking girl. Just wait till I'm out of these cuffs."

But I can't wait. I need him. Now.

I lift and hover over his mouth, gripping the headboard.

"Fucking perfect," he mutters, desperate.

But I don't lower myself—not yet.

"Rosa. Please."

His breath beats against my soaked pussy.

"Beg for it, birthday boy."

His restraints pull taut. He's wild beneath me.

"Rosa Russo. I am begging you. If I could, I'd be on my fucking knees. Sit on my face. Ride me. Please. Please. Please. Fuck my face."

My cheeks flush. My heart pounds.

"Good boy."

He growls, and I finally lower onto his mouth.

His tongue destroys me.

He devours me until I'm unraveling, crying out, trembling from the force of it.

I ride out my climax with no mercy. My screams echo and my grip tightens.

When I finally pull away, I slide down his body. His cock—hard, heavy, perfect.

I lick the piercing and he groans.

"Let me out," he growls.

I smirk. "You promised me two hours."

Then I take him deep. All the way. Until he's swearing and tensing beneath me.

"Rosa. Fuck!"

"Where do you want to come, Luca? Mouth or pussy?"

"Pussy," he grits. "Still trying to put another baby in you."

I straddle him, lining him up and leaning over to place one hand on his throat. Just how he likes it. That's still one of my favorite things, the fact I can choke him, too.

Because damn, it feels so good.

"Yeah. Just like that, baby," he growls.

Before I can lower, he thrusts up hard.

"Oh my god," I cry out.

It's relentless. It's heaven.

"Are you going to come for me?" I whisper. Sparks erupt within me, having this power over him and seeing the way he reacts to it.

"Yes. Now."

Our mouths crash. Our bodies shake. I feel him spill into me, warm and deep. He's taken over ownership of every part of me.

As I collapse onto him, he kisses my neck and sucks. I let out a little moan as he does.

"I love you, Rosa," he rasps.

"I love you more."

His cock twitches inside me, sending aftershocks through my already wrecked body.

"I'm not finished with you yet," I whisper, climbing off him, shedding every last piece of lingerie and spreading my legs for him.

His eyes go wide as I scoop up his cum, push it back inside, and lick my fingers clean.

My eyes lock with his.

"Want a taste?"

He bites his lip.

"Dirty girl." He winks and I blush. "I'll fucking eat you clean if that's what you want."

I need a minute. Just a breath. I don't think I can handle his tongue again; I'll come in ten seconds.

Instead, I grab a few more toys that I stashed in the drawer earlier. Some more presents for him to play with.

"What's that?" he asks.

I show him the pink one. "Vibrating butt plug you control."

Then the purple. "Clit suction."

I tried that one while I was waiting for him. Damn, it's insanely good. He groans, eyes shut. I can't help but grin. His patience is wearing really thin now. I know I don't have long.

I pull out the necklace. Diamond. Elegant. With a hidden clasp—a choker.

His hunger flares. His cock's hard again and I want it all.

"After I'm done with you, I'm yours for the night."

"Best. Birthday. Ever."

I laugh, setting the toys beside him. There is no way this is going to last two hours.

"After I'm done," I remind him, wagging a finger.

Squirting some lube on the plug, I hand him the controller. I hear him groan as I climb on all fours over him, my ass now in his view.

"Now I'm going to slide this in." I press the cool tip against my ass.

"You're trying to kill me."

"No. I couldn't live without you. I'm just trying to turn you on."

"You do that every damn day, tesoro. Always have. Always will."

That steals my breath. This man knows how to get to me in every way possible. Taking a deep breath, I push it in a touch further. I want to impress him. But I also want my husband feral for me.

"Good girl," he murmurs. "Slide it in. Just relax."

His voice—steady, grounding—gets me there. I push it in.

"Beautiful."

The vibration kicks on and I jolt. It's instant and so intense there. At this point I almost don't know what to do next.

I need him. That's all I know. As fun as me being in control is, when he takes over, that's when my world explodes.

He knows every possible way to get me to finish. He can read me better than I know my own body. That man has studied me for years.

Everything he does is for me. And I need him free now.

So I unfasten the cuffs.

In a flash, his hand is at my throat, flipping me onto my back.

"You done with me?" he grins.

I nod.

"Tell me what you need."

He cranks the vibration and I scream.

"You. I need you to fuck me. Own me."

He knows. Always knows.

"You'll always belong to me, tesoro. And I'll always be yours."

He presses a kiss to my lips as his fingers tighten around my neck.

That tattoo on his hand still makes me melt.

"But you're getting punished for keeping me from touching you."

I gasp, breathless.

"What are you going to do about it?"

I draw my knees up, tempting him.

"Remind you who's in charge. Then I'll worship you all night."

His rough hands cup my face.

"This was perfect, Rosa. Thank you."

A kiss to the tip of my nose.

"You've been working so damn hard—with the kids, your business. I thought we needed time. Us time. Before baby number three."

He chuckles.

"You really want another one?"

I nod.

Being a mom changed me. Watching Luca be a dad—it's healing.

We're becoming who we were always meant to be.

Our demons are gone.

"Maybe we need a holiday first."

"You got it, baby. Now stop distracting me from your punishment."

I bite my lip as his rough palms roam.

"Fuck it. I need to be inside you first."

He thrusts deep. Hand at my throat. Mouth to mine.

And the world fades.

Bliss.

Perfection.

And the night's just getting started. Seeing as I've just

missed my period, we can end the night by taking the tests I've brought with me.

I know deep in my heart what the results will be. I felt the same way with Elio and Evangelina. But even if it's not, I know Luca will be dedicated to making it happen.

The End

NEED MORE OF THE BENEATH THE MASK SERIES?
WATCH FOR FRANKIE AND ZARA'S STORY IN *DETAINED*.

PLAYLIST

NIGHTMARE—UNDREAM, NEONI

SILENCE (FT. KHALID)—MARSHMELLO

FLAMES—DONZELL TAGGART

GET YOU TO THE MOON (FT. SNØW)—KINA

DUSK TILL DAWN (FT. SIA)—ZAYN

LET ME DOWN SLOWLY (FT. ALESSIA CARA)—ALEC BENJAMIN

YOU PUT A SPELL ON ME—AUSTIN GIORGIO

BROTHER—KODALINE

SHAMELESS—CAMILA CABELLO

I FEEL LIKE I'M DROWNING—TWO FEET

INFINITY—JAYMES YOUNG

DIRTIER THOUGHTS—NATION HAVEN

MIDDLE OF THE NIGHT—LOVELESS

WE GO DOWN TOGETHER—DOVE CAMERON, KHALID

I WANNA BE YOURS—ARCTIC MONKEYS